The Sense of Honor

Ashley Kath-Bilsky

Highland Press
High Springs, Florida 32655

The Sense of Honor

ISBN: 978-0-9746249-6-9
PUBLISHED BY HIGHLAND PRESS
A Regency Royale Book

DEDICATION

In Memory Of My Mother,
Betty Jane Tucker

Senior Editor – Patty Howell

Junior Editor – Elizabeth Simmons

ACKNOWLEDGEMENTS

This was a long journey, but I was never alone.
I would like to thank my husband, Matthew,
and our sons - Cailean, Sam and William,
for their love and encouragement.
Heartfelt thanks also to:
Leanne Burroughs and Patty Howell
at Highland Press for their patience and
guidance; to my talented critique partner,
Caroline Clemmons; to Dayna, Annette, and Stef
for their friendship, support,
and amazing work on the book cover;
a special hug to Lydia and Aussie Cheryl for
volunteering to read this book
and tell me what they really think!
Thanks also to my kindred spirits,
the Butler's Jewels and everyone at GALS!

PROLOGUE

"For never can true reconcilement grow,
where wounds of deadly hate have
pierced so deep."
~ John Milton (1608-1674), *Paradise Lost*

8 September 1812: No. 7, Royal Crescent ~ Bath

"I must not show fear...not now."

Determined to deny the trembling of her body, Christiana Tatum stared back at a pale, haunted reflection. Against the yawning dark of night, the window seemed more a mirror into the past, a disturbing glimpse into the soul of a long forgotten child.

She hadn't expected this assault on her emotions. Yet, from the moment she entered the lavish Bath residence of Lord Bellewyck, fifteen years of memories had rushed to the surface unbidden and most unwelcome. Memories of a cold, antiquated abbey in Kent—and of hours spent in darkness and shadow, seemingly unending moments of insidious cruelty and deadly treachery. All inflicted upon a frightened, orphaned child.

Anxious at the prospect of seeing his lordship again, she hugged her waist and walked over to stand before the fireplace. Vibrant amber and yellow-gold flames twisted and danced upwards like warring tongues from evil serpents. Here, too, came remembrances, cold and bleak, of a small child forced to sweep chimneys to earn her keep whilst below, in the Great Chamber of his ancestral home, sat Lord Bellewyck. He claimed her unreasonable fear of darkness gave him the idea, but there was another purpose. Quite simply, he wanted her to fall. Even worse, he wanted her to die.

"He will be dead come morning," she whispered. "And his power over me and those I love will end...forever."

Despite the spoken words, it was difficult to accept

anyone as evil as Archibald Bertram, Lord Bellewyck, could die. And yet, a sickly sweet smell about the house affirmed that someone had gone to great lengths to disguise the rank odor of disease and putrid flesh. Indeed, a lengthening abyss of unnatural silence gave eerie testimony to one truth.

The veil between life and death was lifting.

Christiana sensed someone enter and glanced over her shoulder. The earl's valet stood in the doorway, a candle extended aloft as though peering into a cave. She remembered the manservant all too well. Vickers had carried out the cruel commands of his arrogant master with keen satisfaction, always exuding a snobbish indifference that so defined the valet and the man he served. She had little doubt Vickers knew all his lordship's secrets and most of his sins. For that reason alone, she looked upon the valet with contempt.

"His lordship will see you now," Vickers said.

Without another word, the valet turned, clearly expecting her to follow. She gathered the hood of her black cloak to cover her head and shield her face from view. Instinct, more than intent, had taught her to disguise her identity.

With each step upon the stairs, Christiana focused on calming her breathing and strengthening her resolve to show no fear before the man who summoned her. She was no longer a frightened child, forced by circumstance and fate to endure his cruelty. She was a woman of intelligence and strength, and would leave this house the victor.

Unlike the rest of his dimly lit house, his lordship's bedchamber glowed with candlelight. For a moment, the extravagance stole her breath. Then, she noticed Lord Belle-wyck on the bed reclined against several large silk pillows. An effective tactic designed to give the impression death might not be so near. But she knew the man well enough to see through the illusion.

With a whisper of sound, Vickers approached the bed, awakening Lord Bellewyck. After a few awkward moments, the earl's eyes fluttered opened.

"She has come," Vickers announced.

Bellewyck motioned for the valet to leave, a request that seemed to take Vickers by surprise. Once the chamber door closed, Lord Bellewyck turned his attention to her. She tensed as he scrutinized her attire and the deep hood practically concealing what he'd always called her saintly face.

Nay, she was not a saint. He'd best think of her as the angel of death come in his weakest hour to finish him off.

"Have you nothing to say?" His voice sounded surprisingly strong.

"Why have you sent for me?"

"Why indeed?" he murmured, narrowing his gaze. "Come closer."

She hesitated, then stepped toward the bed. "I asked, why have you sent for me?"

"Much has passed between us since you had the unmitigated gall to enter my life." He paused for breath. "Oddly enough, I could not depart this world before I spoke with you one final time."

"Do not think to ease your conscience with me. Seek God if you want forgiveness."

"Bah! Repentance is for cowards."

"Then say what you will and be done with it."

"Now, now, patience is a virtue." His expression was sardonic. "Then again, you have never been particularly virtuous. Indeed, I understand you are quite common now."

She raised her chin. "You are hardly one to judge others."

"True," he allowed and relaxed further against the pillows, closing his eyes. "There is a strongbox beneath my bed. Take it with you when you leave."

"And have your man accuse me of stealing? I think not."

"Such a suspicious creature." His dark eyes opened pinning her with a hard look. "My valet knows nothing about this box or its contents...yet."

Christiana mulled over his words, then shook her head. "I think not, Lord Bellewyck. There is nothing I want from you."

"Do not be so sure. And pull back that damnable hood. I would look upon my enemy one last time."

"You made me your enemy!" Realizing she trembled and that her throat felt tied in knots, she turned away. She'd not give him the satisfaction of seeing her pain.

"Be that as it may," he continued. "I intend to honor the agreement we made long ago. Or have you perchance forgotten what it was you wanted from me upon my death?"

She must be hearing things. Looking over her shoulder, Christiana eyed the figure on the bed. Was it truly possible he intended to honor that long ago promise? The fact he remembered gave her pause. Then again, facing one's mortality might prompt a person to mend his wicked ways.

Hesitant, she returned to the bedside and studied him before kneeling to remove the strongbox. With hardly a care for his infirmity, she placed the box beside his body and frowned at its iron lock.

"Where is the key?"

"Let me see your face."

"Oh, for God's sake!" She tossed back the hood of her cloak. "Now give me the key."

He fingered his bony chest, tapping a gold chain resting upon a soiled nightshirt. "I find I am indisposed. Remove it yourself."

Do not trust him.

"First, tell me what is in the box."

"Freedom," Bellewyck answered with a patronizing grin. "Had you not come, my dear, that box would have been delivered into the hands of my heir."

"You have no heir."

"Ah, but indeed I do."

"What are you talking about? You never married, and God knows you never sired a child."

"Be that as it may, there is a distant blood relation who shall come into an unexpected inheritance upon my death. No doubt it will come as quite a surprise to him. What will he do with Bellewyck Abbey, do you think? He is a man of great power, intellect and influence; a man who holds honor and duty to king and country above all else. Such a man may prove keenly interested in Bellewyck's history...of late."

"Who is he?"

"The Duke of Pemberton."

Christiana suddenly felt nauseous. Was it possible? Bellewyck had unearthed not just a male heir, but a duke. What kind of future would she have with the estate in the hands of such a powerful man? And what would Pemberton do with the abbey and everyone there, especially if he discovered the truth?

Bellewyck smiled. "Ah, I see you have heard of him. Is it not providence my ancestral home will be in such noble hands upon my death?"

"Damn you," she whispered. With nary a moment's hesitation, she yanked the chain from about his neck, ignoring the raspy chuckle he made as she fumbled for the catch. Key in hand, she opened the strongbox and began to search its contents. Satisfied with what she had in her possession, she placed the papers back inside the strongbox and locked it again, pocketing the key.

"You are a most contrary creature, my dear." He sounded amused.

"Because I prefer freedom over bondage?"

"Nay." Bellewyck shook his head in an almost piteous manner. "Because your freedom *is* bondage."

Pulling her hood up, Christiana lifted the strongbox. "Ironic, is it not, that you are the one soon to be bound in the chains of hell for all eternity?"

"How very judgmental." His voice began to waver with apparent weakness. "There is a scripture regarding the casting of stones. The exact quote eludes me, but surely you know of which I speak."

"I know it. But I have always held a fondness for the saying, *death comes like a thief in the night*." With a sarcastic smile, she added, "Alas, here I am."

Bellewyck's lips twisted into a sneer. "Take your freedom, my dear. Guard it well, while you may."

CHAPTER ONE

*"An oath sworn with the clear understanding
in one's mind that it should be
performed must be kept."*
~ Cicero (106-43 B.C.)

Pemberton House, Mayfair ~ London

The Earl of Bellewyck is dead.

No matter how many times David 'Devlin' Grayson stared at the letter in his hand, its meaning remained the same. Another member of his illustrious family had cocked up their toes, leaving no heir to inherit an entailed estate. Some measure of sympathy was warranted—after all, a man was dead. Still, he'd never met Lord Bellewyck or even realized that somewhere in the branches of his ancestral tree they shared a blood relation.

He tossed the letter onto his desk. "I don't know what I resent more, Lord Bellewyck dying or the relation who made it possible for me to inherit the man's estate."

A throat cleared, belatedly reminding Devlin he wasn't alone.

"Bloody hell," he muttered. Suffering the consequences of overindulgence should be a private matter for any gentleman, especially if that gentleman is the Duke of Pemberton. He longed for the quiet oblivion of sleep, the comfort of his darkened bedchamber, and the total absence of any other form of life. Instead, he found himself seated in the library of his town residence at a most ungodly hour of the morning facing his mother, a solicitor by the name of Virgil Higginbotham, and the news of an unexpected inheritance.

He simply couldn't believe his mother, the ever-refined, ever-graceful Dowager Duchess of Pemberton, had sent her coachman to scour London and hunt him down like some escaped felon. And like all of his mother's blindly loyal servants, Nash had dispatched his duty with nothing short of dogged determination. Never was that more apparent than when the man forced his way into the bedchamber of London's leading actress to find his prey.

Thunder rumbled in the distance, prompting Devlin to grimace. "For God's sake, even the elements are against me."

Leaning back in a chair made of butter-soft leather that conformed as perfectly to his body as it had for his late father's, Devlin closed his eyes and gently massaged his temples.

He tried to listen as the solicitor addressed various aspects of Lord Bellewyck's estate. Unfortunately, Higginbotham's deep voice, reminiscent of a bullfrog, made it difficult to remain awake, let alone understand what he was saying. Indeed, the man spoke with such unfettered fluency that he refused to pause, swallow, or even breathe until he neared the point of asphyxiation.

Did the man just mention ale? Cautiously opening one eye, Devlin stared at the stranger in his home, a tactic that did nothing more than cause a searing pain behind his left eyeball.

"Did I mention the estate has brewed ale for centuries?" Higginbotham asked.

Good God, he is talking about ale.

"I daresay Bellewyck Abbey could prosper under the influence and guidance of Your Grace," Higginbotham continued. "Not to speak poorly of the dead, mind you, but 'tis said his lordship was never much interested in the abbey. He died in Bath, you know."

"Lucky bastard," Devlin mumbled. Unfortunately, the impulsive remark brought about closer scrutiny by his mother and Higginbotham. He managed to maintain a sober mien throughout their respective inspections, well aware what he must look like after a night of excessive delights and lack of sleep. Though still wearing elegant evening attire from the night before, his head felt as if caught in a vise. And if his eyes looked as bad as they felt, they were blood red.

"Mr. Higginbotham,"—he cleared his throat—"is there something in particular you wished to bring to my attention? Assuming, of course, the reason for my being summoned home was not to discuss ale."

The solicitor's already ruddy complexion turned a deeper shade of red. "Your Grace, I merely wished to convey that although Bellewyck Abbey is a modest property, the ale brewed by the estate has quite an excellent reputation."

"A bullet to the brain would be less painful, man," Devlin groaned.

"Please excuse the Duke of Pemberton," his mother offered kindly. "I fear he is out of sorts this morning."

Devlin frowned. Granted, his condition was inexcusable, but she knew damn well it was rare for him to get foxed. Besides, a man doesn't celebrate thirty years of life without indulging in some form of celebration. Ironically, last night's revelry proved an epiphany of sorts. He wasn't sure of the precise hour, but some time during the gaming, the drinking, and the requisite debauchery, he'd made a startling discovery.

He was bored.

On the heels of that realization had come the decision to put away his bachelor days and end his wicked ways. Not that he was all that wicked, but the things he'd enjoyed before seemed nothing more than mundane rituals now. He wanted a family; he needed a wife.

Out of sorts? Without question, he was out of sorts. Not only had he come to the daunting decision it was time to find a bride, reason enough to get foxed for any gentleman, but for the better part of an hour he'd been sitting and listening to a corpulent solicitor torture him with nonsensical ramblings about ale and some isolated abbey.

"Enough," he bit out, surprised his thoughts had emerged so harshly from his throat. Judging from the look of incredulity on his mother's face, she was taken aback as well.

Making a concerted effort to sound more composed, he added. "The duchess is quite correct, Mr. Higginbotham. I am, for wont of a better word, most decidedly *out of sorts*. And although I appreciate you traveling a great distance in rather unpleasant weather to inform me of Lord Bellewyck's death, this meeting is over. Be assured, I will take into consideration your views on Bellewyck ale and its importance in the lives of all Englishmen."

"Mr. Higginbotham," his mother said. "Perhaps the Duke of Pemberton should now be informed about the other matter?"

Devlin frowned. "What other matter?"

"Yes, indeed," the solicitor agreed. "Your Grace, this inheritance involves more than property and ale. Put simply, there is a ward."

Incredulous, Devlin quirked a brow. "And just why, pray

tell, was this not mentioned before?"

"There is a reason for my reticence, Your Grace." The solicitor nodded toward the papers resting on the desk. "Lord Bellewyck's Last Will and Testament has but a vague reference to the ward. Indeed, the child is not mentioned by name or gender. The document states only that all details regarding the ward are to be found in a codicil. Of course, you are under no legal obligation to assume responsibility for the child, but I felt certain you would wish to know—from a moral standpoint if nothing else. In situations such as these, since the child's guardianship is not transferable, the Lord Chancellor must be consulted. Before that is accomplished, I feel the matter requires further investigation."

Devlin tensed, the hairs on the back of his neck stood on end. "I have the distinct impression I am not going to like what it is you are about to say, Mr. Higginbotham."

"To be certain," agreed the solicitor. "You see, the codicil is missing. It could not be found amongst any of Lord Bellewyck's papers. Neither could I find the original guardianship arrangement. Consequently, I have no information whatsoever regarding the ward."

A muscle pulsed in Devlin's jaw. "How is this possible? You were the earl's solicitor."

"Your Grace, I was not Lord Bellewyck's solicitor when these documents were prepared. In truth, I only made his lordship's acquaintance when summoned to his deathbed."

"Then I recommend you contact the Lord Chancellor forthwith and obtain his record of the original arrangement."

Higginbotham's mouth opened and closed several times, absurdly reminding Devlin of a codfish gasping for air. "But without the child's name or details concerning its present whereabouts, eyebrows will be raised, questions asked for which I have no response."

"What do you mean—its present whereabouts?"

"As I said, I do not know the name of the child, its age, or where it is presently residing. I should hate to contact the Lord Chancellor when I have no way of knowing if the child is living, dead, or simply missing."

Devlin glanced at his mother. It was now clear why she'd found it necessary to summon him home with such haste. Higginbotham must have made some mention of Bellewyck's missing ward to the duchess. Knowing well what an advocate she was of any child in need, especially orphans, nothing was as important as the unknown fate of Lord Bellewyck's ward. Still, there was no need to further worry his mother's sensibilities.

"The codicil is likely kept at the family seat in Kent," Devlin suggested. "No doubt, the ward is there as well."

Higginbotham shook his head. "When the codicil could not be found in Bath, I traveled to Kent before notifying you of his lordship's death. I, too, entertained the thought Lord Bellewyck's ward might be at the estate and that I might accompany the poor child to London and thence your temporary custody."

Unable to remain seated a moment longer, Devlin strode to the elegantly draped windows of his library. "I take it the child and the codicil could not be found at Bellewyck Abbey."

"No," Higginbotham replied. "And, well, the situation has made me quite suspicious, especially after my visit to the estate."

"What do you mean?"

"Put simply, the servants at Bellewyck Abbey claim his lordship never had a ward. Indeed, they were most emphatic about it."

Glancing over his shoulder, Devlin pinned the solicitor with a hard look. "They are obviously mistaken."

Higginbotham removed his wire spectacles and cleansed the lenses with a wrinkled handkerchief. "Yes, well, the more I questioned them, the more adamant they became. Even more peculiar, I could not find one piece of evidence to support his lordship's claim to the contrary—other than his Will. None of the estate's accounts reflect monies paid for the care of a child. And there was no record of a governess or nurse being engaged, or a school receiving funds for educating a child."

Devlin's gaze returned to the storm-darkened street outside his residence. Scratching the budding growth of shadowed whiskers on his jaw, he speculated. "Perhaps Lord Bellewyck intended to execute a new Will, but, being too near death, was unable to make his wishes known. It's quite possible this ward died years ago, thus explaining why the servants know nothing about the child."

"In truth, his lordship was near death when we met," Higginbotham said. "Yet, when asked, he gave no indication he wanted his Will changed. With regard to the servants, it is my understanding they have been with the family since Lord

Bellewyck's father was alive."

Devlin looked at the solicitor. "What then is your opinion?"

"I am hesitant to say. Yet, in good conscience, I cannot remain silent. Your Grace, I found the reaction of the servants to my questions about the ward most troublesome. By claiming the child never existed, and with no evidence to contradict them, it is their word against the word of Lord Bellewyck. I daresay his lordship would not lie about such a serious matter. No, something is gravely amiss. Even should the child be dead, there would still be some record of its existence. And I believe there was."

"The missing codicil," Devlin murmured.

"Yes." Higginbotham narrowed his gaze toward the papers on the desk. "Does it not seem an odd coincidence that such an important document is missing?"

"Were you able to question Lord Bellewyck about the codicil?"

"I tried. His lordship was in great pain, yet insisted upon speaking with me in private. When asked about the codicil, he became most agitated and bid me go to the abbey posthaste. Then he said something just before he died that has since haunted me." The solicitor looked off into the distance, as if drawn back in memory. "His lordship said, '*Death will not silence me*'."

"Such a cryptic remark?" whispered the dowager duchess, clutching a delicate hand to her throat.

"There is something else, Your Grace," Higginbotham said.

Devlin folded his arms across his chest. "Go on."

Higginbotham donned his spectacles again. "When I arrived at the abbey to search for the codicil, I made some rather disturbing discoveries. You see, not long after he inherited the title, Lord Bellewyck took up residence in Bath. Consequently, the estate servants were given a great deal of freedom over the years. As you know, it is not unheard of for servants in such situations to take liberties with their employer's home."

"You believe they did this?" Devlin asked.

"I do," the solicitor said. "I daresay the condition of the estate is nothing short of scandalous. The property is all but in ruins, stripped of its valuables, and there is a disturbing rumor about the servants amongst the neighboring gentry."

Devlin frowned. "What kind of rumor?"

"Rumor has it they *entertain*. It seems they have an extravagant masked ball at the abbey each Yuletide."

"You cannot be serious."

"I confess it sounds ludicrous, but when one takes into consideration the missing codicil, the claim by these servants that Lord Bellewyck never had a ward, as well as the deplorable condition of his lordship's estate..."

Devlin held up his hand; there was no need to finish. Rubbing the back of his neck, he returned to his desk and began to look over the papers regarding Lord Bellewyck's estate.

A resounding clap of thunder announced the breaking storm. Rain descended from the heavens with tempestuous ferocity. Yet, the turbulent weather outside Pemberton House could little compare to the stormy temperament Devlin now felt as Lord Bellewyck's heir.

The quiet hush of rain lingered throughout Mayfair later that evening. Seated in the drawing room of his town residence, Devlin enjoyed a spot of brandy with his four closest friends. The purpose of this evening's dinner engagement had been to inform them of his departure for Kent in the morning. He had no choice but to resolve personally the many questions he had about Bellewyck Abbey. Honor would not permit him to do otherwise, not when it concerned the welfare of a child.

"I daresay your suspicions are sound." Howard Mitchell flicked a piece of lint off the sleeve of his dark blue superfine coat, then continued to scrutinize his immaculate appearance in a gilded mirror. "One simply cannot leave peasants to govern themselves. God knows what these wretched servants have been up to without the Earl of Bellewyck in residence."

"Well, 'tis damn inconvenient," contributed auburn-haired Walter Duncan as he poured another drink. "What's to become of our four-in-hand racing? Not to mention I have that match with Reggie Simmons in a fortnight. You do realize this leaves me without a sparring partner at Gentleman Jackson's. Have you perchance seen the betting book at White's of late? I'll not be bested by Simmons. There would be no end to that bloody idiot's crowing."

"Hardly an appropriate comment to make at this time," Viscount Lyndon said, staring into the fireplace.

"Just what is it you think to accomplish by visiting Bellewyck Abbey?" The youngest of the group by ten years, Michael Stevenson, the Earl of Wessex made every effort to compensate for that deficit by being one of London's most notorious rakes with an alarming penchant for gaming. "I mean to say, you must have someone in your employ capable of unearthing the truth for you. I hardly think these servants will be any more forthcoming with you than they were with that solicitor chap."

"What then?" asked an incredulous Mitchell. "Do you propose Pemberton remain in town?" Using only his left hand, a gesture sanctioned by none other than his fashion idol Brummel, he deftly removed a bejeweled snuffbox from a coat pocket. "Someone must be held accountable," he continued with a sniff. "The solicitor claimed the abbey was quite barren. If you ask me, the servants have been stealing from Bellewyck for years. While the cat's away, the mouse will play."

"Bah!" Duncan exclaimed. "Left to their own devices, all servants steal. Besides, Pemberton's rich as Midas. He hardly needs Bellewyck's wealth to line his pockets."

Mitchell turned and looked at Duncan as if he were a complete dimwit. "Whether or not a man is wealthy has no bearing on the matter. Have you heard nothing Pemberton said? The manor is in shameful disrepair, stripped bare of its possessions."

Devlin softly cleared his throat. "Gentlemen, let us not forget the more pressing matter—a child is missing."

Duncan frowned. "Yes, well, 'tis a pity about the child. You don't suppose they murdered the tyke and buried it 'neath the roses?"

"What roses?" Mitchell demanded.

"Bloody hell," Duncan grumbled, finishing off his drink. "There's always roses in Kent."

With a soft chuckle, Viscount Lyndon stood and stretched his long arms over his head. "I once saw an amusing play about this very thing."

"The devil you say," Duncan said. "A missing ward murdered by servants?"

Lyndon frowned at the remark. "Don't be a bloody idiot, Duncan. The play involved a nobleman being robbed by servants whilst away from his country estate. Wanting to spy on the culprits and catch them at their dastardly game, he disguised himself as a servant and took up employment in his own household. There they were, drinking his wine, wearing his clothes, stealing from his ancestral home. He exposed their treachery at a party, revealed his true identity, and had the lot of them put out."

"Unscrupulous bastards," Duncan snarled.

"It was a play, Duncan," stressed Mitchell. "A work of *fiction.*"

"Makes no difference," Duncan said. "Miss Drummond says the theatre is but a mirror of life. To quote the fair lady, all the world's a stage."

Viscount Lyndon rolled his eyes. "Withholding comment upon Miss Drummond's rather dazzling intellect, Will Shakespeare penned that particular observation. Still, there seems to be an absurd similarity between that bloody play and what is happening at Pemberton's new holding."

Devlin sipped his brandy and nodded thoughtfully. "*High Life Below Stairs.*"

"There you have it," Lyndon announced with a mock toast. "And a highly amusing farce as I recall."

"Perhaps," Devlin said. "But this is neither amusing nor a farce. Entertaining guests in an employer's home is scandalous. Stealing from one's employer demonstrates dishonesty that is unacceptable. But claiming a ward never existed is treacherous."

"By God, I have it!" Lyndon exclaimed. "Why not borrow from that bloody play? Let them think Bellewyck's heir cares nothing for the property, preferring to remain in London. In truth, you shall be living amongst them as a servant of the duke. To make it more interesting, we could place a wager on the outcome."

"The Duke of Pemberton pose as a servant?" Mitchell snorted. "A hundred pounds he'd not be able to maintain the facade a fortnight."

"Done," Lyndon said. "I shall double that wager and go a step further. I say Pemberton will maintain his masquerade, but will not be able to discover the truth. Sorry, old chap, but you're quite inept when it comes to scandal or intrigue. Even should they not see through your disguise, these servants will never trust a stranger, particularly one sent by the Duke of Pemberton."

"Hah!" Wessex laughed. "Pemberton shall make a perfect spy. Come now, gentlemen, let us be bold. I wager five hundred pounds Pemberton will not only fool the lot of them, but expose their crime in record time."

Stunned, Devlin stood. "Have you all gone mad?"

Wessex grinned. "I have the utmost faith in you, Pemberton."

Devlin snorted in disgust. "This is absurd. Apart from the impropriety, you expect me to disguise myself as a servant and live amongst possible criminals?"

"Well, you were of a mind to go there anyway," Lyndon argued. "And, if nothing else, this will make your inconvenient absence from town interesting for the lot of us, eh?"

Devlin arched a brow. "And what, pray tell, do I gain from this charade?"

Lyndon shrugged. "I suppose you must content yourself with unearthing the truth by reason of your wits, which I might add Wessex values so highly. As for me, I intend to remain in town, anticipating a tidy windfall—five hundred pounds to be precise."

"And just how will you know whether or not my disguise has been revealed?" Devlin remarked. "I could tire of the game."

Lyndon snorted. "You are without doubt the most honorable man I know, Pemberton. You will stay true to the wager, should you accept. Come now, where is your sense of adventure? I daresay none of those wretches have been to the theatre. And since you didn't know you were related to Bellewyck, they have no idea what his heir looks like."

"Servants are predictable creatures," Wessex nodded. "Such a pretense may be your only means of discovering the truth."

For the first time, Duncan appeared interested. "Pemberton posing as a servant? No valet. No footmen. No dressing room rendezvous with Miss Drummond? Hah! He'll not be able to do it, I tell you."

Somewhat insulted, Devlin countered, "I beg to differ. I am entirely self-sufficient and quite adept at matters of intrigue."

Lyndon laughed. "Does that mean you accept our proposal?"

Much as it went against his better judgment to make sport of a serious issue, Devlin had never been one to ignore a wager—especially from one of his closest friends. Besides, what did it matter how he learned the truth? If the servants were treacherous, the disguise might be the quickest method toward finding the child. And Lyndon would lose five hundred pounds.

A slow grin curved Devlin's lips. "Not only will I last a fortnight, but I will expose these servants at Bellewyck's annual masquerade ball. Indeed, you are all invited to attend the Yuletide revelation of their dastardly crimes. In place of plum pudding, the lot of them will be trussed up like a Christmas goose and sent to prison or, better yet, shipped off to Van Dieman's Land."

"What about the missing ward?" Mitchell asked. "I daresay 'twould be in poor taste to place wagers on the fate of a child."

"Unscrupulous bastards," Duncan mumbled.

"No wagers will be placed on the child," Devlin stressed, brooking no argument. "And this particular wager is to remain strictly between us, gentlemen."

"So be it," Lyndon exclaimed. Raising his glass of brandy once more, he saluted his friend.

CHAPTER TWO

"Death has a thousand doors to let out life:
I shall find one."
~ Philip Massinger (1584-1640)

Bunt Head, Goodwin Sands ~ Kent

"The storm blows stronger from the east, Blackjack," Christiana said. "It could be an omen."

As leader of the Ravens, one of the most daring smuggling gangs in Kent, Blackjack Paschal was a suspicious man—one whose authority must never be questioned. She felt the heat of his cobalt blue eyes glaring at her, their manner accusatory.

When she made no attempt to avoid his penetrating stare, he made a sound similar to a growl and turned back to the dark water.

Christiana slowly released the breath she held. *Whatever is the matter with me? I have enough problems without incurring the wrath of Blackjack.*

Still, this truly was madness. The shifting sands were cause for any number of dangers during daylight, but being here at night was like venturing into the lair of a dragon that might wake at any moment.

Swillies, caused by whirlpools in the sand, were unseen in the darkness and deadly treacherous. Like the gaping mouth of some monster, they waited to devour unsuspecting prey. But it was the threat of the returning flood-tide that made her the most anxious. They had but a three-hour interval before the waters returned in force, covering the dense sands where they now stood in mere moments. Even now, the sand quivered beneath her feet—another warning the turning of the tide was imminent.

The more she thought about it, the more she wanted to rail at Blackjack. Apart from the fact they were on the most deadly stretch of the sands, the moon was full, though concealed now and again by swift moving clouds. Thunder rumbled. Lightning flashed.

She wished she were home in bed—not that sleep would come easy. Ever since Lord Bellewyck's death, a specter of doom had haunted her dreams. A disconcerting, foreboding sense of something about to happen. Of course, she knew why she had this sense of dread. Another person had visited Lord Bellewyck before he died, someone who then came to Bellewyck Abbey with far too many questions.

How many hours of freedom did she have before the earl's solicitor arrived at the abbey? She remembered coming home, feeling as if the weight of the world had been lifted from her shoulders. But the joy had soon been shattered by the unexpected arrival of Mr. Higginbotham.

Bellewyck's solicitor had spent hours looking for personal papers to give the duke. He even made an inventory of the estate, laughable under the circumstances and certain to cause a raised eyebrow by the Duke of Pemberton. But when Higginbotham kept asking questions about a ward, she knew what the solicitor searched for at the abbey.

With a shudder, Christiana closed her eyes, determined to not dwell upon the past or the iniquities of her life. She must focus on the present and keep watchful and wary with every step she made. *Take one day at a time. Breathe one breath and then another.* Yet, once again she treaded treacherous waters, standing upon another desolate beach, her life in her hands.

Waiting.

Watching.

Listening.

Hard as she tried to concentrate on the run, she couldn't stop thinking about the Duke of Pemberton and what he might know. Well, she wasn't entirely helpless, not if she remained focused.

Secrecy is essential.

Trust is everything.

"Stay close at hand," said Blackjack. "Be swift. Be silent."

Shoulders tensed and muscles ached from standing in readiness for what seemed hours without end. Dressed from head to foot in black clothing, their faces darkened with pitch, the Ravens were ready to flee or dispatch their duties with order and precision.

Thunder rumbled, closer now, a malevolent warning

prompting the most experienced smuggler to ponder what judgment waited in the hereafter. Yet, if any prayers were offered for the absolution of one's sins, Christiana knew they were done so in silence.

Raindrops began a rhythmic strike upon the sands, a muffled pattern steadily increasing in tempo until, with a deafening crack of thunder and a jagged streak of white fire, the water became briefly illuminated. And in that fleeting heartbeat of time, luggers could be seen navigating the deadly shallows of Goodwin Sands, cutting their way swiftly toward the shore. Seemingly from out of nowhere, shadowy figures emerged from secret crevices and caves, their agility honed from years of experience. Armed guards stood at the ready. Prized contraband would be taken to hiding places—perhaps the sanctuary of a church tower or one of many tunnels leading to places known by but a privileged few.

They worked silently, oblivious to the tempest now raging around them or the weight of rain-soaked, woolen garments. Amidst the weather's wrath and the life-threatening work they pursued before the mighty sea returned to claim the sands, the terrified pounding of a single heartbeat resounded with but one thought that would not, must not, be spoken aloud this night.

Death comes like a thief in the night.

Beyond where ancient Roman roads cross the River Medway, the Duke of Pemberton made his way toward the southeast coast of England and the remote, ancient village of Bellewyck. Seated beneath the shade of a towering oak, he ate an apple and slowly twisted his torso to the left and right in an effort to ease the knotted muscles.

Traveling alone on horseback might not have been so arduous a task had the weather cooperated. His clothing, still damp from the most recent onslaught of rain, now felt like a coarse, horse blanket rubbing his skin raw. Tired of muddy, washed out roads and flea-infested coaching inns, he studied his journey's end with no small amount of relief.

Situated on a remote headland overlooking the sea, the village of Bellewyck appeared serene—picturesque. Drifting in from the gray water of the Dover Straits, a haunting mist wound its way through quiet streets and shuttered shops like the breath of a mythic dragon. To the west was an expanse of countryside, gently rolling hills and rich, fertile meadows.

And on a knoll in the far distance, beyond a wood of dense trees, he saw the gothic spires of Bellewyck Abbey.

At the faint rumble of thunder, he stood, scrutinizing the sky. With a sigh, he gave the remainder of the apple to his prized black hunter. "No time for dallying, Luther. Another storm gathers over the Straits. No doubt the French have willed it our way. We best be off and hope we reach the abbey before nature unleashes its fury upon us."

Once beyond the village, the weather improved. The sky cleared from a depressing slate gray to blue. Stately poplars lined either side of the road, the vast expanse of their branches forming a majestic emerald arch. Here and there sunlight speared down in shafts of gold. In other more densely wooded areas, dappled light twinkled and glistened like stars between fluttering leaves. A soft breeze whistled through the trees. The air was crisp, clean. The forest cool, tranquil. He indulged his senses, inhaling deeply of nature's fragrance.

Every so often a break in the trees allowed a glimpse of meadows glistening with dew or a pocket of rising mist. The conical shape of an oast house and other outbuildings gave evidence to the estate's brewery operation, yet he didn't see a single person. The odd feeling of isolation didn't depart even when the abbey loomed before him. If anything, Devlin thought the deplorable neglect of the estate served to magnify the impression of human abandonment.

Thick, crawling tendrils of ivy encroached upon magnificent stonework, completely shrouding the west facade. Yet, despite the abbey's age and obvious decay, a timeless majesty remained with the gothic structure.

"It has possibilities," Devlin murmured.

Glancing up, he saw most of the windows shuttered. According to the solicitor's report, the estate was understaffed, but the place looked as if it hadn't been lived in for years. His gaze drifted down to the servant's entrance concealed behind an elaborately carved stone staircase to the front door.

"Well, Luther, shall I enter stage right or left?" He patted his mount's sleek neck. "The servant's entrance being stage left, mind you." When Luther expelled a rather telling snort, Devlin chuckled. "Quite right, my friend, let us take care of you first."

After seeing to Luther, Devlin approached the entrance to

the abbey, brushing bits of hay and dust from his clothing.

Ascending thirteen steps to the main entrance, he sounded an iron ring against thick planks of weathered oak. After a time in which no one came to answer his summons, he walked in.

A vast hall greeted him, magnificent in design with an exquisite fan-vaulted ceiling. Two rows of massive stone columns reflected the abbey's Norman influence. Originally the abbey's nave, the long hall separated the front door from a large stained glass window facing east. Six massive columns lined each side of the nave. Every two columns supported elaborate gothic arches leading to another direction of the abbey. If not for light streaming in through the beautifully crafted panes of the east window, the cavernous hall would have been concealed in darkness.

Suddenly, boisterous laughter resonated from a nearby room. Following the sound, Devlin approached what appeared to be the Great Room wherein a handful of servants congregated before an enormous fireplace.

Curious as to what the servants found so entertaining, he quietly approached. They were talking freely, laughing wildly, and not tending to their duties. No doubt, the spectacle provided a fairly accurate picture of what had been transpiring at Bellewyck Abbey for years.

Just then, a cloud of soot sprinkled down, prompting an older couple to step away from the ornate marble chimney-piece, fits of coughing wracking their bodies. They waved their hands in front of their faces until the ash settled upon a small mountain of soot accumulated in the hearth.

"Blast," the man yelled. "What's taking so long?"

Devlin had no idea what the sweep said in response, but the spectators clearly found his comment amusing. Their peals of laughter rang louder than before. More soot rained down a moment later, followed by a fit of sneezing high inside the flue.

"Bloody hell, I'm getting too big for this," a muffled voice yelled.

"In more ways than one," laughed a buxom servant with golden tresses.

More guffaws and laughter followed. The blonde looked over her shoulder to speak to a much younger girl when she noticed him. Whatever she'd intended to say she didn't.

"Caw," she screamed. "Who the devil might ye be? And

what do ye think ye'er about comin' in here without so much as a by yer leave?"

Devlin crooked his brow. "I beg your pardon. Are you addressing me?"

"My, my," she sniggered, tossing a riot of bright curls about her shoulders. "What hoity-toity manners he has."

Suddenly, there came a yell from inside the flue. A body fell to the hearth, landing with a thud. Dressed in black from head to foot, the small sweep didn't move. Stunned, the handful of servants offered no aid, but stared transfixed at the immobile figure.

Fearing the sweep boy had broken his back or neck, Devlin stepped forward and pushed the servants aside. Kneeling down beside the stricken youth, he sighed with relief to find the lad still breathing. But when he attempted to examine the sweep's limbs to determine if anything was broken, an older man forcibly tried to pull him away by the elbow.

"Here now," the man chided. "We take care of our own."

At that moment the sweep moaned and opened his eyes. Although his face was covered with soot, the youth had the bluest eyes Devlin had ever seen. He seemed dazed, unaware of the commotion about his prone body. Staring up the darkened flue, he clearly didn't understand what had just happened to him.

"Merciful heavens," a matronly woman gasped. Leaning over the slender sweep, she said, "Are ye hurt?"

The boy sat up gingerly. "I-I don't think so. Just had the breath knocked out of me is all." He cleared his throat several times, but it did little to alleviate the faint hoarseness of his voice. He rubbed the back of his head. "Leastways I'm not dead."

Devlin's jaw clenched. He had no idea how far up the chimney the boy had climbed, but the hearth was large enough to hold four men standing side-by-side, and tall enough for both him and Viscount Lyndon to stand without striking their heads. Whatever height this young lad achieved, such a fall could easily have meant his death.

Jostled still further away by servants now huddled about the lad and talking all at once, Devlin's towering height allowed him to watch as the boy gathered his wits and stood. The sweep then brushed off the seat of his trousers and placed his hands on his hips.

"Damn," the disgruntled lad muttered as he looked about inside the hearth, searching the thick layer of soot with the toe of his boot.

"What are ye lookin' for?" the older man asked.

Glancing back over his shoulder, the boy was about to answer when he saw Devlin watching him. Their gazes met and held. Devlin tried to determine if the boy had been injured. What the boy was thinking he had no idea, but he seemed afraid. The other servants noticed the youth's expression and turned as one to stare at the uninvited guest.

The plump, older woman stepped forward. With an almost cherubic countenance, her brown eyes appeared wary but kind.

"Pardon me, sir, but have ye business at Bellewyck Abbey?"

"Indeed I do, Mrs. Tatum," Devlin said with a slight smile, most effective when dealing with servants.

The woman paled, quite an odd reaction to be sure. She glanced to the older man, still standing inside the enormous hearth beside the sweep. "No, sir," the woman said softly. "I am Mrs. Lloyd, the cook."

"I see," he replied. "And where might I find the house-keeper?"

"What business have ye with her?" the older man demanded.

Devlin stared at the rude servant. "My business does not concern you, old man."

"I like that," the blonde servant said. She came to stand before him, both hands planted firmly on her hips. "Old man, is it? And just who d'ya think ye are to come in here and speak to our Tom Rooney like that?"

Devlin stared hard at the servant. Who was this chit? She belonged in a tavern—or worse.

"Well?" she barked and stomped her foot.

Clenching his back teeth together, Devlin placed his hands about the young woman's waist, then lifted and set her aside without another word or thought.

"When is Mrs. Tatum expected to return?" he calmly addressed the others.

"Mayhap she won't ever return," interjected a lanky boy with ash-blond hair, large green eyes and an abundance of freckles. His cheeky attempt at bravado lost by the cracking of an adolescent voice.

"This is absurd," Devlin muttered. "I am Mr. Randolph, newly appointed steward to this Godforsaken estate." He enjoyed a moment of devilish satisfaction witnessing the shock on their faces. "Now that I have your attention, unless I receive direct answers to my questions, the lot of you will be sacked here and now."

"Who sent you?"

Devlin had no idea who'd spoken. "The Duke of Pemberton. Indeed, I have a letter from His Grace for the housekeeper. Now, for the last time, when will she return?"

"I *am* the housekeeper," the unfamiliar voice said.

The servants stepped aside to reveal, of all people, the slender sweep from the chimney. The impish, soot-covered sweep slowly approached Devlin with a determined stride. When, at last, the figure stopped before him, violet-blue eyes flashed with defiance.

"You cannot be serious," Devlin said. "*You* are the housekeeper?"

"As you see," she nodded.

The top of her head came to but the middle of his chest. Covered in soot and dark boy's clothing with a black woolen cap covering her head, he saw no womanly attributes. Neither could he begin to guess her age nor what she might look like beneath all that soot. In any event, what the devil was a housekeeper doing climbing chimneys? And what manner of woman would so clothe herself?

Unable to restrain his amusement, Devlin laughed. Unfortunately, his humor wasn't appreciated, especially by the housekeeper. Clearly, she was livid. With each agitated breath, puffs of soot lifted in a smoky cloud about her person. Instinctively, Devlin stepped away and shielded his mouth and nose with a fine linen handkerchief.

Someone gasped. Another person mumbled something beneath his breath. When he looked, it was to see averted faces save one. Mrs. Tatum continued to study him with nothing short of loathing, her palm outstretched as if she were a beggar. She wore black gloves, the fingertips of which had been cut away—no doubt to give her a more secure hold when climbing inside the chimney. Like some damn primate. On closer inspection, he noticed although her fingertips were blackened with soot, her fingernails had been neatly trimmed.

It took him a moment to realize she demanded something of him. Ah, the duke's letter. What unmitigated gall. He targeted the housekeeper with an intimidating glare, but the woman only returned it with matched animosity.

"We can stand here all day if you prefer," she said. "You did claim you have a letter from the duke."

Something about the way she said *the duke* Devlin found rather insulting. Mentally noting her employment would soon end, he reached inside his coat and removed the pristine letter. Soot marred the fine linen parchment as she accepted the missive. After breaking the seal, she began to read the letter, her gaze narrowed as if disturbed or confused.

"It was my understanding you could read, madam. If that is not so, permit me to perform the arduous task for you."

She raised her unblinking blue gaze to meet his with sober regard. "That will not be necessary."

"Indeed," he murmured.

"If you must know, his grace has poor penmanship." She spoke with an educated, imperious tone. "And he misspelled Bellewyck."

"I di—," Devlin began before catching himself and stopping short. "I doubt that," he covered smoothly. He'd penned it with his own elegant handwriting and nothing was misspelled.

She refolded the letter, stuffing it inside a black leather jerkin she wore over a black woolen sweater, patting it for good measure. Then she addressed the other servants.

"Mr. Randolph is indeed the estate's new steward. We are to cooperate with him in all matters. His Grace also requests we obey Mr. Randolph's instructions regarding any changes he feels necessary."

"Polly," the housekeeper said as she looked at the buxom blonde maid. "Please see Lord Bellewyck's bedchamber is made ready for Mr. Randolph. According to this letter, he is to use that chamber during the duke's indefinite absence."

Polly snorted derisively, pinning Devlin with a hard glare.

"Does this mean the Duke of Pemberton won't ever come to the abbey?" the young girl asked.

The child appeared no more than twelve years of age. She looked at him with such despair he wanted to reassure her not to fret, all would be well. He studied the child with a speculative eye. Could she be the ward?

"I am afraid the Duke of Pemberton has little time to spare his new property," the housekeeper said. She added with a sigh, "No doubt there are a great many social engagements which take precedence. It must be quite demanding to be a duke, so many parties, so little time."

"Aye," said Polly. "And 'tis clear enough His Grace wants nothin' to do with the abbey, just like his lordship."

"I hate the Duke of Pemberton," the young girl cried. "I hope he dies a slow death."

"Sarah!" The housekeeper tried unsuccessfully to hide her obvious amusement, then looked at him, no doubt trying to gauge his reaction to the child's murderous statement.

Devlin said nothing, but God help him if this ill-mannered child was the ward. As much as his mother had her heart set on having a child at Fairhaven again, it might prove less troublesome to simply have the child placed with a different guardian altogether.

"You best go about your duties," the housekeeper said to her. Then, with a smile still playing about her mouth, added, "Indeed, we must all see to our duties, else what might Mr. Randolph think of us?"

Devlin breathed a sigh of relief. If Sarah had duties, she couldn't be Bellewyck's ward.

Without another word or glance, the servants quit the room, leaving their new steward alone with the housekeeper. Mrs. Tatum turned and walked to the hearth.

Never had he been treated with such contempt or ambivalence. It was, without question, the most infuriating encounter he'd ever had with a woman. She once more began to feel around in the soot with the toe of her boot. He cleared his throat, refusing to be ignored.

"Your bedchamber can be found on the second floor of the tower, Mr. Randolph," she said without looking at him. "Last door on the left."

As the woman thence disappeared before his eyes, Devlin caught his mouth dropping open like some dimwitted fool. He stepped to the hearth and heard her climbing inside the chimney again. Was the woman mad?

Peering up into the darkened flue, he yelled, "Madam, what in God's name are you doing?"

"What the devil does it look like I'm doing?" she mumbled savagely. He heard her stop in her ascent and sigh. "And I would not stand there were I you, Mr. Randolph. You might soil your fine clothes or breathe in some soot."

She was lithe and strong, despite her gender. Hearing the sound of soot breaking away beneath her feet, Devlin jerked back and managed to avoid having his superfine sage coat sullied by a considerable cloud of soot.

"She did that on purpose," he grumbled under his breath.

Slightly husky, not altogether unpleasant laughter ensued. "I should warn you, Mr. Randolph, voices carry quite well inside a chimney. Even the slightest whisper, so 'tis best to mind your tongue."

Devlin swore under his breath and heard her laugh again.

"Aha," she cried. "There you are."

"Is someone hiding up there with you?"

"Alas, you've caught me now," she answered. "Pardon me whilst I have a spot of tea with the Queen."

Catching his mouth hanging open again at the scandalous impertinence of her remark, Devlin promptly closed it and clenched his back teeth. So much for winning the confidence of the servants by masquerading as one of them. Clearly they resented a steward's presence and were disinclined to accept him into their little circle. While he considered his next move in this curious game of intrigue, his housekeeper must have assumed he quit the room.

"What a prig," she muttered in a vehement tone.

"Mrs. Tatum," he said with deadly calm. "Need I remind you voices carry quite well from this end of the chimney as well?"

No response. She began to scrape the inside of the chimney in earnest. Realizing the woman would like nothing better than to ruin his finely tailored clothing, Devlin moved away from the fireplace.

"One more thing, Mrs. Tatum," he called. "I expect you to meet with me after supper this evening. I shall await your presence in this very room. Do bathe."

CHAPTER THREE

*"Stand still, you ever-moving spheres of heaven, That time
may cease and midnight never come."*
~ Christopher Marlowe (1564-1593), *Dr. Faustus*

Solitary footsteps echoed a steady procession as Devlin
paced in front of the Great Room's ornate marble chimney-
piece. The sound another reminder that he was alone in a
house filled with strangers—any one of whom might be a thief
or worse. Cold, ancient stones, lingering shadows, and
deathly quiet emphasized his sense that something was
terribly amiss at the ancient estate.

He paused to stare into the vibrant firelight, yet felt no
warmth from the flaming heat. This damnable pretense to be
someone else. "How can I stay true to a bloody wager when a
child's welfare might be at risk?"

At the same time, how could he win the confidence of the
abbey servants unless he pretended to be one of them?
Clearly, they resented the Duke of Pemberton and weren't
pleased he'd sent a steward to the abbey. Even now they
seemed to be hiding, especially the ridiculous housekeeper.
He'd not seen the woman since she'd scampered up the
chimney that morning.

"Mr. Randolph?"

Startled, Devlin turned toward the doorway. The cook
entered carrying a tray. Of all the servants, Mrs. Lloyd seemed
the most amiable. Still, she'd been guarded when he'd
questioned her earlier. He studied her demeanor as she
approached and set the tray containing a tankard of ale upon
a sideboard near the hearth.

"I thought ye might enjoy a bit to drink while ye wait
upon our housekeeper. The abbey can be cold as the grave at
night. This is one of the brewery's special blends—a very old
receipt, most comfortin' on a chilly night. With all the storms
we've been havin', the dampness has made the abbey even
colder."

"Thank you. Mrs. Lloyd, do you perchance know how much longer I am to be kept waiting by the housekeeper?"

"No, sir. But I'm sure she will be here as soon as she can."

After the woman left, Devlin surveyed the vast Great Room. Higginbotham hadn't exaggerated when he'd indicated the estate was all but in ruins. This particular room was without adornment, apart from the magnificent fan-vaulted ceiling and chimneypiece.

Recessed shutters provided a stark contrast to expensive silk and velvet window dressings found at other Pemberton holdings. A few pieces of mismatched furniture had been placed about the room without thought for style or design. The room resembled an armory—a dozen suits of armor standing ghostly sentinel.

No marble flooring polished to a high patina, no finely woven carpet or even an oilcloth. The light afforded by a brace of candles on the sideboard and the flickering firelight showed the wooden floorboards, though sound, were faded almost white from washings.

Picking up the tankard, he sipped the ale and found himself pleased by its taste. Not as dark and heavy as the ale served at supper, this one had a slightly fruity flavor, cherry perhaps. Making himself more comfortable, he sat in a chair facing the fireplace, thinking and drinking, drinking and thinking.

One by one, sparks of amber broke away from the fire, pulled by an invisible current up the chimney where they'd be extinguished in the night air. They reminded him of time passing without restraint into eternity, moment by moment, hour by hour. *Time—a precious commodity for any man.* And despite the housekeeper's comment that the Duke of Pemberton was too preoccupied with his social calendar to come to Bellewyck Abbey, nothing could be more removed from the truth.

He had responsibilities and obligations. Did he really have the luxury to continue this absurd masquerade? To play some ridiculous game with people who resented his presence, even as a steward, and were far too secretive?

"I never should have agreed to this blasted wager."

Raising the tankard of ale, he wondered how long he'd have to wait before the housekeeper made her appearance. With a derisive snort, he said, "Perhaps it takes an inordinate amount of time to remove soot from one's person."

Standing in the shadows of a stone column in the Great Room, three women watched the stranger. Even from this distance, firelight reflected on the man's black Hessian boots, polished to glossy radiance. Tight-fitting doeskin pantaloons hugged long, well-muscled legs. At times his head nodded toward his chest, only to lift abruptly fighting the inevitable pull of sleep.

With a shudder, Bertie Lloyd pulled a shawl closer about her shoulders. "Why is it takin' so long?" she whispered.

"He's a big man," Christiana said in a soft voice.

"That he is," said Polly. She nudged Christiana in the side with her elbow. "Just look at them long legs."

Christiana frowned in a reproving manner, but Polly only grinned. "Well, there's no use denyin' it. Not one of us has ever seen a more comely man. Strong too! He lifted me like a sack of feathers. Admit it, he is ever so handsome."

The cook started to argue the point when Christiana shushed their whispered bickering with a finger to her lips. She listened for something—a groan, snore, anything to indicate the sleeping potion was working. Then it happened. His hand dropped, the empty tankard of ale dangling from his fingers.

Polly gasped. "If that thing falls, it'll sound like a cannon blast."

Bertie said, "He'll wake for sure."

"One of us should take it out of his hand," Polly remarked. Her expressive green eyes stared unblinkingly at Christiana, leaving no doubt who that should be.

Christiana sighed and tiptoed toward the fireplace. Never taking her gaze from the man's face, she removed the drinking vessel. She held her breath, expecting he'd move or jump up from the chair and rail at her.

He remained still.

She studied the man's features. Comely didn't begin to describe Bellewyck Abbey's new steward. Hating to admit it, the dashing Mr. Randolph possessed a God-like beauty—despite the fact his pantaloons were scandalous. They hugged his long legs like a second skin. He'd loosened his snowy white cravat, yet his fine lawn shirt and bottle-green, embroidered waistcoat made him the picture of a true gentleman.

She glanced warily at her anxious friends. "Mr. Randolph?"

No reply. "Mr. Randolph?" she repeated louder and patted his cheek. His jaw went slack and Christiana bit back a scream. Had she killed him?

When the drugged ale at supper had no effect, she'd had no choice but to give him a stronger dose. Had it been too much? She leaned down and rested her head against his broad chest, relieved to hear the strong, steady heartbeat.

"Just sleeping," she whispered.

What if he pretended to be asleep? She quickly lifted her gaze to his face. Thankfully, his eyes remained closed, although the dark lashes proved quite fascinating from this angle. And his neck, now exposed from the loosened cravat, was long and strangely seductive, shadowed with budding whiskers. Realizing she still rested her head on the man's chest like a brazen, smitten fool, Christiana chastised herself.

She returned to her friends. "He's dead to the world."

"God in heaven!" Bertie gasped. "We'll hang for sure."

"Don't be daft, Bertie," Polly whispered. "She means the sleepin' draught worked."

Handing the empty tankard to the cook, Christiana feigned a thoughtful mien. "Then again, killing Mr. Randolph does sound tempting—if not for the fact his demise would bring about a most unfortunate and unwelcome visit from the Duke of Pemberton."

When Bertie looked aghast, Christiana kissed the older woman on the cheek. "Dearest, don't look so panicked. I'm not of a mind to risk my immortal soul any more than I have already."

"Well, what do we do now?" Polly asked.

Christiana looked back at Mr. Randolph. "God willing, he'll sleep 'til morning." Turning to her friends, she sighed. "Polly, you'll have to search his belongings. It should not take long; he arrived with little. Most likely the remainder of his things will follow in a day or so. Still, he may have something with him from the Duke of Pemberton. Perhaps the report prepared by that solicitor during his visit to the abbey."

Polly grinned. "I expect ye taught me enough readin' to know the difference between a love letter and somethin' from a bloody duke."

Christiana raised a brow. "And don't make a mess. Take care to put everything back the way it was. If you find anything suspicious, bring it to me."

Polly nodded.

"In the meantime, I must see that the reserve ale has been hidden in the caves until delivery can be made. Tom and I have already secured what contraband we had on hand." She looked at the cook. "Bertie, one of us must keep an eye on Mr. Randolph. Can you do that?"

The cook paled. "What if he wakes?"

"Tell him I came to meet with him, but found him asleep. Believing him travel weary, I thought it best we speak in the morning. I should be back by then, God willing."

"What if ye're not?" argued Polly.

Christiana looked once more toward the sleeping steward. "Then Mr. Randolph will be the least of our worries."

"Is all this necessary?" Bertie asked. "Mayhap he asked questions because he is curious about his new situation."

Christiana arched a brow at the matronly cook. "Did you not tell me Mr. Randolph complained about the abbey and its sparse furnishings when you served him supper? That he became almost irate we had no wine cellar?"

"Well, yes," Bertie answered.

"And did you not also tell me he started questioning you about Lord Bellewyck's ward?"

"Ye did, Bertie." Polly's head nodded for emphasis.

The cook sighed. "Yes, he did."

Christiana embraced the older woman. "Dearest, I know this is difficult for you. 'Tis difficult for all of us, but we simply cannot afford to make any mistakes now. One false step could mean imprisonment or death."

All but hidden within the heavy folds of a man's greatcoat, its three broad falling collars flapping wildly in the wind, and an oversized, weathered tricorn worn low over her brow, Christiana stared hard at the eastern gable of The Eight Bells Tavern.

"Is it there?" she asked above the whining wind.

Gordon Darrow shook his head. Tall and lanky, Polly's widowed father was a handsome man with a still youthful countenance. However, his stern expression said he was far from pleased to be out tonight.

"Wait here," he ordered.

Gordon stepped out from the warren, located on the east side of town. The streets were deserted—most sane people abed at this hour. He crossed the cobbled road, weaving as if drunk, until he stood beneath the tavern's sign. If all was well, a green bottle would be placed in the eastern gable.

Touching the brim of his hat, Gordon Darrow signaled; the bottle was in its place. Breathing a sigh of relief, Christiana ran across the street.

With its low ceiling and waddle and pitch Tudor walls, The Eight Bells appeared much as it had during the reign of Queen Elizabeth. Now, it was a rough tavern frequented by smugglers, highwaymen, and a variety of other unsavory patrons.

A hush fell over the crowded, noisy taproom as they entered. With a nod to Gordon, she walked to a darkened, corner table at the far end of the room and sat so she could watch both the door to the tavern and another door leading to a private dining room.

Gordon handed her a glass of brandy. "Ye best drink this."

"Well, well, if'n it ain't young Christian."

With her shoulders hunched in boyish pose and the glass poised at her lips, Christiana lowered her voice, adapting the persona of the adolescent lad the smugglers believed her to be.

"Bugger off, Snake."

Snake Watkins wiped his bulbous, red nose with the back of his hand and cackled like an old woman. "Now, now, I'm surprised to see ye here is all." Leaning forward, the stench of whiskey about his face, he sneered. "Ain't it past yer bedtime, pup? Tryin' to grow some whiskers, ere ye?"

"SNAKE."

Blackjack's resounding voice made Snake jump and everyone else in the taproom take notice. The Ravens' leader loomed in the doorway of a private room. His eyes narrowed into hard slits as he glared at Snake until the man returned to his table.

Christiana and Gordon watched Snake slink away as a muscular fisherman named Murphy approached their table— his weathered features filled with a piteous look. "Blackjack wants to see ye, boy."

She stood and crossed the room to stand before the giant. He frowned down the great distance between their respective heights, clearly livid at her presence.

"Get in there before I wipe the floor with ye."

Christiana heard men snicker, reminding her rumors

existed that *Christian* was Blackjack's bastard.

Standing before a table laden with a virtual feast, she tensed when Blackjack slammed the door shut behind him. As he walked around the table, he slapped the black tricorn off her head.

"Are ye out of your mind comin' here on a night like this? There's another storm brewin', ye know."

"I cannot control the weather, Blackjack." She picked her hat up off the floor.

From behind his chair, his beefsteak hands bolstered upon his hips, he scowled. "Well, tell me what is so bloody important ye could not wait 'til our meetin' at The Green Dragon."

"The Duke of Pemberton has dispatched a man to the abbey. And this one intends to stay; he came this morning."

"Who is he?"

"His name is Randolph. Pemberton granted him the unenviable position of steward. And a more disagreeable man I've never met. He threatened to dismiss everyone at the abbey less than ten minutes after he arrived."

"And just how did ye get away from this tyrant?"

"I drugged his ale," she said sheepishly.

Blackjack chuckled, a low rumbling reminiscent of distant thunder. "Ye drugged his ale? Where *do* ye pick up these bad habits?"

She smirked as Blackjack tried unsuccessfully to hide his amusement. He sat and resumed eating a meal that could easily feed six men. His hands tore a roasted chicken apart as if it were one of Bertie's fresh baked ginger cakes. "Tell me about this steward," he said between bites.

"Mr. Randolph has complete charge over the estate. Even has permission to sleep in the duke's bedchamber. That's a bit odd, don't you think?"

"I take it as a sign Pemberton has no plans to come to Bellewyck. Then again, p'rhaps the duke has a different fancy for the steward."

Christiana frowned. "Polly did find pink gloves when she searched his belongings. They were soft pink like a baby's bottom."

Blackjack rolled his eyes and downed a tankard of ale. "Lots of dandies in London-town wear pink gloves these days. 'Tis a sign of fashion, I suspect." Bestowing a stern look, he added. "Listen well. A steward we can handle, but a duke is more difficult. Now, I don't care if this Randolph bloke has emerald earbobs and a diamond tiara. Don't give him reason to suspect anythin'."

"You've not met the man. He behaves as if he already suspects us. Bertie told me he did nothing but complain at supper, especially about our not having proper china or a silver service."

Blackjack shrugged again, wiping his greasy mouth with the back of his hand. "More than likely he believed the estate would have such things. We both know it did once."

"Even so," said Christiana. "Why would the steward become so upset we had no wine to offer?"

"P'rhaps he found his ale a trifle bitter tonight, eh?"

Hardly amused by his teasing remark, she shook her head. "You are missing the point. Bellewyck Abbey is an ale-making estate, and a poor one at that. Why would we have a wine cellar? For God's sake, it's all we can do to produce the ale."

She sat, trying to calm herself. Finding it to no avail, she jumped up and paced the small room. "I trust my instincts. There is something about this Mr. Randolph that is not right. He disturbs me."

The giant scratched his black, silver-laced, full beard. "Ye think Pemberton sent him to spy?"

"I don't know what to think." Realizing her female voice might be heard outside the room, she lowered her tone. "Maybe he's just what he claims to be. But I still don't like the idea of him living at the abbey watching us all the time."

"Has the man accused ye of anythin'?"

"No, but he only just arrived today. And, well, I've been avoiding him."

Returning to the table, Christiana gripped the back of a chair. "What if the Duke of Pemberton comes to the abbey next? Lord Bellewyck might have said something to Mr. Higginbotham about the smuggling. We already know he said something about a ward."

Blackjack shook his head and tore brown bread into pieces, using a large chunk to dunk in a bowl of steaming stew. "If Pemberton suspected somethin', he'd be here now. He wouldn't send some damn steward. If ye ask me, Pemberton is only bein' responsible about his new property. Don't go lookin' for trouble."

"I am not looking for trouble. It simply has a peculiar way

of finding me." She sighed in frustration. "What am I supposed to do with this man?"

"For one thing, stop druggin' his ale. If he's a drinkin' man, he'll start wonderin' why a mug of ale knocks him flat on his arse."

"But, if this man *is* a spy for the duke, if Pemberton finds out what we've done, what I've done—"

"Don't let your imagination run away from ye."

The anxiety she felt would not go away. "You must let me quit the Ravens, now before it's too late."

Blackjack shook his head. "It's already too late. Ye know too much."

A soft smile came to his cobalt eyes. "Do ye remember when ye found me in the grotto? Ye were no more than a babe, scared and afraid of comin' face-to-face with a real giant."

"I was six years old. And you were the one who was alone and wounded as I recall."

Blackjack rubbed his brow. "I never should have let ye join the Ravens when ye came to me five years ago, but what's done is done. I am sorry, Christi, ye cannot walk away now. No one walks away and lives to tell the tale."

He shook his head. "We all face the same risks, all reap the same rewards. That's the way it is, now and always."

She stared at him, contemplating his words and the sadness in his eyes when he spoke. Though his words denied her the one thing she wanted more than anything else, she could only nod her understanding. It was not that Blackjack would ever harm her if she quit the Ravens, but loyalty of others only went so far.

"At least ye have that damn strongbox now," he said.

Christiana scoffed. "For all the good it does me. Pemberton is far too rich and much too powerful."

The giant stared hard into her eyes. "Keep in mind, 'tis one thing to be suspicious of others and another to arouse their suspicions. This Mr. Randolph could be just what he claims and nothin' more."

"I hope you're right," she whispered.

"Give the man the benefit of the doubt for now." Blackjack refilled his tankard from a pitcher of ale and took another long drink, wiping his glistening whiskers with the back of his hand. "Damn good ale, if ye ask me."

Christiana tried to smile, but it was a feeble attempt at

best. Strange how the choices one makes in life can become a prison, forging walls of iron with no hope for escape.

"Bloody hell," he said. "If it'll make ye feel better, I'll have some friends of mine see what they can find out about this Randolph bloke in London."

She all but leapt from her chair and ran over and kissed his bearded cheek.

The smuggler gruffly cleared his throat. "Enough of this damn chatter. Get back to the abbey before ye're missed."

With a nod, Christiana walked across the room to the door, straightening her greatcoat and the brim of her hat. She felt like crying or sleeping for a week—didn't know which appealed more at the moment. At least one thing was in her favor. Blackjack would have his London contacts ask about the new steward to determine if Mr. Randolph was a spy.

"One more thing," Blackjack called.

She turned, not knowing what to expect by his stern expression.

"If ever I see ye in The Eight Bells again, I'll take a strap to ye."

The harsh tone of his voice gave her pause. Would he really raise a hand to her? She knew it was forbidden for her to come to The Eight Bells, but Blackjack had never hurt her or so much as boxed her ears—despite promises to the contrary. He must have seen the question in her eyes for he shook his leonine head and snickered softly.

"Just don't come here again. It's one thing to fool the men on a midnight run. It's another in a well-lit tavern. I'll not be so forgivin' next time."

"You won't forget to find out about Mr. Randolph and let me know straightaway?"

Standing, Blackjack crossed the room in three strides and looked down into her eyes. His voice was low. "I'll keep my word, but don't make him suspicious—and watch yer damn temper. At least make it look like ye're willin' to work with the man. Remember, I'm lookin' out for ye just as I always have."

She offered a tremulous smile. "Little good that does me when 'tis at the abbey where I feel the most danger now."

CHAPTER FOUR

"All men by nature desire to know."
~ Aristotle (384-322 B.C.)

"Where the devil is the woman?"

Standing at the base of the abbey's staircase, Devlin rubbed his jaw and glanced about the empty Great Hall. In sore need of a shave, his disposition wasn't fit for man or beast. In fact, his head felt as if it weighed a ton, throbbing with an incessant rhythm.

Movement on the stairs caught his eye. The blonde maid descended carrying a basket. A white ruffled mobcap covered all but a few unruly curls, and made her look almost demure.

"You there," he called. "Where is the housekeeper?"

"Um, she's about some—"

"—where," Devlin interrupted. When the maid gaped, he snorted derisively. "Yes, I've noticed how everyone says the same thing each time I ask her whereabouts."

The woman paused on the bottom step, not venturing a response. Noting the basket of linen resting against her hip, he frowned. "Why do you not use the servant stairs?"

Although she remained silent, he caught the flicker of distraction in her green eyes. Someone else had entered the hall, someone now approaching from behind. Before he could react, a hauntingly familiar voice spoke.

"The servant stairs burned down six years ago, Mr. Randolph. Lord Bellewyck never saw fit to replace them and I doubt His Grace, the Duke of Pemberton, will either."

Devlin clenched his back teeth, ready to have it out with Mrs. Tatum once and for all regarding her disappearing act yesterday and the thinly veiled sarcasm in her voice whenever she spoke about him—or rather the Duke of Pemberton. Unfortunately, the moment he turned, all such intentions took flight.

Gone was the filthy chimneysweep and in its place stood a young woman of unadorned beauty. Raven hair glistened, a vibrant blue-black hue set aglow by morning light streaming in from the great stained-glass window of the hall. Her pale skin was flawless, the color of ivory or Devonshire cream.

His eyes greedily took in the delicate features comprising a truly unforgettable face. She had a petite and utterly feminine nose, tempting rosebud lips, and radiant, luminescent violet-blue eyes framed by dark lashes that curled up in an exotic manner.

Unlike the maid, his housekeeper wore no mobcap. Her hair was neatly braided into a thick coronet on top of her head, exposing a long, graceful neck and delicate ears that needed no jewelry for adornment. Her black bombazine gown, although better suited for one in mourning, was quite serviceable for a housekeeper. She even wore a ridiculous white apron, crisply starched.

"I believed you much older, madam," he said, clearing his throat.

"Why is that?"

"Why?" he repeated, floundering a moment to gather his wits. "Well, I believe Lord Bellewyck's solicitor, Mr. Higginbotham, mentioned something to the effect—to the Duke of Pemberton, that is."

"Curious." She pursed her lips together thoughtfully. "Then again, Mr. Higginbotham does wear spectacles."

Devlin crooked a brow. "Higginbotham is not blind, madam. Spectacles help one see better."

"Yes, well, I daresay that is the theory, but you cannot prove it by me."

Devlin narrowed his gaze at the departing figure of Polly. Was the impertinent maid laughing at him? By God, he was in no mood for humor. Indeed, he couldn't remember feeling more out of sorts or surly. The only explanation was that he'd either caught some ague on his journey or became foxed last night on Bellewyck's damnable ale—perhaps both. In any case, the first thing he intended to do was purchase some wine, even if he had to ride as far as Canterbury to do so.

"Mrs. Tatum," he said, rubbing the knot of tension between his closed eyes. "I've been trying to locate you for hours."

"So I've heard."

Devlin lowered his hand and studied the woman. What the deuce did she mean by that? Did someone tell her he was looking for her or had she heard him calling her name and

45

chosen to deliberately ignore him? He had the unnerving feeling it was the latter.

"You were to meet with me after supper yesterday."

"Did you sleep in your clothes, Mr. Randolph?"

"What?" Devlin frowned at the abrupt change in subject and looked down at his clothing. "Oh, I fell asleep before the fire in the Great Room—waiting for your arrival I might add. Which reminds me, why was no candle left burning in the hall for me?"

"The abbey is quite frugal. As such, we do not waste candles."

"Frugal, is it," he said with a dubious tone. "Regardless, I had a devil of a time finding my room when I woke before dawn."

"You woke before dawn?"

"What?" Peeved to find himself distracted again by her stellar beauty, he bristled with indignation. "Madam, what difference does it make when I awoke? Henceforth, keep a candle with an appropriate shade burning at all times in the hall and on the stairs. I am not accustomed to retiring with the sun. I care not about the expense. Besides which, I was under the impression this estate is entirely self-sufficient."

"Self-sufficient?" She blinked at him with a surprised, doe-eyed look. "Is that what Lord Bellewyck's solicitor told the Duke of Pemberton?"

Aware he must be staring like some besotted youth, Devlin rubbed the back of his neck and tried to recall her last words.

"Do you have trouble hearing, Mr. Randolph?"

"No, I do *not* have trouble hearing."

"I meant no insult. It is simply my nature to be curious about a great many things. And, well, you do keep answering *what* to everything I say. My remark was merely an observation, nothing more."

Devlin approached until they stood toe-to-toe. Irritated by her unwavering impertinence and patronizing attitude, he spoke in a deceptively calm voice. "You would do well to let me make the observations henceforth, Mrs. Tatum. Need I remind you I have the authority to dismiss anyone I consider inefficient or insubordinate?"

The light of rebellion wavered in her eyes. She said nothing, but her full, pink lips pursed together as if fighting the urge to either kiss him or retaliate with some shrewish retort. She was far too willful, and far too beautiful. Damn the woman.

"Now then," he said, clasping both hands together behind his back. "You will show me about the abbey today. After dinner, we will start reviewing the estate's accounts. I understand you are responsible for the entries."

She nodded. He was again taken aback with how young she was to hold such a position of responsibility and authority. And where was her husband? Not that it surprised him she was married. A woman as exquisite as his housekeeper would be wed. Then again, perhaps she was widowed? A wave of masculine interest swept over him at the notion.

"How old are you?" he asked.

She bristled with obvious indignation. "Sir, I hardly consider my age any of your business."

"Ah, but it is," he said, making a point to speak in a low, cajoling voice. "You see, His Grace is quite meticulous when it comes to how he likes his properties managed. And since this particular estate is in such shameful disrepair, he may decide to close Bellewyck Abbey."

"Close Bellewyck Abbey?"

"Permanently," Devlin stressed, opting to ignore her unguarded dismay. "Even should His Grace decide to keep the estate open, there is the distinct possibility the position of housekeeper may be deemed too demanding for someone of your tender years. Then again, marriage does have a way of bringing about a certain degree of, shall we way, *worldly* wisdom. You are worldly, are you not, Mrs. Tatum?"

"I beg your pardon?"

"I meant no insult," he said, employing the words she'd used a moment ago—and with just about the same amount of sincerity. "It is simply my nature to be curious about a great many things. And speaking of curiosities, where is Mr. Tatum?"

"Mr. Tatum?"

"Your husband?" he prompted with a raised brow.

Noting the obvious confusion on her face, Devlin's heart raced with the notion her husband no longer existed.

"I see." Insinuating his body a step closer, he watched a rush of color blossom high on the arch of her flawless cheeks. "Did he go soldiering and die?"

"Mr. Randolph, I am *not* a widow."

And just as quickly, Devlin's spirits plummeted. Oh well, it never would have worked. After all, she was a servant under his employ and, subsequently, his protection. And the day would come when this masquerade must end. Still, he wanted to be sure.

"Then your husband is alive?"

"Mr. Randolph," she said with a sigh that conveyed all too clearly her utter exasperation with him. "I have no idea what you are talking about. How could I have a husband, living or otherwise, when I have never been married?"

For reasons he didn't fully comprehend, Devlin's heart pounded in his ears, his mouth turned dry, and a rush the likes of which he'd never known shot through his body to settle heavily in his loins. That is, until another thought hit him hard in the stomach.

"You deceitful little witch." He ignored the contemptuous narrow-eyed look she directed at him. "You deliberately deceived me from the moment I arrived at this estate. Did you or did you not present yourself to me as Mrs. Tatum?"

"I never said I was *Mrs.* Tatum." She bolstered both hands defiantly on her slender hips. "I said I was the house-keeper. You assumed I was married."

Already on the verge of lecturing about honesty, he stopped short and closed his mouth. Rubbing the back of his neck, he frowned. "By God, you're right. And yet, I could have sworn Higginbotham said the housekeeper was named Mrs. Tatum."

He started to pace, then caught her studying him with a peculiar expression. "What is it? You look as if you've just thought of something that might explain my confusion. If so, pray enlighten me."

She hesitated a moment. When she spoke, her voice was soft and low. "Mrs. Tatum was housekeeper at the estate until her death two years ago. Lord Bellewyck wasn't inclined to hire a new housekeeper at the time and offered the position to me. It would seem Mr. Higginbotham assumed we were the same person."

"This woman was a relation to you?"

She nodded, her eyes lowered to blink away tears that appeared like liquid crystals upon thick, black lashes. "She was my—my dearest mother."

Somewhere in the vicinity of his heart, Devlin felt a stab of pain. He knew what it was like to lose a parent. The void in his life after the sudden death of his father eight years ago had yet to go away.

"My sympathy at your loss," he said with a slight bow. "To lose a parent is difficult at any age, I know."

The surprise in her eyes made him uncomfortable. Perhaps expressions of sympathy were not addressed between servants? He must remain ever conscious to conduct himself befitting a steward and nothing more.

"Yes, well. In any event, you are still quite young to hold such an important position."

"His lordship never thought so."

Devlin frowned as a more disturbing thought came to mind. What kind of relationship did she have with the late Lord Bellewyck? Perhaps Miss Tatum had been his lordship's mistress. Despite maintaining his residence in Bath, the earl must have come home to his family seat from time to time. It was difficult to believe any man could live under the same roof with this woman and not want her in his bed.

"You are rather forthcoming where Lord Bellewyck's good opinion is concerned."

Her chin lifted at a defiant angle. "I only wished to convey his lordship never voiced any complaints about my age or the quality of my work as housekeeper."

Ah, there it was again. Another reference to Lord Bellewyck and what he thought about her abilities. In light of the estate's disgraceful condition and the unknown where-abouts of Bellewyck's ward, such remarks were suspect.

Approaching her, Devlin looked into her eyes. "Be that as it may, Miss Tatum, I prefer to reserve judgment of your housekeeping skills for myself. Now then, how old are you?'

She looked at him with a provocative, if not challenging expression. "I shall be twenty come December."

Stepping back, Devlin folded his arms across his chest. The masquerade might prove more a challenge than first anticipated, particularly since he now had to fight a damnable attraction to a beautiful servant who might very well be a thief or worse.

Damn, but this is vexing. Who would have thought the estate's housekeeper would be nothing short of a temptress? As a rule, housekeepers were unattractive women of no particular consequence and possessed perpetually sour dispositions. Prudish spinsters or plump widows, sullen women who spent their lives organizing the homes of their employers because they had no prospects whatsoever for romance or marriage.

"Did Lord Bellewyck arrange for your education?"

"The vicar's wife liked me. Mrs. Snow taught me many things, including how to read and write."

"And did the vicar's wife also instruct you in speech and deportment? You are quite well spoken—for a servant, that is."

"I taught myself," she answered. "As a child, I paid particular attention to my elders, especially members of the gentry."

"Well, if nothing else, that is to your credit."

"You are too kind."

Devlin's brow arched at her caustic tone although, for some strange reason, he wanted to smile at the young woman's audacity. No one would ever contradict the Duke of Pemberton or dare question his opinions on any matter, especially women. In truth, unmarried women, especially those of the servant class, rarely looked him in the eye. Yet, this young woman had no qualms whatsoever about not only staring him in the eye but speaking her mind. In a strange way, he found it quite refreshing.

Of course, impertinence in a servant wouldn't be tolerated. And he still had suspicions about her involvement in some manner of treachery, as well as possibly having had an intimate relationship with his predecessor. For some unexplainable reason, the latter proved a more disturbing notion.

"No more falsehoods, Miss Tatum. Whether or not you remain housekeeper depends entirely upon my good opinion. Do you understand?"

She nodded, continuing to stare unflinchingly at him.

"Very well, then." He tried to straighten his disheveled clothing. "Please see that a hot bath is prepared in my chamber straightaway. Henceforth, I should like for you to take your meals with me. We will employ that time discussing the estate. The first thing I want to know is the complete background of every person employed at the abbey and their duties."

The moment he turned his back, Christiana clenched her fists. *Take my meals with him? When pigs fly!* A slew of ripe profanity rattled through her brain as she watched the odious new steward ascend the stairs. With back and shoulders straight, his scandalously clothed legs took each step with the precision of a general. He must have realized she watched him, for he issued one final command without even turning his head to see if she had quit the hall.

"A word of caution, Miss Tatum. Do not wander off again. You *will* show me about the abbey today."

Christiana closed her eyes and slowly counted to ten. The man was a beast. Just who did he think he was to come here and order her about? And how dare the fates deign to send such a handsome man?

She recalled all too clearly the moment yesterday morning when she'd first seen him in the Great Room. Bathed in a shaft of sunlight from a high window, he'd reminded her of a knight in shining armor—much like the fanciful musings of her youth. But the enchantment ended after introducing herself as the housekeeper. The man had the temerity to laugh at her. It made no difference that she'd been covered in soot. His amusement was cruel, yet another reminder how the world beyond Bellewyck Abbey would see her now.

She'd hoped he might extend a more gentlemanly manner toward her today, especially after making a special effort with her toilette this morning. Little good it did. He found fault with her age and seemed suspicious of her abilities as housekeeper. Even his compliments about her manner of speech had been laced with condescension.

Who was this man? Was he a steward or a spy for Pemberton? Despite the fact he resembled a well-bred London dandy with a penchant for the latest fashion, Mr. Randolph didn't have the pasty white complexion one expected from a gentleman who spent idle hours sitting around in gaming clubs on Pall Mall. Quite the contrary, his skin was slightly bronzed, as if he preferred being outdoors.

Remembering what Polly had said last night, she had to agree. There was no denying Mr. Randolph was the physical embodiment of masculine perfection. Well over six feet tall, with broad shoulders and a narrow waist, he had a face and form that could send any woman's heart racing.

He had unusual eyes that seemed to change color with his moods. Yesterday, they'd been a blue-gray. Today, they appeared a vivid green color. He smelled heavenly too—like fresh morning air and sunlit forests, sandalwood and something unexplainably male. His chin was strong, his nose straight—almost patrician—with slightly flared nostrils. And intriguing dimples resembling long, deep creases on each cheek—which would seem to indicate the man not only possessed a keen sense of humor but had a tendency to smile often. Not that he'd afforded anyone at Bellewyck Abbey the consideration of a smile. Heaven help her if Mr. Randolph ever did smile at her.

What did it matter? She had no intention of being charmed by Mr. Randolph.

"I may not have much, but my virtue is still in tact." And Mr. Randolph's reference to worldliness proved he had no qualms about dallying with a woman he knew nothing about and cared for even less.

"No doubt, he thinks I'd jump at the chance to bed down with the likes of him." A sudden wave of breathlessness washed over her at the notion. "Don't even consider it. He's the duke's man and you'd best not forget it."

Heading toward the front door she muttered under her breath. "And if he so much as alludes to absconded silver or missing wards, I'll kick the ever so handsome Mr. Randolph and damn the consequences."

CHAPTER FIVE

"Shun the inquisitive person, for he is also a talker."
~ Horace (65-8 B.C.), *Epistles*

Torn between disgust and amusement, Devlin crossed his arms and leaned against a wall in the abbey's ancient gallery. "Not that I'm surprised, mind you, but it appears Bellewyck's artwork has also mysteriously disappeared."

Miss Tatum walked to the center of the room and turned away from him in profile. Her lips pursed together as if fighting the urge to argue his point. If nothing else, her restraint was admirable, especially considering the woman teetered on the edge of losing her temper with him for most of the day.

"Come now, Miss Tatum," he continued. "You must agree 'tis rather odd the estate has nothing of value within its walls—or on them for that matter."

She turned to face him, one eyebrow arched. "What I find odd is your preoccupation with it."

Devlin couldn't help it. He laughed at the woman's un-wavering determination to challenge everything he said. More intriguing, however, was her reaction to his amusement.

A vivid pink blush colored her cheeks, and a coquettish look of transfixed wonder lit her expression. He found it not only endearing, but seductive. If she continued to look at him that way, he'd not be responsible for the consequences. A moment later, however, the determined tilt of her rebellious chin returned and her lips compressed into what he'd describe as a mutinous line.

"Now, now, don't bite my head off," he said with a lingering smile. "I merely made an observation. We stand in a gallery with not one painting to document the noble lineage of Lord Bellewyck or the history of this ancient estate. You need only look at the faded framing shadows to know that once upon a time a great many works on canvas graced these walls, some of quite impressive size."

"I wouldn't know," she said. "I was not here *once upon a time*." She proceeded toward another set of gothic-style doors.

Touché, he mused to himself. As a rule, he preferred wit in his women. Damn, but where did that come from?

Following, he studied the womanly sway of her skirts, inviting yet forbidden. Miss Tatum definitely possessed some rather enticing dimensions of her own, although they'd been artfully hidden by that damnable chimneysweep attire yesterday. An even greater curiosity to him was despite her character being suspect and her honesty highly questionable, he enjoyed her company.

All too late, he realized the woman had stopped walking and stood glaring at him. Gruffly clearing his throat, he glanced up at the ceiling.

"I see the roof leaks in this part of the house as well."

"You are nothing if not observant, Mr. Randolph."

"There's a double meaning there," he said with a winning grin he'd perfected long ago—equal parts tease and seduction. Most women found it irresistible; Miss Tatum clearly wasn't one of them.

He switched to a more stoic demeanor. "Yes, well, the roof should be repaired as soon as possible. 'Tis fortunate no one has been injured or killed."

"Mr. Randolph, such repairs would be astronomical in cost."

Her hands clasped in a rigid pose which, in his opinion, the young Miss Tatum must consider an expected stance for a responsible, mature housekeeper. On her it was simply adorable. Damn, he needed to get control of himself.

With a shrug, he walked over to one of the many tall windows and looked out at the expansive, emerald grounds. "The Duke of Pemberton takes his obligations seriously, Miss Tatum. It matters not if that obligation is to his title, his properties, his tenants, or the people he employs. I am confident he will find it unconscionable how neglected this estate has been."

"This estate has *not* been neglected."

Devlin turned about, surprised by the anger in her tone.

She sighed, a womanly sound that could indicate either impatience with him or regret about her emotional outburst. "Mr. Randolph, including myself, three women and four men are employed at this estate. What little profits the brewery made his lordship confiscated, with no thought for necessary repairs to Bellewyck Abbey. Yet, we have tried to maintain the house and the brewery to the best of our abilities."

"Is that so?"

"Yes, and it should be obvious, even to you, that an estate of this size by rights should employ at least five times its present number."

"At least," he concurred with a nod. "Pity Lord Bellewyck did away with his tenancies. Apart from the land not being properly farmed, he might have made arrangements with the tenants to ensure the upkeep of his estate. Labor in exchange for credit on rents is not uncommon, especially when an estate experiences financial difficulties."

"You will soon learn Lord Bellewyck never had much interest in the estate, the village, or its people. Indeed, 'twas often said he wanted nothing more than to see Bellewyck Abbey in ruins."

"Do you believe that?"

"I have no idea what Lord Bellewyck's motives were regarding the estate. But were I to venture an opinion, then yes, I believe his lordship hated Bellewyck Abbey with a great passion."

She spoke calmly, yet with conviction. There might even be some truth to what she said about his lordship's lack of regard for his family seat. The pile of debts owed at the time of Bellewyck's death gave a disturbing picture of how poorly the man had managed his affairs. Had the earl been equally negligent in the care of his ward? If not, where was the documentation about the poor child or at least someone who knew its fate or present whereabouts?

He quelled the impulse to contact his secretary in London with instructions to initiate a thorough investigation into Bellewyck's personal affairs. Honorbound to learn the truth on his own, the rules of the wager prevented him from corresponding with anyone or even traveling back to town to conduct any research. Allowed the assistance of only one servant during this masquerade, that man needed to be someone of much stronger disposition. God knows there was little his secretary, the bookish Jacob Filbert, could do in a pinch. Remembering how his mother's coachman had impulsively stormed Louisa Drummond's bedchamber to find him, Nash would make the best ally—all things considered.

Returning to current matters, he said, "Perhaps now

would be a good time to explain the duties of each servant and how long they have been employed."

"As you like. You already know Mrs. Lloyd is cook; she's been at Bellewyck Abbey for nigh on thirty years. Tom Rooney's duties are varied. Whenever his lordship was in residence, Tom performed the duties of butler. Most of the time, however, he maintains the grounds. He was head gardener here for many years and lives in the old gatehouse. Then we have the Darrow family. Gordon Darrow is our cooper; he came to Bellewyck thirteen years ago with his two children, Billy and Polly. Today, he is delivering ale to market in Folkestone. His son, Billy, tends what little farm animals we have—a few dairy cows and a number of sheep."

"Where does the Darrow family reside?"

"In a small cottage on the grange. But Polly lives in the manor with the women of Bellewyck Abbey."

"Ah, yes, Polly." Just the mention of the loud, insolent blonde gave him a headache. "And what, pray tell, are her duties?"

"She has many duties, primarily the laundry and the kitchen garden."

"Which brings us to you, I believe."

"Yes." She raised her chin at a determined angle. "In addition to the customary duties one expects of a house-keeper, I clean the guest chambers as necessary. Prior to your arrival, these rooms were closed. Bellewyck Abbey rarely has guests. This allows me to maintain the estate's accounts and work closely with Jasper Collins down in the brewery."

"I see," Devlin replied. "And this Jasper Collins?"

"Jasper is our brewer and has been at Bellewyck Abbey all his life. His family has managed the brewery operation for generations. Advanced years and poor health prevent him from coming up to the house. He lives at the brewery."

Devlin frowned. "The women live alone in the house?"

"Yes."

Having no man in the house seemed reckless to his way of thinking. If danger were to present itself, no one would be close enough to offer protection to the three women. At least a competent butler or footman should live in the house. Perhaps Nash could act as butler until a more qualified person could be retained.

Remembering what his housekeeper had just said, he crooked a brow at her. "I was under the impression Polly cleaned my bedchamber."

At least that's whom he assumed had rifled through his belongings, even going so far as to damage the top of his new traveling desk. Had the chit not been so hasty, she would have noticed he'd left it unlocked. Thank God his signet ring had been concealed in a specially made pocket inside his boot.

"No," said the housekeeper. "She cleaned the duke's bedchamber."

Devlin bit back another grin. Miss Tatum's wit wasn't only quick, but intriguing. He'd found that women of beauty rarely had anything between their ears. As if God deemed it only fair to slight them in some way. To find beauty and intelligence in a servant woman was nothing short of miraculous.

"My dear, Miss Tatum, I am inordinately pleased you recognize Pemberton's authority. He is indeed the new owner of Bellewyck Abbey and everything here does belong to him."

"Not everything," she murmured.

"I beg your pardon?"

"I do not belong to him."

Devlin frowned. "Yes, well, that goes without saying, but I presume His Grace can rely upon your loyalty."

"I am exceedingly loyal to this estate." She took a few steps toward him, her expression one of keen interest. "But what about your loyalty, Mr. Randolph? Does it rest with the estate or the Duke of Pemberton?"

"I consider them one and the same, Miss Tatum."

"Not necessarily. There may be times when one must choose between doing what is right and what someone orders them to do. I am curious—would you obey the duke without question? Even should Pemberton ask you to do something you find personally disagreeable, perhaps even reprehensible?"

Devlin blinked. Were they speaking the same language? Why did women with any measure of intelligence try to impress men by spouting convoluted scenarios and hypothetical situations?

"I suppose there are limits concerning duty to one's employer, Miss Tatum—especially in such an instance where one's sense of honor might be compromised."

"One's sense of honor," she whispered as if testing the words on her tongue. She stared at him a long moment, her violet-blue eyes reflecting a certain degree of respect, perhaps even admiration. It made him wholly uncomfortable.

"Yes, well...back to the bedchamber I am using with the benevolent permission of His Grace. Did you clean it?"

"I was a bit preoccupied when you arrived."

Devlin grinned, remembering their first meeting. It had been a mistake not to advise the servants of his impending arrival. The controlled fury in Miss Tatum's eyes had been something he'd never forget. Of course, he now understood the reason for her upset. No woman would ever consider making the acquaintance of a gentleman when not at her best. Two sisters had taught him that much.

"Was there a problem with Polly cleaning the duke's chamber?" she asked.

Devlin chuckled. "My dear Miss Tatum, for the sake of conversation, mightn't we refer to it henceforth as *my* chamber?" She smirked at the suggestion, prompting him to laugh. "Why does it bother you so much that I am permitted to use the duke's bedchamber?"

"Because it simply is not done," she argued. "Stewards do not occupy their employer's bedchamber. 'Tis exceedingly improper. You should have refused the privilege."

Devlin studied her thoughtfully. Did she consider it improper because he used the bedchamber or because a man now lived in the house who could better watch her activities?

"Ironic you are so concerned with propriety, Miss Tatum," he said. "I daresay your mannish attire and rather colorful language upon my arrival could hardly be deemed proper for a woman let alone a housekeeper."

She paled, and he noticed a slight quivering of her chin. *Well, that was a bloody mistake.* He'd meant to cajole her into a smile, but somehow the words came out as a condemnation.

"Forgive me," he said, taking a step toward her. "Since your mother's passing, you've carried a great weight upon your shoulders. I commend you for taking it upon yourself to clean the chimney. I doubt many women would be courageous enough to attempt such a dangerous task, especially knowing they could have delegated the chore to another."

Tears spiked her long lashes. Dear God, if there was one thing that left him at a complete loss, it was a woman's tears. He offered her his handkerchief. "You care a great deal for the people employed here, do you not?"

"Yes." Her voice was a faint whisper.

58

A moment of silence followed as they looked at one another. What was this aching attraction he felt for her? And why, with all the doubts and concerns he had about the estate and its people, was he thinking about taking her into his arms and kissing her soundly? For God's sake, the woman was a servant in his home. He couldn't involve himself with her, especially in light of the suspicions about everyone and everything at Bellewyck Abbey.

"Tell me about your father," he said, changing the subject.

She returned his handkerchief. "I do not remember my father."

With a slight frown, Devlin watched her turn away, her manner once more aloof. The ensuing silence proved awkward and he thought only to break it by enquiring about the one person they had not yet discussed.

"Tell me about Sarah."

She looked over her shoulder at him, an expression of unguarded surprise upon her face. "Sarah?"

"The young girl who wished the Duke of Pemberton a slow and painful death?"

The trace of a smile curved the corners of her mouth. "You must forgive Sarah's impulsive remark. She can be a bit dramatic, but she would never cause injury to anyone or anything."

"I am relieved to hear that." Taking pains not to frighten her, he slowly approached. "You mentioned she had duties at the abbey yesterday. Is she a servant here as well?"

His housekeeper shook her head. "Sarah is Mrs. Lloyd's granddaughter. She came to the abbey when her parents died. She helps Bertie from time-to-time in the kitchen, but we try to give her an enjoyable, carefree childhood. In truth, she is more like a little sister to me."

"To you?"

"And Polly and Billy Darrow, of course."

"Of course." He nodded, but his thoughts whirled with possibilities, especially since Sarah was the only child living at the estate. "When did Sarah's parents die?"

Miss Tatum's violet eyes took on a faraway glint. "She was two years old at the time, so it's been almost ten years now."

A rush of excitement assailed Devlin. Bellewyck's Will had been dated ten years ago, the very document mentioning a ward. Good God, in little more than twenty-four hours he'd learned the truth.

It made perfect sense. Didn't Miss Tatum admit she cared for the people employed at the estate? And there was no denying the tender emotion in her expression at the mention of young Sarah. The close-knit servants were likely fearful Sarah might be removed from their midst—most astute of them in fact.

"Come now, Miss Tatum." Employing his most cajoling tone, he closed the remaining distance between them. "No need to deny the truth a moment longer. Sarah is really Lord Bellewyck's ward, is she not?"

Such a look of contemptuous indignation came to Miss Tatum's face he felt the need to protect his nether region in some way. Good God, her temper was quick as lightning.

"You are very skilled at placating people to get what you want, Mr. Randolph. I was actually beginning to believe you a man of conscience, honor and integrity—someone who might truly care for this estate and its people. In truth, you are a slithering snake waiting for just the right moment to strike. Tell me, do you intend to interrogate everyone like this?"

"If I must." He bit back the urge to defend his actions.

"I see," she said with a curt nod. "Well, since you have repeatedly commented upon Mr. Higginbotham and his recent visit to the abbey, you already know he questioned everyone about the estate and this mysterious ward. I daresay the subject is becoming rather redundant and tedious."

Devlin clenched his jaw. *Redundant and tedious?*

"Be that as it may,"—he tried to rein in his outrage at her cold indifference to such an important matter—"the Duke of Pemberton requested I look into the matter. You see, His Grace does not believe Lord Bellewyck made false claims about having a ward. And where a child's welfare is concerned, learning about that child takes precedence over anything else I am here to do."

"There...is...no...child."

"So you say," Devlin answered softly.

He stared at her, and she at him.

"Have you nothing more to say on the matter?" he asked.

"No," she replied succinctly.

"Very well, but I give you fair warning, Miss Tatum. I cannot, nay I will not, let the matter rest until I am confident about the truth, one way or another. No doubt, you will find my pressing on about this particular subject even more redundant and tedious in the days to come."

"Mr. Randolph," she said with a grievous sigh. "I am quite sure I have no control over what you intend to say or do in the days to come. We told Mr. Higginbotham the truth, the same truth I now tell you. Whether or not you choose to believe us is entirely up to you."

The woman was not only beautiful, but clever and damnably exciting. Then again, she sounded so adamant and confident about her statement perhaps she spoke the truth. What if the servants were innocent of theft and treachery? What if the Earl of Bellewyck had lied about having a ward?

A wave of frustration swept over him. Swearing under his breath, he returned to stand before the window. How could he permit himself to be so easily swayed because of an absurd attraction he felt to a servant woman he knew nothing about?

By God, there was no earthly reason why Lord Bellewyck would claim a ward that didn't exist. A child did exist. Not just a child, but a child who remained his responsibility until its fate could be determined by the Lord Chancellor. Even now, its life could be in grave jeopardy.

Folding his arms across his chest, he considered his next course of action. Seduce the housekeeper? It would prove no hardship to bed the woman. Then again, the day would come when his identity must be revealed. As Duke of Pemberton, he neither needed nor wanted a romantic entanglement with a servant.

The fact of the matter—and one that deserved further consideration—was that his housekeeper seemed keenly interested in what the Duke of Pemberton intended to do with Bellewyck Abbey. No doubt, the servants were concerned for their situations. Could he could use Miss Tatum's feelings of concern for the abbey and its people as a means to win her confidence and trust? Say what she will about his placating people to get what he wanted, it had never been known to fail—especially with women.

"The Duke of Pemberton is rumored to have an appreciation of fine architecture," he said, surveying the sprawling grounds outside the window. "It might prove an intriguing challenge for His Grace to restore Bellewyck Abbey into some semblance of its former glory."

"You have a great deal of faith in both the Duke of Pemberton and his pocketbook, Mr. Randolph."

The sound of her slightly husky voice drifted over him like a honeyed caress. He swallowed hard, desperate to quell his rising, impudent desire. Now that he'd decided not to seduce the young woman, he could think of little else.

She came to stand beside him, so close their bodies almost brushed against one another. With but the slightest effort on his part he could turn and...

Devlin closed his eyes, determined to think of anything but the unruly lust possessing his body. Even now, the throbbing head of an aching arousal tented his trousers in a way that left little to the imagination. It would not do for Miss Tatum to know how she affected him.

Perhaps he should behave in a more churlish manner toward her. If they were constantly at odds, treating one another with barely restrained animosity, he just might be able to conduct himself in a gentlemanly manner and find the missing ward. It was the only rational alternative at this point, especially since his libido was spiraling out of control.

Opening his eyes, he took a deep, steadying breath and tried to ignore her delicate scent—to no avail. A strange fever possessed him. His heart drummed with lustful need, so swift and loud it sounded ready to jump out of his chest. His breathing, now ragged and heavy, waged its own desperate struggle to deny a virulent passion. Even his palms were sweating.

What the devil is wrong with me?

He turned his head, intending to employ his most intimidating glare, the same look that had sent any number of individuals running from his presence in the past. Unfortunately, the afternoon light streaming in through the warbled glazing of the thick window panes illuminated her face with a warm, golden glow. No blemish marred her pale skin, not even a freckle. She had high cheekbones and striking, long lashes that curled and framed her violet eyes. In a word, she dazzled him. Even worse, he now saw her breathless desire for him.

The moment grew intense with intimacy. It was one thing to be strong when a woman didn't seek or welcome a man's advances. But when a woman looked at him with such a seductive, yet innocent expression, breathless—trembling with obvious passion—it was nigh on impossible to resist.

Good God, this is madness.

Had the woman bewitched him? What manner of man forgot a child was missing? Or that a strong likelihood existed all servants at the estate, including this housekeeper, were thieves and liars?

"Mr. Randolph?"

Looking out the window again—anywhere but at her—Devlin latched onto the gist of their conversation. "Repairs to the roof are essential, Miss Tatum. I do not anticipate the expense to be a financial hardship for His Grace."

"You know him so well?"

Ah, there it was. She hadn't come to stand beside him because she felt the strange connection between their souls. She wasn't speaking in that soft, seductively breathless tone because she quivered with desire for him. Nay, she was suspicious about his relationship to the duke and, in all likelihood, trying to seduce him into revealing information about Pemberton.

He snorted with disgust for thinking this young woman might be innocent in any form or fashion. She was nothing—nothing but a servant of little consequence with no breeding or family. He'd be wise to stop thinking of her as anything beyond that.

Clenching his jaw, he considered how best to proceed. One way or another he would have the truth from the servants at Bellewyck Abbey, beginning with Miss Tatum. Just then, a movement in the distance caught his eye. A coach led by four high-stepping bays approached the abbey and it was imperative he greet the driver alone.

"Pray excuse me, Miss Tatum. It appears my luggage has arrived."

CHAPTER SIX

"Though thy enemy seem a mouse,
yet watch him like a lion."
~ Proverb

With hands clasped behind his back, the steward stood on the crushed shell drive, his posture erect as the magnificent chocolate brown coach rolled to a stop. Taking a step closer to the mullioned window, Christiana watched as Mr. Randolph stood ready to greet the occupants of the elegant carriage.

"That coach delivers more than luggage," she said.

Raising a trembling hand to her lips, she waited to see if the Duke of Pemberton had decided to visit Bellewyck Abbey after all. Then again, perhaps Mr. Randolph was married and his wife had come to join him? Oddly enough, the thought he might have a wife seemed more disturbing than having to come face-to-face with the rich and powerful duke.

Beneath her gaze, the coachman doffed his hat and approached Mr. Randolph, making no attempt to open the carriage door. The two men appeared to know one another and whatever the steward said, the driver seemed to find of keen interest.

With a quick glance to the gallery windows, Devlin saw a shadow step back out of view. She'd been spying on him, just as he'd thought. Returning his attention to the coachman, he said, "Remember my instructions, Nash. My identity must not be revealed unless I give you leave to do so. I am simply Mr. Randolph, a steward hired by the Duke of Pemberton."

"As you wish, Your Grace—I mean, Mr. Randolph, sir."

Upon re-entering the house, Devlin saw Miss Tatum step out of the shadows from the staircase into the hall. The woman must have raced down the stairs; there could be no other explanation for her timely arrival. Noting Nash's interest in the striking beauty, Devlin murmured, "House-keeper."

"Miss Tatum," he called. "Permit me to introduce Nash, newly arrived from London with my luggage."

"Welcome to Bellewyck Abbey, Nash."

"Thank you, Miss Tatum." Nash doffed his hat, his bright amber eyes staring at the housekeeper like a besotted youth.

Devlin could little help but notice Miss Tatum had chosen to all but ignore his presence, preferring to focus her attention on the coachman. "Might I enquire who owns that beautiful carriage, Nash?"

"It, uh..." Nash stammered.

"The Duke of Pemberton," Devlin contributed. "His Grace has dispatched it for my use at Bellewyck Abbey. A good thing, too, since the estate has no such conveyance."

Miss Tatum turned her attention to him then, a mocking twinkle in her eyes. "Yet another generous gesture from His Grace. You don't suppose he is trying to buy your loyalty, do you?"

"I hardly think so," Devlin replied with a sarcastic edge. "The Duke of Pemberton is one of the wealthiest men in England, Miss Tatum. He owns a great many carriages much finer than this one. I doubt he will even miss it."

"That seems an ungracious remark in light of the duke's generosity toward you." She turned to the coachman. "Do you not think so, Nash?"

The coachman looked back and forth between the man who paid his wages and the inquisitive housekeeper. Devlin nodded, encouraging him to answer the damn question.

Nash shrugged. "To be honest, I cannot say His Grace is a generous man—especially toward his servants."

Devlin glared at him. "Perhaps it depends on the servant."

Looking back at his housekeeper, Devlin found her watching him with a somewhat satisfied gleam in her eyes. *She couldn't possibly have surmised my true identity in so short a time.* It seemed more likely Nash's comment had validated her already poor opinion of the Duke of Pemberton. Still, the woman was perceptive.

"By the by, Miss Tatum," he said. "The Duke of Pemberton has requested Nash remain at Bellewyck for a time to oversee the stables, such as they are."

She nodded and glanced down at the trunk beside Nash's feet. "Does that belong to you, Mr. Randolph?"

"Yes." Her interest in the finely carved chest was tangible, but unless the woman was proficient at picking locks, it should be safe for the time being. "Have that Rooney fellow bring it up to my chamber straightaway. I daresay he's lurking about the grounds. I have yet to see the man doing anything constructive."

She bristled, her eyes narrowed. "Tom Rooney does not lurk."

"No need for that, Mr. Randolph, sir," Nash interrupted. "I've brought it this far, I can carry it up to your room myself." The coachman then picked up the cumbersome chest and balanced it over one broad shoulder. "Miss Tatum, if you would kindly direct me?"

"I would be happy to."

"Not bloody likely!" Devlin snapped. Seeing the startled faces of his housekeeper and coachman, he added, "That is to say, there is something I must retrieve from my room. I shall escort Nash to my chamber, Miss Tatum."

Noting the ill-concealed amusement on Nash's face, Devlin mumbled, "And afterwards I'll direct you to the stables, Nash. You'll be bedding down in the groom quarters."

Redirecting his attention to the housekeeper, Devlin noted her shrewd, clearly intrigued expression. No doubt baffled by his relationship with the coachman, she likely calculated how much information she might glean from Nash in private.

"Miss Tatum, since you are so very impressed with the duke's fine carriage, I leave it to you to see it housed in a suitable manner. Not that I expect you to lift anything heavy, mind you. After all, you are just a woman."

A contemptuous look passed across her face and she mumbled something that sounded like "One, two, three."

"What did you say?"

She shook her head and smiled—the picture of innocence.

Turning toward the stairs, Devlin noticed Nash's admiring gaze reluctantly leave the stunning Miss Tatum. He hoped having Nash here wouldn't prove a mistake. Now that he thought of it, the man did have a reputation amongst the female Pemberton servants for being a charmer. Best keep Nash and Miss Tatum apart as much as possible. Nash could charm that harpy, Polly.

Devlin glanced back at his housekeeper. "Miss Tatum."

"Yes, Mr. Randolph."

"Pray do not wander off as is your wont to do. I intend to see the accounts today and am in no mood to search for you."

She nodded without comment, but no sooner had he started to ascend the stairs when he heard her mumble under her breath. "Four, five, six, seven."

Pausing, Devlin looked over his shoulder. "Are you counting, Miss Tatum?"

Those sinfully long lashes blinked at him like a wide-eyed child. "I was merely commenting that working with you shall be heaven."

Devlin eyed her doubtfully, biting back a laugh as she walked away with her little chin lifted mutinously in the air.

"She was counting," he said with a soft chuckle.

"Aye," Nash agreed. "That she was."

Several hours later, after tending to the duties she'd put aside yesterday, plus finding suitable quarters in the stables for Nash, an exhausted Christiana watched the steward walk to the desk in the library. When he issued yet another command with the wave of a long, muscular arm, she glared at his back. As fate would have it, he looked at her then and caught the mutinous expression.

"Come, come, Miss Tatum," he said, snapping his long fingers. "I am nothing if not curious about your writing skill. As I recall, you made a point to comment upon the Duke of Pemberton's fine hand when I arrived yesterday."

Remembering Blackjack's caution to mind her temper, she watched the steward remove his swallow-tail coat. A white shirt and gold embroidered waistcoat emphasized the insufferable man's fine form, from his broad shoulders to his narrow waist. It was a sin for any man to be so blessedly handsome—especially this man.

Removing two cumbersome ledgers from the bookcase, she placed them before Mr. Randolph on the desk. He bestowed a cursory glance at the books then shook his head. "I think not, Miss Tatum. I want to see the books for the past ten years."

Ten years? Why did he want to see the estate books for the past ten years? She bit her tongue and turned to gather the other ledgers.

"A moment, if you please," he said. "What is this?"

She had no choice but to return to the desk and see what he questioned. A wave of heat swept over her to be in such close proximity to him. Even more disturbing was the strangely exhilarating effect the dreadful man had on her. It must be the distinctive scent about him. A mysterious blending of sandalwood soap, freshly laundered linen, the clean air, the deep green of the forest, the spray of the sea on a moonlit night, and something indescribably, distinctly male.

He stared at her with that damnable eyebrow quirked, clearly waiting for an explanation of some sort. She cleared the annoying catch out of her throat. "Those are expenses paid during Michaelmas."

"Indeed," he said.

"Yes, we hire additional labor at harvest."

"This expense is for labor?"

"It also includes the annual Harvest Home celebration."

"Harvest Home," he echoed. With a mocking grin, he leaned back in the chair and crossed his arms. "And just whom did you feed at this celebration? Judging by this outrageous sum, there must have been a virtual army in the fields."

"Everyone helps!" She cringed inwardly at the defensive sound of her voice. In an effort to calm her upset and not raise his suspicions any further, she closed her eyes and took a moment before continuing—counting silently to ten.

When she opened her eyes again, he looked very amused. What a horrid, horrid man.

"The villagers close their shops and businesses," she said quietly.

He said nothing, just continued to stare with that smirk on his face.

"Even fishermen from Folkestone and Deal come to work the fields. They camp out on the grange. Some bring their families."

Again, no response.

"Harvest is hard work, Mr. Randolph. The Harvest Home supper is a traditional celebration, a means of saying thank you for the efforts by so many laborers. It would be miserly for the estate not to provide this gesture of goodwill. I might add, Lord Bellewyck rarely did anything nice for anyone, the village included, yet he sanctioned Harvest Home. He knew we could not possibly harvest the fields without additional help. And a good harvest is necessary for the operation of the brewery."

The insufferable steward said nothing, but continued to study her, his gaze slowly roaming up and down her body in such an intimate way she felt her clothing stripped away. The thought not only prompted her to become more flustered, it conjured a strange tingling sensation deep in her belly.

"Do you even know or care about tradition?"

"There is no need to rail at me for simply asking a question, Miss Tatum. I have made an understandable observation, nothing more. Judging from the expense spent on this *tradition*, 'tis little wonder all England does not come to Bellewyck at Michaelmas. In any event, what pray tell does Bellewyck harvest?"

"Primarily hops." She walked away from the desk and stumbled in her haste to create a greater distance between them. Unfortunately, the beast clearly saw her stumble since he started to chuckle, taking no pains to subdue his amusement this time. Incensed, she put her hands on her hips, unable to hold back her temper a moment longer. "Permit me to enlighten you, Mr. Randolph, since you are obviously dimwitted on the subject."

Opting to ignore the abrupt end to his amusement, as well as the dark look that came to his stormy gray eyes, she continued, "It should be obvious, even to you, that we do not have enough staff to harvest the hops ourselves."

"Sounds rather suspicious," he grumbled, directing a now sober mien to the ledgers. "A great deal of expense and very little profit in return. There are other areas of Kent suitable for the growing of hops, Miss Tatum. I saw any number of them on my journey to Bellewyck. It might be wise to purchase hops from such a farm. If nothing else, it will be far less costly than growing hops at the abbey and hiring a damn army to harvest it."

How dare he come here and criticize the way they did things? Buy hops from another farm indeed.

"Mr. Randolph, I find it just as suspicious you know nothing about the operation of a brewery, yet have been hired to manage an estate that produces ale. Then again, I understand you do not particularly care for ale. If we made wine, might you show some interest?"

He stood slowly. "My preference in drink is irrelevant, Miss Tatum. And whether or not I am familiar with brewing ale has nothing to do with my ability to manage this estate. It is a matter of business acumen."

"Hah! I know not what your business acumen might be, but 'tis obvious your qualifications for this estate are sorely lacking. I suggest you peruse Bellewyck's informative, albeit limited, library on the subject of ale-making. There are a number of tomes you might find enlightening."

Having spoken her piece, Christiana turned and walked toward the door.

"Miss Tatum, you have not been dismissed."

She stopped, her back stiff, and slowly turned to face him. "Contrary to what you think, Mr. Randolph, I have duties to perform as housekeeper of this self-sufficient estate. Those duties do not include being at your beck and call all day long. Neither do they require my tutoring you in the brewing of ale or the cultivation of hops."

A moment later she was running down the ancient hall of the abbey toward the stairs. Suddenly, a hand grabbed her hard from behind, pulling her into a darkened archway between two massive stone columns. Fingers bit into her arms as she struggled to break free.

"Let me go!"

"Not until we understand one another," Mr. Randolph said in a heated whisper. "By God, I'll not tolerate impertinence."

She could barely see his face, which only made matters worse. It simply wasn't fair for this man to appear at Bellewyck Abbey now, the image of a maiden's knight in shining armor. Ah, but this was no knight, and he was not here to rescue her. No, Mr. Randolph was here to laugh at her, to find fault with everything she ever tried to do at the abbey.

Couldn't he see she was more than a housekeeper with calluses on her hands? Everything she'd done had been for the good of the abbey and its people. And she was tired; tired of fighting battles everywhere she turned. Bellewyck Abbey was her home—a home earned through blood and tears. And no one had the right to come here and tell her what to do. Not now. And not this man.

"I am not impertinent," she bit out between clenched teeth, struggling anew.

"Stand still, damn you!"

The thunder of his voice instantly made her stop wiggling. All too late she realized her struggle had brought their bodies in closer contact. He towered over her, holding her close against his broad chest, imprisoning her within solid, muscular arms. And it was that nearness, that physical power he so easily wielded that proved most frightening of all.

Somewhere in the back of her mind she held onto a thought that had always been a source of strength. When a man knew he had power over a woman, she was lost and couldn't be taken seriously again as an ally or adversary. Although stronger physically, defiance to his authority must not waver.

She must not show fear. Then again, it wasn't exactly fear she felt at this moment. No, this was something far more disturbing, something over which she had no control. A person could overcome their fear much as she'd conquered her childhood fear of darkness. Unfortunately, she had the strange sensation that what this man provoked in her was something she couldn't conquer, would never conquer.

The power of his taut, muscled body shifted to trap her between him and the cold, stone column at her back. He was fire and she was instinctively drawn to his seductive heat. Her body trembled with a desire she found both confusing and exciting. A strange, rhythmic pulsing deep inside the core of her womanhood compelled her to shamelessly arch toward him rather than pull back.

Dizzy with anticipation, her breathing sounded as if she'd just scaled a cliff off Dover. *Dear God, he mustn't know the power he has over me, a power I don't need or want.* Closing her eyes, she concentrated on calming her senses, gathering some measure of composure.

Then she realized his breathing sounded just as labored. He groaned, angling his hips in such a way as to press the hard ridge of his arousal against her. Even through the layers of her clothing, the gesture communicated in no uncertain terms that he desired her as a man desires a woman. When one of his large hands lowered to cup her bottom and lift her body ever so slightly in closer contact with his, a small, involuntary, whimpering noise escaped her throat.

What is happening to me? This man spies for Pemberton. He cares nothing about me and merely wants to satisfy his own lust. Well, I'll be no man's whore.

With renewed strength and a cry of outrage, she struggled anew. "Let me go you pompous, arrogant wretch."

"Wretch, am I?" He chuckled, a low, seductive laugh that reverberated through the darkened hall. Angling his head even closer to her face, he whispered. "Has anyone ever told you that you have a tongue like a viper and the stubborn disposition of a jackass? I've a good mind to send you packing."

"Do it then." She answered savagely, desperate to break free of his embrace. "I should like nothing better than to never see you again or suffer your arrogance a moment longer."

Silence. With a heavy sigh, he pulled back although he seemed unwilling to release her completely.

"If it were possible for me to leave Bellewyck Abbey this night, I would," he said. "Has it not occurred to you that I may be able to improve your lot and that of the other servants? You help yourself when you cooperate with me. Fight me and you only make it difficult for everyone else."

"Y-you do not want to be here?"

"No."

"But, then, w-why have you come to Bellewyck Abbey?"

"I had no choice in the matter."

"I don't understand," she whispered.

"For God's sake, there is nothing for you to understand. You can wish me to hell and back, but it'll not change a damn thing between us. I have a job to do and so do you. It will be easier for the both of us if we at least try to be civil toward one another."

She swallowed hard and nodded. "Yes," she said, her voice now a weak thread. "We must try to be civil."

Devlin tried to concentrate on anything but the woman in his arms or the intimacy of their situation. Unfortunately, his senses were too finely attuned in the shadows of the ancient nave. Of its own accord, his hand moved slowly to her waist. She wore a half corset—so much easier to remove—the thought further inflamed his lust. As if burned by an iron poker, he removed his hand only to have it, quite by accident, brush beneath the swell of a full breast. He longed to capture its weight in his palm, but raised his hand instead to cup the delicate curve of her cheek.

He swallowed hard. Heaven help him, but he wanted to kiss her. Just one brief taste, he told himself. Just as he lowered his head, she turned away, preferring the cold touch of the stone column to the heat of his kiss or the touch of his hand.

Though disturbed more than he would admit by her rebuke, he admired her restraint. "You smell of soap and flowers—and something else," he whispered hoarsely. "I cannot place it."

"Lemon," she responded. "It-it works best to remove soot and the smell of ash."

At once, the image of his housekeeper bathing her creamy skin with lemon juice assailed Devlin. What he wouldn't give to see such a sight, to watch her bathe before the amber glow of firelight in his bedchamber above stairs. He would approach her slowly, lift her from the bath and lay her down upon his bed, sipping the drops of moisture from her pale skin. Her feminine sighs would fuel his desire to fever pitch, yet his lovemaking would be excruciatingly slow. He would coax and seduce until she joined him in an erotic dance building in tempo and intensity causing them to soar together beyond the confines of all earthly restraint.

Devlin swore under his breath. He'd never been a man ruled by lust. Neither did he have affairs with unmarried women or servants of his household. It made no sense whatsoever that he should desire this perplexing, infuriating, impertinent servant with such intensity. *I must gain control of myself and focus on the only reason for my being at Bellewyck Abbey. It certainly is not to dally with a servant, no matter how beautiful I might find her.*

Abruptly walking away, his boots sounded a hasty tattoo until he was once again in the library. He slammed the heavy oak door, securing its iron latch—more to keep himself in than to prevent anyone else from entering. Seated behind the barrier of his desk, he tried to come to grips with the realization a war now waged between reason and a desire that challenged every bit of self-control he possessed.

CHAPTER SEVEN

"No sooner met, but they looked, no sooner looked, but they
loved, no sooner loved, but they sighed, no sooner sighed,
but they asked one another the reason."
~ Shakespeare (1564-1616), *As You Like It*

"How long do ye think to hide from him?"

Leaning against the open doorway to the laundry house, Christiana stared at the library windows where Mr. Randolph had been sequestered all morning. Then, remembering her friend's remark, she looked over her shoulder at Polly. "I am *not* hiding; I'm thinking."

With a delicate snort, Polly continued to hang the steward's freshly laundered and starched cravats on a rack before the fire. "Well, could ye think about getting' the man to stop wearin' these damn neck cloths? I swear he goes through them six a day."

Christiana joined her friend and examined a cravat. "He claims they're not properly starched. He cannot tie them; they're too limp or some such nonsense."

"Limp is it?" Polly anchored her hands on her full hips, clearly insulted. "Not starched properly? A bit demandin' for a steward, don't ye think?"

"I do indeed," Christiana murmured.

Polly returned to her work, a slight smile working about her mouth. "So, why are ye hidin' from him?"

"I told you—"

"I know what ye told me," interrupted the maid. "And I know what I see. Pretend all ye want, but I know different. I might even be able to help. I've a sight more experience with men."

Christiana arched a dubious brow at her friend.

"Well, p'rhaps not a sight," Polly said with a giggle. "But some."

"Just because you let Freddie Tompkins steal a kiss at his sister's wedding does not make you a woman of the world,

Polly." With a soft laugh, Christiana walked back to the door, turning her attention once more to the library windows.

A moment later, Polly appeared at her side, pure exasperation on her doll-like face. "Just tell me what happened!"

"If you must know, we had an argument."

"What kind of argument?"

"He wanted to see the estate accounts for the past ten years. Then, the first thing the horrid man did was start making snide comments about Harvest Home. So, I lost my temper."

"Ye lost yer temper about Harvest Home? With all we have to worry about?"

"Well, what gives him the right to judge everything I do?" Christiana frowned at her friend. "And he laughed at me. In truth, he seems to make a habit of it."

"Mind ye, I don't like the man bein' here any more than ye, but the duke sent him here and there is nothin' to be done about it. If ye ask me, he likely feels insulted knowin' a woman was doin' his job before he came here. And a right fine job, too."

"Have you gone daft, Polly? Look at this place. I know not what the monks put in the mortar to hold these stones together, but 'tis all that keeps the walls from falling down about our heads."

With a shrug, Polly blew a fat, riotous curl out of her eyes. "What old house doesn't have some aches and pains? This abbey will be standin' when all of us are dust. A few repairs are all 'tis needed to set the place to rights. Besides which, didn't yer Mr. Randolph say the Duke of Pemberton has enough blunt to fix everythin'?"

"He is not *my* Mr. Randolph," Christiana insisted. "In any event, when the Duke of Pemberton learns all that needs to be repaired, he will close the house and build a grand new manor in its stead. 'Tis what the rich do these days."

"What is so bad about that? I'd rather fancy workin' in a grand new house."

Christiana started to respond then stopped mid-breath. What was so bad about that? If Pemberton closed the abbey, renovations wouldn't take place. All the passageways and underground tunnels would never be discovered, yet she could still come and go as she pleased. She could even live in the Shadow Walk if it became necessary.

"Now what are ye thinkin'?" Polly asked.

Christiana tapped a finger against her pursed lips. "Were I to persuade Mr. Randolph to recommend the manor be closed, how could I be sure Pemberton would not close the brewery as well? A meager livelihood is better than no livelihood at all."

With a mischievous grin, Polly said. "I know a way ye could have Mr. Randolph eatin' out of your hands."

"Do not be daft," Christiana said.

"He fancies ye. With a smile here and a wink there, ye could win the man's heart and mayhap his loyalty away from the duke. Or, do ye not find Mr. Randolph a fine lookin' man?"

"Looks can be deceiving." If only she could be sure he was just a steward and not a spy. It would mean the difference between night and day, between fear and trust.

With a sigh, she shook her head. "He is the duke's man."

"Even so, I have seen his face when ye enter a room, and I have seen his face when he knows not where ye are. He has been like a hound with a thorn in his paw since ye have taken to avoidin' him these past few days. Why do ye not just take yer meals with the man like he asked?"

Christiana tried to ignore the sudden rapid beating of her heart. She looked down at the clean, but worn dove gray gown that hugged the womanly shape she sometimes forgot she possessed. Turning over a palm, she rubbed a thumb across calluses earned by scaling chimneys as a child and rocky cliffs as a smuggler.

"If ye ask me, Mr. Randolph is half in love with ye already."

"Do not confuse lust with love, Polly. Mr. Randolph made it quite clear that he does not want to be here. He had no choice in the matter. I daresay he waits for the first opportunity to leave."

"Ah, so that is what bothers ye," said Polly. "Ye're afraid of what ye feel for him."

Feeling her face heat with embarrassment, Christiana covered her cheeks with her hands. She could deny it, but Polly would see through the lie. "It makes no sense, Polly. I barely know him and yet he makes me feel things, think things, want things."

Closing her eyes, she took a steadying breath. "I feel as if trapped between two worlds. This man could bring about our doom, yet the sound of his voice touches my heart in ways I do not understand." She looked at her childhood friend. "I *am* hiding from him, Polly, but 'tis because when I see him I must deceive him. Not just to protect the truth anymore, but to protect myself."

Polly took hold of Christiana's hands and squeezed them. "As brave as ye are, as brave as ye have always been, how can ye be afraid to fall in love?"

"Look at what I have become! If he knew the truth about me, he would turn away in disgust. You saw how he reacted when he learned a filthy chimneysweep was the house-keeper."

"I know that hurt," Polly sympathized. "But, to be honest, there wasn't a speck on ye that wasn't covered in soot. Think instead how he acted when he saw what ye really look like. And when he learns ye're as beautiful inside as ye are on the outside, the man will be beside himself, wantin' ye with him always."

Christiana shook her head, determined not to waste one more moment dwelling on things she couldn't change or dreams that would never come true. "It will never come to that, because the more I fall under his spell, the more I must—"

"The more ye must what?"

"The more I must resist."

"What if he is the one?" Polly asked.

Christiana shook her head. "The man is handsome, educated, and refined. He could easily win the affections of a titled lady or some spoiled young heiress. Besides which, he's been given a fine situation from the Duke of Pemberton. In truth, I cannot help but feel there is more to his connection to Pemberton than we know. He sleeps in the duke's bed, uses the duke's carriage. I have never heard of such a thing. Either Pemberton is the most generous nobleman that ever lived or there's another reason."

"What other reason?"

"Perhaps Mr. Randolph is the by-blow of someone important, possibly an acquaintance of Pemberton? He could have been sent here to learn about running an estate, even offered the challenge of making this one thrive again. Or, he might have squandered away his inheritance and this position is some type of punishment."

Leaning her head against the open doorway to the laun-dry house, Christiana frowned. "Then, there is the fact he is so curious about the ward and claims Pemberton asked him to find it. For God's sake, he might even be related to Pemberton himself."

Polly inhaled sharply. "If Randolph is a relation?"

"Then he could very well be here to spy on us. So tell me, Polly. How can I possibly fall in love with a man I cannot trust?"

"What will ye do?"

"I must know the truth. There is still time to keep my appointment with Blackjack at The Green Dragon. I must know if he has learned anything about our steward."

Staring at a decade's worth of ledgers, Devlin had the overwhelming desire to toss the lot of them into the fire and wash his hands of Bellewyck Abbey once and for all. With a growl of disgust, he leaned back in his chair and pinched the bridge of his nose with his thumb and forefinger. After almost a week, he'd not garnered one piece of information that might prove treachery at the estate.

"More than likely the answer is staring me in the face," he muttered.

He tried to focus on the matter, but gave up in frustration and got to his feet. Hands on his hips, he paced the confines of the library, dimly aware he was talking to himself.

"First sign of madness," he said with a snort.

Looking at the desk, he rubbed the back of his neck. "Those damn books are perfect. By God, they're almost too perfect."

Devlin narrowed his gaze at the disarray on his desk. Returning to the mess, he sat and began to compare entries made ten years ago with the most recent ledger entries. Here and there in the older ledgers an error was noted, simple human mistakes. A word spelled incorrectly. An amount entered in error and subsequently corrected. Yet, the more recent ledgers, those prepared by the lovely Miss Tatum, were entirely without error. Meticulously perfect.

Leaning back in his chair, Devlin spoke softly into the empty room. "Miss Tatum's fine hand appears in the ledgers five years ago. Rather odd since she did not become house-keeper until her mother's death two years ago."

Thumbing through the ledgers, he looked for the name Tatum under household staff. At any given time there'd been only one Tatum listed. Up until two years ago, the name

Tatum had been prefaced by the name *Reliance*.

"Her mother," he mused aloud. The name stopped being recorded two years later. More recent entries record the housekeeper as *C. Tatum*.

"Question," Devlin said aloud. "Why would Mrs. Tatum's daughter handle the estate's accounts when not yet employed by the estate—at all but fourteen years of age? And on who's authority?"

Devlin frowned. Even if simply a matter of Miss Tatum beginning an unsalaried apprenticeship five years ago—perhaps in exchange for room and board—he found it doubtful she'd been so gifted in mathematics she never erred —not once—in five years time.

"Bloody hell, maybe I am imagining things. The woman is quite intelligent."

And a female might be gifted in mathematics. "Then again, what if the books for the past five years are not what they appear to be? What if the numbers have been deliberately contrived to hide theft or embezzlement?"

With a sudden flash of insight, he said. "There could be another set of books."

Damn, he didn't want to believe Miss Tatum guilty of such duplicity. But the woman's behavior was suspicious; her manner too guarded. More importantly, she alone had been responsible for the estate's books. Still, if Bellewyck had suspected Miss Tatum or anyone else had been guilty of theft...

"Why did he not punish the lot of them while still alive?"

Rubbing the edge of his forefinger against his bottom lip, Devlin stared hard at the ledgers until his eyes caught sight of something else. Removing the vellum document from beneath a stack of papers, he sighed. "Bellewyck's Will."

Standing, he paced about the room. "Were the servants aware of some scandal involving the earl? Some secret shame that—if revealed—could have ruined the man's reputation? The secret might be that his lordship's ward died under mysterious circumstances, a ward the servants now claim never existed. Was their silence given in exchange for the license to steal from the man's estate? Is this simply a matter of blackmail?"

A knock upon the library door interrupted his thoughts.

"Come," Devlin said.

Nash stood before him, hat in hand. "Sir, you might want

to come down to the stables."

"Has something happened to Luther?"

"No, sir, 'tis only that Miss Tatum is goin' ridin'. The thing is—well, her attire is most odd and she seems a bit anxious to flee before ye find out."

CHAPTER EIGHT

"Common sense is not so common."
~ Voltaire (1694-1778)

Good God! Dressed like a boy—again. With his arms folded across his chest, Devlin leaned against the stable door watching his housekeeper adjust the girth of her saddle with familiar proficiency. Her state of concentration so intense, she never noticed his presence until mounted upon the sorry beast—astride. Even then he had to step in front of the woman to block her exit.

"What the devil are you doing?"

She gasped with surprise, then stared fixedly at his attire in a rather disapproving manner. Granted, he was a bit under-dressed, but it was nothing compared with her scandalous clothing. Although he'd left his coat and cravat in the library, he was still presentable in white shirtsleeves, crimson waistcoat and black pantaloons.

"Did you hear me?" he continued. "What the devil are you doing?"

"What the devil are *you* doing?" she retorted.

Gritting his back teeth, Devlin narrowed his eyes. "Get off that horse."

"I will not!"

Not accustomed to being denied anything, Devlin took hold of the mare's bridle and held the horse in place. "Do not argue with me, Miss Tatum. I demand to know what you are about and, rest assured, I am prepared to stand here all day until you tell me."

Without a moment's hesitation, she said. "I have an appointment in the village."

Determined not to lose his temper, Devlin took a deep breath. "For someone who places such value on propriety, you must know how scandalous it is for a woman to ride unaccompanied—let alone astride. Need I remind you, as a servant of the Duke of Pemberton you represent him wherever you go?"

"I beg your pardon, but Bellewyck does not have a ladies saddle. Now, if you would be so kind as to release my mare, I am in a bit of a hurry."

Opting to ignore her sarcasm, he asked. "What of your duties?"

"There is nothing for me to do here until after dinner."

"Do you go to meet a lover?"

She gasped. "*That* is none of your concern."

Devlin watched in frustration as she turned her face away. He would have been blind not to notice the way her lips trembled. *Is she going to cry?*

He gentled his voice. "I realize you have been avoiding me, Miss Tatum. I can only assume it is because of what happened in the hall."

Acute awkwardness made Devlin flounder a moment, searching for the proper words to make reparation. His overtures in the hall had been unconscionable; his only defense that he'd been driven by uncontrollable lust—not that he would ever admit that to her.

"Miss Tatum, permit me to tender my sincere apologies. My behavior was unseemly. It will not happen again. Indeed, it must not happen again—ever."

She turned her head and looked at him, her violet eyes resembling sparkling jewels. The woman had no idea how beautiful she was or the feelings she so effortlessly conjured in him.

"In truth, I pray for the day when I am able to resume my former life in London." Grumbling under his breath, he added. "Or at least find a willing wench in the village."

She inhaled sharply, obviously having heard his remark. Her gaze narrowed, as if he were an insect under glass. "Mr. Randolph, I command you to release Blossom at once."

Suddenly, he wanted to laugh. She was dressed like a boy, mounted astride the most pathetic looking animal he'd ever seen and issuing orders at him like a queen. Even clothed as she was, his housekeeper managed to look as beautiful as a goddess. Somehow the thought of returning to the library and those damnable ledgers seemed pure hell.

"Would you perchance permit me to accompany you?"

"I prefer you did not."

"Reconsider," he said, flashing his most effective grin. "Take pity upon a poor soul. I have been shut up all morning in the library with the accounts. 'Tis a fine day and I would very much enjoy your company as well as a bit of fresh air. Besides which, I have been meaning to stop in at The Green Dragon. A man can only drink so much ale, you know. I am of a mind to buy myself some port or brandy, if they have it."

She eyed him with a wary expression. No doubt she believed him truly intent on finding a wench in the village. How laughable. From the moment he saw her the morning after his arrival, no other woman had entered his thoughts, waking or sleeping.

At long last she sighed with obvious exasperation. "Oh, very well, since it appears to be the only way I might continue on my way. But do be quick about it, will you?"

"Hardly the most cordial concession," he remarked with a wry grin.

Several moments later, he rode at the most sedate pace he'd ever sat a horse. For someone who claimed to be in such a hurry she went about it strangely. He lost count of the times he had to pull Luther back from gaining too much ground ahead of his riding companion. Besides which, the woman absolutely refused to acknowledge his presence. In fact, whenever he glanced her way, she steadfastly looked ahead— anywhere but at him. He wanted to laugh at the energy Miss Tatum expended to ignore him. Alas, he had no alternative but to direct his scrutiny to her sorry mount.

"How old is that animal?"

"Old enough," she snapped. A heartbeat later she looked at him and narrowed her gaze reprovingly. "Tell me, Mr. Randolph, do you make a habit of asking the age of every female you meet?"

Devlin started to laugh; there was no help for it. He might have known the first comment she made to him would be a chastisement of some sort. Most decidedly, his housekeeper was unhappy about his decision to accompany her into the village. Still, she was talking.

"I fail to see the humor," she huffed indignantly.

"I am rather sure you do not."

"Has anyone ever told you that you are an impossible man?"

"Impossible but *astute*," he said with a wink and a smile. Feigning a conspiratorial whisper, he added. "I hate to mention this, my dear Miss Tatum, but it might have been faster had you simply walked to the village."

"Perhaps,"—she returned her attention to the road—"but Blossom enjoys the exercise."

"Ah," he said with a nod.

More silence ensued. It was all he could do not to laugh as she nibbled on her plump bottom lip, once again avoiding his presence. When it seemed she'd not speak again, she did.

"Do you breed?"

Devlin almost choked. He stared at his housekeeper, her face as guileless as a nun. It seemed an eternity before it dawned on him that she meant breed horses. Still, why would she ask such a thing? He glanced down at Luther and then at the pathetic Blossom.

They were riding abreast of each other. The thought occurred to him that with very little effort he could lift Miss Tatum off her sorry mount and into his lap. Instead, he leaned a bit toward her and grinned. "I can say without any reticence that Luther would never be interested in, ah yes, Blossom. Lovely name, by the way. It suits her."

"I am not dimwitted. I know the difference between a rich-blooded stallion and a tired mare. I simply thought you might have been raised around horses. I understand you pay particular attention to Luther despite the presence of Nash to now tend the stables."

"I see," Devlin said with a thoughtful nod. "In other words, you are surprised I not only know how to care for Luther, but that I prefer to do it myself."

"I am only surprised you did not prefer the position of stable master at Bellewyck Abbey rather than steward. You seem better suited to that position."

"I should be insulted." Devlin masked his amusement with a frown. "You might at least try to hide the fact you believe me incapable of doing the job for which I was hired."

She arched a brow. "I am nothing if not—"

"—astute," he interrupted with a grin.

A twinkle of amusement danced in her eyes. With what could have passed as a come-hither expression, she said, "I was going to say honest."

He simply didn't know what to make of her. Male vanity entertained the thought she flirted with him, but it seemed just as likely she tried to arouse his temper.

"Honesty is a virtue," he murmured. When he caught her looking askance at him, he added, "Or so they say."

"You still have not answered my question." She clearly

tried not to laugh.

He smiled, pleased she not only conversed with him but found some element of humor in their conversation. "I assure you, the Duke of Pemberton has the utmost faith in my abilities as steward. He as much as told me, to my face mind you, that he would trust no other man with this endeavor. Indeed, I daresay His Grace trusts me with his very life."

"How gratifying for you," she said with an edge of sarcasm.

When she promptly turned her attention to the road again, he couldn't help but smile. What an intriguing young woman. He found himself fascinated with what she might say next and how she felt about a great many things. Of one thing he was fairly certain. Miss Tatum didn't like the Duke of Pemberton, which was a bit awkward under the circumstances.

"Back to your question about—ahem—breeding. Do I look like I have the coin to breed horses?"

"You might." She continued to look straight ahead. "If I were to judge you by appearance, much as you are inclined to judge others."

Oh-ho! So she considered him pompous as well as unqualified for the job. Devlin feigned a thoughtful expression. "You may be right. By jove, I think you are. I do possess a tendency to judge people by their appearance."

There was an almost indecipherable shaking of her head as she studied the road.

"Looks can be deceiving, can they not?" he continued with a low, seductive tone. "After all, the first time I saw you I believed you a boy."

She pulled back on Blossom's reins and came to a stop. He followed suit. She turned slightly in the saddle to study him. "What a curious coincidence?" she said, her expression pure innocence. "When I first saw you, I believed you the kind of man that preferred the company of boys to women."

Devlin almost became unseated for the first time in his life. "You cannot be serious. You thought that I—me—that I..."

With a soft laugh, she nudged her mare and continued on her merry way.

Initial shock gave way to a struggle between laughing hysterically and being highly insulted. He caught up with her easily.

"Might I enquire what made you think I was attracted to

men?"

"Well, 'twas rather obvious."

"Was it indeed?"

She nodded and coerced Blossom to proceed at what must be the mare's interpretation of a trot.

"For one thing, there is your manner of dress."

"You are hardly in a position to critique fashion, Miss Tatum, but I vow I am exceedingly curious."

"Very well," she said with a sardonic grin. "Your shirts are far too elegant, impractical and costly for a steward. In truth, I have not seen members of the gentry wear such finely made shirts. And your trousers are, well, a bit tight-fitted. I can only presume you want to emphasize certain masculine features— the length and power of your limbs perhaps?"

Devlin had to look away, yet couldn't prevent his shoulders from shaking with mirth. It was true some men padded their clothing; however, he'd never had the need to resort to such deceptive methods. And if she was as observant about his body as she claimed, she must have noted the struggle he had with a rather unruly part of his male anatomy—especially in her company.

"Are you laughing at me?"

He could hardly hide it now, but forced himself to concentrate on the road. When he finally controlled his amusement, he managed to speak. "And this is what you base your theory upon? My shirts are finely tailored and my trousers emphasize certain—um—what was it? Oh yes, masculine features. I must say, I am flattered you have taken the time to notice so much about my—ahem—appearance, Miss Tatum. I was under the impression you detested me— *pompous, arrogant wretch that I am.* Those were your exact words, I believe?"

And then he heard her laugh. It shot through him like fire branding his soul. Church bells seemed to be pealing across the countryside. Beams of sunlight rained down from the heavens and the entire world seemed brighter, more in harmony. He turned and stared, his mouth agape, astounded that so simple an emotion could conjure such magic.

At the same time, Devlin found he could no longer laugh or even smile. The seductive sweetness of her womanly laughter washed over him like warm honey, igniting his desire anew. He studied every aspect of her face and form.

It was a crime against nature to hide such a lush body

beneath dark trousers and boyish clothing. The black woolen cap covering her raven hair was nothing short of sinful. Suddenly, it dawned on him that she was wearing her chimneysweep clothing. Then he noticed the satchel tied to Blossom with telltale canes and brushes of a sweep's trade. Why hadn't he noticed that before?

Reaching over, he took hold of her reins and brought them both to a stop. "You are not employed by Bellewyck Abbey to clean chimneys in the village, Miss Tatum."

"My free time is my own." She tried to slap his hand away.

"Not when you use tools provided by Bellewyck Abbey."

She pinned him with an affronted expression. "Bellewyck Abbey did not provide me with my brushes, Mr. Randolph. If you must know, they were given to me as a gift."

"A gift from whom?"

"From the man who taught me to sweep chimneys." She jerked the reins from his grasp and turned her face toward the narrow cobbled bridge leading into the village. "He left them to me when he died."

Devlin didn't know how to respond. What could he say? For all he knew the man had been a relative. Perhaps she needed the extra coin earned by sweeping chimneys? In truth, the pitiful wages Bellewyck paid his servants was unconscionable and the first thing he intended to remedy— provided the servants weren't thieves, of course.

Sadly, the brief moments of lightheartedness had ended. They continued on their way in silence, both looking ahead, but very much aware of the other's presence. It wasn't until they came to the village green that he felt comfortable enough to broach the subject again.

"Miss Tatum, if it is perchance a matter of an increase in wages, I could write Pemberton on your behalf."

She directed Blossom into The Green Dragon's stable yard. A lanky stable boy ran out to greet her arrival, all eagerness to please, especially when she bestowed a radiant smile upon the youth. After dismounting, she looked at Devlin with an enigmatic expression.

"Why would you ask Pemberton to increase my wages? You have taken every opportunity since your arrival to threaten me with dismissal."

She would toss that in my face.

He dismounted, watching her remove the canes and brushes then rest the cumbersome bundle over one slender shoulder with practiced ease. With a carefree tone, he said, "Perhaps you have since impressed me with your diligence."

She eyed him dubiously, her lips pursed together as if fighting off another round of laughter. He had the uncomfortable feeling she might think him mad. In truth, the longer he remained at Bellewyck Abbey, madness seemed a distinct possibility.

"Write Pemberton, if you wish," she said with a delicate shrug—considering the weight of the sweep tools upon her shoulder. "He will do nothing. 'Tis obvious Bellewyck Abbey holds little interest for him; the servants even less."

"Why do you think so poorly of Pemberton?"

"Why do you think so highly of him?"

Stunned, Devlin stood immobile as he watched her approach the tavern door. Then, in two strides, he was at her side.

"Miss Tatum, perhaps you should learn more about the Duke of Pemberton before you pass judgment. Did you not just accuse me of judging people by appearances? You do the same about Pemberton without knowing him."

She looked up at him. "I know a great deal about the Duke of Pemberton. After Lord Bellewyck died we were understandably curious about his heir."

"You were? Might I enquire what it was you learned about Pemberton that has so earned the man your disfavor?"

"Not that it will lessen your good opinion of him, but the Duke of Pemberton is a noted rake."

With her vivid violet-blue eyes fixed upon him, and her expression reminiscent of some affronted spinster, she continued in a conspiratorial whisper. "A friend told me London papers are ripe with tales of his romantic exploits. 'Tis said he keeps mistresses all over England. And a man who loves so recklessly does not know how to love at all."

Her words had the effect of being punched in the stomach. He'd been called a rake before, but coming from this particular woman it seemed exceedingly offensive. Just because a man had a healthy appetite toward sex, didn't mean he was a lecher. And when did this absurd rumor commence about him having a harem of mistresses? Poppycock!

Realizing they conversed openly on a public street, and were beginning to gather the interest of others, he drew her aside. Determined to thwart her low opinion of him, or rather the Duke of Pemberton, he said, "Perhaps love does not come easily to some."

"I daresay it has not a prayer to find men such as Pemberton when wealth and power blinds them to real emotion."

Folding his arms across his chest, Devlin arched a brow. "My dear Miss Tatum, I find your viewpoint exceedingly cynical. Are you saying you believe the Duke of Pemberton incapable of love?"

She laughed softly, the seductive sound causing the hairs on the back of his neck to stand on end. "You believe he is?"

"Yes," he said emphatically. "In truth, I believe all people desire to love and be loved in return, regardless of their station in life."

She grinned impishly. "Ah, but true love knows no station in life, Mr. Randolph."

Devlin snorted with derision. "That, my dear Miss Tatum, is nothing but romantic drivel and well you know it. You do not actually believe a simple flower girl and a nobleman could fall in love, marry and live happily ever after."

"I do, if they truly love one another."

"How like a woman," he said, shaking his head. "Has it ever occurred to you in these absurd flights of feminine fancy and nonsensical romantic musings, that once the bloom of love fades, they'll have naught in common? The differences between their stations, family connections, indeed their very manner of speech, would ultimately destroy any affection they might once have felt toward one another. Family connections, breeding, society, even education—these things matter more than you realize. Why, the very foundation of British civilization is based on strict principles of conduct and structure."

"And you call me cynical?"

Stepping forward, she touched his forearm with her hand. He could have sworn his heart slammed to a halt in his chest.

"Love is always a struggle, Mr. Randolph," she said softly. "Then again, perhaps that is why the rich place such little value on it. I am not ignorant to the ways of the world. The wealthy merchant has no greater desire than to marry his spoiled daughter off to a titled gentleman. And the peerage would never deign to converse with one in trade unless, of course, their family's fortunes were in grave jeopardy. Alas, true love is for the peasants, I fear. 'Tis the price we pay for the little happiness we find in life."

Devlin studied her thoughtfully. "Are you deliberately

trying to vex me? I cannot help but notice you delight in making disparaging comments about the peerage and especially the Duke of Pemberton."

A sad smile curved her lips. "An even more curious question is why you find my viewpoint so unacceptable?"

"What I find unacceptable is blatant disrespect toward the Duke of Pemberton. He is our employer, Miss Tatum. As such, he deserves our loyalty."

"My loyalty is to Bellewyck Abbey and that should be enough for a spoiled duke who cannot be bothered to visit his new estate. Besides which, I have good reason for being suspicious of any heir to Lord Bellewyck."

She then turned toward the inn, but paused and looked over her shoulder at him. "I am truly sorry if my words offend your sensibilities, Mr. Randolph. Yet, I believe respect is earned by deed and not bestowed simply because of someone's birthright. You cannot force someone to respect you any more than you can force someone to love you."

CHAPTER NINE

*"You are a king by your own fireside,
as much as any monarch on his throne."*
~ Cervantes (1547-1616), *Don Quixote*

He was finishing breakfast when she arrived, immaculately attired and smiling as if the sun and moon were out in unison. Goodness, but the man had a fickle disposition.

On the return trip home yesterday, he'd been in a foul mood. Those brief moments of lightheartedness on the ride to the village had vanished. His disgruntled expression after seeing her once more covered in soot had been quite apparent. In fact, the man had ordered her to ride a fair distance behind him on the long way back to the abbey. He made not one attempt to converse. Even after entering the abbey, he glared and grumbled beneath his breath, his distaste over her unacceptable appearance most vocal.

"I trust you are well this morning, Miss Tatum."

"Indeed I am, Mr. Randolph."

"Excellent," he replied. Leaning back in his chair, hands steepled prayer-like, Mr. Randolph studied her for what seemed an eternity.

"I dislike dining alone, Miss Tatum," he said, smooth as velvet and soft as silk. "I believe I told you to dine with me. Had you done so, there would have been no need to seek you out yet again."

"I shall keep that in mind, Mr. Randolph."

He frowned, clearly displeased with her reply.

"Yes, well, I would like for you to accompany me this morning during my meeting with Jasper Collins. Afterwards, we shall make a complete tour of the brewery operation."

"As you wish," she said and turned to leave.

"One moment, Miss Tatum. I have also made a decision regarding your duties and obligations as housekeeper at Bellewyck Abbey." Rising, he walked across the length of the dining room to stand directly in front of her. "First off, you will no longer clean chimneys."

When she started to speak, he interrupted her by boldly placing a fingertip against her lips. "Not at Bellewyck—nor anywhere else. Bellewyck is understaffed and your good health is essential to perform your duties here as housekeeper. Should you disobey me in this matter, I am afraid your employment at Bellewyck Abbey must end. My decision is final. Do you understand?"

Christiana never felt more like kicking someone than she did at this moment. How was she to get away from the abbey without raising suspicion? Wearing chimneysweep clothes had always been her best disguise, especially when she had to meet with Blackjack or venture off the estate on smuggling business. Had Mr. Randolph not chosen to accompany her into the village yesterday, she would have been able to meet Blackjack as planned with no one the wiser. Instead, she actually had to clean chimneys at The Green Dragon.

"But who will clean the chimneys?" she asked.

"When chimneys need sweeping, I shall see that someone else is hired to do the job. I am quite sure we can entice a master sweep from London to relocate to the village. Fear not, I will think of something."

"But Mr. Randolph," she began, hoping to sound calm. "It makes no sense to pay someone else to do the job when I can do it. I have cleaned chimneys most all my life."

His eyes lost all warmth. "You have cleaned chimneys most all your life?"

"Well, only when his lordship was in residence," she quickly amended. "And, of course, I assisted Mr. Hartwell when he was alive. So you see, it really makes little sense at this point in time to—"

"Who was this Mr. Hartwell?"

"Mr. Hartwell was the master sweep who lived in the village. I apprenticed with him as a child and—"

"This Hartwell trained you?" His nostrils flared and his jaw clenched so tightly she could see it pulsing.

"Yes, but—"

"Was he a relation?"

"No." She paused to see if he would interrupt yet again. As she was about to comment, he spoke.

"Why would this man teach you to be a sweep? Surely there were boys in the village, far more suitable candidates to apprentice with the man. Billy Darrow, for example, is but a year or two younger than you. Why not him?"

Christiana sighed, holding onto her temper by a thread. "Because, Lord Bellewyck wanted *me* to clean the chimneys. Really, Mr. Randolph, I do not see why all this matters now. I assure you Billy Darrow had other responsibilities at the abbey."

"Why, in God's name, would his lordship choose you to do such a thing? The concept is ludicrous. It makes absolutely no sense."

Her temper faded to see his distraught, if not horrified, expression. Indeed, the steward seemed a trifle pale, one might even say in a state of shock. She studied him carefully as he turned and walked away. He stopped at the far side of the room, looking down at the floor. She could tell by the rise and fall of his shoulders that he was becoming quite agitated. Then, when he finally turned to look at her again, disbelief rather than anger etched his features.

"Are you actually claiming Lord Bellewyck made this master sweep—this Mr. Hartwell—train a small child, indeed a little girl, to clean the chimneys on this estate?"

Clearly, he didn't believe her interpretation of the facts.

"Mr. Randolph,"—she said soothingly—"Bellewyck Abbey is a poor estate. His lordship required everyone to earn their keep."

He stared a moment longer, then walked to the fireplace, mumbling. With one hand resting on the carved chimney-piece, he stared into the flames burning steadily in the hearth.

"Exactly how old were you when you began this *apprenticeship*?"

"About five or six."

Christiana saw him briefly close his eyes. Her answer seemed to cause him physical pain. Consequently, she was speechless when he returned to her, lifting her chin gently with a thumb and forefinger until she was forced to look him directly in the eyes.

"You will never clean chimneys again. Is that under-stood?"

The quiet strength in his voice not only comforted, but fascinated her. He was rather disarming when he looked at her this way. Genuine concern lit his wondrously handsome features, reflecting and warming his striking blue-gray eyes to such an extent her heart skipped a beat. At once, she remembered the way he looked at her after she'd fallen into the hearth the day he arrived at the abbey. She realized now he'd been afraid for her then, just as he was afraid for her welfare now.

"Why does it bother you so?" she asked in a near whisper.

He hesitated, then said in a low voice, "I saw a sweep boy fall to his death when I was quite young. He-he died in my arms. I've never forgotten that boy or the despicable waste of a human life. I've long considered the practice of using children in such a manner to be cruel and barbaric. To learn Lord Bellewyck encouraged the use of children as sweep boys at his estate is most disturbing."

She nodded. "Thank you for telling me. And thank you for caring about my welfare, Mr. Randolph."

Stepping away, he shrugged. "My concern is for Bellewyck Abbey, Miss Tatum. After all, you are the only servant able to read and write with any proficiency—quite miraculous under the circumstances. Should you become injured or ill from inhaling all that soot or falling to your death, the estate would suffer and I would be hard-pressed to replace you."

The temptation to kick him almost overpowered her—fortunately, restraint prevailed.

The man considered the brewing wizard of Bellewyck Abbey was perhaps the most ancient man Devlin had ever encountered. In fact, he could barely move without the aid of a walking stick. And although the physical limitations of advanced age seemed not to affect the man's mind, his disposition was another matter entirely. Jasper Collins was gruff and, like all the other servants, clearly resentful of any enquiries—particularly those concerning the brewery or his productivity. It was also quite apparent that where Miss Tatum was concerned, the old man had a soft spot in his heart.

"Did you remember to eat breakfast?" she asked.

"I remembered," replied Jasper with an element of uncertainty in his watery gaze.

"Bertie baked some tasty meat pies this morning." Miss Tatum smiled at the old man. "We could have a picnic luncheon together here in the brewery."

"If you like," the brewer replied with a shrug.

Without asking his opinion on the matter, Devlin watched Miss Tatum quit the brewery.

"Miss Tatum is rather fond of you," he remarked.

"Aye," Jasper said, taking a slow draw upon his pipe.

"I daresay you are fond of Miss Tatum as well."

Jasper looked at him and said nothing. The man's gaze through those ancient, knowing eyes was oddly unsettling.

"Miss Tatum is dedicated in her duties as housekeeper," Devlin continued with a slight grin. "I can well understand why Lord Bellewyck placed such trust in her."

Standing at the mention of Lord Bellewyck's name, the brewer hobbled over to the door, peeking outside. Was he desperately hungry or just anxious for Miss Tatum to return? In all likelihood, it was the latter. Clearly Jasper Collins didn't want to talk with the new steward—nor did he want to be alone with him.

"Why is Miss Tatum concerned whether or not you have eaten? Do you not take your meals with the other servants?"

"I live here," the old man said. "And I am set in my ways. I like livin' alone and I like makin' my own food. Christiana frets over me, but I'll not change my ways now."

"Christiana," Devlin said. "So, that's her name. I'd wondered what the initial stood for in the ledgers."

Jasper made a disgruntled sound under his breath and returned to the table. He rubbed his heavily lined forehead in a weary manner.

"Christiana," Devlin whispered, relishing the sound of his housekeeper's name. "It suits her," he added thoughtfully.

He studied Collins, curious why the old man seemed more upset. Was it because he'd inadvertently revealed Miss Tatum's given name? If so, why should that upset the man?

"I understand Miss Tatum's mother was also housekeeper at Bellewyck Abbey until her death," Devlin continued. "What can you tell me about her father?"

"He's dead," Jasper grumbled.

Devlin glanced at the closed door, determined to find out as much as possible about his lovely housekeeper's background before she returned.

"Miss Tatum said Mr. Hartwell from the village trained her to be a chimneysweep at Lord Bellewyck's request."

Jasper gave a curt nod and, with a shaky hand, poured himself a mug of ale.

So, it was true. Lord Bellewyck had all but forced a small child to clean chimneys to earn her keep at the estate. What cruelty! Did he not consider the child might have earned her keep in ways far less dangerous? Some little insignificant task to make her feel she was contributing. Were the man alive, Devlin feared he might beat Lord Bellewyck to a bloody pulp.

Disturbed by the information about Lord Bellewyck's character, Devlin struggled to gather his thoughts. "It is rare to find a female servant so well educated."

"Is it?" Jasper's pale eyes held a quality of censure.

"I thought perhaps Miss Tatum had studied with his lordship's ward as a child, but she told me the vicar's wife instructed her to read and write. I should like to meet this paragon of Christian charity. I believe her name is Mrs. Snow."

"She is dead."

Devlin rolled his eyes and offered a silent prayer for patience. Naturally, anyone who might provide an honest answer was long dead.

"I wonder," he rubbed his chin. "How did Miss Tatum find time to study with Mrs. Snow, or the means by which to travel for lessons into the village? After all, 'tis a far distance for a child to travel afoot alone and still perform her sweep duties at the abbey."

The brewer remained silent, staring at Devlin.

"The courtesy of a reply would be appreciated, Mr. Collins."

"What difference does it make how the child found time for her lessons?" the old man all but barked. "She did and 'tis a credit to her that she hungered to learn. Bein' a servant does not mean ye're an idiot, ye know."

"There is no need for upset," Devlin said. "I merely thought Miss Tatum had befriended the earl's ward and perhaps accompanied the child to the vicarage for lessons with Mrs. Snow. 'Tis a natural observation since there was no nurse or governess on staff at the abbey."

His comment was met with steely determination on the old man's part to remain silent. The only sign Jasper Collins had heard the comment was when the man began to pull absent-mindedly at a long strand of wiry gray hair on a bushy eyebrow.

"The duke is most curious about the ward," Devlin continued.

Stony silence. A hard glare.

"The ward mentioned in Lord Bellewyck's Will," Devlin said with a crooked brow. Leaning forward, he stared directly into the brewer's ancient gaze. "His Grace will not let the matter rest, I assure you. Come now, Jasper, you have been at Bellewyck Abbey longer than anyone else. I daresay there are a great many secrets you have gleaned over the years. I seek the answer to but one."

Silence lingered in the room like the pall of death. Yet Devlin could not, would not relent. "What happened to Lord Bellewyck's ward?"

"Lord Bellewyck never had a ward," Jasper said.

"Lord Bellewyck did have a ward, a ward mentioned in a legal document. For God's sake, man, why would his lordship make such a claim were it not true?"

"Mayhap ye should ask more about Lord Bellewyck and less about a ward," the brewer said. "His lordship did a great many things that made no sense to my way of thinkin'."

Before Devlin could question Jasper further, Miss Tatum returned with a basket of food. The aroma made him realize the extent of his hunger. During the impromptu meal, discussion covered the ale-brewing process from the days when the monks used herbs and spices to the practice of adding hops.

"Jasper's family has been brewing ale at Bellewyck Abbey for six generations." Miss Tatum smiled lovingly at the old man.

For some unexplainable reason, the obvious affection between Christiana and Jasper Collins irritated him. How could she look upon this cantankerous, old man with such open adoration?

Devlin snorted and sipped his ale. "For the life of me, I cannot fathom why anyone would want to remain here a month, let alone six generations."

Encouraged by the attention his statement garnered, he continued. "I mean to say, there are situations where one might earn better wages, if not far more comfortable accommodations."

The brewer and Christiana exchanged glances.

"Come, Miss Tatum," Devlin said. "You are an intelligent, attractive young woman. Your ability to read and write could serve you well elsewhere. Why not seek a better situation for yourself? Were you to travel to London, you could find work in a respectable house or even a shop."

"I have no desire to leave Bellewyck," she answered. "My family is here."

Devlin blinked. "I was not aware you had family yet

living."

"Family is not always related by blood." Leaning forward slightly, she graced him with a gentle smile. "I can well understand that Bellewyck Abbey seems a cold relic from another time to you, stripped of all the luxuries and furnishings one expects in a home of this size and history. But the abbey is much more to us, Mr. Randolph. This is our home. Because of that, its beauty is not diminished in our eyes. We have worked and toiled this land, some of us for generations. Some have died and some will never have an opportunity to travel beyond the village. We have a tie to the past here at Bellewyck Abbey and to all the people who have gone before us."

She rested her delicate hand atop Jasper's aged, freckled hand. "Each one of us is family here. I daresay a person can live in a palace and never know such love and devotion."

Devlin glanced about the ancient brewery with its earthen floor and odors of old wood, the musk of dirt, and pungent ale. Pouring himself another mug of ale, he spoke in a distracted manner. "No doubt such idealism is why people like you are content with what little you have. But if you had a clear understanding regarding the importance of position and wealth in the world, you would not be so easily content with your situation, such as it is."

"Luncheon is over," his housekeeper said, coming to her feet. All at once, she began to place the dishes back into the basket in a haphazard manner.

"What the devil."

He studied her change of temper with great interest, a bit miffed until he realized how his objective viewpoint must have sounded.

"I meant no offense, Miss Tatum."

She yanked his mug out of his hand and tossed its contents onto the dirt floor with almost savage intensity. "Then you are quite possibly the most ignorant, overbearing, judgmental, obnoxious man I ever met."

Incensed by her verbal outrage, Devlin slowly came to his feet, resting his palms flat against the table's surface. "Guard your tongue, Miss Tatum."

She shook her head. "Is it beyond your thinking that *people like us* have feelings?"

"My remarks were of a general nature." He attempted to hide his increasing temper.

Despite the calm challenge of her stare, he noted the rapid rise and fall of her breasts above the neckline of her gown. He could almost read her thoughts in those expressive deep blue eyes. Damn if she wasn't considering her options before she spoke again in anger, and rightly so.

Waiting for an apology, he wasn't prepared when she turned her back on him without another word. It was a moment he'd not easily forget. Granted the woman did not know his true identity as the Duke of Pemberton, but never in his life had anyone addressed him in such a disrespectful manner—or turned their back on him. This woman made a habit of it.

Just when he believed she would say nothing more, she paused at the door and pinned him with a look that could melt iron. "And I daresay I have a better understanding of the importance of position and wealth in the world than you will ever know."

The heavy door slammed in her wake with such force it flew open again. Stunned, Devlin looked at Jasper Collins, only to find the old man staring at him with that damnable enigmatic gaze and a slight grin upon his ancient face.

CHAPTER TEN

"'Tis not the many oaths that make the truth,
but the plain single vow that is vow'd true."
~ Shakespeare (1564-1616), *All's Well that Ends Well*

"What *are* you doing?"

Startled half out of her skin, Christiana looked toward one of many open windows at the stone malting house. So much for thinking the boorish steward might be off doing some task expected of his position. Instead, the man leaned upon his elbows, his handsome head and broad shoulders framed in the open window like a portrait.

How long had he been standing there watching her? For that matter, why did he always seem to have this amused glint in his gray eyes? It was unnerving.

Returning to her work, she remarked, "Turning the barley. It keeps the rootlets from binding together."

"Ah, yes, the rootlets."

She shook her head and looked at him. "You have no idea what I am talking about, do you?"

"I know you are malting," he answered with a smile.

Refusing to be distracted by either a seductive grin or the amusement in his eyes, she tried to think of a sarcastic retort, but he disappeared from the window before she could utter a word. The deep timbre of his laughter floated on a soft, morning breeze. For some idiotic reason, the sound proved a most wretched form of torture—like a brief glimpse of sunshine taunting someone on a bleak, gray day.

With a delicate snort, she returned her attention to her work. "Well, unlike some people who like to dally, I have no time for such nonsense."

Just then his shadow passed by the other open windows, and she realized he was in a direct route to the cottage door.

Desperate to gather her wits and prepare for yet another confrontation, Christiana closed her eyes. After taking a deep breath, she looked up to see Mr. Randolph enter the small house, bending at the waist as he adroitly avoided striking his elegant head on the low lintel of the doorway.

Folding his arms across his chest, the infuriating man leaned against the wall—clearly a favored pose—and said not a word. Then, with a quirk of his right eyebrow, he grinned. "I am here to cry peace, Miss Tatum."

She eyed him dubiously.

"I simply cannot have you avoid me every time we have a tiff," he said. "Besides which, I was up half the night considering your remarks in the brewery."

Christiana could do nothing more than watch as he pulled away from the wall and slowly approached her. His eyes appeared more gray this morning, like molten silver, and the expression on his face caused a feverish reaction to ripple through her body. What was he looking at so intently?

At once, she realized the beast was surveying her appearance, obviously pleased by what he saw. Self-conscious, she glanced down and fought the urge to blaspheme. Not intending to see the horrid man today, she'd opted not to wear her matronly housekeeper's garb. Instead, knowing she would be in the stuffy Malting House, she'd selected a lightweight gown of mint-green, sprigged muslin. Much too fine to wear while malting. Still, it was the coolest gown she had. She'd also gathered her hair into a thick single plait that extended down the length of her back. Mortified, she remembered she'd even fastened a green silk ribbon.

Faced with his heated perusal, a wave of embarrassment swept over her. No doubt he thought she'd dressed thusly for his benefit.

"You look exceptionally lovely today, Miss Tatum."

"Mr. Randolph, I have much work to do."

"Yes, I can see that," he remarked with a lazy grin, stopping before her.

"Then you understand I have no time to converse about anything, particularly your sleeping habits."

She'd hoped he would take the hint and leave, but Mr. Randolph did something that took her breath away. He placed his large, masculine hand atop hers, sending tingling shivers of delight coursing through her body. How strange that the touch of this man's hand could cause such a tumultuous reaction inside her.

"I need very much to speak with you." His voice was low and intimate. "Much as I detest admitting to any flaw in my character, I concede there may have been some truth to your words." Leaning closer, he added in a whisper. "Remember, I am nothing if not astute."

"Mr. Randolph, I do not think—"

He stopped what she was about to say by placing a finger to her lips, just as he'd done the other morning in the dining room when he'd told her she must never clean chimneys again. It was quite bold, highly inappropriate, and very effective. She could barely think, let alone speak.

"I dislike being at odds with you."

"You do?" she murmured against his fingertip.

He laughed softly and tapped her lips a final time. "You were quite right when you gave me that set down in the brewery. I have been overbearing, judgmental and at times obnoxious." With an easy smile, he added. "However, it would be remiss of me not to point out that you have also been overbearing, judgmental and at times obnoxious."

She couldn't help but smile at the man's roundabout apology. "Perhaps, but a gentleman would never say as much."

"My dear Miss Tatum," he said, placing a hand dramatically over his heart. "I know not whether to be flattered you consider me a gentleman or insulted by such a thinly-veiled criticism regarding my lack of manners." He lowered his head a degree, his gaze remaining fixed on her. "Admittedly, where you are concerned, my manners have a tendency to take flight."

A wave of breathlessness swept over her to such an extent she felt faint. Never before had she sensed herself in such danger, not even on a smuggling run. *Do not think to engage in conversation with this man. Mr. Randolph is far too dangerous and much too experienced with women.*

With a delicate shrug, she turned her attention back to her work. "In my defense, I must say 'tis your own fault. You have an unnerving habit of making everyone at Bellewyck Abbey feel defensive."

"Defensive because of my presence or defensive because of my questions?"

"Both, I suppose."

A soothing breeze swept into the room, caressing the nape of her neck. She turned her face toward the gentle wind, savoring the cool respite. Then, feeling his gaze upon her, she studied his expression. She saw no humor banked in his eyes.

He seemed genuinely interested in what she had to say.

"You must understand," she continued. "We have been left alone for years without interference from anyone. A person in such circumstances becomes accustomed to not having others breathing down their neck and scrutinizing everything they do."

"I see," he murmured low. "And is that what I have been doing? Breathing down your neck?"

"To a fashion." Hearing the breathless quality of her voice, she made a conscious effort to speak with some measure of decorum. "Your questions seem more an attack than a curiosity. I tried to tell you in the brewery what Bellewyck Abbey means to us. You truly have no idea the struggles we have endured just to keep this estate going."

"You are mistaken," he said, mesmerizing her with his kissable mouth. "I do realize things have been difficult. Yet I have a job to do as well."

Their gazes held for what seemed an eternity. The more he looked at her, the more she remembered long abandoned dreams of love and romance. She looked away.

"You may not believe me," he said, "but I have never thought of myself as ignorant or insensitive to the feelings of others. Leastways, no one has ever accused me outright of being an insensitive brute."

"Until me?"

"Until you." His seductively low, velvet voice caressed her from the inside out, raising gooseflesh upon her arms.

Intrigued more than she was willing to admit by the timbre of his voice and its effect on her, she looked up at him. There was a powerful intensity to his eyes, and he was standing much too close. The confines of the small stone house, as well as the quiet intimacy of their aloneness, made it all too easy to become lost in his quicksilver gaze.

"How long will this take?"

"How long will what take?" she whispered, unable to stop looking at the enticing curve of his upper lip.

He glanced at the barley.

"Oh." She tried to focus on her duties. "Several days. The temperature must be watched closely while the rootlets grow."

Devlin groaned inwardly, trying to ignore the hedonistic effect Christiana's words conjured. *Think about anything but sex, you fool.*

"How..."—he paused to clear his throat—"how does one watch the temperature?"

A faint smile curved the corners of her mouth. "Do you feel the cool breeze from the windows?"

"Not really," he said. "It seems damnably hot in here to me."

Beneath his steady gaze, a rush of color blossomed upon her cheeks, a telling sign that had nothing at all to do with Miss Tatum's labors and a great deal to do with the undeniable heat between them. He knew when a woman wanted him, but never had it mattered so much. A soft sigh escaped her slightly parted lips. Desire became an aching torment. He was hard as stone, determined more than ever to taste her lips—here and now.

He lowered his head until he was but a breath away, his intent obvious, but she surprised him again. She stepped away and walked over to a large wooden tub whereupon she began to clean the shovel she'd been using. Far from pleased by her resolve—and unable to even move, so painful was his arousal—he could only watch dumbfounded as she set aside the instrument then proceeded to close a few of the windows. When, at long last, she turned to face him, her composure was restored.

"Would you care to visit the hops?" she asked.

Good God, is she going to pretend nothing whatsoever is happening between us? It was a brave attempt, but hardly the best tactic to employ—especially with a man whose experience at seducing women was rather extensive.

"My dear Miss Tatum," he said, unable to suppress a grin. "You are the most single-minded woman I have ever met. Indeed, let us go and visit the hops."

Summer had started to wane, yet the morning was clear and warm, a breathtaking day of golden sunlight and gentle breezes. Studying her demeanor as they walked, he listened half-heartedly as she pointed out the various outbuildings on the estate.

He found himself caught in a strange fascination watching how the sun's radiance affected her violet-blue eyes, making them sparkle like the rarest of jewels. Wisps of long, raven hair danced in a teasing manner about her face, pulled free from the unrelenting tug of the wind. But what struck him most was the serenity of her countenance, the absolute joy upon her face as she walked beside him and spoke of

Bellewyck Abbey.

When had he felt so at ease in the company of a woman? For that matter, when had a woman kept him so enthralled by her presence? There was no rhyme or reason to it. She wasn't clothed in the latest fashion, although her gown today was rather fetching. Neither was she skilled at games of seduction men and women employed when alone together. Miss Tatum didn't pretend to be coy, her manner not the least bit contrived.

He got the sense she was comfortable just walking with him, at times not saying anything for the sake of conversation. They were contentedly silent for long periods of time, completely different and yet alike in so many ways. At one point she stopped walking, closed her eyes and simply smiled.

"What are you thinking about?" he asked.

"Listen. Do you hear the gentle swooshing of the wind through the trees? I love it. 'Tis my favorite sound." She looked at him then with the innocence of a child. "Do you have a favorite sound?"

"I-uh-do not believe I have given it much thought."

"Do you have a favorite color?"

"Violet-blue," he said without hesitation as he looked into her eyes. "And what, pray tell, is your favorite color, Miss Tatum?"

She pursed her lips together and frowned. "I-uh-do not believe I have given it much thought." Then, her eyes twinkled with mischievous laughter; it proved contagious.

How can such an exceptional woman be involved in treachery? Unfortunately, she was the one person the other servants looked to for direction in all matters regarding the estate. As a result, it seemed only logical he could best learn the truth from her. One problem existed. His quest to discover the truth now had him walking a fine line between desire and duty.

Never before had he felt this way about a woman. It was a combination of things. She had a keen mind and a tempestuous spirit. She cared deeply about others. Even her devotion to this decaying estate was admirable. These were traits he not only admired in a woman, but wanted in a wife. Stunned by his musings, Devlin stopped walking.

For God's sake, he must remain focused on what he needed to do. He had an obligation here that took precedence over everything. Later, when he had all the answers—and provided she was innocent of any wrongdoing—then and only then could he consider a more amorous acquaintance with Miss Christiana Tatum.

Firm in his resolve, he returned to her side in two strides. Consequently, it was with no small amount of amazement he heard himself say, "Have you ever considered leaving Bellewyck Abbey, Miss Tatum?"

She glanced at him with what he considered a somewhat amused expression. "You are indeed brave to ask me that question, especially after our argument in the brewery."

He took hold of her elbow to stop her. "I must know. Have you never thought about it?"

"No."

"Do you not wonder about life beyond Bellewyck?"

"What is so wonderful beyond Bellewyck?"

"London," he replied.

She visibly shuddered and pulled away from his grasp. "What I know of London, I do not like. Filthy water and air fouled by the stench from the Thames. Too many people, too many carriages, sickness, poverty, resurrection men, rat-infested prisons, orphaned children left to the mercy of deviates who prey upon their innocence or perhaps find themselves placed in asylums no better than prisons."

"Who told you such things?"

She said nothing, but turned and entered one of several majestic arbors containing neat rows of sturdy vines and blossoming hops. The dense foliage transformed the chestnut-colored arbor into a shelter from the rest of the world. Private, cool, intensely aromatic and very intimate.

He followed after her. "Did Lord Bellewyck tell you such horrid atrocities about London? Did he threaten to send you to London as a child if you did not clean the chimneys and earn your keep?"

She made a great show of checking the hop vines. "I rarely saw his lordship. I spoke with him even less."

Devlin took hold of Christiana's shoulders and turned her about to face him, glimpsing something in her quickly averted eyes. "You are hiding something from me. If you know anything about the earl and his ward, tell me now."

She twisted away from his grasp. "I told you—"

"I know," he interrupted with a growl of frustration. "The Earl of Bellewyck never had a ward. Can you not at least phrase your answer differently? Or, is one required to use the prescribed response?"

"Has it occurred to you that it is the truth?"

"Bloody hell, I am no fool. Someone is lying!" Frustrated more than he was willing to admit, Devlin ran a hand through his hair and looked about the enclosed arbor. Glancing back at her, he saw she held a large hop leaf.

"Forgive me, I did not mean to raise my voice," he said. "But I must know why there is so much confusion about so simple a matter." When she didn't respond, he continued, "Lord Bellewyck's Will was dated ten years ago and it mentioned a ward."

"So you have told me," she murmured.

"Yes, well, the codicil containing particulars about this ward is missing."

She glanced at him. "Perhaps Lord Bellewyck lied about having a ward."

Devlin frowned, reining in his temper. "One does not make claims of guardianship if it is false, particularly if that someone is an earl."

Her response was to walk deeper within the arbor, giving him no choice but to follow.

"You must realize 'tis only a matter of time before Pemberton locates the codicil. Should His Grace learn you deliberately deceived him, his anger will be most profound."

His words had no effect whatsoever. Amazing.

"You never heard talk about an orphaned child? Come now, think carefully. Perhaps you overheard your mother and the other servants discussing the earl's ward?"

"For heaven's sake," she exclaimed and turned to face him. "You cannot obtain the answer you want simply by asking the same thing over and over again. How many times must I answer this question? By my soul, you would try the patience of a saint."

"I am trying to find a child," he said with deadly calm.

She sighed, her expression almost sympathetic. "I know you are concerned about a child, and I wish I could tell you what you want to know."

"But?"

Her lips parted as if she wanted to say something then decided against it. When she would have turned away, he cradled her face in his hands and held it fast.

"You must tell me."

"There is nothing to say," she whispered.

It was as if a great sadness had cast a shadow over her heart. A sadness that pierced his soul. And in their private arbor of dappled sunlight and lingering shadows, with the heady scent of the hop blossoms surrounding them, the lovely Christiana Tatum proved too enticing to resist any longer.

He lowered his head, hesitating a moment before pressing the most gentle of kisses upon her soft mouth. She did not demure, but sighed sweetly against his lips.

With a groan, he pulled her hard against his body, well aware she could feel his rousing sex pressing against the layers of her clothing.

Gently stroking the tender flesh of Christiana's half-parted lips with his tongue, he coaxed with finesse and patience until she opened her mouth, just enough for him to venture within and deepen the kiss. Though skittish at first, she moaned with pleasure, twining her fingers through his hair. An adventurous novice in the art of kissing, her sweet but eager response made him burn with desire such as he'd never known.

Unable to deny a moment longer the physical effect she had on him, Devlin mimicked the act of lovemaking with a subtle thrusting of his hips. However ungentlemanly his actions, he wanted to make damn sure she knew where such unrestrained intimacy led.

A wild tattoo drummed throughout his body; his breathing turned ragged, his restraint failing fast. Another moment and he would be lost. As if struck by a bolt of lightning, he suddenly knew why.

This was more than lust, more than a man's physical desire to satisfy sexual urges with a woman. He would not put a name to it, but what he felt for Christiana Tatum seemed stronger than any emotion he'd ever known. It was this startling, somewhat numbing, realization that made him pull away from a kiss—for the first time in his life.

He looked down at Christiana's upturned face, noting her dreamy, half-lidded gaze and passion-swollen lips. She was an innocent, incapable of treachery. He knew it in the depths of his soul. That instinctive knowledge made him forget all doubts he harbored about her. He didn't give a damn about anything but possessing her completely.

What was it she said on their ride into the village? *True love knows no station in life.*

Does a man who never believed he would need or want

love dare toss it aside because the most remarkable woman he'd ever met happened to be without family or fortune? He was a duke, born to power and privilege, with a family history of wealth and influence in Britain that dated back to the days of William the Conqueror. What need had he of family connections—even did she have them? He certainly had no need for a fortune. And as far as society was concerned, he neither courted, nor wanted, its approval.

Dear God, was he actually considering marriage to this perplexing woman? If anything, Christiana was better suited for the role of mistress. The possibility brought a smile to his lips. Could he persuade her to consider such an arrangement?

Gently cupping the sides of her face, he kissed each dainty, delicate eyelid, the petite bridge of her nose, meticulously making his way down the soft side of her neck toward her décolletage.

"No more," she whispered, resting the palms of her hands upon his chest. "Upon my soul, I cannot breathe."

"High praise indeed," he murmured, about to kiss her again when the sound of whistling distracted him. Damning the intruder, Devlin released the temptress in his arms and walked over to the arbor's vine-canopied entrance. Tom Rooney steadily approached the one hop arbor where they just happened to be sequestered.

"Bloody hell," Devlin mumbled under his breath.

What in God's name was the man about now? And what was that ridiculous tune? It hardly sounded like a melody at all—more like a bird call or signal, repetitious and peculiar. Doubt pricked at the back of his brain; he looked over his shoulder. With her back to him, Christiana stood still as a marble statue. Had Rooney been signaling her? Warning her about something? At once, his reason for being at Bellewyck Abbey struck him with startling clarity.

With hands resting low on his hips, Devlin waited until Rooney noticed his presence and stopped advancing toward the arbor. A silent test of wills ensued before the old man reluctantly returned from whence he came.

Despite an almost overwhelming desire to make love with Christiana, he would go no further. Some dark secret lay at Bellewyck Abbey. It involved not just the missing ward, but the condition of the estate, even the carefully recorded ledgers. As a result, everyone must be held suspect— especially Christiana. Until she was willing to be honest with him, to tell him all she knew, there could never be anything more between them. And, by God, he wanted more.

Rubbing the back of his neck, he looked about the odd-looking vineyard, searching for the right thing to say. Perhaps he should take his cue from her behavior in the malting house and pretend nothing had happened at all.

"So this is hops," he said inanely.

"Yes," she replied in a near whisper.

"They're quite aromatic."

Christiana faced him. "They become more fragrant as harvesting nears."

Obviously, they were both trying to compose themselves after the heated intimacy. Bloody hell, he could still taste her sweet lips. Trying not to notice the high color on her cheeks, his gaze drifted to the rapid rise and fall of ivory breasts above the rounded neckline of her gown. And though it pained him to close the door on the passion they so recently shared, he begrudgingly accepted the inevitable.

"I should not have kissed you," he said.

She nodded, then directed her attention to the fertile vines, gently caressing a cylindrically shaped cone. "The cones become lighter in color as they mature."

"I am sure you agree that any intimacy between us would be a mistake, particularly when so much uncertainty exists about—well—everything."

"We use the leaves for tea," she continued and plucked a leaf from a vine. "There are medicinal purposes to hops—many people do not know that."

He closed the distance between them, stopping just behind her. As if with a will of its own, his hand reached out to stroke the length of her heavy braid, but instead he closed his fist against the impulsive gesture.

"So many secrets surround you," he said. "Surround everything and everyone here at the abbey."

She walked still further into the arbor, prompting him to follow again.

"If you would just tell me the truth, things could be different between us. And I *do* want things to be different between us."

"Do you have a family?" she asked in a quiet voice.

He frowned at the change in subject. "Are you asking whether or not I have a wife?"

"Actually I am asking if you have a family—parents,

brothers, sisters." She looked down at the hop leaf now all but shredded in her hand. "But, do you have a wife?"

"No," he said, amused by her attempt to be cavalier about whether or not he might be married—especially after engaging in passionate kissing a few moments ago. "I am not married. And as for my family, there is but my widowed mother and two sisters already wed."

She nodded. "Do you love them?"

"What?"

"Do you love them?"

"Do not be ridiculous," he muttered.

She turned then and studied him in the shadows of the arbor. "I find it more ridiculous that you are embarrassed to answer. Very well, let me rephrase it. If your family needed you, if their very lives depended upon you, could you turn your back and walk away?"

"Of course not."

With a sad smile, Christiana gently touched the side of his face. "Neither can I," she whispered.

Stunned, Devlin could do nothing but watch as she quickly quit the arbor. He knew one truth now—Christiana was protecting someone. No doubt, in her mind, to divulge the truth to him would be an act of betrayal against those she loved. Although he admired her loyalty, he could not be swayed by such a dilemma. He was here to learn the secrets of Bellewyck Abbey and nothing, not even desire for her, would prevent him from doing just that.

CHAPTER ELEVEN

"He is not a lover who does not love forever."
~ Euripides (480-406 B.C.), *Troades*

'I should not have kissed you.' So said the man of my dreams. Lured by seductive enchantment, I fancied myself falling in love, amazed at the whirlwind of emotions soaring through my body. Suddenly, I doubted every rule by which I have lived. Tempted to bare my soul to a stranger, I almost spoke of what I have never voiced aloud. It grieves me how close I came to abandoning those I love.

Christiana blotted the ink from her carefully scripted words then blew on the vellum page for good measure. It seemed rather pointless to keep a journal. No one would ever read it for no one ever ventured beneath the abbey into the ancient, winding labyrinth known as the Shadow Walk. And yet the small book had become so much a part of her life, it would be impossible for her to stop writing in it.

Within the pages of her diary were recorded the dreams and desires she'd idealistically once believed would come true. At other times, it proved instrumental in purging her soul by bearing witness to all she had seen and heard. And when, on occasion, she was too weary or worried to write, a quote or thought had been inscribed to bring solace, hope, or a greater understanding of life itself and her place in the world.

With a sigh, she closed the red book and gently placed it inside the strongbox Lord Bellewyck had given her before he died. Gathering a gray woolen shawl closer about her narrow shoulders, it did little to ward off the chill that always came when she thought about the evil man who had taken pleasure in tormenting others.

Why had his lordship given her the strongbox? Was it simply to lull her into believing she might be free and confuse Pemberton at the same time? How does one understand the workings of such an evil mind?

"I wonder," she said softly. "What would Mr. Randolph do if I were to suddenly gift him with this box and its contents?"

More than likely, the steward would leave at first light and deliver it into the hands of Pemberton, nevermore casting his eyes upon Bellewyck Abbey or give another thought to those he'd left behind, especially her.

"It matters not," she whispered. "The secret is mine to protect; the truth—mine to give."

Standing, she walked past cases of leather-bound books to a gilded painting resting against the wall, pulling off a black velvet cover on the canvas. A distinguished looking gentleman stared back with a somber expression. His hair was a soft shade of light brown; his eyes dark and large as the buttons on a man's greatcoat. His manner of dress proclaimed him a man of wealth and influence; even the hound at his feet looked at its master with reverence. Yet, as familiar as she was with the man in the portrait, he remained a stranger.

It was to an adjacent smaller portrait she felt more connected. Gently revealing its subject, she looked upon a face that might have been her own. How strange to look upon one's mirror image and have no recollection of that person—to never have known the sound of her voice, the lilt of her laughter, nor the touch of her hand.

She told herself there had been no sentiment involved when saving these two portraits from the clutches of Lord Bellewyck. In truth, her heart ached for the absence of this man and woman—and the difference they might have made in her life.

Are they watching now from heaven? Does a golden window open from time-to-time, a portal through time and space? Do those that sleep in death ever visit loved ones still living?

Even should they visit this very moment, shame prevented her from wishing for such a reunion. At one time she'd looked upon the portraits and engaged in one-sided conversations about her day. But she no longer whispered for guidance or invoked prayers for understanding at what she'd become. Pausing a moment more, she studied the faces, searching for the blink of an eye or a quivering breath. Nothing happened. She covered the images again.

Extinguishing the lamp upon a table, Christiana placed a basket in the cradle of her arm and walked out of the secret chamber that had been her private sanctuary since childhood. The light of a flickering, solitary candle formed an eerie halo about her head. Without a backward glance, she walked into the vast darkness of the Shadow Walk, her steps sure and certain.

Iron sconces, forged in another time, were strategically placed along the walls although their torches remained unlit now. She had no need for their light; far too many times since childhood had she traversed the Shadow Walk.

The trickling sound of water echoed as she ascended the steep inclining path winding above the underground lake. She paused at the turning point, reflecting on the alternate path she'd taken as a child, and where she'd found Blackjack in the hidden grotto. So much about the Shadow Walk had played a role in the person she'd become today. It seemed this secret place harbored not just her past and her present—but perhaps her future.

Leaning against the high stone wall surrounding a secluded knot garden, a blade of grass clenched between his teeth, Devlin watched Tom Rooney pause from trimming a box hedge to wipe his brow. It was then the old gardener noticed he wasn't alone.

Devlin suspected Rooney knew some intimacy had happened between the housekeeper and the steward in the hop garden. Of course, he could only speculate whether the old man had told anyone else. It seemed likely. *Why else would the other servants be eyeing me peculiarly all week long—or rather more peculiarly than usual?*

Was that why Christiana had been avoiding him, too? Was she embarrassed because the servants knew about their stolen kisses in the arbor, or hurt by the inept way in which he'd handled what happened afterwards?

Pulling away from his position at the wall, he followed a narrow turf path among neatly manicured box hedges and vibrant flowerbeds, making a point to admire the color and variety of the many blooms.

"It appears you spend a great deal of time here, Rooney."

Continuing to study the flowerbeds, a sickening thought came to mind. Remembering the morbid reference Duncan had made about burying someone 'neath the roses in Kent, the thriving flowerbeds took on new meaning. After contemplating Rooney and his elegant garden for a few awkward moments, Devlin finally dismissed the notion as absurd. Still, it could not hurt to enquire why this particular area was so well tended.

"I daresay there are a number of other areas about the grounds also requiring attention," he said. "The ivy about the west façade resembles a jungle."

When the gardener said nothing in response, Devlin tried to decipher the expression on the older man's face. Like everyone else, Rooney resented him. But today there seemed more than resentment in the man's eyes. There was contempt.

Having made a complete turn about the garden, Devlin noted a series of leafy Hornbeam arches leading to a second walled garden, this one larger and secured by a heavy iron gate. Peering between the ironwork he saw an enclosed orchard.

"Are those lemon trees?"

When there was no response from Rooney, he glanced back at the groundskeeper. "For Miss Tatum, I presume?"

The older man's stern frown conveyed all too well he didn't appreciate the new steward enquiring about Miss Tatum. Walking back toward Rooney, Devlin stopped directly in front of the disgruntled servant. With an unwavering stare, he said, "Surliness is unacceptable behavior for a servant to possess."

Realizing the man must be in his early sixties and would likely have trouble finding a new situation, Devlin sighed. "Then again, you are not paid for your conversational abilities. You are obviously skilled as a gardener. However, I suggest you perform your duties with the least amount of animosity directed at me."

The sound of iron creaking distracted Devlin. He turned to see the woman who'd been haunting his days and nights emerging from the orchard. She stopped short, surprised at the sight of him.

"Where the devil did you come from?" he asked. Before she could reply, he stood before her. "I looked in that orchard a moment ago and saw no one."

She glanced down at a basket of pears she carried. "Obviously, I was out of your view."

"Impossible," Devlin muttered and walked behind her into the orchard.

A few moments later, as he sat on a stone bench trying to

deal with the effect Christiana had on him, the sound of the gate opening drew his attention. He looked up to see her approach, the skirt of her gown brushing soft blades of freshly cut turf with but a whisper of sound. She stopped before him, her body casting a shadow upon his face and making her presence rimmed in an almost ethereal golden light.

"The view from the gate can be deceptive," she said. "It is possible for a person to be in the orchard and still not be seen from the gate."

Devlin stared hard at her.

"You simply made a mistake," she said with a gentle, if not, sympathetic smile. "There is no need for upset or ill temper."

"I am not upset," he bit out. "And I do not make mistakes."

"Ah," she said with a nod. "Indeed, it must be a great hardship to be so perfect. Are you quite certain you are not royalty in disguise?"

"Just what the devil do you mean by that?" he snapped.

"Nothing," she said and took a step back.

Devlin closed his eyes and tried to rein in his temper. *What the bloody hell is wrong with me?* This is the first time they'd spoken in days; the first time they'd been in each other's company since the morning in the hop garden. He'd gone over in his mind a million times the things he would say and how differently he would act if given another chance. This churlish behavior was not in the scenario.

Why was he so angry? And suddenly he knew. It was because she seemed so unaffected by his presence. His first instinct—after recovering from the shock of seeing her—had been to pull her into his arms and kiss her senseless. One thing was certain. He couldn't pull her close, then push her away each time they met. Either he wanted her or he didn't. She was guilty or innocent. Did he listen to his head or his heart?

Well, when all else fails, change the subject.

He looked about the orchard. "I have often wondered what the grounds would look like if maintained properly. And to think, I believed Rooney did nothing at Bellewyck Abbey— apart from making my life miserable, of course."

Christiana walked over to stand beneath the canopy of a cherry tree, the soft rustling of its leaves casting delicate shadows upon her face. "Why are you always so suspicious about everyone and everything?"

He watched as she selected a pear from her basket and bit into the ripened fruit. There was an innocent sensuality about her, an almost coquettish glint in her enchanting eyes. If he didn't know better, he would think her flirting with him. Indeed, he was half-tempted to look over his shoulder and see if some other gentleman stood behind him.

Is this the same woman who had avoided his company for days at a time? The same woman he'd feared had been wounded by their amorous encounter in the hop field?

She had every right to be angry with him, but her demeanor now was quite the opposite. She seemed to want his company. In truth, she could have returned to the abbey, but instead had followed him into the orchard where they were alone.

"Human nature, I suppose." He joined her beneath the shade of the tree. "I might ask the same of you. Why are you so suspicious of me?" A stray lock of silky hair danced about her face on a soft breeze. He gathered it in his fingers, inhaled its floral scent, and tucked it in place behind a delicate shell-like ear. "You *are* suspicious of me, are you not?"

"I think perhaps I have reason to be."

Devlin grinned. "Our suspicions could be nothing more than two people trying to deny something else."

"And what might that be?"

"As to that, my dear Miss Tatum, permit me to demonstrate."

Lost in the beauty of her eyes and the lush shape of a rosebud mouth, he lowered his head. There followed a delicate yet sensuous melding of their lips and tongues. Remembering her tentative, virginal response to his kiss in the hop garden, and the skill she now demonstrated under his private tutelage, he smiled against her mouth, savoring the lingering taste of pear juice upon petal-soft lips.

Her pear and the basket fell upon the ground with a soft thump. Her arms circled his waist in a delicate grasp. Groaning low, he deepened their intimacy. From that point on, the kiss became wildly erotic—to such an extent it seemed they both might burst into flames.

Womanly gasps lifted from parted lips as he kissed the side of her soft neck. "If you ever think to hide from me again, I shall tear this abbey apart stone by stone."

"I-I was not hiding," she said with a soft shudder.

He pulled back slightly and looked into her eyes. "I thought you hurt or angry over what happened between us in the hop garden."

"Nothing happened in the hop garden," she said, looking away from him.

Devlin crooked a brow, unable to hide his amusement. "Is that so? I have never known a woman to deny her first kiss. I am nothing if not wounded."

An adorable look of righteous indignation came to her face. "And what, pray tell, makes you think that was my first kiss?"

"An experienced man knows these things." He proceeded to nibble on a velvety earlobe, drawing it into his mouth and prompting an exquisite gasp of pleasure from her.

"Is-is that why you regretted kissing me?"

With a laugh, he backed her up against the trunk of the tree. "Is *that* what I said?"

"Yes, more or less."

A breath away from her sweet, succulent lips, he whispered, "You mistook my meaning, my dear Miss Tatum. In truth, I would like nothing better than to kiss you again, right here, right now."

Pulling her into his embrace, he covered her mouth in a slow, deep, wet seduction that effectively intimated what he wanted to do with a far more potent part of his anatomy. Much to his delight and amazement, she skillfully engaged his tongue in a dance as effective and erotic as a houri in a harem.

The world seemed to spin out of control. Between the intensely erotic sounds of their kissing, heavy breathing and soft moaning, he found himself unable to wait a moment longer to bury his unyielding heat deep within the honeyed harbor of her lush, welcoming body.

CHAPTER TWELVE

"When lovely woman stoops to folly,
And finds too late that men betray,
What charm can soothe her melancholy,
What art can wash her guilt away?"
~ Oliver Goldsmith (1730-1774), *Vicar of Wakefield*

One more moment and I will end this heavenly madness, Christiana said to herself. But before that moment came, she felt her suddenly weightless body lowered to the soft green grass, guided by the strong arms of Mr. Randolph. He came with her, his hard, lean body covering hers yet angled in such a way the brunt of his weight didn't crush her.

Speckled rays of sunlight glistened like jewels through the leaves above her head. A soft breeze sang sweetly about them and the very ground beneath her seemed to tremble.

They kissed over and over, feeding on each other as if seeking nourishment found only in the joining of lips. The cadence of their breathing became a melody unto itself. He whispered words of passion and guidance, and she acquiesced willingly.

Despite the thrill his passionate kisses evoked, she moaned with keen frustration, needing something more. Wanting to probe beneath the layers of his clothing and caress the naked breadth of his powerful shoulders, her fingers began pulling at the fabric. He must have understood, for he pulled back long enough to hastily remove his jacket, waistcoat and shirt, tossing them carelessly aside onto the emerald turf.

He returned to her again with drugging kisses that melted any lingering reason. Then, with a startled gasp, she realized all the while he'd been kissing her mouth, at times nibbling upon her neck or laving the pulse point in the hollow of her throat with his tongue, he'd quite effortlessly lowered her gown and even loosened the ties of her half-corset, thereby freeing the constraints of her breasts. Though stunned by her immodesty, she grew enraptured by the heated desire in his expression as their gazes met.

He gently squeezed and caressed her breasts, now faintly visible through the simple linen chemise. It proved a scandalously thin barrier between her flesh and his eyes. She bit her bottom lip as the pads of his large thumbs teased the sensitive nipples until they resembled cold, ripened berries beneath the fabric. Then he lowered his head and ringed the taut tips with his tongue, prompting a strange, mewling sound from her lips that oddly corresponded with a tingling sensation at the juncture of her thighs.

Again and again, he adored each breast with his mouth and tongue until she trembled with uncontrollable need. The flimsy linen undergarment soon resembled a second skin; only then did he slide the inconsequential barrier below her now aching breasts.

Flicking the berry-sized nubs with his tongue, he teased and nibbled playfully, a wicked smile curving the corners of his lips. Just when it seemed she'd accustomed herself to the erotic torture, he drew hard upon a distended nipple, prompting a gasp of exquisite delight.

Surprised by the force of his ardor, yet thrilled by the desire spiraling uncontrollably throughout her body, she arched toward the source of maddening pleasure. Gathering thick strands of his sable hair in her fingers, she held him close against her breast. It was then she realized his other hand had brazenly moved beneath her gown, drifting slowly toward the hot, wet place between her thighs.

She started to stay his hand, but maidenly shock took flight when he cupped the heat of her blossoming womanhood. His fingers deftly stroked and plied the honeyed petals, then slipped inside her very core with a thrilling rhythm.

Wanting to focus on what she was feeling, she closed her eyes and heard the labored sound of his breathing. Was he in just as uncontrollable a state as she? Opening her eyes, his expression appeared one of both exquisite pleasure and aching torment. Pulling his head to her mouth, she kissed him with all the need that pulsed and vibrated through her body.

His skilled hand continued its merciless ministration, insidiously finding some hidden pearl deep within her woman's flesh and manipulating it in such a way she found herself shaking with need, approaching yet another portal of erotic ecstasy.

The elusive horizon drew near until it seemed she no longer possessed a will of her own, restraint, or even control of her body. Unable to speak, she could do nothing more than embrace the magic conjured by this man and pray she survived. And when it seemed she could endure not one moment longer of this strange pleasure-pain, she took flight in undulating waves of rapture.

Christiana knew not how long it took for her to return to some semblance of her former self. When it seemed her spirit had returned to her body, her eyes fluttered open. The first thing she saw was his beautiful face smiling down at her with an expression of pride and something else, something very powerful.

Angling his body in such a way he rested the brunt of his weight upon an elbow, he cradled his free hand about the nape of her neck with such gentleness it made her want to weep. More than anything, she longed to confide in him, to trust him with her very heart. If he truly cared for her, if this was not merely reckless abandon, he would tell her what she needed to know and set her fears to rest.

Ask him now, before it's too late.

His eyes darkened as he leaned closer, his lips brushing against hers with an exquisite tenderness. Almost with a will of its own, her voice lifted from her throat. "Why are you really here at Bellewyck?"

He pulled back, his breathing labored. "What?"

"Please, tell me why you came here." She spoke quickly, hoping that by speaking the words in haste he might answer just so.

He looked at her as if he had never seen her before. A heartbeat later he all but jumped to his feet, roughly adjusting trousers she'd not realized were even unfastened. Lifting his shirt from the ground, he shook it out, then turned and glared at her.

"I am nothing if not curious, my sweet. Why the devil do you think I have come here?"

Sitting up, she awkwardly corrected her chemise, trembling with the realization she'd just made a horrible mistake. Not only had she shattered the beauty of their intimacy, but if he was truly just a steward, he now had more reason to suspect her than ever before.

As she struggled to tighten the front lacings of her corset

and situate her gown, she studied his profile. His jaw clenched so hard she saw it pulsing; his breathing expelled hard and fast. As if feeling her avid attention, he turned to her. The contempt in his eyes was palpable; she wanted to disappear. Death itself seemed enticing.

Though still trembling, she managed to stand, bolstering her shoulders back and feigning courage she no longer felt. It was difficult to bring some measure of calm to her voice, but she owed him some sort of explanation.

"I-I am sorry, but I-I just happened to recall how you said you did not want to be at Bellewyck Abbey."

"You happened to recall? And just when, pray tell, did you happen to recall that remark?" His voice became more forceful, but still a deadly quiet. "Do tell me, my sweet. At what point during the throes of passion did that particular thought come to mind?"

Retrieving his waistcoat and jacket from the ground, he donned the garments in haste. Facing her again, his eyes narrowed into hard slits. "Did you think by gifting me with your body I would be so besotted by the honor I would forget my duty to this estate?"

"Can you not try to understand?"

He held up a hand to silence her. "I believe I understand well enough, thank you."

"Do you?" she snapped. "I think not. You made it quite clear from the moment you arrived that you do not like being at the abbey. You have no interest in ale-making and, judging by the way you are now behaving, I strongly suspect you do not even like me. Am I simply a diversion whilst you are here? A comely country wench to dally with during your exile from London?"

"Oh-ho," he exclaimed. "That's a woman for you. Do not even think to twist this around to me, my sweet. You and you alone are responsible for this little fiasco. You started this encounter when you followed me into this orchard. And, I might add, you were hardly reticent about accepting my advances. Or was this entire scenario planned?"

Angry now, Christiana put her hands on her hips. "Dare I remind you, my dear Mr. Randolph, that you kissed me and then you, you, you..."

He arched a brow and smirked, taunting her for an explanation.

"You know what you did," she charged. "You were touching me in, well, in a most ungentlemanly manner." She tried again, gesturing madly at his face, his hands, and the rest of his body. Yet all that came out of her mouth was. "You, you, you."

With his arms folded across his broad chest, he smiled sardonically. "Do go on. You were saying?"

Unable to complete her thought, Christiana closed her eyes and counted, silently but quickly, to ten. She refused to behave like some stuttering dimwit. By sheer force of will, she opened her eyes. "You know what you did," she calmly continued. "And I would not have followed you into this orchard had you not been so upset about my coming out of it."

He stalked toward her until her back was once more against the trunk of the cherry tree. This time, however, he stopped an arm's length away. "Since the only way one might reach the orchard is through the knot garden where, incidentally, I was conversing with Rooney, I was understandably curious how you happened to fly over a stone wall and into this orchard without my notice."

She glared at him. "You are mad!"

"And you are guilty as sin!"

Christiana felt the blood drain out of her body. "What?"

"You heard me."

She swallowed with difficulty. "And of what precisely am I guilty?"

"I have my suspicions," he mumbled.

"I am all amazement," she said, forcing an imperious tone she didn't feel. "Would you care to be more specific?"

"Permit me to enumerate," he said with a forced smile. "You disappear for days then appear as if from nowhere. You are damn secretive. You are guarded about everything I ask. I still have not ruled out the possibility you and the others have stolen from the estate, hence explaining its sparse furnishings. I also suspect that you, my impertinent little housekeeper, have falsified the books to cover theft. In general, I have not believed a damn word any of you has said."

She tried not to show how terrified she was, but it soon became impossible. A wave of dizziness swept over her at the implications of his words. Apart from the fact he was too close to the truth, there was one other reality she could no longer ignore. It cut through her heart.

Mr. Randolph was spying for Pemberton.

Feeling trapped, she managed to side-step away from the tree. Bile rose in her throat. She was going to be sick. No, she was going to faint. Tears stung her eyes, but she refused to cry in front of this man. Instead, she raised her quivering chin, praying he wouldn't notice, and said nothing.

He looked at her, his expression cold and unwavering in its contempt. "Mark my words, I intend to make it my life's work to learn what you are hiding."

Trembling so hard, she was shaking, Christiana could only watch as Mr. Randolph stormed out of the orchard. She heard the gate slam shut. Only then did her knees give way, allowing her to collapse upon the ground. Stunned by what had just happened between them and the condemning things he'd said, she didn't even try to stop the tears.

CHAPTER THIRTEEN

*"Curiosity is one of the most permanent and certain
characteristics of a vigorous intellect."*
~ Samuel Johnson (1709-1784), *The Rambler*

He missed London, the daily rituals of a well-ordered life, the comforts of his home in Mayfair, and the noise of carriages ambling through Hyde Park. He longed to discuss politics in tobacco-scented sanctuaries of masculinity on Pall Mall, or take an early morning ride along Rotten Row. Even the social whirl of parties, musicales and gaming dens seemed of another time, another life. And though he missed the sexual satisfaction experienced as the Duke of Pemberton, his desire was now focused on someone much closer than London, someone with breathtaking blue eyes and raven hair.

Four monotonous days had passed since his passionate rendezvous and tumultuous argument with Christiana in the orchard. Accompanying those days, four grueling nights found him unable to do anything but think of her. He couldn't sleep, could barely eat. And were there anything more substantial to drink than Bellewyck ale, he would likely find himself foxed every night.

It was guilt. It had to be. No matter how justified he felt at the time, he was appalled at his loss of temper and cruelty in the orchard. She'd done nothing more than ask a question about why he came to Bellewyck Abbey. In retrospect, his anger had been more at her timing than anything else. Yet rather than handle the situation in stride, perhaps even humor, he made threats and cruel accusations.

"What if I am wrong about her—about all of them?"

He still had no proof about the existence of a ward. And despite suspicion and speculation, he'd not found one shred of evidence that might condemn the servants of any wrongdoing. Even his theory about another set of books was mere conjecture.

Every servant at Bellewyck Abbey worked extremely hard,

performed a variety of duties, and received pitifully low wages. They woke before dawn and retired early. No doubt exhausted, the entire household slept peacefully at an hour when he would ordinarily be going out for an evening of social delights in town.

Flat on his back, hands clasped behind his head, Devlin stared at the collection of nubile nymphs cavorting shamelessly on the gauche French toile bed hangings. But the only figure he wanted to see anywhere near his bed, cavorting or otherwise, now wanted nothing to do with him. Like a bloody fool, he'd destroyed the fragile steps he'd made toward earning her trust.

Giving up on sleep, he rose from the bed. "Perhaps if I got one of those damn books on brewing ale, I could strike up a conversation with her on estate business."

A moment later, holding a brace of candles to light his way, Devlin strode down the long, darkened corridor toward the staircase. At the head of the stairs a whisper of movement made him turn.

What appeared to be the figure of a monk walked down the hallway in the opposite direction. Wearing a traditional long white robe, a deep cowl covered the back of the monk's head. The apparition seemed to float on air until it turned the corner leading to the tower's third floor.

"What the devil?" he whispered.

He quickly followed, but by the time he reached the corner where the ghostly figure had turned, there was no one in sight. Focusing his gaze on the ancient stone walls, a curious thought came to mind. *The same stone as the walls enclosing the orchard.*

Then he noticed a fragrance lingering in the air—a subtle mixture of lemon and rose-scented soap. A slow, knowing grin curved his lips. "I'll be damned."

Bertie Lloyd listened with a gentle smile as she sat with Christiana in the kitchen. A moment later, however, the matronly cook's expression sobered as her gaze went to the doorway.

"Good morning, Mrs. Lloyd," Devlin said, entering the warm kitchen.

Christiana looked over her shoulder at him, a rush of color rising to her face. This was their first face-to-face encounter since the orchard.

"What are you doing here?" she asked.

"Good morning to you as well, Miss Tatum. Did you enjoy the sunrise? I certainly did. It was spectacular."

He walked about the kitchen, making a pretense of scrutinizing the stone walls and various cooking accoutrements, knowing full well both women watched him. Stopping before the hearth, he warmed his hands, then looked inside a pot of bubbling porridge.

"Is there somethin' I can do for ye, Mr. Randolph?" asked Mrs. Lloyd.

He turned and clasped his hands together behind his back. "I have decided to heed Miss Tatum's advice. Indeed, I was up most the night contemplating a great many things, particularly the unique history and architectural design of the abbey."

"I see." The cook frowned to see the housekeeper staring at the table's scarred surface. Returning her attention to him, the older woman smiled in a nervous manner. "Would ye like a cup of tea, Mr. Randolph?"

"Thank you, yes." He sat at the head of the thick oak table. "Tell me, Mrs. Lloyd, is the abbey haunted?"

Although he directed the question to the cook, he kept his gaze fixed on Christiana. Obviously perceiving his stare, she blushed beneath his scrutiny and swallowed hard. Still, she refused to look at him although he did catch a flicker of curiosity in her eyes.

"Haunted?" Mrs. Lloyd squeaked. "Ye mean as in ghosts?"

He accepted the tea from the cook. "Mind you, I am not given to fanciful musings, but I believe I saw the ghost of a monk last night walking down the corridor outside my bedchamber."

"What were you doing outside your bedchamber?"

The accusatory tone in his housekeeper's voice prompted Devlin to quirk a brow. "If you must know, I was in the process of retrieving a book from the library."

"Oh," she whispered.

The ensuing silence proved most curious. He sensed Mrs. Lloyd caught the tension between him and the housekeeper, as she made a concerted effort to prepare breakfast, to check on bread baking, and to keep her back toward them. Miss Tatum seemed determined to stare a hole through the wall, no doubt praying one of them would disappear. He had a sneaking suspicion he knew whom that someone might be.

"Tell me, Miss Tatum," he said. "Have you ever seen anyone suspicious wandering the halls?"

"No!" Her tone clipped, she still refused to look at him.

Devlin hid his amusement. "No ghosts?"

"I suppose 'tis possible." She turned her narrowed gaze to him. "But since I am not in the habit of wandering the halls at night, I have never seen anyone suspicious."

"Caw, what is he doin' here?"

"Good day, Miss Darrow," Devlin said without looking at the maid who seemed determined to ruin his clothing in the laundry.

"Mr. Randolph was just telling us he saw a ghost last night," Christiana remarked. "Said it suspiciously wandered the hall outside his bedchamber."

"The devil ye say!" Polly exclaimed.

After a cursory glance in his direction, Christiana continued, "Apparently, while going to retrieve a book from the library, he saw the ghost of a white monk walking down the hallway."

"Caw," Polly gasped.

"Caw, indeed," Devlin murmured. "I suspect the ghost was trying to communicate with me about something. Naturally, I followed." He paused for effect, noting the way all three women stared open-mouthed at him. "Alas, it vanished without a trace."

No one spoke. Whereas Christiana appeared irritated, the cook and maid looked stricken with terror. Mrs. Lloyd held a shaky hand to her throat, and Polly's gaze darted about the kitchen as if she expected a ghost to suddenly appear demanding breakfast.

Why would Mrs. Lloyd and Polly be so frightened unless...

Clearly, they had no knowledge of their friend's nocturnal activities, which meant—much to his great disappointment—Christiana was guilty of not only deceiving him, but the friends she loved so well.

"Surely you do not believe him?" Christiana scoffed. "Do you not see what he is trying to do? Mr. Randolph thinks to frighten us with ghost stories. No doubt, he considers this entire conversation quite entertaining. I suspect what he really wants is to take his meals with us rather than continue to dine alone."

"Do you really think so?" he asked with feigned innocence.

Christiana tossed him a dark look. "Yes, I really think so."

Leaning forward until his face was but a kiss away from Christiana's mouth, he whispered, "I never said it was a *white* monk, Christiana."

Never taking his eyes from her, Devlin slowly sat back in his chair and finished his tea, aware that Polly and Mrs. Lloyd had no idea what he'd just whispered for Miss Tatum's hearing alone. Judging from Christiana's high color, they likely assumed he'd made some flirtatious remark to their friend.

Let them. He now had every reason to believe his suspicions about the beautiful, obstinate, fascinating housekeeper were valid. No ghosts walked the halls of Bellewyck Abbey, but mischief and treachery were most definitely afoot.

Although impatient for the proof he needed, one small part of the puzzle had been solved. The sudden disappearances and appearances of his housekeeper were now explained by the magical appearance of a ghostly white monk last night. Quite obviously, passageways were riddled throughout the ancient abbey—passages Christiana used to hide from him and where the proof of what he needed to know might be hidden at this very moment.

"This is ridiculous," she said, coming to her feet. "There is far too much work to be done to engage in such idiotic nonsense."

"Very well," Devlin said as he stood. "Where shall we go first?"

"We?"

"As I mentioned before, I have decided to take a more active interest in the daily operations of the estate. And since you know so much about the estate and its workings, the best way for me to achieve my goal is to be your shadow."

"You cannot be serious. You intend to follow me about and watch me work?"

He did nothing more than smile.

She narrowed her eyes at him and spoke through what sounded like clenched teeth. "I prefer not to be alone with you, Mr. Randolph."

"He can follow me around and watch me work," suggested Polly.

Christiana shot her friend an exasperated, somewhat

comical, look. "I think it best we each do our own duties—unaccompanied."

"Ah, but it is imperative I accompany you, Miss Tatum," he said in his most cajoling manner. "My duty is to learn as much about this estate as I can, and I believe you are the proverbial key to unlocking all the secrets of Bellewyck Abbey."

CHAPTER FOURTEEN

"No man is a hero to his valet."
~ Mme. A.M. Bigot de Cornuel (1614-1694)

Will he never leave me be? Christiana had deliberately put off cleaning his bedchamber all day, hoping he would tire of this ridiculous game and grant her some privacy. God knows she didn't want to be alone with him anywhere near a bed.

As if the man hadn't been enough of an irritant all day long with his constant questions, he now had the audacity to turn a chair from its position of facing the fireplace to better study her with unrelenting intensity. He just sat, watching her work. The Beast!—she wanted nothing more than to slap that silly grin off his face. With another snap of the bed linens, she vowed to ignore his presence altogether.

"Ahem. Miss Tatum, I am still waiting for you to explain how you knew the monk's habit was white."

She faced him. "What is so fascinating about my saying it was a white monk? Bellewyck was a Cistercian abbey. One of the more discriminating facts about the Cistercian order is that they wore white habits rather than the brown of the Benedictine order. My remark was perfectly reasonable."

"Why then are you so flustered?"

"I am not flustered."

"I beg to differ," he said.

"Well, if I am flustered 'tis because you have followed me about all day. And I did not appreciate being forced to take supper with you. You did nothing but stare at me during the entire meal. I know you suspect me of something. You made that abundantly clear in the orchard. So, why not just accuse me of whatever it is you think I am guilty and be done with it? What are you waiting for?"

"The truth," he said quietly. "You are hiding something from me, my sweet. And this may come as a surprise to you, but I know you were the mysterious white monk last night."

Christiana felt faint.

He smiled—that purely masculine, slow, heated smile that melted her insides. She swallowed hard and tried to concentrate. Was this a seduction or an interrogation?

"A unique scent lingered after you vanished," he said with a crooked brow. "And since you are the only one I know who smells of lemon and rose-scented soap, reason dictates..."

She paced, her thoughts whirling with any number of possible explanations to thwart his logic.

"Call me intrusive," he continued in a casual manner, "but I should very much like to know why you wander halls in the dead of night dressed as a monk. I should also like to know from whence you came, although I have a fairly good idea. Of course, I could try and locate the secret passageway myself, but that might take some time."

She stopped and looked at him, barely catching her jaw from dropping open. He knew about the secret passageway. *Dear God, it's only a matter of time before he starts snooping and discovers the Shadow Walk.*

The erratic beat of her heart was uncontrollable and somehow it had jumped from her chest to lodge in her throat.

"For all I know a sinister plot may be afoot." With a gleam in his eye, he added, "I might even wish to participate, if I find it intriguing enough."

"So now I am involved in some sinister plot? Do enlighten me, Mr. Randolph. What is it you think I am hiding?"

"Call me Devlin," he said with a rakish wink.

"Devlin for devil?" she asked with intended sarcasm.

He chuckled softly. "Actually, Devlin is Irish for David."

"You are far too bold if you think I shall ever call you by that name."

"Am I indeed? Time will tell, but back to the matter at hand. You must realize the reason for my suspicion is because you have a peculiar habit of becoming defensive whenever I question you about the estate or the duke's ward."

"So, now it is the duke's ward?"

"I hasten to remind you, my sweet, the Duke of Pemberton legally inherited Bellewyck Abbey. As a matter of honor, and until the Lord Chancellor determines otherwise, part of that inheritance includes the temporary guardianship of Lord Bellewyck's ward. I assure you, His Grace takes such things seriously."

"The Earl of Bellewyck never had a ward," she wanted to

scream.

She noticed from the direction of his intense gaze that her white muslin fichu was askew. More to the point, her breasts looked ready to pop out of her gown. Turning, she repaired her disheveled appearance.

When finished, she prayed her voice sounded calm and her manner more composed. "You have seen for yourself in all the estate's accounts that there has never been any reference to or provisions made for the care of a ward. It stands to reason that if a ward existed, arrangements would have been made for the care of the child. It is absurd to think she would be exiled here."

"Who said the ward was a *she*?"

The deadly quiet of his voice caused sheer panic to sweep over her like the cutting cold from a mid-winter squall. Attempting to hide it, she went to the window. "I merely tried to make a point. Why must you read something into everything I say?"

She fussed with the velvet drape, absently smoothing the faded crimson fabric. "No evidence supports Bellewyck ever had a ward."

"Evidence can be misplaced. And as far as the estate's accounts not reflecting expenses paid for the care of a ward, books can be wrong."

She looked over her shoulder at him. "So can Wills."

"True," Devlin replied. With his arms folded against his flat belly and his legs stretched out, he gave every indication of being bored. "The rub, my dear, is that Pemberton believes there *is* a ward."

They were at an impasse. *Damn Pemberton.* She faced Devlin, her hands clasped behind her back to control their shaking. *Please God, do not let him ask any more questions. 'Tis difficult enough to be in the same room alone with the man, but now I am beginning to feel like a cornered animal.*

"Tell me about his lordship," he said.

She blinked at the change of topic. "Tell you what?"

Devlin grinned. "What was he like? How often did he come to Bellewyck Abbey? You said it was his lordship who all but commanded Mr. Hartwell to train you to be a chimneysweep. Well, now I would like to hear what you thought about Lord Bellewyck."

"Why?"

Devlin shrugged. "Perhaps it will help me understand

why an earl would claim to have a ward when everyone says he did not."

She looked away, collecting her thoughts. Something on the floor caught her attention. Four clean neckcloths were scattered beneath the pier glass mirror. She retrieved them and shot him an exasperated look. "Must you toss these things so carelessly about? Polly's fingers are raw from laundering and starching them to your absurd satisfaction. She has other duties, you know."

Devlin wanted to laugh. She was such a champion for her friends and entirely correct in her condemnation in this regard. How does a man admit he hasn't the patience to tie a cravat properly? Unbeknownst to Christiana, he'd decided this morning to cease wearing them altogether while at Bellewyck Abbey.

"We were discussing Lord Bellewyck," he said, determined to return her to the subject at hand.

After neatly folding the cravats, she set them on the dressing table and walked over to stand before the window. He was struck by how small and pale she looked before the tall gothic panes of the bedchamber. Waning sunlight through diamond-shaped Flemish glass formed a surreal altar that bathed her in a warm glow.

"I saw his lordship but a few times in my life," she said, her voice quiet. "If you want to know more about him, you should ask someone else."

"I am asking you."

She said nothing and the silence seemed to stretch on endlessly. The woman was truly an enigma. She had strength and intelligence—and a will of iron. Yet, she was also a beauty who could appear seductive as a temptress one moment and innocent as a child the next. She was heaven in his arms, an extraordinarily sensuous woman, but much too guarded for her own good.

And now he might know the reason why.

It happened after her spectral appearance in the corridor last night. He'd returned to his chamber, unable to sleep, and contemplated every conversation he'd had with her since coming to the estate. Pushing aside his attraction to her, he'd managed to piece together enough unguarded remarks from their ride into the village, their argument in the brewery, and their conversation in the hop garden to glean one recurring truth.

Christiana considered the people at Bellewyck Abbey her family. She'd admitted as much in the brewery. In the hop garden, she even said she couldn't walk away from those who needed her. It was impossible for her to be behind the treachery. No, she protected someone. He would accept no other possibility.

Loyalty to one's friends was an admirable trait—especially in a woman. Indeed, he'd rarely encountered such compassion amongst women of society. Most women he knew preferred to gossip about one another.

"He was not an attractive man."

It took Devlin a moment to realize she'd answered his question about Lord Bellewyck. He could do nothing more than nod.

"Fairly tall and quite thin." Her eyes took on a faraway glint. "Small, dark eyes—much like a rat. He appeared a most sickly looking man, always very pale." She directed her gaze to Devlin. "I loathed him. Whenever he came to the abbey, I would hide. Then again, so did everyone else."

"I can see why," Devlin said under his breath. And now that he knew about the secret passageways, he could well imagine where and how his dear Christiana had hidden.

"What did your mother think of him?"

She frowned. "My mother?"

"She was the man's housekeeper. She must have made some comment about him from time to time—his likes, dislikes, traits."

"No one was fond of his lordship. He was not a nice man. I suppose the only good thing I can say about Lord Bellewyck is that he rarely came to the estate."

"Why is that?"

She didn't respond.

"Oh well, I suppose he had his reasons." He feigned an interest in his fingernails. "When his lordship did come to the abbey, how long did he stay?"

With a sigh, she walked over to the bed and sat—an action he found disconcerting to say the least. Too many nights he'd dreamt of having her in his bed, and now she was sitting with her feet dangling over the side, looking altogether too fetching for words. His body came alive with need.

Bloody hell, how do I remain objective now?

"I believe that is my bed." His voice sounded hoarse, strained by lust.

"Actually, 'tis the Duke of Pemberton's bed." When he just stared at her, she added, "Well, if you are going to interrogate me, I prefer to be seated. Now then, what was it you asked?"

What was it I asked? How the devil should I know? All I can think about now is getting into that bed with her. Gruffly clearing his throat, Devlin focused on the conversation.

"How long did Lord Bellewyck stay when he visited the abbey?"

"No longer than a few days, a fortnight at the most."

"And what did he do during these visits?"

"He took things."

Devlin frowned at the unexpected response. "What things?"

"Anything of value."

A slow rage began to build inside Devlin, try as he might to conceal it from her view. The more he learned about Bellewyck, the more he detested the man. If Christiana spoke the truth, which he suspected she did, then the earl himself was responsible for stripping the estate of its valuables. And in just a few moments, he'd also learned there had been a ward at one time—a little girl. The sudden pallor on Christiana's face had been far too dramatic to be anything but an admission she'd never intended to reveal.

Had the poor child died at the hands of an unscrupulous Lord Bellewyck? If so, why deny she existed now? He no longer knew what to think.

"I understand Lord Bellewyck maintained his residence in Bath," he said. "Is it not possible he wanted these items from the abbey placed there on a temporary basis?"

She made a comical face and rolled her eyes heavenward. "I am quite sure this will shock your sensibilities about the peerage, but Lord Bellewyck had a nasty habit and needed constant funding to support it. Thus, when his lordship came to the estate it was for one purpose. A most disagreeable man was often with him. They would drink together, discussing which items from the estate could bring the best price in London. I caught them at it when I was quite young. That was when they decided to have some sport with me."

Devlin's stomach clenched. "What kind of sport?"

She appeared reluctant to speak, but then her words lifted into the room as if pulled from somewhere deep inside, a painful memory perhaps.

"He would make me climb the chimney in the Great Room, over and over again. He even made wagers on how many times I could do so without falling. At first I did as he bid me, but then I found a narrow lip inside the chimney where I could rest my feet. When they became bored waiting, or too drunk to notice, I would sneak back down."

"I am surprised he did not light a fire and burn you alive," Devlin muttered.

She smiled faintly. "Ah, but then Lord Bellewyck would have had to exert himself. His lordship never did any manner of physical labor, and no one else here would have lit the fire."

"What about after your appointment as housekeeper? How often did you communicate with the earl?"

"Rarely," she said.

"Did Jasper know his lordship well?"

She narrowed her gaze. "Why do you not ask him?"

Devlin snorted. "Jasper will not be forthcoming with me. In truth, you are the only one who speaks to me at all. For some odd reason, I do not think anyone else around here likes me very much."

A bubble of laughter escaped her, but she quickly covered her mouth with her hand.

"You find that amusing?"

"Well, you have hardly been friendly toward anyone. In truth, you have done nothing but accuse us outright of theft and treachery. And, I might add, you have done absolutely nothing to exert yourself other than perhaps turn that chair around to watch *me* work. You are quite an arrogant man. 'Tis as if you look upon yourself as being our better, which is quite laughable under the circumstances. Dare I remind you, the duke is also your employer? If you are always so rude toward people, I wonder that you have any friends at all."

Highly insulted, Devlin came to his feet and walked a circle about the room, rubbing the back of his neck. Did she truly think so ill of him? It was all he could do to sleep at night with images of her lemon-scented body tormenting him.

He stopped short as another thought came to mind.

Good God, the wench is trying to distract me, to turn me away from questioning her about the earl. And it had worked. Damn, but she's clever.

He turned about to find her smoothing the wrinkles in the silk embroidered counterpane. Well, he could be quite adept at distraction, too.

"I suppose you do not find me attractive either."

She straightened and faced him.

He folded his arms across his chest and smiled. "Many women find my company quite agreeable."

"How fortunate for you."

"Do you really expect me to believe you do not find me the least bit amiable or charming?"

She smiled sardonically. "I think it rather obvious you do not need me to point out your finer qualities, Mr. Randolph."

He took three steps closer to her. "Ah, but you have aroused my curiosity with your comments. As I recall, you were not repulsed by my attentions in the orchard."

Her face blossomed with color. "The orchard was a mistake."

"Was it?" He stopped before her, staring into her eyes.

"I'll not discuss the orchard." She looked down, clearly uncomfortable with the subject. "Indeed, I prefer we never speak of it again."

Irritated by her refusal to admit most of what happened in the orchard had been glorious, he lifted her chin with his thumb and forefinger and made her look at him. And in her eyes he saw the truth. Despite the impropriety of their impetuous behavior, she couldn't forget the wondrous intimacy they'd shared.

She'd found pleasure in his arms, and he had no doubt whatsoever it was the first time she'd ever found such pleasure. Even now, she was visibly breathless, her eyes resembling amethyst pools of desire.

"Do you really dislike me so?" he whispered.

"I never said I disliked you."

With a teasing grin, he asked, "Well then?"

She sighed with apparent resignation. "Very well, if it makes you feel any better, you are a most attractive man."

"A most attractive man," he repeated with a crooked brow. "In other words, you *are* attracted to me."

"I said you are attractive, not that I am attracted to you."

Employing his most seductive smile, one that left most women melting into his arms, he cupped her delicate face in his large hands and shook his head. "Must you always be so adamant in your denials?"

"Do not do this," she whispered.

"Do what, my sweet?"

"Pretend you care about me."

Suddenly, he had no desire to tease or jest a moment longer. Instead, he stared at her and came to terms with the strange feelings this woman conjured in him. Try as he might to deny anything more than intense passion, he recognized the truth. More importantly, he felt compelled to tell her that truth.

"Christiana, what would you do if I said you torment me day and night? Or that I believe you the most beautiful, exciting woman I have ever known? Shall I confess I cannot sleep for want of you? That I was in bed until the wee hours of this morning rock hard with need of you, contemplating all the many ways I would like to pleasure you, to taste you, to take you."

"Do not speak it," she pleaded, the hint of tears glistening in her eyes.

"Do you not think I have tried to deny what I feel? I even told myself this was only lust." He laughed caustically. "Nothing could be further from the truth, Christiana. Whatever is happening between us is beyond our control as mere mortals. Admit you feel it, too."

"All I know is I cannot trust my feelings for you." She pulled away and crossed to the hearth, her arms wrapped about her slender waist. "Neither can I forget what you said to me in the orchard."

Devlin ran a hand through his hair in acute frustration. "Devil take it, I spoke in anger. I was upset. I would sooner forfeit my life than cause you pain or see you harmed in any manner. Is it so difficult to accept that not every man is like Lord Bellewyck?"

"I know you are not like him," she whispered.

"Then why can you not trust me?"

She spun around and looked at him, her exquisite violet-blue eyes glistening with unshed tears. "Because when someone knows only shadow and darkness, it hurts too much to look into the light."

The stark pain in her eyes was almost more than he could bear, the meaning of her impulsive words causing a strange ache in the vicinity of his heart. He knew not what to say, how to respond. They simply stared at one another, the sound of their breathing—fast and shallow—lifting into the quiet room.

It seemed he stood upon a precipice, facing a decision that would alter the remainder of his life—a decision between suspicion and faith, between logic and love. And in the time it took from one beat of his heart to the next, the choice became clear.

In two strides he pulled her into his arms and kissed her lips slowly, tenderly, wanting to prove the depth of emotion he felt for her. Only then did he pull back enough to whisper against her slightly parted lips. "One cannot find dreams in shadows, Christiana." He would have said more, but she pressed two fingertips against his lips and smiled through her tears.

"Then show me how to dream, Devlin," she whispered. "Now, before the darkness returns and the shadows fall."

CHAPTER FIFTEEN

"All this, and Heaven too!"
~ Matthew Henry (1662-1714), *Life of Philip Henry*

His kiss transcended time and space, and swept her into an enchanted kingdom ruled by desire and passion. Yet, awareness of so many details endured, from the quiet of the room to the sighs and cadence of their breathing. The texture of his clothing and the muscles she felt contracting in his back with each movement. And, of course, the scandalous sensation of his arousal pressing against the skirts of her gown.

He kissed the side of her neck, resulting in a most curious reaction. A fluttering feeling deep inside her belly grew more insistent; slick moisture gathered between her thighs. A moment later, his seductive lips slid down to place open-mouthed kisses upon the swells of her bosom, prompting her to clutch his upper arms and direct a rather unfocused gaze to the ceiling.

Do not faint.

Then, he stopped. Pulling back, his breathing harsh, ragged gasps, he flicked his hand and—much to her startled amazement—her gown slid to the floor. How had he accomplished such a thing without her knowing?

Standing before him in her half-corset, she had little time to think about the gown. His long, large masculine fingers began to release the lacings with a skill that made her blink. Pulling it off her body, he grinned. "I do so like the shorter version."

"How did you learn—"

Shaking his head, he pressed a fingertip against her lips to stop her question. "You do not really want to know, do you sweetheart?"

"No." She did not want to think about past lovers. Their vaporous images sprang up anyway, making her feel gauche, inept, and ignorant. As if he knew the direction of her thoughts, he led her to the side of the bed.

"Sit."

Not knowing what he wanted or expected from her, she could only watch as he slowly removed her shoes and stockings. Her chemise remained the only article of clothing and he seemed to be debating whether or not to remove it.

Perhaps he expected her to remove it? She looked to the open draperies allowing so much light into the room. Then again, he'd seen most of her body already in the orchard. For that very reason, she stood and brazenly opened her chemise enough to let it slip from her body and pool about her feet. That action seemed to stun him.

Determined to convey a sense of worldliness, she kept her arms at her sides and waited for his slow, heated inspection to conclude. His breathing sounded labored and he swallowed hard; his nostrils flared slightly like an animal on the scent of its prey.

He moved toward her—one step, two steps. A hairs-breadth apart when he turned her about and kissed the curve of her shoulder, one hand flat against her belly while his other hand cupped one of her breasts. He groaned low, pulling her back against his chest, the hard ridge of his still confined erection pressing against her naked skin.

"You do not play fair, my sweet," he whispered into her ear.

She tilted her head slightly and saw their reflection in the pier glass mirror. His eyes were closed, his brow tense as if a great pain had been inflicted upon his person. She suddenly realized he was struggling to gain control of himself, the heavy intensity of his breathing conveying the difficulty of the task.

It thrilled her to see the effect she had on him. Curious to learn the extent of her seductive powers, she placed one of her hands atop his and guided it further down her belly. A wicked grin curved the corners of his mouth. "You play with fire."

"Do I?" her voice a shaky whisper. She arched against him as he cupped that part of her aching for his touch. Less than a moment later, she panted and whimpered as he pleasured her with his hand. Yet before she could find release, he took his hand away, leaving her bereft and tense.

She looked again at the mirror, curious as to why he'd stopped.

He stared back at her in the reflecting glass. "Do you want more?"

"Yes," she answered on a sigh.

In one sweeping motion, he lifted her into his arms and placed her on the bed. "Do not move," he said.

Breathless with anticipation, she watched him bolt the door. Facing her, a heated look in his eyes made her heart flutter. Slowly crossing the room, keeping his gaze steadily upon her, he removed his jacket and waistcoat, dropping them along the way.

Everything this man does is erotic, even so simple a thing as undressing.

She bit her bottom lip to keep from screaming for him to hurry. When at last he'd removed his shirt and bared his chest to her view, she drank in the sight of him. From the smooth breadth of his shoulders to the narrow of his waist, he embodied masculine perfection.

Draping his fine lawn shirt over the back of the chair, he sat to remove his boots, the well-defined muscles in his arms contracting, prompting her mouth to turn dry.

"It is not too late to change your mind," he said without looking up.

"I have waited too long for this moment and for the right man to share it with."

His gaze lifted to hers. "And are you certain I am that man, Christiana?"

"I see no other."

He dropped a boot onto the floor and laughed, the rich resonance causing her heart to beat faster.

I love this man. A startling realization, yet to the depths of her very soul she knew it was true. Try as she might to fight it or focus on the misgivings she had about his loyalty to Pemberton, she could not. Like the haunting refrain of a heavenly tune, love beckoned her to this man, whispering words that unlocked the most guarded chambers of her heart.

Lingering in the back of her mind a voice of reason whispered what dire consequences befell a lady who compromised her virtue. This was scandalous behavior, impulsive, wild and reckless—even for her.

Her well-guarded virginity was all she had left—the one aspect of her person that belonged to her alone, pure and untarnished. Did she really want to compromise that virtue now with a man who'd made no profession of love? Then again, he knew nothing of her love for him. Perhaps it would be best if they didn't speak of such things.

Of one truth she was certain. This might be her only opportunity to know passion, to make love with a man of *her* choosing. It was that simple. She mustn't deceive herself into believing they might have a future together. They would not marry and live happily ever after. And since this was her only hope to experience intimacy, she wanted it to be with the only man she'd ever love.

Devlin Randolph had resurrected long abandoned girlhood dreams of love and romance. He was her courtly knight and Bellewyck Abbey their castle. She could even imagine this to be their marriage bed and make the dream complete.

"What are you thinking?"

"Huh?" She blinked, caught off guard by his question. "I...um...am just...well, admiring your exceedingly fine form."

"Ah," he said with a crooked brow. "Pray continue, my sweet."

She smiled and proceeded to peruse his body with a discerning eye. His chest was well-defined and smooth, except for a dusting of dark hairs that narrowed rather enticingly into a fine line beneath the waistband of his trousers. Her gaze fell upon the undeniable evidence of an exceedingly healthy arousal.

Devlin slowly approached the bed, a sinful promise of untold pleasure in his eyes. "I see you've noted the scandalous fit of my trousers."

"They do appear rather confining."

He climbed onto the bed with all the stealth of a lion stalking its prey. "Only when you're about," he whispered against her mouth. "You have no idea the self-control I've had to master around you, my dearest Miss Tatum."

She shuddered, breathless, as he nuzzled the side of her neck. "I...um...I must say at times you look decidedly un...uncomfortable."

Devlin chuckled low and nibbled playfully on her earlobe.

She tried not to giggle, but he truly reminded her of a lion—king of the bedchamber. Misunderstanding her amusement, he tickled her until both of them were laughing and twisting about on the recently made bed covers. Just as quickly they both sobered, very much aware of the intimacy of the moment and where they were.

"Christiana, I am not in the habit of seducing—"

"Servants?" she asked with a mischievous grin.

"I was going to say virgins." His gentle smile faded. "You

understand that our making love will complicate matters between us. We will likely still argue. I will not abandon my search for the truth about the abbey. What I am trying to say is I cannot promise you anything."

Christiana swallowed hard. A wave of disappointment washed over her. She never believed he would consider marriage, but to have it put so boldly caused deep pain in her heart.

She envisioned the woman he would one day marry, likely a breathtaking picture of femininity and impeccable taste. Without doubt, no one would mistake her for such an epitome of fashion or maidenly grace. Despite her guarded virtue and cultured tones, she was a housekeeper who—on occasion—climbed chimneys and dressed in mannish clothing. Harsh realities returned. Her dreams of love and marriage must remain dead and buried.

"I am not asking for promises," she said.

Devlin slowly lowered his head until he was a breath away, the color of his eyes more green now—like emerald fire burning with uncontrollable desire.

"So be it," he said.

From the moment their lips met, the kiss erupted into a wildly passionate volcano of need. He pressed forward, his tongue slipping between her lips and joining with hers in an erotic dance of seduction. Inarticulate, mewling sounds emerged from her throat, her thoughts focused on a singular desire to join with this man.

Pulling back slightly, he caressed the curve of her cheek, his thumb smoothing her bottom lip. "You are more beautiful each time I look at you." Swallowing hard, his gaze then followed the slow movement of his hand as it moved further down her chest to her pale breasts. Cupping a full breast in the palm of his hand, he tongued the aroused nipple, prompting a gasp of pleasure as she arched toward him. His gaze lifted to hers and a devilish smile curved his lips.

One moment he flicked the sensitized puckered berry playfully with his teeth, and the next he employed rapid spirals of moist heat. He alternated between soothing and teasing until she felt pulled taut as a bow, panting and quivering down to her pointed toes. Only then did he draw the hardened nub into his mouth, suckling at her breast and prompting her to cry out with exquisite pleasure.

Sensations too numerous to consider made it difficult to

focus on any one thing. She felt the erotic thrill of his hands moving all over her body. His mouth moved from her breasts, to the curve of her shoulder, the length of her arm, a hand, her fingers, even the inside of her wrists It became too much—endless sensual awakenings building layer by layer, yet denying her the release she desperately needed.

By the time he returned to her mouth, kissing her with an intensity that made her want to weep, she writhed uncontrollably. At the same time, she wanted to taste him, to kiss and explore the mysteries of his body. She tried to push him onto his back. "Let me," she pleaded against his delicious mouth.

"Not just yet," he rasped, refusing to relinquish himself. Rather, he deftly rolled her onto her back again whereupon his mouth began a slumberous descent down the flat planes of her belly, placing wet, open-mouthed kisses upon now feverish skin and drawing ever near the moist heat pulsing between her thighs.

Closing her eyes, she remembered the ecstasy he'd conjured with his fingers in the orchard, anticipating a repeat performance. However, an entirely different sensation made her almost jump out of her skin. Her eyes opened to see his dark head situated between her thighs, his mouth pressing the most intimate of kisses upon her glistening womanhood.

"Devlin!" she gasped. "What are you..."

Initial shock and maidenly embarrassment at the brazen yet glorious adoration quickly vanished. She never imagined such scandalous delights possible. Moaning helplessly, her fists clutched handfuls of the silk counterpane.

"Yes," she sighed, more a breathless plea than an affirmation. Still, it echoed into the bedchamber, making her leonine lover all the more voracious in his attentions. When she thought she could stand no more, he immediately found that elusive, mysterious pearl hidden within the supple shell of her sex. At once, wave after wave of blinding pleasure swept over her. She cried out in undulating ripples of wild abandon.

Drifting slowly back to self and reality, she opened her eyes to see him removing his trousers. The length and width of his erection made her dizzy with anticipation and no small amount of apprehension. He was magnificent in every way. Truth be told, she wanted nothing more than to adore his body as he had done hers. Indeed, the temptation proved so strong that when he returned to the bed, she brazenly stopped him and gently maneuvered him onto his back.

"What *do* you want, my sweet?" he asked, a strained but teasing gleam in his eyes.

"To look at you," she said. "To touch you as you have touched me. I have never seen a naked man before, you know."

A low, seductive laugh lifted from his throat. "Very well, but take down your hair first. I have long imagined it loose and draped about your body."

Beneath his steady gaze, she unpinned her hair, then released the braided tresses until they fell about her shoulders and waist in rippling waves. He twined a skein of hair about his fist and pulled her toward him, kissing her deeply.

Releasing her, he cupped his hands beneath his head. "I am at your mercy. What will you do with me?"

"I have no idea."

He arched a brow. "Well, this should prove interesting."

With a somewhat strained smile he watched her fingertips caress his body with the gentlest of touches. Then, like a sculptor molding a bit of clay, she kneaded his taut muscles. She wanted to learn by touch the shape of each sinew, the length of each bone, from the breadth of his shoulders to the shape of each heel.

Curious if he found pleasure from her touch, she glanced up for his reaction. The smile had vanished; his expression now tense. He studied her through half-lidded eyes, his breathing labored. Clearly, he was no longer amused. In fact, the muscles of his flat belly contracted hard beneath her touch. If he felt even a fraction of the excitement she'd experienced from his touch, she must go further still and reciprocate in kind the wondrous pleasuring he'd given her.

She came to that part of him saluting her and lifted her gaze to find him exerting great discipline to allow this erotic inspection. She kissed the broad, glistening head of his mysterious sex and his entire body tensed. At the single, swirling stroke of her tongue she heard him inhale sharply.

"Perhaps this isn't such a good idea," he rasped.

Curiosity compelled her to continue, but just when she'd discovered a particularly effective technique, Devlin growled low in his throat and all but tossed her onto her back.

His beautiful, hard body loomed above her, the expression on his face so feral she began to reconsider this aspect of sexual intimacy. "You are about to learn what happens when someone plays with fire," he said between racing breaths.

Before she could think or breathe, he quickly positioned his body and, with one swift, conquering thrust, pressed forward. Tearing pain sliced through her from the totality of his possession. Afraid to move lest she make it worse, she concentrated only on the erratic beating of her heart. Refusing to cry like some wounded, simpering virgin, she listened to his labored breathing as he remained motionless inside her.

"I'm sorry, sweetheart," he said. "There will be no more pain, I promise."

She squirmed to find a more comfortable position.

"Remain still," he soothed. "Just give it a moment."

Mindful of the rigid, pulsing length still buried inside her body, she waited. The burning sensation began to subside, followed by a strangely comforting, even reassuring intimacy from being joined with him. Realizing he'd still not moved, she hoped he recovered soon because his weight on her made it difficult to breathe. A sudden thought occurred to her. Polly said there would be blood when a woman's maidenhead was rendered.

"Oh, no!" she gasped. "The counterpane."

"Pain?" Devlin lifted his face from nuzzling her neck, confusion etched across his furrowed brow. "What pain?"

"The counterpane is silk," she whispered. "It will be ruined."

"Forget the damn counterpane, and try to remain still a bit longer." He closed his eyes and moaned something about her being so tight.

"Oh, no," she gasped. "Devlin, please tell me you have not become stuck."

A slow, seductive grin curved his lip. Then he began to laugh, soft and low. And when he laughed, she gasped from an altogether different sensation. Unfortunately, it was then he began to withdraw from her body, a fraction at a time until he was almost unseated. She clutched at his shoulders, feeling strangely abandoned. But he returned and began to repeat the process in an erotic, rhythmic manner.

"Ahhhh," she gasped. "Oh my, Devlin, this is—"

The sexual awakening Devlin saw reflected in Christiana's eyes inflamed his already desperate hunger, driving him to thrust with almost savage intensity. Instinctively, she met him, undulating against him like a skilled courtesan.

"That's it," he said, groaning low in his throat. "Come with me, move with me just like that, again, again."

All the while he moved inside her, Devlin watched Christiana—learning what she enjoyed, amazed by her lack of inhibition. Erotic sounds lifted from her throat. Indeed, he'd never known such a vocal lover—or one so responsive and eager to please. His own restraint was failing fast, yet he focused on bringing her pleasure first. When she suddenly arched upwards, licking the straining cords of his neck, he knew he'd never felt such exquisite torture.

Even the ancient bed creaked in protest.

"Oh God, oh God," she cried out, quivering uncontrollably.

Determined they find release together, he quickened his thrusts, each penetration hard and deep. She cried out, holding fast to his shoulders, panting wildly, and rising up to each downward thrust in such a wildly sensuous way he quickly lost all rational thought.

He must withdraw. Now, before it was too late. Yet, within him a supreme sense of possession drove him onward with unrelenting intensity to claim her so completely that no other man would ever take his place.

With tenuous control, he waited until she crested the horizon, contracting wildly around his painfully engorged shaft. Illogical, lust-induced madness possessed him; he soared with her—inside her. The force of his release so intense he could almost visualize his seed flooding the very depths of her womb.

After the rhythmic pulsing had subsided, their bodies— resplendent and tranquil amidst the lingering warmth of sexual satisfaction—separated. Gathering her gently into his arms, he held her close. For the longest time, neither spoke. Instead, he lifted the delicate hand resting on his chest and kissed it.

She faced him, balanced on an elbow. "I have never felt anything so wondrous before, Devlin. Is it always just so?"

"The degree of pleasure depends on the lovers and the passion they feel for one another." When she didn't respond, he glanced at her. Lifting her chin with his forefinger, he kissed her lips. "And no, I have never known such pleasure before."

She cuddled against him, resting her arm across his chest.

"Can we do it again?"

With a low chuckle, he kissed her brow. "I see no need for the dream to end just yet."

Closing her eyes, she sighed. "For certain the male body is a marvel."

Devlin knew he'd lost himself in sexual excess, tutoring Christiana in various sexual positions and ways to find pleasure in the act of lovemaking. Again and again they came together. He explained she would be tender, that they should be mindful of how new she was to such intimacy. She refused to listen, wanting him with a desperation and hunger that mirrored his own.

It wasn't until night had descended like a black velvet blanket across the starlit sky that—thoroughly sated and physically spent—Devlin let Christiana settle down to some semblance of sleep. They'd not even emerged from their haven for nourishment, preferring to feed their passion for one another. Perhaps later they would sneak down to the kitchen. For now, Christiana needed sleep; he only hoped she'd not regret making love with him in the morning.

He looked down at her head nestled against his shoulder. "Why did you gift me with your innocence, Christiana?"

"I wanted you to be the one, Devlin."

A lump formed in his throat to see the glistening of tears in her luminous eyes. He stroked the raven strands of her luxurious mane of hair, cupped the back of her neck and pulled her to him. Their lips met again with a soft, sweet, abiding tenderness that eclipsed the wild passion of recent lovemaking.

"Sleep beside me now, sweetheart," he whispered. "The night is not yet over and this dream has only just begun."

How can I possibly lose her now or let any other man take my place in her bed? She is part of my very soul. She belongs to me—now and forever.

Unable to sleep, Devlin stared at the ancient carved canopy above his head. With startling clarity, he understood why he'd remained a bachelor for thirty years. This was what he'd waited for, to find the one woman he was destined to love the remainder of his life. He didn't want a marriage where he searched endlessly in the beds of other women to find something missing in his married life. God knew he'd already had his fill of clandestine affairs and mistresses.

He wanted Christiana—now and always. He wanted her to look at him in ways only he understood—whether they were dining alone at Fairhaven, his family estate, or in a crowded ballroom. He wanted to hear her laughter when she was happy. Wanted to comfort and protect her when she was sad. Wanted her soft touch on his skin, her breath mingling with his. He wanted more than just one night—he wanted a lifetime. A lifetime to feel their passion-crazed bodies entwined together in the throes of lovemaking. He wanted to see her belly swell with his child. This last powerful realization proved the depth of his regard for this perplexing woman and the future he wanted with her.

Looking down at the woman sleeping contentedly in his arms, he smiled. Christiana Tatum would not be his mistress. She would be his wife.

CHAPTER SIXTEEN

"Tell me what company thou keepest,
and I'll tell thee what thou art."
~ Cervantes (1547-1616), *Don Quixote*

With a startled gasp, Christiana bolted upright in bed, her eyes quickly adjusting to the darkness of Devlin's bed-chamber. Even the fire in the hearth was almost out.

Dear God, the smuggling run!

Quickly looking to her side, she saw Devlin sleeping, his breathing slow and steady. She ached to touch his shadowed jaw, to kiss his sensuous lips now at rest, but feared he might wake and pull her once more into his arms. As much as she hated to admit it, the dream was over and life's reality had returned—cold and stark.

As quietly as possible, she left the warm bed and searched for her discarded clothing. Donning her chemise, she draped her gown and corset over her arm, then gathered her stockings and shoes. She stood before the window, looking out at the clear yet cold moonlit night. The familiar cry of the wind beckoned like the wailing of a banshee.

Tears sprang to her eyes. "Damn you, Blackjack."

Devlin awoke when Christiana slipped from his bed. At first, he thought her embarrassed or perhaps concerned about what the other servants might think were she to spend the entire night with him. Now, however, he wanted to know only one thing.

Who the bloody hell was Blackjack?

Feigning sleep, he watched Christiana walk to the door of his bedchamber, slowly pulling back the latch. When he thought she would slip out the door, she returned to the hearth with a deliberate stride. Kneeling, she placed her bundle of clothing on the floor. She gathered her cloud of raven hair, swiftly braided it into one thick rope, then twisted it around until she'd fashioned a tight knot at the base of her neck.

Perhaps sensing being observed, she glanced back at the bed, but Devlin quickly closed his eyes and concentrated on his acting. He even feigned a soft snore. Then he heard a strange sound—like the muffled rumbling of distant thunder. A moment later, a whoosh of cold air made him open his eyes.

The secret passageway.

Oblivious to his nakedness, Devlin leapt from the bed. By the time he reached the panel, it was sealed tight. Not knowing the mechanism Christiana had used to operate the wall, he looked to where she'd been kneeling. The control must be inside the hearth. He swore under his breath. Apparently on her way out, his darling Christiana had stoked the fire to such an extent she now made it impossible for him to reach inside and search for the hidden latch.

"If she thinks I'm not about to follow, she's in for a rude awakening," he muttered. He'd not let her slip away so easily. Dressing quickly, he silently vowed to find out exactly what Christiana was up to this night. Granted, he may not be able to access the secret passageway, but how difficult could it be to find someone named Blackjack.

Stunned silence filled The Mermaid Inn when the tall stranger entered. All eyes followed as he caught the eye of a voluptuous serving wench and sauntered over to an empty table.

Seated in a corner booth, a disguised Christiana almost choked on the brandy wine she'd been drinking. She couldn't take her eyes off the man who'd been sleeping when she'd left his bed but a short while before. A sharp elbow in the side, however, brought her attention back to her smuggling companions.

"What's eatin' at ye, Christian?"

She frowned at Henry Tucker, another member of the gang just a few years older than her nineteen years; but whereas *Christian* remained in a perpetual state of adolescence, Henry was now a strapping young man.

"What?" Her feigned boyish voice sounded halfway between a croak and a whisper.

"Ye look as if ye've seen a ghost," Henry said.

Christiana couldn't help but watch Devlin flirt outrageously with Millie Piehler. When he pulled the strumpet down onto his lap, an onslaught of jealous rage swept over her so badly she absent-mindedly broke the bowl of the glass in her hand. Inhaling sharply between clenched teeth, she shuddered from the bitter pain. Biting back tears, she picked a piece of jagged glass from her palm.

"Would'ya look at that? 'E's jealous," laughed Davey O'Toole. "I didn't know ye was smitten with Millie, Christian."

"Hey, yer bleedin' all over the table," Henry said.

Christiana shrugged off the injury, too preoccupied by whether or not her smuggling disguise would deceive Devlin. Still wearing an oversized cocked hat worn by all the Ravens, her long hair had been knotted and hidden under a bag-wig purchased by Blackjack for her in London. And thankfully, she'd yet to remove the mannish greatcoat, making a pretense to the others that the wind had been biting cold.

"Did ye hear me, Christian?" Henry asked.

After gruffly clearing her throat, she nodded and walked over to the bar, quietly asking for a towel from Silas Wynne, the proprietor.

"Ye're bleedin' like a stuck pig," Silas said. "Best let Millie see yer hand, lad. Ye might have glass still in the wound."

"Just give me a towel," she whispered with boyish impatience.

When Snake came to stand beside her, it was all she could do not to scream.

"Don't ye be faintin' now, boy," the pesky older man joked with a liquor-laced cackle. "Oooh, look at all that blood. Best get me needle and sew ye up right quick."

Christiana turned to glare at the wiry man, but caught Devlin watching her with a puzzled expression. God help them both if he recognized her now. She swallowed hard and turned back to face the bar, wrapping a towel about her hand.

"Bugger off, Snake," she mumbled. "I'd as soon sew it myself as have ye touch me."

With another round of loud cackling, Snake wandered about the room, telling everyone that the young bugger had stuck his hand. Over and over again, the smuggler laughed. "How d'ya think he'll climb those cliffs now, eh?"

Devlin narrowed his gaze on the youth, watching as the boy in the greatcoat and cocked hat returned to a corner booth where two other young men sat.

"Don't mind 'im," Millie said. "Snake teases Christian like the devil, 'e does."

"Christian?"

"Aye," said Millie. "We don't see 'im round 'ere 'cept when

Blackjack wants 'im. Old Snake likes to 'ave a bit o' sport with the boy, leastways 'til Blackjack shows up."

"Where is Blackjack now?" Devlin angled his head to get another look at the boy, but some men had walked over to stand beside the table and blocked his view.

Millie trailed a finger down his cheek. "Are ye 'ere to ask questions 'bout Blackjack or 'ave a bit o'fun?"

Devlin crooked a brow and eyed the bountiful breasts of the barmaid all but spilling out of the confines of her faded gown. He only wanted to bed one woman, the same woman who'd shared his bed a few hours ago, a woman who'd left him for someone named Blackjack.

Asking about his unknown rival at The Green Dragon led him to the most disturbing collection of men he'd seen outside the rookeries of London. Every one of them had a nasty firearm resting on the table before him.

Just then the men previously blocking his view returned to their table and Devlin looked across the taproom at Christian. Much to his surprise, the boy stared at him.

"Bloody hell," he muttered as his eyes locked with the unmistakable jewel-like orbs of Christiana. Judging by the sudden frown she directed his way, and the barely perceptible shake of her head, she knew he'd recognized her.

What the devil was she doing in a place like this? Dressed like a boy, and drinking with men named Snake and Blackjack?

His jaw clenched. He couldn't wait to drag her out of the tavern and give her a piece of his mind. Better yet, he'd turn her over his knee and make sitting an uncomfortable experience for a month.

Enough is enough. Christiana was going to tell him what she was involved with before this night ended. At least that was his intention before Millie started fondling him.

"I think 'tis time we 'ad ourselves some private sport," the barmaid said with a lusty giggle.

Devlin glanced back at Christiana. The expression on her face could only be described as livid. Her eyes shot daggers at him, so much so that she'd caught the attention of her table mates. It didn't take long for him to understand the cause of her anger, especially with Millie fawning all over him. Christiana was jealous.

"Quite right, Millie," he said in a voice loud enough for everyone to hear. "Let's go have a bit of sport."

Christiana wanted to shoot someone, preferably Devlin Randolph, especially when she saw him saunter off like a cock on the walk with Millie on his arm. Shaking off Henry's restraining arm, she all but raced across the room toward the stairs. Devlin and Millie were nowhere in sight.

"Damn the man for a fool," she mumbled under her breath.

Quickly locating Millie's chamber, she threw open the door, effectively stunning both its occupants. There they were —the man she loved flat on his back and a wicked tart straddling his hips.

"Bloody 'ell," the barmaid screeched. "Ye scared the wits out o' me, Christian."

"Put the knife away, Millie." Christiana kept her disguised voice calm but stern.

Devlin quickly lost his cocky smirk and crooked a brow. "Knife?"

"He's a friend," Christiana said as she approached the bed.

"Then why is 'e askin' 'bout Blackjack?"

"I don't know," Christiana said, arching a brow at Devlin, intimating she too wanted to know the answer. "Like as not, he has a meeting with Blackjack. And you know how Blackjack feels about his friends, Millie. Best let this one go."

Millie drew the arm she had hidden behind her back forward, revealing a lethal knife in her hand. She touched Devlin's cheek with the tip of the deadly blade, careful not to apply enough pressure to cut him. "Is that true, luv?"

Devlin's eyes glanced from Millie to Christiana. Although he'd been lounging back on his elbows, slightly amused by the interruption, he now realized just how bloody close he'd come to having his throat slit. He managed to smile at Millie and nod.

"Bloody 'ell," exclaimed the barmaid as she jumped off the bed. After straightening her gown, she slid the knife back into a hidden pocket.

"Go back downstairs, Millie," Christiana said. "And if anyone asks, the stranger is a friend to Blackjack."

After Millie quit the room, Christiana whispered, "What the devil are you doing here?"

Devlin jumped to his feet. "What am *I* doing here? What the devil are *you* doing here, *Christian*? And who the bloody hell is Blackjack?"

"You best not bandy that name about. Just because I said you were Blackjack's friend does not mean you will leave this place alive—not yet."

"What in God's name are you talking about?"

"Do you have any idea where you are? Any idea what those men downstairs are capable of doing? And just how, might I ask, did you come to be here?"

Devlin cleared his throat, reluctant to admit he'd followed after her in a fit of jealousy, especially since he now wanted to know what she'd been up to in her damnable disguise. She certainly wasn't here to clean chimneys.

"I merely asked someone at The Green Dragon where I might find an establishment with an accommodating wench." A lie, of course, but he preferred not to discuss his real reason for being here until after they'd returned to the abbey.

Her mouth dropped open and her eyes blazed. "You wanted an accommodating wench? Forgive me, but I believe I was exceedingly accommodating earlier this evening."

Devlin said nothing. As excuses went, it had been a poor one.

Christiana shook her head, eyeing him with a combination of hurt and disgust. "I should have let Millie kill you."

She walked over to the door and put her ear against the weathered wood. With a weary sigh, she looked back at him. "You best come with me—and for God's sake—go along with whatever I say. Do not say a word."

Aware she had him at a disadvantage, Devlin bit his tongue and came to stand beside her, noting the seeping crimson stains saturating the cloth of a makeshift bandage. "Your hand is bleeding; let me look at it."

She rolled her eyes. "Are you daft? We've no time for that."

He could do nothing more than follow her downstairs in silence, his thoughts filled with a bitter disappointment at how blind he'd been to Christiana's true nature.

"Wait by the door," she whispered.

He did as told, but kept a careful eye on her as she walked across the taproom. The proprietor stared hard at him, then turned his attention to the person he believed a boy named Christian.

She said nothing to anyone, except the young man she'd spoken with earlier. When she turned around, Devlin swore under his breath. She had a damn blunderbuss in her hand.

Nodding at the proprietor, she walked the length of the taproom and returned to his side. What amazed him more than anything else was how everyone seemed to accept her as this youth named Christian. Truth be told, it was impressive the way she carried out her disguise, from the boyish manner in which she walked to the surly attitude she projected.

Once outside, however, his attempt to give her a piece of his mind died a quick death. She darted toward the stable yard at breakneck speed. Having no other choice, he followed.

"You are fortunate Luther is still here," she said, pointing to his horse in a stall. "And that he is still saddled. After Millie killed you, they would have given him to Blackjack as a gift."

"There's that name again," he said with no small amount of sarcasm.

She ignored his remark and focused on leading an impressive roan gelding out of a stall. Hands on his hips, he watched her quickly saddle the roan. "Where is Blossom?"

It soon became obvious if he didn't collect Luther post-haste, she'd ride off without another word. Gathering Luther's reins, they led their mounts outside. After taking to the saddle with the proficiency of a seasoned dragoon, she looked about the deserted street before kicking her horse into a mad run out of the village.

"Bloody little savage," he muttered, taking to Luther's saddle and racing after her. He followed closely, not the least bit surprised by Christiana's exceptional riding ability.

They rode through dense woods and darkened paths that made it impossible to glean any idea of where they headed. He thought he heard the sea. Were they riding toward the coast? Perhaps the sound was simply the echo of waves pounding against the shore from a distance?

Rather than lose her in the darkness, he kept Christiana's cloaked figure in sight, contemplating all the things he intended to say once they returned to the abbey. Sometime later, after giving up trying to discern where the bloody hell they were going, she took him down a steep path to a deserted beach and the white cliffs of Dover Strait.

To his amazement, she rode toward the chalky cliffs, finding a barely visible fissure through which she adroitly maneuvered her mount. The passageway, wide enough and tall enough to ride a mount in single formation, would only be accessible when the tide was low. After riding a fair distance through the passage, they emerged into a beautiful, sheltered grotto set aglow with moonlight and an abundance of stars.

They dismounted. Neither spoke.

With his hands resting low on his hips he began to pace, gathering his thoughts and trying to control his temper. It was to no avail.

He turned and glared at her. "Who the bloody hell is Blackjack?"

"Do you know *anything* about Kent?"

"Obviously not enough," he replied.

She sat on a large, smooth rock, looking both ridiculous and adorable in her dark, boyish clothing, the greatcoat dwarfing her woman's body.

"Blackjack is the leader of the Ravens."

"Regrettably, that means absolutely nothing to me."

She turned away, her chin set at a mutinous angle. Clearly, she didn't want to have this conversation.

"Make no mistake, Christiana, you will answer my questions."

As if resigning herself to the situation, she looked at him. "The Ravens are a smuggling gang, one of many that operate along the coast off Kent and Sussex. The Ravens control the stretch of coast from Deal to Folkestone and have a very faithful following. You would be hard-pressed to find anyone who does not support their activities."

"Hence the reason for Millie wanting to kill me, I presume."

Christiana nodded. "You stumbled into a den of thieves tonight, Devlin. Asking questions about Blackjack targeted you as a spy, perhaps even a member of the militia. Millie's father and two of her brothers were killed by spies posing as sympathizers; consequently, she tends to kill anyone who seems suspicious. You would not have survived another sunrise had I not been there to stop her."

The gravity with which she spoke told Devlin all too well that she told the truth. Of course, as a man he was hardly flattered to hear the woman he loved believed him incapable of protecting himself—or her.

She looked at the placid water of the grotto. "You should be safe here until dawn."

"What do you mean—*you?*"

She ignored him. "When the tide starts to turn, you must follow the beach road south until you come to St. Margaret's Bay."

"And just where do you think you are going?"

"Back to The Mermaid Inn." She stood, brushing wet sand off the back of her greatcoat.

"You cannot be serious," he bit out. "I am not about to let you go back there, Christiana."

"I belong there," she said, her voice quiet.

"You most certainly do not."

"Do you not understand?" she cried. "I'm one of them!"

Devlin felt the blood drain from his face. In all his imaginings about what Christiana might be involved in he never expected something like this. For God's sake, smuggling was punishable by death. And if she was involved—

"Is the estate also involved?"

"No one is involved but me."

"I find that hard to believe. Then again, you are the only one here. Might I enquire what possessed you to join these cutthroats?"

"I have my reasons."

Devlin snorted. "And that is all you intend to say about it? You have your reasons? You do know smuggling is against the law. 'Tis considered an act of treason, Christiana. You trade with France, I presume?"

Although pale, her manner appeared controlled. "It is not something I am proud of, Devlin. But sometimes one must do things because it is the only way to survive. You cannot understand because you have not lived my life."

"You are right," he snapped. "I cannot understand treason. There is no possible defense you could offer in my opinion."

Pacing, he contemplated the quandary of loving a woman he knew so little about. Good God, he'd actually decided to marry her earlier that evening. Then, in the midst of churning disgust came one prevailing thought. Something didn't make sense. Apart from the fact it contradicted everything he believed about her, when one engaged in illegal activity it was usually for material gain. She lived in virtual poverty. Why then would she risk her life and gain nothing in return?

He looked over his shoulder and caught her wiping tears from her eyes. When she saw him looking at her, she turned away.

"I must go," she said.

He folded his arms across his chest and shook his head. "You cannot possibly believe I will allow you to continue this activity. Your involvement is over, my sweet."

She walked over to her horse then led it toward the rock upon which she'd been sitting. "It is not that simple. If I do not return within the hour, my life is forfeit. The Ravens will think I have betrayed them. I have no choice but to return."

Devlin felt his heart shudder to a stop. "And just why, pray tell, would they believe you've betrayed them?" When she said nothing, the truth hit him hard. "Because I came there tonight."

She nodded. "Blackjack will know a stranger came looking for him, a stranger I saved from Millie's blade and then left with before he could meet the man. I have to be there to defend my actions."

"And then what? You assist them in another smuggling run? Christiana, soldiers watch the coast for smuggling activity. These men are trained by His Majesty's Royal Navy to shoot first and ask questions later. Why the bloody hell do you think they built that damned canal? Do you have any idea how many disgruntled British soldiers are spoiling for the chance to catch a band of smugglers in the act? Those men would rather be out at sea in some glorious battle. They're none too happy about having such unglamorous naval posts in this war."

"You seem to know quite a bit about them."

"I rode to Kent on horseback," he said with deadly calm. "I saw them. Spoke with them. For God's sake, the Duke of Pemberton was one of the most vocal advocates for the canal being built."

"Now why does that not surprise me?"

Seeing her prepare to mount and ride out yet again into the night, he quickly went to her side. "You are not going back there, Christiana. Rather, you will return with me to the abbey whereupon we will calmly discuss the extent of your involvement—and determine the best way to extricate you from this mess."

Keeping her back to him, she whispered, "I cannot."

Grasping her shoulders, he pivoted her to face him. "And I cannot allow you to risk your life on a damn smuggling run."

"Do you think I enjoy this?" she cried, tears gathering in her eyes. "I am terrified each time I go out, knowing what could happen, knowing this goes against everything I was taught as a child. I hate it, Devlin. But that doesn't change what I am."

Pulling her into his arms, he said. "We can fix this, Christiana. Whatever your reasons for joining these men, we can find a solution. We have come so far this day, have we not? Only think of what we have found together and believe in me."

She pushed away from him. "Believe in you? A man who made love to me only to wake and look to slake his lust with any willing wench?"

Devlin grabbed her again by the shoulders. "I did not go there looking for a woman. If you must know, I went looking for you."

She made a soft, scoffing sound. "And just how did you think to find me there?"

"I was awake when you left my bed," he admitted. "I heard you say something about this Blackjack fellow."

"You were sleeping. I heard you snoring."

Devlin made a snoring sound, then arched his brow.

"Very convincing," she murmured.

"This is why you have been so secretive, guarded and suspicious about my coming to Bellewyck Abbey. Why you have been so defensive to all my questions. You did not want me to learn about the smuggling."

A faint smile curved her lips. "Well, if nothing else, you are persistent. Very well, yes, I did not want you to find out about this. Good heavens, what shall we talk about now?"

"Rest assured, my sweet, we have a great deal to talk about."

"I can well imagine," she said under her breath.

"Christiana," he said gently, "I can help you, but you must trust me."

"There is nothing you can do," she argued.

"You don't know that."

She turned away.

"For God's sake, how can you still not trust me after everything we shared this night? I realize this is new to you, but what happened in my bed was more than lust. What we shared was not some hasty bedding between two people who care nothing for one another."

"I know that," she said in a raw whisper.

"Then you must also see the wall between us no longer exists."

Keeping her back to him, she said, "When walls come down they often leave ruins." She swung around. "You have already put yourself in danger because of me. If you had been killed tonight, if I had not reached you in time—"

She briefly covered her mouth with her uninjured hand, tears glistening in her eyes. It took a moment for her to gain control of her emotions. Shaking her head, she spoke in a strained voice. "I want nothing to happen to you because of me. You cannot fix this, Devlin. No one can."

"That is it then? You expect me to simply accept this as your destiny and forget what happened between us tonight? Forget you could be injured or possibly killed?"

She didn't respond.

Frustrated with her quiet resolve, he tried another tactic. Looking down at her clothing, he said, "For God's sake, how can you hope to keep up this ridiculous disguise? I recognized you within ten minutes."

"Only because when first we met, you found me dressed as a sweep. The Ravens know me only like this; I am just a boy who has been with them for five years. Besides, they know how Blackjack feels about me."

Devlin crossed his arms, his disposition becoming more irritable by the moment. "And just how does this Blackjack feel about you?"

"He loves me," she replied matter-of-factly.

Devlin clenched his jaw. "Does he perchance know you are a woman?"

"Yes."

"I see,"—he nodded curtly—"and I suppose he thinks to be your lover. And what of that young man you were sitting with tonight? He seemed rather solicitous to your needs."

She smiled at his inference. "Henry? We are friends, nothing more. If anything, Henry treats me like a little brother."

"So you say. I cannot help but note you have a great many male friends, my dear."

"You are not jealous?"

"What if I said I am jealous? What if I said I want you to abandon this foolishness for me? This may come as a complete surprise to you, but I hoped we might have more than one night together." He cupped the sides of her face. "You know what will happen if you are caught. Hanging is not pretty."

"And that is why I never wear a necklace," she said. "In truth, I never put anything about my neck—not a bit of gold—

not a bit of rope. You might say 'tis a motto I live by."

Her attempt to make light of dire circumstances failed miserably. With a sad sigh, she pulled away from his touch. Then, standing upon the flat stone, she took to her saddle. "If you truly care about me, you will understand and let me go."

Devlin put his hand on her foot, noting how small it was encased in a boys' black half-boot. "Do not do this, Christiana. I can gain your release. I can protect you from these men. You must listen to me. Trust me."

Crystallized tears spiked her long, black lashes. "And I prefer you not die because of me." Leaning forward, she put her uninjured hand atop his. "I am sorry, Devlin. Perhaps in time you will not think too harshly of me."

"For God's sake!" he said between clenched teeth.

"I understand this places you in a difficult position, and that your loyalties are first to Pemberton. If you prefer, I shall not return to the abbey. Polly can assume my duties under your guidance."

"Oh, no," he scoffed. "You shall not escape me so easily, my sweet." Touching the side of her face, he said. "How can I possibly let you return to that inn? You claim this Blackjack loves you, yet fear to be killed if you do not return to prove your loyalty to the man. What hypocrisy is this? Return with me to the abbey or let us face the Ravens together. I am not without skills. Do not presume me incapable of defending you."

"You are such a lion," she said with a sad smile. "But now is not the time for misplaced chivalry. You are one man against a hundred. Can you not see? If you follow me back, you endanger my life all the more by your very presence. They do not know you, Devlin. They will not trust you. Besides which, it is not Blackjack who would harm me, but the other members of the Ravens. Honor among thieves is no exaggeration."

"Forgive me, but you have a rather distorted view of honor."

She looked down at her hands, wincing slightly at the blood-soaked bandage covering her wound. "I suppose I do," she whispered.

The sadness in her voice made him frown, but at least she recognized the inherent wrong in her actions. Recalling the dark suspicion with which he'd been regarded upon entering The Mermaid Inn, Millie's attempt on his life, and the menacing looks directed his way when he left with Christiana, he conceded his unexpected arrival might very well have put her in danger tonight.

Would he compromise her safety if he returned with her now? And if she didn't return, would those blackguards seek her out and thence discover her true identity? Would that not make them more blood-thirsty and suspicious about the reason for her boyish deception?

As much as he disliked the idea, perhaps the best tactic would be for the Ravens to continue thinking her a boy, then get her out of the gang as that boy. He only wished she didn't see him as a steward—and an ineffective one at that. She had no way of knowing he was not only rich and powerful, but possessed great skill in fisticuffs and firearms, was quite deadly with a sword and, if necessary, adequate with a bow.

Perhaps he should tell her the truth now?

"Christiana, there is something you must know about me. It may very well change how you feel about going back to the inn."

"There is no time, Devlin," she stressed. "I have been too long away as it is. I will see you in the morning. We shall talk then, I promise."

She started to leave the grotto, but stopped and glanced back over her shoulder to give him one last endearing smile. He stood like a damn fool with his hands resting on his hips, feeling utterly useless and more confused than ever.

"Damn it, Christiana, if you are not back by dawn..."

She smiled softly. "For what it is worth, I love you, Devlin Randolph."

Her declaration of love took him by complete surprise, the softly spoken words slamming into his chest with all the force of a crossbow's arrow. Not until after she'd gone could he speak past the lump in his throat.

"God help me, Christiana. I love you, too."

CHAPTER SEVENTEEN

*"Dangers bring fears, and fears more
dangers bring."*
~ Richard Baxter (1615-1691)

Alone in his bedchamber, a shadowed jaw resting in one hand, Devlin sat before the window. Each monotonous hour had lengthened in numbing silence until morning passed and afternoon waned. Still, Christiana had not returned.

All day he'd waited, at times going so far as to saddle Luther and go search for her. One thought restrained him. Would he put her in greater jeopardy if he returned to The Mermaid Inn? He couldn't very well enquire about a woman. And asking about a boy named Christian would only put fuel on the fire of suspicion and risk exposing her disguise. In addition, she might return in his absence, injured and in need of medical attention. Another possibility was that word might come of her capture and, if so, he must be present to intercede on her behalf.

"Bloody hell," he muttered and stood. "This waiting is driving me mad." Why was he sitting at home wasting precious time? There must be a way to find her or at least gain some insight into her whereabouts.

With sudden clarity, he looked to the fireplace. Remembering Christiana had knelt to open the hidden wall panel, his fingers searched for the release mechanism, mindless of the cold, gray ash quickly caking his hands. Through dogged determination, he located a loose stone behind which was an iron ring. Once pulled and turned counterclockwise, the ring released the panel; a slight rumble followed.

Darkness loomed in the revealed space. He stood before the threshold, hands on his hips. Why would anyone voluntarily enter such a yawning void? Silent as a tomb, the passageway was no doubt ancient as the foundations of the abbey itself and perhaps structurally unstable now. Then again, the cold air smelled fresh.

Where did it lead? Would he be able to find his way out again? Bloody hell, it made no difference—not if the labyrinth provided the means to find Christiana.

Before he could act upon his intentions, a knock sounded on his chamber door. Paused at the entrance to the secret passageway, he returned to the hearth and turned the ring once more to close the panel. Dusting his hands off, he flung wide the chamber door. Unfortunately, the person he most wanted to see was not there.

Unable to meet his eyes, Polly Darrow stared at her feet. "Mr. Randolph, ye've not eaten all day. Bertie wants to know if ye'd like a tray of food."

"Thank you, no."

Polly nodded, then looked beyond his shoulder. "I could clean yer chamber and set yer bed to rights."

Devlin followed her gaze to the askew linens and silk counterpane half off the bed. Remembering all too clearly what transpired there yesterday with Christiana, he wanted no one to touch it.

"I would rather wait upon Miss Tatum." Realizing how that sounded, he added, "That is to say, I understand she is responsible for cleaning my bedchamber."

Polly's eyes looked to him then, but the fiery temperament he expected had been replaced by a far more subdued demeanor. Earlier this morning she'd been glib, airily pronouncing each time he asked, that Miss Tatum was about somewhere. At one point, she actually lied, saying the housekeeper was in the brewery. He let it go at the time, opting to watch from his chamber window the activities of the servants. One thing was evident. Polly wasn't glib now.

A feeling of dread washed over him. "You have not seen Miss Tatum all day, have you Polly?"

Polly swallowed hard and shook her head.

Rage unlike anything he'd ever known made his body tense. "Inform the other servants I want to see them, including Jasper, in the library. Those who are not present will no longer be employed."

A pathetic looking group, hardly capable of deception, had assembled. Still, their silence was condemning. Either they protected Christiana out of loyalty or because they too were involved with smuggling. How could he discern the truth from these people short of threatening their very lives?

Despite their guarded manner and the doubts he had about their honesty, he'd actually come to care for this little group of misfit servants. He knew their personality quirks and traits. Touched by their more than obvious affection for one another, he'd been equally impressed by their diligence and work ethics. He knew their strengths and weaknesses. Ironically, both seemed to come from the same source. And since their beautiful, reckless captain wasn't present to lead, they now appeared as lost and helpless as a group of children adrift at sea.

Jasper Collins, withered and aged, leaned heavily on a walking stick. Tall and lean, the balding Tom Rooney looked straight ahead, his manner as defiant as ever. Young Sarah Lloyd held her grandmother's hand while Polly stared a hole through the library's already worn carpet. Even Devlin's loyal coachman, Nash, was present, his hands clasped together behind his back, his posture straight and strong. Gordon Darrow and his son were absent.

Devlin returned to his desk chair, studying each person in silence. He looked at his timepiece. Now was the hour when they completed their duties for the day and prepared to retire for the evening. In truth, they did look exhausted.

Glancing up at the pitiful group, a wave of sympathy gave him pause. They loved Christiana; he could well imagine what fears they had regarding her present whereabouts—especially if they knew about the Ravens. Well, the time had come to learn exactly what they knew, and he wasn't about to settle for less than the absolute truth.

"I know Miss Tatum is involved in a very dangerous, illegal activity," he began. "Furthermore, each one of you has been covering for her absence all day. Consequently, I believe many, if not all, of you are also involved in this activity."

Tom Rooney glanced at Bertie Lloyd, a curious look exchanged between the two.

"The Duke of Pemberton is also suspicious," Devlin continued. "Regrettably, you have done nothing to put those suspicions to rest. Quite the contrary, your behavior has had the opposite effect."

That got their attention. The mere mention of the duke and they all paled with terror. How laughable. God, but he wanted to proclaim himself as the Duke of Pemberton.

"I have questioned each of you individually; your answers have always been the same. I can only presume you lie for one another and have done so for quite some time. In view of the absence of Miss Tatum—and others—I will question each of you again now. I warn you, this is your last opportunity to speak truthfully, and your only hope for pardon."

Directing his attention to the cook, he asked, "Mrs. Lloyd, where is Miss Tatum?"

"I do not know, sir."

"I see, and what can you tell me about a man named Blackjack."

Mrs. Lloyd paled. "I-I know of no such man, sir."

"Am I then to assume you know nothing about a smuggling gang that frequents the area called the Ravens?"

"No sir, Mr. Randolph," she said in a near whisper.

Devlin noticed Sarah squeeze her grandmother's hand. The poor child looked terrified. "Sarah," he said gently. "Come here, please."

The young girl looked at her grandmother, then walked forward until she stood in front of his desk.

"You seem particularly upset," he said.

"I-I do not know what ye want us to say," she choked out.

"The truth," Devlin said, making sure he kept his voice gentle, his words strong. "Surely you do not want to see anyone suffer needlessly. Stealing from one's employer, whether creating false books or engaging in acts of smuggling during a time when a country is at war, these are crimes punishable to the full extent of the law. The courts will not seek to understand why a person has done something wrong, Sarah. They consider only the facts and impose judgment. Smuggling is punishable by death. Would it not be tragic to see people you know and love come to such a horrid end?"

Visibly trembling, Sarah looked imploringly back at her grandmother. When she turned her attention again to him she cried. "I-I-I—"

Polly Darrow stepped forward and put an arm about the young girl's waist. "Stop torturin' her!"

"I am not torturing her," Devlin said. "I am telling Sarah the truth, which is something that should have been done long ago. You do the child no service when you lead her by the hand into a web of lies."

Undaunted, Polly returned Sarah to her grandmother's loving embrace whereupon the child immediately burst into muffled sobs. Then, returning to stand before the desk, Polly clenched her fists. "There is not a one of us has done wrong.

We only did what his lordship always told us to do. Ye cannot come here and threaten us for doing what was expected."

Devlin frowned at the convoluted statement. Standing slowly, he leaned forward. "Why then is Miss Tatum not here doing her job? I daresay she is employed as a housekeeper at Bellewyck Abbey, not a smuggler named Christian."

His words clearly stunned the maid.

"And if you truly know nothing about Miss Tatum's smuggling activities, why have you lied to me regarding her whereabouts all day? Has it not occurred to you that your friend might need assistance, Polly? What if, at this very moment, she has been captured or worse?"

The fear amongst the servants became tangible. Glancing at his servant Nash, he caught the coachman's slightly narrowed eyes. He only hoped Nash went along with what he was about to do—however cruel the tactic might seem.

Picking up a quill from the desk, his fingers idly stroked the length of the plume. "Miss Tatum is a member of the Ravens, a smuggling gang led by a man named Blackjack."

He watched closely for any reaction to his statement; there was none.

"I discovered this quite by accident. Last night I happened to come upon Miss Tatum in some rather disagreeable company. It was then she told me of her involvement. I tried to impress upon her that she must return with me to Bellewyck Abbey, but she refused. She said her life would be forfeit if she did not return to her comrades in crime, that her absence would raise all manner of suspicion and could expose her disguise as a boy. Because of this possibility, I honored her request and did not follow her back to join the Ravens." Under his breath, he added, "Much to my regret, I must say."

Jasper Collins hobbled over to a chair before the fire and sat down. Whether the weight of his years, his poor health, or what he'd just heard, the man seemed drained of what little strength he possessed.

"She promised to return this morning," Devlin continued. "She did not. I have questioned the lot of you all day as to her whereabouts or where I might find her. Rather than tell me that you did not know or have not seen her, you deliberately lied to me."

"Who is to say she does not hide from ye?" accused Tom Rooney.

"There is no reason for her to hide from me. When she

told me of her involvement with smuggling, I vowed to help her. Despite what you think of me, I have no desire to see Miss Tatum hurt in any way. Now, I appreciate what a cruel taskmaster Lord Bellewyck was to all of you. As such, I can well understand how Miss Tatum might have been drawn into smuggling out of desperation. Perhaps she became involved with these cutthroats because she wanted revenge against the earl and his estate."

"Is that what ye think?" asked Rooney. "Ye think she risks her life for revenge against Lord Bellewyck and his bloody estate?"

Devlin rubbed his brow. "I can only speculate, Mr. Rooney. We were to discuss her reasons this morning. Perhaps you can tell me why she became involved in this madness."

He received no response. With the exception of Jasper, the servants simply stared at Devlin without the slightest expression.

"Very well," Devlin said, his temper rising. "If not revenge, why would she become involved in such a dangerous association? From what I have seen of her limited wardrobe, she does not appear to be making a profit from her participation."

The fact they continued in their silence became frustrating to the extreme. Devlin could think only of Christiana and where she might be at this moment. He began to pace, rubbing the back of his neck. Stopping before the fireplace, he stared at them. "I will not tolerate insolence or secrecy regarding this estate or anyone employed here a moment longer. You do not help Miss Tatum by your continued silence."

Looking down at the oldest servant, he sighed. "Come now, Jasper, you know more about the estate and its people than anyone. How can we locate Miss Tatum?"

"I do not know," the brewer said.

"Rather like the way you know nothing about Lord Bellewyck's ward?"

Devlin turned to Polly. "Where is your father, Polly? For that matter, where is your brother? Odd they both are missing; one might even consider it highly suspicious."

Polly closed her eyes tightly, as if willing away the threat of tears. Her posture remained stiff, her hands clenched at her sides.

Devlin frowned hard at the maid, his patience at an end. "You think this loyalty? Your father, brother and friend are all missing, and you will not say a word to help them? So be it, but if blood has been shed, it is on your hands not mine."

Polly's eyes snapped open. "Blood! The last time I saw Christiana she was in yer company. She went to yer bedchamber. Mayhap there is another reason why she is of a mind not to show her face today. 'Tis because ye shamed her. Ye took her to yer bed."

"Polly, no!" Mrs. Lloyd gasped.

"I saw his bed." Polly cried, turning to look at the cook. "The linens were twisted and him not carin' who might see."

Devlin bit his tongue rather than reprimand the maid. She already trembled with the clear realization of what she'd just said, a mistake compounded by the presence of other servants.

"What did or did not happen in my bedchamber is not your concern," he bit out slowly. "The issue at hand is that she is now missing. She has not returned when she promised me she would. Do you understand? Your friend is missing. Your father and brother are missing. Just like the Bellewyck ward is missing. Needless to say, I find all these disappearances a rather disturbing coincidence."

With considerable effort, Jasper Collins stood and, leaning heavily on his walking stick, studied Devlin with an enigmatic expression. "And just why would that be a disturbin' coincidence, Mr. Randolph?"

Folding his arms across his chest, Devlin crooked a brow. "I am of the opinion it has something to do with the precious secrets everyone guards at Bellewyck Abbey. I do not doubt you all know what happened to the earl's ward. Mayhap that knowledge was used as a means to blackmail. Theft in exchange for silence perhaps? It stands to reason his lordship could do nothing during his lifetime for fear of public scandal and reprisal, but after his death he wanted you all to pay and pay dearly."

Mrs. Lloyd moaned softly. He looked to her and saw the older woman appeared almost as if she would swoon. A shaky hand rested upon her throat.

"Lord Bellewyck never had a ward," bit out a stone-faced Tom Rooney.

"And if he said he did, he was just makin' another one of his cruel jokes," Polly Darrow added with an abrupt nod for emphasis.

"Another one of his cruel jokes," Devlin echoed. "I hardly think so." With a telling look to Nash, Devlin returned to his desk and began to look through some papers until he found a letter with a broken seal.

"This letter is from the Duke of Pemberton, delivered by Mr. Nash. It seems the Lord Chancellor has located the original guardianship papers of Lord Bellewyck's ward. As such, it is only a matter of time before the duke knows the truth."

Deathly pale, the servants stared at the piece of parchment. One might think he held their death warrants in his hand.

"There *was* a ward," Devlin proclaimed. Remembering the slip of tongue Christiana had made regarding a girl child, he added, "And I have been instructed not to stop until I know what happened to her."

"Ye're too late!" cried Polly, slapping her palms down upon the desk.

"What the bloody hell does that mean?" Devlin stared hard at the maid.

"What she means is that the ward no longer exists."

The sound of Christiana's voice made everyone turn with a start toward the open doorway. Beautiful, although a trifle pale, she stood regal as a queen. And standing protectively behind her were Gordon Darrow and his son, Billy.

Devlin's initial reaction had been joy to see Christiana alive and well—his first instinct to pull her into his arms and cover her with a thousand kisses. In the presence of the other servants, however, he restrained himself.

"Your absence today has been a source of great anxiety to us all, Miss Tatum."

"So I heard," she replied, a delicately winged eyebrow arched.

"Come, join our meeting." He motioned for the three servants to enter. "Mr. Darrow, welcome to our little gathering. Billy, do come in and join us as well."

Christiana lowered the deep hood of a black woolen cloak and slowly came forward to stand beside Polly. Long, wayward strands of ebony silk framed her pale face, which told him her hair hung loose about her shoulders and waist. But her eyes seemed different today, as if shadowed by a sad, painful resignation.

Separated by the width of his desk, Devlin studied her stiff demeanor. "Miss Tatum, what do you mean the ward no longer exists?"

"It is quite simple really." Her voice was somber and quiet. "You see, I killed her."

CHAPTER EIGHTEEN

*"Often the test of courage is not to die
but to live."*
~ Vittorio Alfieri (1749-1803), *Oreste*

Someone sobbed hysterically, young Sarah Lloyd by the sound of it, but Devlin couldn't remove his stunned gaze from Christiana long enough to see. What struck him more than anything, her startling confession contained not the slightest hint of sorrow or regret.

"I will tell you everything, provided you put an end to these bullying tactics." She glanced at her friends and a small sigh escaped her parted lips; the sound conveyed both resignation and heartfelt concern for their welfare.

Raising her chin in that defiant tilt he would always associate with Christiana, she said, "The others are innocent of any wrongdoing. They have no part in anything I have done or anything I am involved with. In truth, they have done nothing but always endeavor to protect me."

Devlin glanced at the servants, noticing for the first time the extent of their emotional turmoil. Mrs. Lloyd stood pale and distraught, still comforting her granddaughter. Polly had silent tears streaming down her cheeks as she stared at her friend. Even Tom Rooney and the Darrow men were teary-eyed. Yet, for some unknown reason, the ancient Jasper Collins looked at Christiana with what could only be described as pride. The brewer seemed to be willing the housekeeper to continue.

"Very well," Devlin said, "but I prefer we discuss this in private."

After the servants filed out of the room, Devlin frowned at the still open door. Since Rooney had been the last one out, clearly the gardener hoped to eavesdrop on the conversation. Not bloody likely. Without comment, he closed the door, then studied Christiana, his arms folded across his chest.

It was, without doubt, the most absurd confession he had

ever heard, and one he didn't believe for a moment. She could never cause the death of anyone, especially a child. This was a woman who, if nothing else, had continuously impressed him with her devotion and compassion for others. It seemed far more likely her confession was another attempt to protect someone, even if it meant taking the blame for their actions.

His heart ached, arguing with reason. Needing to better study her almost rigid demeanor, he walked to the front of the desk and sat down upon the edge of the polished surface.

"I must say, you hardly look capable of murder. Then again, you hardly resemble a smuggler or a chimneysweep."

"Looks can be deceiving, can they not?" Her voice was almost a whisper.

"Indeed," he murmured.

Devlin frowned. She stood still as a statue, staring at a point behind the desk. He maneuvered himself until he sat directly in front of her. For one brief moment their eyes met and he saw yet another truth. She trembled with fear.

Gentling his voice, he enquired, "Tell me the truth, Christiana. Are you actually claiming the Bellewyck ward is dead because of you?"

"Yes," she whispered.

He rubbed his jaw distractedly. "What happened?"

Christiana nibbled on her lower lip. "I am afraid 'tis rather long and complicated."

"Then perhaps you should start at the beginning."

With a nod, she swallowed hard and took a steadying breath. "The truth begins with his lordship's father, William Bertram. Do you know anything of him?" When Devlin shook his head, she continued. "He traveled extensively, living a rather self-indulgent lifestyle far removed from his wife and son. Does that surprise you?"

"Not necessarily," Devlin said with a slight shrug. "Few marriages are a love match, especially among the peerage."

Christiana studied Devlin's enigmatic expression, disturbed more than she would ever admit by his apparent indifference to the issue of loveless marriages.

"Go on," he prodded, his brow crooked.

Realizing it would be easier to not look at the man she loved, she walked to the shuttered windows. "What people did not know was Lady Bellewyck suffered from an illness of the mind. Her family concealed this from Lord Bellewyck when contracting the marriage. By the time his lordship suspected something, she had conceived their only child."

"Archibald Bertram?" Devlin asked.

She nodded. "Lady Bellewyck's illness worsened, violent tendencies followed by long periods of deep melancholy. Wanting to protect his young son from the often erratic behavior of his mother, William sent the boy away."

Cradling her bandaged hand beneath her cloak, Christiana stepped to the fireplace. Staring into the vibrant flames, she began to relax. The flickering firelight seemed to coax the story from the depths of her soul.

"With his wife confined to the abbey and his son away from home, William traveled throughout Europe. Even after the death of Lady Bellewyck, he preferred to be anywhere but here. During one of his travels to Russia, he met a young, beautiful, accomplished woman. She was also married to a much older member of the aristocracy. Whether the affair was based on lust, love or need, I do not know, but a child was conceived. As fate would have it, the mother died in childbirth. The woman's husband, old and bereft by the loss of his young wife—and having no children of his own—recognized the newborn infant as his legitimate daughter. Sadly, he became gravely ill not quite two years later and arranged for the child to be given over to the guardianship of her true father, William Bertram, the Earl of Bellewyck."

Christiana turned and looked across the room at Devlin. His expression was attentive, void of any condemnation, and so she continued.

"William doted upon his young ward, preferring to remain at the abbey for the first time in many years. The bond he shared with the child was one of great affection."

"Did no one suspect the child's true parentage?"

"There was no resemblance. His lordship introduced his ward as the daughter of Count Alexander Petrovsky, a widower he'd befriended whilst living in Russia. Even the two Petrovsky servants who accompanied the orphaned child to England bore witness to this fact."

Devlin frowned. "What happened to these servants?"

"The nurse spoke very little English. She returned to Russia after seeing the child settled. The English-born manservant made a solemn promise to Count Petrovsky that he would always look after the child. Impressed with this servant's devotion to the child, William hired him on at the estate. And that is how Tom Rooney came to Bellewyck

Abbey."

Devlin blinked. "Tom Rooney brought the child to England?" When she nodded, he snorted with derision. "I knew the man was lying to me. Might I enquire who else at the abbey knows this truth?"

"Everyone, I am afraid," she said in a near whisper.

With a sardonic laugh, Devlin shook his head. "I suspected as much. Still, it is disconcerting to hear you admit it." When she made no comment, he asked, "Did Lord Bellewyck's son know the truth about the child's parentage?"

"Not until his father was dying," she said. "William wanted his son and heir to assume responsibility for the child. I suppose he felt there would be a greater sense of obligation if his son knew the child was his half-sister. His son also learned that Count Petrovsky had provided quite generously for the child's future."

"Was this request witnessed?"

"There were five other people in the room," she said. "Mr. Stafford Evans, an old friend and solicitor to Lord Bellewyck, and four servants of the estate—Reliance Tatum, Bertie Lloyd, Jasper Collins, and Tom Rooney."

Devlin began to rub the back of his neck. "So, this child was never the legal ward of Archibald Bertram. Rather she was the ward of his father, William."

"Yes."

"Do you perchance know if papers were ever filed in England appointing guardianship of the child to Archibald Bertram?"

"I do not think so. I believe it was more a request, an understanding between father and son."

"Whereupon the son failed to honor his father's wishes," Devlin murmured.

She nodded. "But since it had been made in the presence of others, it was not something the new earl ignored outright —especially while Mr. Evans was alive. Although sworn to secrecy about the child's true parentage, Mr. Evans suspected the new Lord Bellewyck would not do his duty by the child. Evans then prepared the codicil. But when he died, there was no one who knew the truth about the ward or the deathbed promise between father and son—except for the essentially powerless servants of the abbey."

Devlin couldn't remove his gaze from the beauty standing before the stone fireplace. There was something about the way Christiana spoke that prompted him to believe she saw more than she remembered at this moment.

"Then you and the ward were children together?"

She did not respond, but continued to stare at him in a breathtakingly sad manner.

"What happened to her, Christiana?"

"Before I say anything more, I must know something. You claim to know the Duke of Pemberton well. What will he do about all this now?"

"If, as you say, the incident was an accident, I feel certain the Duke of Pemberton will be just and understanding. Of course, there will need to be an inquest."

"Why?"

Devlin's gut wrenched at the cruelty of her words. How could he have been so wrong about her? "For God's sake, Christiana, a child is dead." He tried to calm his temper. "Frankly, I am astonished Lord Bellewyck never pursued such a course of action. Despite his obvious lack of affection for the child, did he never question what happened to her?"

"His lordship was very much aware what happened to her."

"Yet he did nothing?"

"You would do better to ask yourself what Lord Bellewyck had to gain by remaining silent."

Devlin rubbed his brow. "Christiana, I am in no mood for riddles."

"I am trying to make a point." Gingerly removing her cloak, she draped the garment across the back of a chair, briefly caressing its worn fabric. "The Earl of Bellewyck knew what happened to his father's ward yet did nothing. Why?"

"I apologize for being obtuse, but do tell."

"He wanted her dead, Devlin. And he did everything in his power to see it accomplished. With Mr. Evans dead, Lord Bellewyck had access to a virtual fortune. So, he abandoned his half-sister at the abbey whilst he lived in comfort at a new residence in Bath. He never sent funds to see to her welfare, never took measures to see her educated or groomed to take her rightful place in the world. Although her true parentage could not be made public, she was still the legitimate daughter of a Russian count and an heiress in her own right."

Returning to the desk, Christiana shook her head at Devlin. Her bosom began to rise and fall above the rounded neckline of a periwinkle gown with increased agitation. "You want an inquest now? You expect me to believe the rich and powerful Duke of Pemberton cares what happened to that child after all this time? If, as you claim, Pemberton is remotely concerned about the Bellewyck ward, why did he not come to Bellewyck Abbey himself?"

Devlin considered Christiana's impassioned words. He now understood her animosity toward the Duke of Pemberton. She believed Pemberton no better than Archibald Bertram, simply because he didn't come to the abbey in person to see about the missing ward. The irony was the Duke of Pemberton did come—albeit in disguise.

Yet, he sensed something more to her resentment, a deep pain that stirred within him such a startling possibility it sent chills rippling down his spine. Like dying embers refusing to be extinguished, the disturbing thought ignited in his brain, blossoming into blazing flames of incredulity.

"When did the child die, Christiana?"

A log slipped in the hearth, the sound distracting him. In that single breath of time a picture flashed through his mind, the image of an innocent child abandoned at Bellewyck Abbey amongst servants. The child had raven tresses and dazzling violet-blue eyes. Apprenticed with a chimneysweep to earn her keep, the child climbed inside the black hell of soot-filled flues. A child who learned to speak properly from years spent hiding in the shadows and listening to members of the gentry. A child educated by the vicar's wife in a manner more befitting the daughter of a gentleman rather than a servant. She'd blossomed into a young woman whose loyalty to the villagers and servants of Bellewyck Abbey seemed almost noble.

His heart seemed to seize up in his chest as his throat closed with burning emotion. Looking to Christiana, he whispered, "Dear God, it's you. *You* are the ward."

She said nothing, but in her glistening eyes reflected a world of truth. He watched the workings of her delicate throat as she swallowed hard.

"For God's sake, why have you done this to yourself?"

"It is called survival, Devlin."

The sight of her nobly fighting back tears was more than he could bear. He went to her side and gently pulled her into his arms. Inhaling deeply of the fragrance from her hair, he kissed her temple and damned himself for a blind fool. Before he could capture her lips in a tender kiss, she pulled away, stiff and rigid, as if determined to distance herself from him.

Though confused by her sudden aloofness, he fought to understand. "Why the elaborate deception, Christiana? Pemberton will eventually learn of your existence, especially once he locates the codicil."

When she nibbled on her bottom lip and looked away, he knew yet another truth.

"You have the codicil."

She nodded, wiping the stains of tears from her face. "I saw my *brother* before he died. He summoned me to Bath and gave me a strongbox filled with all the papers regarding my identity, including the codicil. There is even a letter written by William Bertram, acknowledging himself as my true father. But it no longer mattered. I had already given up any claim to my true identity. All I ever wanted from my brother was freedom to remain with the people I love. I foolishly believed Archie's parting gift had been sincere."

"Perhaps it was a gift," Devlin said. "Is it not possible that upon his death he wanted to leave the door open should you wish to reclaim your birthright?"

"You did not know him,"—Christiana laughed bitterly—"he wanted me dead for as long as I can remember. If not for the people here and in the village, he might have succeeded. Their love and devotion was a weakness he used against them. He made them do things they never would have done if not for me."

"The smuggling?" Devlin asked.

She nodded. "Lord Bellewyck discovered the servants had been stealing ale from the brewery and selling it under another name. They used those funds to care for me, wanting to give me some semblance of what my life might have been or could be someday. Mrs. Snow taught me of books, languages, and music. I even had a dance master for a time."

She smiled faintly at the memory, but quickly sobered. "But having lost my inheritance and desperate for funds—and with nothing more at the estate he could sell to moneylenders in London—Archie forced the people who loved me to engage in smuggling."

Devlin frowned. "How did he force them?"

"He had dealings with many unsavory people. One of them ran a brutal smuggling gang from Calais that operated along the coast several years ago. The abbey's brewery was used as a means to hide and transfer contraband. Specially made barrels with false bottoms were used to bring the contraband to either London or Bath. If the servants and villagers did not participate in the madness, his lordship threatened to take me away from here. And the place he had chosen for me was such that I would have had no hope whatsoever for a life of decency or virtue."

Devlin swore under his breath.

"You must understand, I only learned of the smuggling five years ago," she said. "I was terrified for them. I knew what would happen if they were caught."

She looked imploringly at him. "Was I to do nothing and let them continue to risk their lives because of me? I had to get them out of the Calais gang. There was only one person who could help me. On a chance meeting years earlier, I had befriended Blackjack. He knew he could trust me, and I knew I could trust him. I needed someone powerful on my side. Not only did Blackjack help our people get out of the Calais gang, the Ravens are now the only smuggling operation in this area of Kent. Unfortunately, Lord Bellewyck had grown accustomed to the income smuggling afforded him. He threatened to see everyone hanged, accusing them not only of theft from the brewery, but of stealing the very items he took himself to sell in London. My friends were getting old; their health had suffered terribly. They had given all they possibly could because of me. It had to end. So, I took their place in smuggling by joining the Ravens."

"And you have been a Raven for five years now?"

"Yes. The only thing I asked from Lord Bellewyck was proof of my identity upon his death. But when that Mr. Higginbotham came to the estate asking questions and looking for the ward, I knew Lord Bellewyck still wanted to make us suffer. If discovered, the truth about stealing and smuggling still meant imprisonment or death to the people I love. And he also knew I did not want my life controlled by another nobleman."

"Because all noblemen are like Lord Bellewyck?" When she said nothing, he shook his head. "Considering everything he put you through, your feelings are understandable. And yet, I do not think his lordship was trying to make you or anyone else here suffer when he gave you that strongbox. He could have simply told Higginbotham you were the ward, or that the servants were thieves."

"Ah, but where is the revenge in that?" she scoffed. "He

knew my greatest fear was to be taken away from the people I love. That was his intent by this cat-and-mouse game."

Devlin folded his arms across his chest, his lips pursed together thoughtfully. "Yes, it does seem a cat-and-mouse game. However, I do not believe you or your friends are the mouse."

"I am sorry, Devlin, but I knew his lordship better than you. He never did anything for anyone. The only person Lord Bellewyck ever cared about was himself."

"Perhaps you are right," Devlin said with a slight shrug. He studied her a long moment in silence. "So Bellewyck never had a ward, eh? Quite a clever play on words, my dear."

"I thought so," she said with a faint smile. "After all, you were talking about Archie, not his father. Besides, I did tell you there was no child."

Devlin snickered softly, but quickly sobered. "My God, do you comprehend the life you could have had? Well, if nothing else, you can now end this charade and take your rightful place in the world."

"My rightful place? If the Duke of Pemberton learns I exist, he shall take charge over my life—my very future."

"And you hold that against him?"

"Do you not understand? The moment he meets me, the moment he learns about the things I have done, he will want to rid himself of the obligation. Oh, I am sure there will be some kindly pretense about finding me a suitable husband, but the truth is Pemberton will not want me underfoot. I would be a scandal, an embarrassment. I have nothing to offer any man of good family. It will likely cost Pemberton a small fortune just to marry me off."

"You forget I know the Duke of Pemberton," Devlin argued. "He would never force you into a marriage you do not want. His own sisters married for love. Besides which, as isolated as your life has been here, no one need ever know about the past. With very little effort, you can learn how to behave as a lady befitting your true station in life. You already know a great deal. I have no doubt you could make a stunning transformation."

"And thus begin a whole new deception?" Christiana smiled sadly. "I am too far removed from that world now, Devlin."

"Nothing you have been forced to do changes who you truly are, Christiana."

"I would rather die in servitude with people who love me than go to London and be made to feel a fool amongst snobbish people who will never accept me. Can you imagine what Pemberton and his set would do if I showed up now? The man is looking for a child, not a troublesome, uncivilized hoyden who rides astride and associates with smugglers."

"For God's sake, the Duke of Pemberton is not Lord Bellewyck." Devlin ran his hand through his hair with obvious frustration. "Think of your parents, Christiana. Do you honestly believe this is the life they wanted for you? Even Count Petrovsky cared about your future happiness."

"I have no memory of Count Petrovsky or my parents. What they wanted is of little consequence now."

"What of love and marriage? Do you not want children? A husband and family of your own?"

"I did once"—she retrieved her cloak and draped it over her arm—"but I stopped believing in knights in shining armor and living happily ever after a long time ago."

"Forgive me for being blunt, but there is the distinct possibility you have already conceived a child—my child as it so happens."

The serious regard in his expression was disconcerting. Did he find the possibility of her carrying his child reprehensible?

"Do you regret what happened between us, Devlin?"

His lips compressed into a firm line. "Do I regret it?" With a curt nod, he said, "I regret not that it happened, but how it happened. The truth is, had I known you were the Bellewyck ward, I would not have bedded you."

She tried to ignore the pain in her heart. "Yet, you had no problem seducing me when you believed me only a servant. Is that it?"

"Do not put words in my mouth, Christiana. Contrary to what you think of my character, I am not in the habit of seducing virgins—be they servants, wards, or ladies of the *ton*. The point is I had an obligation to find the Bellewyck ward, not seduce her."

It took little time to realize that biting her bottom lip until it started to bleed would not ease the anguish his impulsive words caused. "I am so much a fool," she whispered.

"What did you say?"

"Only that you need have no fear I will cast aspersions upon your honor, Devlin. I will not tell Pemberton you unwittingly seduced the mysterious Bellewyck ward."

He shook his head with obvious disgust. "Why am I not surprised you think nothing of deceiving Pemberton about that as well? Tell me, Christiana, what if you have conceived a child?"

"Have no fear, Devlin. I'll not trap you into marriage. I have known from the day you arrived at Bellewyck Abbey that you have higher aspirations for yourself than remaining a mere steward. And God forbid you lose the favor of the Duke of Pemberton."

Though insulted by her words, they caused Devlin to remember his own deception. Dear God, not only had he fallen in love and bedded the missing ward of Bellewyck Abbey, but he'd seduced her whilst pretending to be someone else. Bloody hell.

"I need a drink," he mumbled savagely. Oblivious to anything but the blinding truth of his own despicable lack of honor, he opened a desk drawer. Removing a bottle of whiskey he'd managed to purchase at The Green Dragon the day they rode to the village together, he poured himself a glass. After downing the drink with one quick swallow, he studied the young woman before him.

"Devlin, I wanted to tell you the truth, but I was afraid."

He said nothing, just stared at her.

Turning, she crossed the room. "The others were only protecting me. I do not want them punished for the past or blamed for the decisions I have made in my life. Right or wrong, they were mine."

"Might I point out the decisions you've made have put your life in great danger? You could have died last night, and for what? Was the plunder worth it? Do forgive me, but I do not understand why you continue to smuggle. After all, Lord Bellewyck is dead and buried. The threat of exposure no longer exists. You could have stopped after his death and I might never have learned about it. Thus, I cannot help but wonder what you find so damnably intriguing about this life of crime. If it is a question of income, God knows there are other far more pleasant ways for a beautiful woman like you to earn some extra coin."

Christiana paled at his remark and Devlin immediately regretted his words. "Forgive me, Christiana. My head is spin-ning. I am trying to understand, but there is much to consider. I think it best we talk more about this in the morning"

She nodded uneasily and went to the door. Pausing once more, she looked at him. "Devlin, please do not tell Pemberton I'm the missing ward. Let him think me dead. What harm can it do now? Please, will you keep my secret?"

Bloody hell. She truly thinks Pemberton is no better than that monstrous half-brother of hers. The irony is—without realizing it—she'd just told the Duke of Pemberton everything. Emotion burned like a fiery poker embedded in his damn chest, forcing him to gruffly clear his throat even to speak. "I promise you, the Duke of Pemberton will not learn who you are from me, Christiana."

Tears glistened in her eyes and she offered a tremulous smile. Then, without another word she walked out of the library and into the darkness beyond.

CHAPTER NINETEEN

"He that will win his dame must do
As love does when he draws his bow;
With one hand thrust the lady from,
And with the other pull her home."
~ Samuel Butler (1612-1680), *Hudibras*

Unable to sleep, Devlin sat before the fireplace in his bedchamber, chin resting in the palm of his hand. His head felt as if about to explode from everything he'd learned about Christiana over the past twenty-four hours. Revisiting in memory all the things he'd said and done since beginning this masquerade only added to his surly mood.

"How could I have been so blind?"

He'd been looking for a child, ignoring the fact Lord Bellewyck's Will had been dated ten years ago and that children grew up. How many times did I see frustration in Christiana's eyes when I asked about a missing child?

With no small amount of chagrin, he realized what a pompous fool he'd been since first coming to the estate. The thought a servant might be the ward had never crossed his mind.

"Bloody hell, have I always been such a judgmental bastard?"

Loath as he was to admit it, there was another reason why he never suspected the beguiling Christiana might be the ward. Quite simply, he had other things on his mind where she was concerned. From the morning he saw her standing at the foot of the staircase, he'd thought of little else but bedding her. Not only did he think of it, he'd acted upon it.

Had he concentrated on learning the secrets of Bellewyck Abbey and not permitted himself to be distracted by passion, he might have behaved more like a man of honor. Instead, he'd taken every opportunity to touch her, to kiss her, to seduce her.

It made little difference now that he'd fallen madly in love with her, mad being the definitive word. His behavior had been disgraceful and dishonorable. Even worse, he'd practiced his own brand of deceit by pretending to be someone else. The fact she preferred to remain an impoverished servant for the remainder of her life—rather than tell the truth about her very existence—spoke volumes of her hatred for the Duke of Pemberton.

What a quandary. He needed to soften her heart to a man she knew, but didn't know, to make her see him for the man he is and not the villain she believed him to be. The task would require patience, gentle words, and courtly manners—made all the more complicated because he simply couldn't make love to her again until she knew him as the Duke of Pemberton.

"First things first," he said. "I must get her safely away from those bloody smugglers. This Blackjack fellow is in for a rude awakening if he thinks to stop me."

Standing, he paced before the fireplace. "Then there is this absurd idea she has about denying her birthright and not believing in happily ever after. By God, knights in shining armor do exist and I care not how many damn dragons I have to slay to prove it."

Huddled in her narrow bed beneath layers of blankets, Christiana stared at the ceiling and fretted over what Devlin would do next. Would duty and loyalty to Pemberton prompt him to tell the duke the truth? Then again, he did say the duke wouldn't learn the truth from him. She found comfort in that.

With a sigh, she closed her eyes. Just then the sound of footsteps paused outside her chamber door. Before she gathered wits enough to ask who was there, the door opened and a tall shadow loomed in the doorway.

She must be dreaming. He wouldn't come to her room. For that matter, how did he know which room was hers? She squeezed her eyes shut, held them that way for the count of three, and looked again. It wasn't a dream.

Holding a candlestick, Devlin wore those scandalous pantaloons. His fine white shirt, opened at the collar, showed an indecent and rather enticing amount of masculine chest. He didn't enter, just searched the darkened room from the threshold until he located her in bed.

"Ah, there you are."

Clutching the bedcovers to her chin, she gingerly sat up, trying to appear as graceful as possible. A ridiculous gesture, especially since she'd been naked in his arms just yesterday. For some reason, however, she felt more exposed tonight.

"Did you think I would run off again?" she asked.

Devlin entered and proceeded to examine the dimensions of her small cell of a room. She heard him swear under his breath as he tapped a thin layer of ice already starting to form in her wash basin.

"I knew it," he grumbled. "This room is cold as the grave. Get up! I'll not have you freeze to death."

He walked to the narrow window, frowning at the panes of glass laced with frost. "I should have known your room would be a dreadful hovel."

Christiana looked about her chamber. In truth, it was small and sparsely furnished. Still, she'd grown accustomed to it. When she looked back at him, she found he watched her.

Setting the candlestick on the bedside table, he stretched out his hand and smiled. "Come with me."

Her pulse began to race. "With you?"

"I want you to sleep in my bedchamber."

Each rapid beat of her heart pounded in her ears. "Y-you want me to sleep with you?"

He grumbled. "Um, no actually, I intend to sleep elsewhere."

Feeling the blush of embarrassment, Christiana nodded. "Thank you for the offer, but no. Quite honestly, the thought of being alone in Lord Bellewyck's bed does not inspire sleep."

"Then think of it as my bed, but you will not remain in this room another night."

He walked over to an old wardrobe and searched its contents. A moment later, he removed a soft, woolen dressing gown and placed it in her lap.

"This is not necessary," she murmured.

"Christiana, I cannot in good conscience sleep when I know you are in this room. Until I decide what must be done about everything, you will obey me."

She fiddled with the dressing gown. "But where will you sleep?"

"Before the fire in the Great Room." He folded back the numerous blankets and started to pull her up by the hand. She gasped in pain.

"What is it? Are you hurt?"

Christiana closed her eyes, gritting her teeth. "I am all right."

"The hell you are!"

Opening her eyes, she stared at him, noting his upset.

"What happened? Good God, is this why you were late today?"

Her bottom lip quivered and she looked away.

Torn between shaking her and holding her close, he said. "Tell me what happened."

"I fell," she said in a near whisper.

"WHAT!"

"Well, my hand was bandaged," she argued. "That does tend to impede one from getting a firm grip when climbing a cliff."

"You fell off a cliff?"

"Not all the way down. Hardly any distance at all really."

Devlin sat gently on the edge of the bed, studying her as if he didn't know where to begin searching for injuries. "Did you strike your head? Your back?"

"Nothing is broken, Devlin. I just have some bumps and bruises. I would have been home this morning, but Blackjack gave me a bit too much laudanum."

Devlin's posture stiffened. "You were with Blackjack all day?"

"I was unable to ride. While I slept, he sent word to Mr. Godolphin at The Green Dragon. 'Twas Godolphin who contacted Gordon Darrow to fetch me."

He snorted in disgust. "I suppose it never occurred to you to send word to me."

"I was asleep, Devlin."

Somewhat pacified, he nodded. "Are you certain you are all right? Perhaps I should summon a physician?"

"I do not require a physician."

"Is this why you kept your body so stiff in the library?"

She didn't respond; there was no need.

Ever so gently, he helped her stand. "Come, I refuse to let you remain in this room another night."

"This does not seem fair, Devlin," she said. "I feel guilty. What about Polly?"

He rolled his eyes heavenward. "God forbid you have feelings of guilt where I am concerned, eh? Then again, for propriety's sake, I suppose it would be best if we found a room for Polly in one of the guest chambers."

"And Sarah, too?"

He shot her an exasperated look. "I thought Sarah rooms with her grandmother off the kitchen."

"Yes, but, well, there is a lovely bedchamber I have often thought would make a perfect room for a young girl. I am quite sure Sarah would enjoy a nice, cheery room all to herself."

"Good God," he mumbled, although he was more touched than he would ever admit by Christiana's sense of generosity and consideration toward others. Her transformation into a duchess would be most intriguing, especially when his very proper mother tried to explain rules of behavior between servants and their employers.

With a slight grin, he said, "If it will make you quit this room tonight, we shall move all the servants to the guest chambers of the abbey. God knows there are more than enough rooms to spare. It might even make this place seem less a tomb."

The smile she graced upon him made Devlin ache to hold her close, to kiss her senseless. Instead, he could only watch as she tied her dressing gown.

"Of course, Tom will not want to move from the gate-house," she continued in a distracted manner. "And Bertie is quite content in her quarters."

"Fine," he said.

She followed his lead as they walked downstairs to his bedchamber. Upon entering, she sighed. "Oh, 'tis so warm and cozy in here. And, look! You built up the fire by yourself."

"Imagine that," he said, biting back a grin.

She stood before the fireplace and warmed her hands. It proved impossible to resist the sweet picture she made. He took her delicate hands in his and kissed them.

"I promise you this much, Christiana. You will never be cold again."

The longer he held her hands, the more difficult it became not to stare at her enticing pink lips. More than anything, he wanted to pull her into his arms, to divest her of the prim bedclothes and make love to her. Yet, until she knew the truth about his identity and they were legally wed, he vowed not to make love with her again.

"Climb in bed," he commanded gruffly.

"Are you quite sure you do not mind?"

"Oh, I mind, but there is nothing to be done for it now."

With a shy smile, she carefully removed her dressing gown and climbed into the high bed. Once situated under the covers, she eyed him curiously. "This is quite nice of you."

"I am only doing what Pemberton would expect."

"Oh," she said in a quiet manner. "You like him very much, do you not?"

"Who? Oh, Pemberton you mean?"

She nodded.

Believing this might be the perfect opportunity to begin singing the Duke of Pemberton's praises, Devlin feigned a thoughtful mien. "Yes, I do like him. Indeed, I should say that I admire him very much. Pemberton is quite intelligent and very honorable."

"What does he look like?"

Devlin shrugged, hoping to appear nonchalant about the subject. "Many women consider him handsome. It is quite well-known that throngs of beautiful women compete for his favor wherever he goes."

She made a sour expression. "How old is he?"

"About my age, I suppose."

Christiana sat in his bed, her bandaged hand outside the covers resting in her lap—the picture of innocence. She wore a simple, white nightdress buttoned high on her neck, prim enough for Mrs. Lloyd. But, the wide flounce of a linen cap shadowing her eyes and long, twin plaits of raven hair reminded him of a young girl. The thought made it easier for him to leave her alone.

He laughed softly. "You look like a child in that big bed."

She frowned, clearly affronted by the remark.

"Can I get you something before I leave? I have no laudanum, but I do have that bottle of Scotch whiskey in the library." He snapped his fingers. "By jove, I have it. I shall fetch you a glass of warm milk."

"Thank you, no." She raised her chin at a haughty angle and arched a delicate eyebrow. "Goodnight, Devlin."

Lips pursed together in an effort to stave off laughter, Devlin presented a courtly bow and left. Once outside, he couldn't hold back his laughter as it echoed through the ancient hallway.

CHAPTER TWENTY

"God is not averse to deceit in a holy cause."
~ Aeschylus (525-456 B.C.)

The unmistakable song of morning called and Christiana reluctantly answered. It took a moment to realize she wasn't in her little bed. Smiling, she wiggled her toes and stared at the drawn bed curtains. Curious as to the hour, she leaned forward on an elbow to peek through the toile curtains. Startled by someone snoring, she fell out of bed—landing with a hard thud on the floor. Wincing at the pain to her already bruised ribs, she rose to her feet then stared in disbelief.

Devlin slept on his belly, his face turned toward her. A strange, swooshing-type sound emerged from his slightly parted lips. Was he drooling? Recalling another time when he'd feigned sleep by snoring, she poked him in the arm. He didn't move. She poked him again with more force. He grumbled, then turned to face the opposite direction, remaining asleep.

Looking toward the window, she frowned. She'd always been an early riser, ready to start the day well before dawn. Everyone would be looking for her, anxious to know what had happened between her and Devlin last night.

Donning her dressing gown, she went in search of Polly and found her friend entering the abbey carrying Devlin's freshly laundered shirts.

"Where have ye been?" Polly cried. "I came to yer room this mornin' but yer bed was empty. I thought mayhap ye were down in the brewery. Why are ye still in yer bedclothes? Are ye not feelin' well?"

With a finger to her lips, she motioned for Polly to follow her into the Great Room. After securing the heavy doors, she turned to her childhood friend. "Mr. Randolph came to my bedchamber last night."

"The devil ye say!"

Stirring the fire in the hearth, Christiana noticed an old

drinking horn on the floor. Without thinking, she knelt down to pick it up, placing it on a nearby sideboard.

"Tell me what happened," Polly demanded.

"Mr. Randolph claimed he could not rest knowing I slept in such a cold room, but I think there was another reason. Now that he knows I am the Bellewyck ward, he is behaving most strangely—almost like a guardian himself."

"Ye told him the truth then?"

She explained to Polly all that transpired between her and Mr. Randolph, up to and including waking this morning and finding the fully dressed steward in her bed. The maid eyed her suspiciously.

"Are ye sure nothin' happened after he got in bed with ye?"

"I believe I would know if it had." She placed a hand against her sore ribs. "Besides which, he made it clear last night he never would have seduced me had he known the truth. It seems as the ward, I am no longer a desirable woman. The last thing he said before he quit the bedchamber was that I looked like a child."

Indignant, Polly frowned at her friend. "Well, he did not think ye were a child night before last. I suppose now that ye're the long lost ward, he is frettin' over what Pemberton will do to him."

"He did nothing I did not want him to do," Christiana said in a quiet voice.

"Do ye think he plans to tell Pemberton?"

"I do not know." She watched Polly set the laundered shirts down on a chair. "He did say Pemberton would not learn the truth from him. I suspect he wants me to step forward and tell the duke who I am."

"That'll never happen," Polly said with a delicate snort. Folding her arms beneath her ample bosom, a speculative gleam came to the maid's eyes. "I know a way ye can stop Pemberton and stay here with us."

Christiana arched a brow. "And what might that be?"

"Marry Mr. Randolph before the duke finds out the truth," Polly said with a definitive nod. "Then Pemberton would have no say in yer future."

"Give a false name in marriage?" Christiana shook her head. "Even should Mr. Randolph want to marry me, he would never agree to that. He is exceedingly loyal to Pemberton."

"But he compromised ye!"

"I will not force him to marry me, Polly." With a sigh, Christiana absent-mindedly touched one of Devlin's shirts. "When he learned about the smuggling, he was so angry—so disappointed in me. But then he vowed to help me. He was so dear, so loving. I began to believe he might actually love me. I just do not understand how his feelings could change so much because I am the ward."

"'Tis because of Pemberton," Polly grumbled. "Mr. Randolph loves ye. I am sure of it. Ye should have seen the way he stalked about here lookin' for ye, askin' where ye were. When he was not pacin', he was in his chamber. We all saw him sittin' by the window watchin' the road to the village. I only managed to do a quick job of strippin' the bed when he talked with ye in the library."

"Is that why the counterpane is missing?"

Polly smirked like a prim, spinster aunt. "'Tis missin' because I plan to keep it safe until he does right by ye. I'll wave it in front of Pemberton's nose if I must."

Christiana made a comical expression. "I hardly think that necessary."

"Well, I say if the duke tries to take ye away against yer will, we show him proof that his comely steward compromised yer virtue."

"There may be other proof to show Pemberton."

It took a moment for the light of understanding to dawn in her friend's eyes. "Caw," Polly gasped.

Crossing to the fireplace, Christiana studied the marble chimneypiece, its elegant carvings documenting the noble lineage of the Bertram family—her family. "Polly, I have been thinking perhaps I should come forward as the Bellewyck ward. That is to say, if Mr. Randolph believes I should."

"Tell Pemberton ye're Christiana Petrovsky?" Polly asked.

"If I could have a future with Mr. Randolph, then yes."

Polly's green eyes glistened with understanding. "Well then, ye best remind Mr. Randolph ye're a woman. Seems to me he is actin' like a fish flounderin' on a hook. Now is the time to put the net under him."

With a laugh, Christiana hugged her friend.

"Did I not tell ye he was the one?" asked Polly.

"Yes," Christiana whispered. "He is the one."

Out of the corner of her eye, Christiana saw the door to the cellaret open and frowned. She walked over to the cabinet and studied five bottles of ale, two of which were now empty. "Dear God," she whispered. "This explains why he is sleeping so deeply. He found the drugged bottles of ale."

Polly paled. "If he drank those two bottles, he'll not remember how he got into that bed with ye or what happened afterwards."

"I wonder," Christiana whispered with a mischievous grin. "Now might be the perfect opportunity to remind my darling Mr. Randolph I am not a child."

Devlin groaned as bright sunlight filled the room behind his eyelids. Who the devil had the gall to come into his room and open every damn curtain? Covering his eyes with a forearm, he tried to return to sleep. It was futile. Stretching his arms to his sides, he slapped the mattress in frustration. It was then he realized he still wore clothing from the night before. Even more odd, his shirt was open and his trousers unfastened.

"Good morning," said a lilting voice.

With a start, Devlin turned his head and saw Christiana standing beside the bed—a vision of loveliness. Her black hair, no longer in plaits, glistened in the sunlight, falling loose about her hips. She smiled with what could only be described as an invitation to seduction.

As he admired her womanly form, Devlin found himself grinning like a besotted fool. Then he realized she wore one of his shirts, and nothing else. Sitting up quickly, he cradled his aching head with his hands, waiting for the dizziness to subside.

He looked again at her attire, swallowing hard to see shapely limbs and bare pink toes. "Why are you wearing my shirt?"

"I had nothing else to wear." She bit her bottom lip and looked down at the floor.

"What are you talking about? What happened to your bedclothes?"

When she continued to stare at something on the floor; Devlin followed her gaze and saw her prim nightdress, torn from collar to hem, completely shredded. Swearing under his breath, he all but jumped out of bed, fastening his trousers and looking at the nightdress as if it were a dead snake.

"How the bloody hell did that happen? What are you saying, Christiana?"

She looked at him with wide-eyed innocence. "I have said nothing but good morning, Devlin."

"What happened last night?"

"Do you not remember?"

He swallowed hard, trying to think clearly through the muddled shadows of his mind. The last thing he remembered was leaving this room and her in his bed. He rubbed the back of his neck. "I fell asleep before the fire." Pointing with an outstretched arm at the hearth in his bedchamber, he added, "And not that fire, by God."

She studied him with a wary expression.

"I remember distinctly stirring up the logs in the fire downstairs. I found some bottles of ale in the sideboard and thought the ale would warm me. But I most definitely had no thoughts of seducing you."

Agitated and confused, he looked at Christiana—lovelier in his white shirt than any woman at St. James' Court dressed in the finest silks and jewels. *Is it possible I got so foxed last night I made love to her without her consent?*

When his heated gaze devoured her, Christiana knew without any doubt that Devlin still desired her as a woman. She enjoyed a brief measure of triumph that her little experiment had worked so well. But just as quickly, anguish crossed his features.

"I vowed it would not happen again." He spoke in a pained whisper.

He sounded upset, even ashamed at the thought he might actually have bedded her. She watched in stunned silence as he sat down in a chair and cradled his head in his hands. The sting of tears burned her eyes, yet she was determined not to cry. "I am such a fool," she whispered. "What was I thinking? Bind him to me so that he will not tell the duke."

"What did you say?"

She quickly looked up and found him studying her with a suspicious expression. "Nothing," she said.

"You said something about not telling the duke."

"No," she cried. "Do not tell the duke."

Devlin's expression turned hard. He crossed the room and took hold of her shoulders in a firm grasp. "You were seduced against your will and still you will not speak the truth."

"You do not understand," she cried.

"Oh, I understand. I understand I came back to this room

and bedded you like some foxed lecher."

The look of self-loathing on his face nearly destroyed her. Tears cascaded down her cheeks. She made no effort to wipe them away or hide them.

"And now I have made you cry," he said in a hoarse voice. Releasing her shoulders, he stepped away. "I swear to you, Christiana, I do not remember."

"Please," she pleaded, anxious to calm his temper. "Listen to me, Devlin. I have not accused you of anything. You have done nothing against my will."

He laughed caustically. "Oh, I am quite sure I employed sufficient tactics to seduce you. I am not an animal after all, just a dishonorable bastard who cannot control his bloody quimstake."

Stunned by his crude language, she couldn't think of what to say as he walked across the room to the door.

Pausing at the threshold, he looked back at her. "Bellewyck took your childhood and I have taken your innocence, not once but twice. Clearly, I *am* no better than that evil monster."

She ran across the room, desperate to stop him from leaving. "You are not a monster," she cried. "You are nothing like him, Devlin Randolph."

Devlin laughed. A harsh, cynical sound. When he sobered, he looked at her with pity. "My dear Christiana, you know nothing about me."

Ashley Kath-Bilsky

CHAPTER TWENTY-ONE

*"Courage is that virtue which champions
the cause of right."*
~ Cicero (106-43 B.C.), *De Officiis*

How could I not remember making love to Christiana?
Again and again, the question repeated in Devlin's head.
After riding hard and fast about the countryside all morning,
the question remained unanswered. Even more disturbing
was that this hadn't been the first time he'd wakened under a
cloud of uncertainty, not knowing where or how the previous
hours had been spent.

By the time he reined in at The Green Dragon, it was
midafternoon. Still wearing yesterday's clothes, his face had
stubble from a dark beard. Thank God none of his mother's
friends could see him now. Even Hastings, his valet, would
have a fit of apoplexy. He found an empty table in the corner
of the common room and ordered a Scotch whiskey, refusing
to look at anyone.

No one approached, but apparently Mr. Godolphin, the
proprietor of The Green Dragon, found his presence of
particular interest. At times Godolphin whispered rather
loudly to a heavyset man Devlin recognized as the village
smithy. As the day wore on, other men came to the tavern and
joined in the discussion, clearly bemused by the abbey's new
steward's unkempt attire and surly disposition. More and
more of the conversation drifted to Devlin.

"Appears a might burdened, don't he?" the smithy asked.

Godolphin then approached, carrying a bottle of whiskey,
an expression of wary concern on his weathered features.

"Is there somethin' I can do for ye, Mr. Randolph?"

More sober than he appeared, Devlin clenched his back
teeth at the fictitious name. Damn this idiotic charade. He
never should have accepted that blasted wager. Had he come
to Bellewyck Abbey as himself, like he'd planned, none of this
would have happened.

199

I tried to fight it. I never intended to get involved with her, no matter how beautiful she is or how deeply she touched my soul.

"Blinded by lust," he grumbled aloud.

"Beg pardon, Mr. Randolph?"

Devlin stared at his half-empty drink. When did he lose control of his life? Had it started with their first kiss in the hop garden? In truth, that first sweet taste had weakened his resolve. It ultimately gave way to more intense erotic musings about Christiana that kept him awake, painfully aroused, and in sore need of release. Then, when they finally gave in to temptation and made love, it was beyond his greatest expectations.

But his feelings for Christiana were more than mere lust. From the moment they met, the exasperating, impertinent, absurdly secretive housekeeper had challenged his mind and chiseled away at his heart.

Christiana had conquered him completely—mind, body, and soul.

He looked at Godolphin. "I just learned the identity of the Bellewyck ward."

With a quick glance over his shoulder, the innkeeper took a seat at the table. "And is that what ails ye, Mr. Randolph?"

Devlin quirked a brow and studied the innkeeper. In another life, the man would be chastised for having the audacity to take a seat in the presence of the Duke of Pemberton—let alone engage in conversation with him. Now, however, he welcomed Godolphin's cheek.

"What ails me, Mr. Godolphin, is that I failed to realize the truth before now. No doubt, the entire village thinks me a damn fool. The signs were there all along; even covered in soot there was—"

Uncomfortable speaking in public about his problems, Devlin frowned. "Well, it bloody well doesn't matter now."

"No need to feel embarrassed, sir," Godolphin said. "Love is blind, they say."

Barely managing to not choke on his whiskey, Devlin opted to remain silent about Godolphin's impertinent remark. Just how much did the people in the village know about his relationship with Christiana? For that matter, to what extent were they involved in the more secretive, quite illegal, goings-on at the estate?

According to Christiana, the villagers had been involved

in protecting her from Lord Bellewyck, as well as maintaining the deception about her identity. Neither could he forget that it was Godolphin who very agreeably directed him to The Mermaid Inn the other night—or that Blackjack had contacted The Green Dragon's proprietor when Christiana had been injured and needed to be brought home. Therefore, logic dictates Godolphin must be involved in the smuggling operation. Still, he best be certain.

Draining the whiskey from his glass, Devlin leaned forward in a somewhat conspiratorial manner. "I know about the smuggling."

A frown creased Godolphin's brow.

Devlin grinned. "You know, I actually believed his lordship had killed the ward and was being blackmailed by the abbey servants." Tapping his temple with his forefinger, he added, "I had it all charted out in my mind. The earl could do nothing about the blackmail for fear the servants would expose the murder of his ward. Clever, eh?"

"Aye," Godolphin said.

"Ah, but then I discovered, quite by accident mind you, that the beautiful Miss Tatum is a pistol-wielding smuggler and, even more amazing, the missing ward of Bellewyck Abbey."

With a hard stare at Godolphin, he added, "Which reminds me, you almost got me killed the other night. If not for the timely intervention of a smuggler named *Christian,* I might very well be dead at this moment."

Godolphin's coloring paled. "Ye do not believe I wanted ye dead, Mr. Randolph?"

Devlin said nothing.

"I am sorry 'bout that, Mr. Randolph, but ye did come in here sayin' ye wanted to speak with Blackjack."

"True." He nodded. "I suppose I cannot fault you for obliging my request."

The older man sighed with relief. "I knew ye was a fair man the moment I met ye, sir."

"Indeed," Devlin murmured.

Godolphin leaned forward and spoke in a barely audible whisper. "If ye do not mind me askin', sir, what is it ye plan to do with all ye know?"

Devlin stared hard at the innkeeper. "That depends."

"Depends?"

"On how honest you intend to be with me hereafter."

"Well, as to that, knowin' how our dear lady feels 'bout ye, there'll be no more secrets between us. I can promise ye that, Mr. Randolph, sir. I am an honest man, ye see."

Leaning back in his chair, Devlin crossed his arms and crooked a brow. "Is that so? Then you shan't mind telling me about his lordship and this smuggling business."

Godolphin turned and motioned for a serving wench to bring him a glass. Glancing back at Devlin, he grinned. "I hope ye are not in a hurry to get back to the abbey just yet."

"Not at all."

They waited for the serving girl to bring the glass. Godolphin poured a drink, then took a long draught of the whiskey. "Beggin' yer pardon for being blunt, sir, but his lordship was a sorry bastard. He'd have seen the child in a grave without a second thought. Make no mistake 'bout that."

"We have no argument there," Devlin said.

"Right, then." Godolphin nodded. "So, ye see, there was nothin' the White Monks wouldn't do for our little girl."

Devlin blinked. "White Monks?"

"Aye," Godolphin said with an easy grin. "Reliance thought up the name, God rest her soul. Ye see, long ago there was a monk from the abbey. He'd come down at night and do good deeds for those in need. No one knew his name. Those that caught a glimpse of the man only saw a white monk. 'Twas Reliance who said we should do like the legend and help Miss Christiana, but instead of bein' just one white monk to do a good deed, there were many."

"How many?"

"The entire village," said Godolphin. "And what servants yet lived at the abbey o'course."

The innkeeper paused to take a long sip of his whiskey, savoring the aftertaste with a sigh. "Reliance told Reverend and Mrs. Snow how his lordship was treatin' the child, 'specially after that fine Mr. Evans died. So, we all agreed Miss Christiana would become our ward. We vowed to protect her, feed her, even teach her the things she'd need to know when she became a fine lady one day. Most things we tried to do on our own, but other things—well, we did need some blunt now and again."

"Hence the smuggling?" Devlin asked.

"Not at first," the innkeeper said, shaking his head. "Old Jasper had this special ale named after the monks. We sold it here and there—nothin' grand, mind ye. 'Twas when we started sellin' to the big merchant ships that we turned quite a profit. Men from the village helped at the brewery to meet demand."

"I see," Devlin murmured. "Was that when Lord Bellewyck learned of the profit you were making and threatened to take Miss Christiana away unless you smuggled for him?"

A contemptuous expression came to the innkeeper. "Aye, and for a murderin', ruthless smugglin' gang out o' Calais. They wanted barrels of ale, special made with a false bottom. The top was filled with ale, the bottom was—"

"Contraband?"

Godolphin finished off his drink and poured another. "Gold, spices and some jewels—mostly books and papers wrapped in oil skins. Never got a good look at it myself, but there was more to what that Calais gang smuggled than lace and brandy. Aye, 'twas all we could do to survive back then. Still, any profit went to his lordship, may he burn in hell."

Raising his glass to his lips, the older man paused. "Mind ye, I'm not complainin'. There's not a one of us who would not do it again to keep our young lady safe from the clutches of Lord Bellewyck."

Devlin nodded, at a loss for words when the innkeeper— suddenly overcome with a rush of emotion—fought back tears and blew his nose loudly with a handkerchief.

"I've no doubt you saved her life."

Godolphin's chest swelled with pride. "Ah, but she's worth it. Never had a daughter of my own, but Miss Christiana is like a daughter to us all. She sings like an angel too. Sometimes, when she comes to The Green Dragon, I coax her to sing me a tune. And there is not a more generous soul that walks God's earth than Miss Christiana. I suspect she gets that from Reliance; the woman was a saint."

With a guarded look, Godolphin whispered. "Promised I would ne'er tell of it, but just to prove how generous Miss Christiana is—I've caught her many a time in the village doin' some act of kindness for one of our poor families in need. Why, just the other night she was here wearin'—"

"The habit of a white monk?" Devlin interrupted.

"Ye know about it then, eh?"

Devlin nodded. So, Christiana had decided to perpetuate the legend of the original white monk. He could well imagine her venturing into the village under disguise to do some act of charity for the people she so loved. It also explained what she did with her share of earnings from smuggling now, and why she continued to engage in the activity even after Bellewyck's death.

"How did Miss Christiana learn about your smuggling?"

When the innkeeper tried to pour them both another drink, Devlin realized the need to keep a clear head and covered his glass with his hand. Godolphin leaned across the table and whispered. "Damned if she didn't recognize us."

"How did she recognize you? Did she follow you on a run?"

"No, no, no." Godolphin shook his head for emphasis. "It happened at the birthday ball." Obviously noting Devlin's confusion, the innkeeper grinned. "Do ye mean to say ye've not heard about the birthday ball?"

"I am afraid not."

"Miss Christiana's birthday is Christmas Day," the innkeeper said. "So, every year we had a grand masquerade ball at the abbey—to celebrate. It started when she was a tiny thing. After all, we did not want her thinkin' she was forgotten and alone. We all pretended to be friends of her dead parents, come from far away to keep a promise to wish her well on her special day. Ah, but it was a grand affair."

Devlin stared down at the table's scarred surface, finding it difficult to swallow. This was the rumored masked Yuletide ball? A birthday celebration for the Bellewyck ward?

"We fooled her easy enough in the early days." Godolphin said. "But she recognized Giles Yates five years ago."

"Giles Yates?"

Godolphin jerked his thumb in the direction of the smithy. "Giles Yates."

Spying the behemoth of a blacksmith across the room, Devlin nodded. Yates was the size of a bull. No matter the costume, it would prove difficult, if not impossible, to hide his true identity.

When Godolphin concentrated more on his drink than their conversation, Devlin prodded, "You were saying she recognized the smithy."

"Aye." Shaking his head, Godolphin chuckled. "She demanded to know how we could afford the ball each year and where all the costumes came from that everyone was wearin'. Coaches lined the drive, ye see, each one pulled by fine horses with liveried footmen. There was music and feastin', tables set with silver and crystal. Just as fine as what you would see in the grand homes of the gentry. Well, we felt she deserved it."

"You told her the truth about the smuggling at that time?"

Godolphin nodded. "We had no choice."

"Did the White Monks disband?"

"Well, 'twasn't as simple as that. Lord Bellewyck was involved, ye see."

Devlin nodded. At least everything Godolphin said confirmed what Christiana had told him last night. Seeing the innkeeper looking worried as if he might have revealed too much, Devlin grinned. "Nothing you have said alarms me, Godolphin. The lady told me herself about Blackjack, and I know he contacted you after she was injured on the run. I am merely curious how she convinced Bellewyck to let her take the place of the White Monks in smuggling."

Godolphin hunched over the table and whispered. "First, she made up another set of books; they cleared the servants of any wrongdoin' in the brewery. Told him she was goin' to do it with all the books. Clever, eh?"

"Ingenious," Devlin murmured.

"Then, she faced Bellewyck. Gordon and old Rooney took her to Bath. But his lordship still threatened to see the lot of us hanged as thieves. And if we spoke about the smugglin', the Calais gang was told—by his lordship mind ye—to kill us all. Well, hearin' that, Christiana went to Blackjack. Lord Bellewyck didn't know she was acquainted with him, ye see."

"How did Christiana come to know Blackjack?"

"She saved his life." Godolphin nodded for emphasis. "No more than a child, she found him badly wounded and hidin' in the grotto."

"She brought me to a grotto the other night," Devlin mused aloud. "Is this perchance the same grotto?"

Godolphin arched a curious brow. "Only one grotto I know 'bout. It feeds from the sea into a cave 'neath the abbey. There is a bloody lake under there, too."

So, she deliberately rode in an absurd, serpentine manner to confuse his sense of direction. And all the while, the grotto had been beneath the abbey itself. Devlin smirked at the revelation and reached for the bottle of whiskey. Most likely, one of the secret passageways could have taken him to his bedchamber. Then again, had she told him they were already safely returned to the estate, he never would have permitted her to ride back to join the Ravens.

"Clever little witch."

Neither man spoke for several moments. Oblivious to the churning emotions and whirlwind thoughts racing through Devlin's mind, Godolphin appeared content to simply sit back and savor his drink. Under the circumstances, it might have been better had the man remained silent, but Godolphin was far too relaxed with their amiable conversation to mind his tongue now.

"Did she tell ye about the books then?"

"The false books?" Devlin asked.

"Not those," Godolphin replied with a snort. "The ancient books she found at the abbey when she was a child. I saw one of them once; couldn't read a word of it."

Devlin nodded although he had no idea what the man was talking about.

"She brought 'em to Reverend Snow; he helped translate 'em." All at once, the plump innkeeper started to laugh so hard tears came to his eyes. "God rest his soul, Reverend Snow adored Miss Christiana. They spent many an hour readin' those old books from the holy brothers and comparin' them to scripture. One book was about healin'—had all sorts of receipts for potions and herbs to cure bellyaches, and the like. There is one receipt she has used many a time, 'specially when his lordship came to the abbey. It can make a man sleep like a babe for hours."

Bells began to peal inside Devlin's skull and a nauseous feeling started to rise from the pit of his belly. "She drugged Lord Bellewyck with a sleeping draught?"

"Ye best keep to drinkin' whiskey 'round our Miss Christi. Hey, that rhymes!"

Devlin offered a feeble smile and rubbed his brow. "Does Miss Christiana still use this ancient receipt to drug a person's ale?"

Godolphin laughed, then drained his glass, answer enough for Devlin. Suddenly the strange, hazy confusion this morning took new meaning. He'd been drinking ale in the Great Room the night he arrived at the abbey, waking the next morning with the same bloody haziness. She must have drugged his ale that first day. And it had to be the same batch of tainted ale he drank last night.

"Those monks were a strange lot." Godolphin finished off his whiskey. "Do ye know, they even had a receipt for invisible ink, though what cause the holy brothers had for invisible ink is beyond my thinkin'."

"One does wonder," Devlin murmured, still reeling over the fact the woman he loved actually had the audacity to drug him. More to the point, if he'd been drugged last night, then it was impossible he'd made love to her. In truth, he probably stumbled back to his bed just as the draught took effect.

By God, she staged the entire scenario earlier that morning. She deliberately wanted him to think they'd made love again. At once, her reaction to his anger made sense. She'd been crying, desperately trying to tell him nothing had happened.

"Showed me a secret letter once," Godolphin continued. "The special ink was written between the lines of the real ink. 'Course ye couldn't see it unless ye held up the letter to heat."

Devlin held his breath a moment, somewhat afraid to ask his next question. "I suppose she found plenty of uses for that ink, eh?"

"Aye," Godolphin replied. "She's likely saved our necks time and again with her special letters. Not six months ago, there was this one young lieutenant smitten with her. He confided in her 'bout the maneuverin's of his men, and she would tell Blackjack. The funny thing is this lieutenant carried two coded letters for Blackjack to me here at the inn. Damn fool, eh?"

Devlin narrowed his eyes, his jaw clenching at Godolphin's unwitting revelation. All he could think about was what might have happened had Christiana been caught writing coded letters. Clearly, the village had been under suspicion for involvement in smuggling. For all he knew they were still under suspicion.

"Damn," Godolphin whispered, obviously noting Devlin's sudden change of mood. "Didn't tell ye about the letters, eh?"

"No," Devlin replied, his voice a deadly calm. "But she will."

CHAPTER TWENTY-TWO

"I am perplexed whether to act or not to act."
~ Aeschylus (525-456 B.C.)

By the time Devlin returned to the estate, twilight—that enchanting hour separating light from darkness—had cast Bellewyck Abbey in half-shadow. A strange sense of urgency possessed him. Confronting Christiana in the uncompromising light of day would have been much more effective. Instead, dusk had fallen and within the abbey, shadows would soon lengthen to merge with the night.

He should have been home hours ago, but the truth about the past and the sacrifices of so many people had affected him in unexpected ways. Namely, how quick he'd been to judge these people. How easily he believed them to be treacherous thieves and even murderous villains. For a man considered honorable by his peers, even a philanthropic humanitarian for the poor, he'd been blinded by prejudice and preconceived notions. It was a most unwelcome facet of his character, and one he would move heaven and earth to change.

To that end, he would do whatever necessary to help Christiana and the people of Bellewyck. Christiana's days of denying her birthright and engaging in dangerous activities—however noble her motives—must end. He had to make her understand and accept that despite her best intentions, no one was safe. Ironically, the most imminent danger had nothing to do with Pemberton or the monstrous machinations of a dead and buried Lord Bellewyck. The biggest threat to everyone now was Christiana herself.

After learning the drastic measures she willingly pursued to champion her cause, it was a wonder she'd escaped capture, imprisonment, or even death. In Christiana's mind, the lie seemed safer than the truth, which meant action must be taken posthaste. If necessary, he would pull her—kicking and screaming—out of this web of deception.

The house was quiet. The servants would soon retire for

the evening after finishing their daily duties. Unable to find anyone about, he headed toward the staircase. Much to his surprise, Polly Darrow entered the hall, stopping short at the sight of him.

Well, he'd learned one thing at Bellewyck Abbey. Never let his opponent know what he was thinking.

"Hello Polly," he said with a smile. "Did Miss Christiana tell you to find a room for yourself among the guest chambers?"

"I-I-I don't want one." Her green eyes looked big as saucers.

"Come now," he teased. "Surely you have no fear for your virtue around me?"

Her mouth dropped open, then abruptly slammed shut, prompting him to bite back a grin.

"Would you be so kind as to locate Miss Christiana? I wish to speak with her in the Great Room before she retires for the evening." Remembering his unruly attire, he frowned and rubbed his coarse jaw in a distracted manner. "And ask her to make arrangements for a bath to be prepared in my chamber straightaway."

Bestowing him with yet another appalled expression, the blonde maid stormed toward the kitchen.

Realizing the need to act quickly, he took the stairs two at a time, looking in each guest chamber until he located the room Christiana had selected. Quite expectedly, after their strained encounter this morning, her meager belongings had been placed in the chamber farthest from his own.

A cursory inspection revealed a few articles of clothing, but no strongbox or treasured books in Latin. However, just as he was about to leave, he glimpsed something red peeking out from beneath a pillow on the bed. It was a journal. Thumbing through the pages, he immediately recognized Christiana's distinctive script.

Placing the journal in his coat pocket, he walked past the window and caught sight of Polly sprinting across the drive toward an obviously surprised Christiana. Even in the quickly fading light of the courtyard, he could see Polly waving her arms about like a windmill. The maid's agitated behavior had Christiana shaking her head, as if making some sort of adamant denial. No doubt, Polly denigrated him, sagely warning her friend to return to the servants' quarters with all due haste and lock her door against the lecherous Mr. Randolph.

"You are too late, Polly. Your dear friend is about to have another lesson in what happens when one plays with fire."

Christiana closed her eyes and took a deep breath, hoping it might steady her nerves. Self-consciously, she looked down at her gown, smoothing out the faded green sprigged muslin. Satisfied with her appearance, she knocked on the Great Room doors and heard Devlin's deep voice bid her enter.

Standing before the fireplace, the immaculately attired steward closed his timepiece and tucked it away. "I am pleased you decided to join me. Come, sit down."

Her legs, as if with a mind of their own, seemed unwilling to move. Yet, somehow she managed to approach the massive hearth and took the large chair he indicated, the one he'd fallen asleep in the first night he'd come to the abbey.

No sooner had she settled her skirts about her when he spoke.

"I wanted to tell you I shall be leaving Bellewyck Abbey within the week."

She looked at him, swallowing the bitter bile of terror his words conjured.

"Consequently, you must send word to this Blackjack villain. I wish to meet with him as soon as possible and end your involvement in his smuggling operation."

"Why are you leaving Bellewyck?"

"I have business to attend in London."

She jumped to her feet. "You go to the duke!"

Devlin arched a brow. "I have already promised Pemberton will not learn your identity from me. Now, do sit down and listen."

Christiana eyed him warily and, against her better judgment, sat in the chair. It was then she noticed a small red book in his hand. She actually felt blood drain from her face, her breath stilling inside her lungs for what seemed a hellish eternity.

Struggling to remember when last she saw her diary, she blinked through the haze of confusion. She'd gone down to the Shadow Walk to retrieve the strongbox for Devlin. Before leaving the locked box in his bedchamber, she'd opened it to check the papers inside. Only then did she realize she'd placed her diary in the box after its last entry. Before she could return the diary to the Shadow Walk, a red-faced Billy had dashed into the room saying Jasper had fallen. With no other choice, she'd hidden the book in her new bedchamber. The only way Devlin could have her diary in his possession now was if he'd been snooping about her new bedchamber. How rude!

Just then, he opened the little book and began to flip through the pages. An involuntary cry of distress escaped her lips.

Devlin raised a brow. "Whatever is the matter, Christiana? You look positively ill."

Unable to speak, she watched in helpless horror as he pocketed the diary and stepped over to the cellaret. After pouring himself a drink, he returned to her side. Unable to take her eyes off the item in his pocket, she frantically contemplated how to pinch it without his knowing.

Hearing Devlin clear his throat, she looked up and found him extending a glass of ale.

With a quick glance to the cellaret, she bit back a gasp at the subtly marked bottle of ale.

He moved the glass a fraction closer to her lips. "Drink this," he said.

She shook her head. "Thank you, no. I am not thirsty."

"I did not ask if you were thirsty, Christiana. I want you to drink this because you look unwell. And since there is no brandy or port about, needs must and all that."

Not wanting to raise his suspicions, she gingerly accepted the glass. Then, under his watchful gaze, she took a tentative sip, shuddering slightly at its taste. When she looked at Devlin, it was to find him reading her diary again.

"By the way, I spoke with Mr. Godolphin today."

"Oh?"

"We had a most enlightening conversation."

Raising a hand to her forehead, she tried to think. Although quite curious about what Mr. Godolphin had said that might be considered enlightening, nothing mattered but getting her diary back. Not only did it contain her personal thoughts, a great many of which were about Devlin, but there were entries regarding the Ravens, the identity of its members, and her involvement in various runs.

"He told me about your childhood and how the villagers adopted you, so to speak." He raised his gaze from the pages of the book and smiled. "Incidentally, you must sing for me sometime. I understand you have a lovely voice."

"W-what else did he tell you?"

"Oh, a great many things," he said. "About Reliance and how she organized the White Monks to care for you." Another moment of perusing the pages and he closed the book, returning it to his pocket.

Folding his arms across his chest, he studied her with a thoughtful expression. "By the way, you really should be more careful—especially if you want to remain anonymous about your charitable acts in the village. It seems both Godolphin and I have seen you wandering about in your white monk's habit."

"You talked about that?"

Devlin grinned. "He also told me about the annual ball to celebrate your birthday. I hope one is planned this year. I so love masquerades."

Christiana inhaled so quickly she started to cough.

"Come now, take another sip. God knows you have expounded its benefits to me since first I arrived at the estate." Kneeling before her, he shook his head. "You truly do not look well, sweetheart. And is it any wonder what with all the stress and dangers you have endured protecting everyone."

She felt ill. Devlin had an unmistakable air about him that said he knew everything. As if that wasn't enough to make her hysterical, she'd imbibed the drugged ale and he intended to depart for London within the week. Determined to conquer the nausea sweeping through her body, she swallowed hard.

"What will you do?"

"Pardon?"

"In London, what will you do?"

With a shrug, he stood. "As I said, personal business. I should return within a fortnight."

"Y-you are coming back?"

Devlin smiled. "Of course, I am. Did you think I would abandon you when there is still so much to be settled between us?"

An impulsive cry of relief escaped her lips just as a single tear slid ever so slowly down her cheek. Before she realized what was happening, she began to weep in earnest, whereupon he pressed the glass of ale once more to her lips.

"There, there," he said. "My mother often says a good cry is necessary for a woman. A means to purge the soul of all its worries and concerns, so to speak."

With an absent-minded nod, she took several large sips,

somewhat surprised when he abruptly took the drink away.

"No more," he said, glancing at the half-empty glass before setting it on a nearby table.

Before she realized what was happening, she found herself being escorted toward the doors. The combination of potent ale and medicinal herbs warmed her insides with a curious, relaxing feeling. Within the gathering mist of her mind, she felt the effects of the draught. She tried to fight the inevitable pull of sleep. She must tell him the truth—now—before it was too late. Once Devlin read her diary, his anger would know no bounds.

"Devlin, you must understand I *had* to protect them." Her head felt like an unwanted weight upon her shoulders and she struggled to see her diary. "I-I could not bear for the White Monks to suffer because of me. It isn't as if I took pleasure in smugglin'."

He nodded. "I quite understand."

"The earl would have put them in prison."

"At the very least," he replied.

"Then you understand why Pemberton must never know. It will be difficult to make full rest...tution for the loss of rev...nue, but I have a sub, sub—" Why could she not make her mouth work properly? Determined to speak coherently, she tried again. "I have a substantial amount tucked away."

"Do you now?"

"Yes." She nodded. "I think you'll be im...um...im—"

"Impressed?" he queried.

"Yessss," she said with a heavy nod.

"Oh, my dearest Christiana, I am exceedingly impressed."

She stumbled against him, prompting him to offer support. Stopping at the base of the staircase, he studied her with narrowed eyes. "How do you feel, sweetheart?"

"Strange," she said in a whisper.

She felt herself adrift, helpless under the spell of the sleeping draught.

"Curious," he said as he lifted her into his arms. "That ale had the same effect on me. Then again, I suspect you already knew that."

CHAPTER TWENTY-THREE

"Courtship to marriage is but as the music in the playhouse
'til the curtain's drawn."
~ William Congreve (1670-1729), *The Old Bachelor*

A woman should not do certain things upon waking; screaming is one of them. Nevertheless, Christiana pulled open the bed curtains and screamed.

With a hand placed against her heart, she said, "Good God, you frightened me."

"That makes two of us," Devlin murmured.

"I am not accustomed to having men in my bedchamber, you know."

"I am inordinately pleased to hear it."

Seated in a chair beside the bed, a rather tedious book about crop rotation in his hands, he studied her. Concerned the drugged ale had been too potent for her, he'd been tormented with guilt, and spent most of the night worrying about her welfare and what possible ill effects might result. In the wee hours of the morning, once assured she rested peacefully, his guilt slowly but surely turned to anger.

She'd done this to him. Rather than meet him face-to-face, she'd opted to simply drug him. God knew how many others she thought to practice this witchery upon. Decidedly dangerous, since she could not know how each person might react to the drug.

Resting his hands on the spine of the tome, he crooked a brow. "Feeling rested?"

She nodded, but he saw the wariness in her expression.

"Imagine my surprise when, in the midst of our conversation last night, you fell asleep. So asleep, in fact, that I feared for your health. Of course, I had no choice but to carry you upstairs to your room."

Christiana looked down at her bedclothes, a slight frown marring her brow.

What happened next took her by complete surprise. He

all but leapt into bed beside her. She tried to inch away until he adroitly maneuvered himself very nearly on top of her. "We really must do something about your bedclothes." With practiced skill, one hand began to toy with the collar of her prim nightdress. "This simply will not do."

He began to caress her breasts through the fabric, squeezing the soft fullness within his palms. Circling the responsive nipples in a languid manner with a fingertip, he said, "Bedclothes are a nuisance. Personally, I prefer you wear nothing at all."

Her breathing hitched, then turned shallow. As his hand moved slowly down the front of her gown, ever closer to her now clenched thighs, he kept his gaze upon her, watching every nuance of arousal and desire in her expression. Then, through the barrier of her nightdress, he suddenly and quite possessively cupped her woman's mound, prompting her to inhale sharply.

The fabric of her nightgown, combined with the agile movement of his fingers, created an erotic friction. In no time at all, she trembled and quaked with uncontrollable desire. Yet, just as she was about to peak, he removed his hand.

Panting and confused, she swallowed hard and looked to him. Gently brushing a strand of unbound hair away from her face, he whispered against her slightly parted lips. "Do you want to know why I stopped?"

"Yes," she sighed.

"Sex can be wonderful and very addictive, but it must never be forced. It is not just a matter of consent. Both lovers must want to make love. Yesterday, it appalled me to learn I had not only forced myself upon you in such an uncontrollable manner, but could not even remember doing so. Then there is your reputation to consider."

"Devlin."

He silenced her with a brief kiss. Pulling back, he grinned. "But since you have no desire to claim your identity as the Bellewyck ward, I see no reason to deny ourselves enjoyment of one another. You obviously do not mind making yourself available to me whenever I want, so perhaps now would be a good time to discuss the arrangements."

"Arrangements?"

He began to trail a fingertip down the front of her nightdress again. "A man has needs and I am without a mistress at present."

"You want me to be your mistress?" She eyed him suspiciously. "Have you been drinking?"

With all the melodrama of an overzealous actor, he pressed one of her hands against his chest. "I am drunk with desire, my pet. You are the air that I breathe, the ground beneath my feet. And when two people enjoy such a wild, impulsive passion for one another, it would be nothing less than a sin to deny it."

"You *have* been drinking."

"Is this not what you want from me, Christiana? To be so enticed by your charms that I have no will of my own? To be so undone I would drink myself into oblivion, then slake my lust with you—whether you are awake or asleep—willing or not?"

He saw the exact moment when she realized his act. Her eyes narrowed and she tried to push him off the bed. "I think it despicable you make sport of me in such a cruel manner."

Devlin came to his feet, all pretense of seduction gone. With his hands resting low on his hips, he tried to control his temper. "You dare speak of despicable? You drugged me, Christiana."

She paled. "What are you talking about?"

"Is it your intention to claim ignorance? Very well then, let me remind you. The ale you drank last night was the same ale served me the day I arrived at the abbey. I understand now why you were so surprised I woke before dawn after being heavily drugged."

She averted her gaze, paying particular attention to smoothing the bed covers about her body. "I am quite sure I do not know what you mean."

"And I am quite sure you do. You lied to me yesterday morning. Or, do you not recall the devious trick you played? We both know nothing happened in that bed, yet you wanted me to believe otherwise."

"I am not to blame for what you believe. I merely said good morning."

"You did more than say good morning, my sweet. I can say, with absolute certainty, that I have never had the need or inclination to tear a woman's clothing from her body—not even when deep in my cups. That was your doing, Christiana. You wore my shirt in an effort to infer, in no uncertain terms, that I had stripped you bare and bedded you. And let us not forget you attempted to undress me as well, though why you

216

did not complete the task remains a mystery."

Noting her significant blush and averted gaze, he shook his head. "I hope you have a reasonable explanation for this eccentric, if not scandalous, behavior. Just what in God's name did you think to gain by employing such a manipulative trick? Do you have any concept of the insult you paid me as a gentleman?"

"And what of the insult you paid me?"

"When did I insult you?"

"You said I looked like a child!"

Devlin blinked. "*That* is the reason for your calculated maneuverings? I said you looked like a child?"

"I gather that does not seem a cruel insult to you, but it is to me."

He stared at her as if she had two heads.

"I did not mean to upset you. I only wanted to prove a point. How was I to know you would become half-crazed at the thought of bedding me again? And just what is this mysterious vow you made? Are you so concerned with Pemberton's good opinion that you now think to act the man's puppet?"

He pinned her with a hard stare, biting back what he'd like to say.

"I am sorry, Devlin," she said softly. "'Twas a deceitful, manipulative and childish trick. You have every right to be angry."

With a derisive snort, he went to the window.

Christiana buried her face in her hands. Could this possibly get any worse? Through a break in her fingers, she peeked at the man she loved. He stared out the window—arms folded across his chest—a familiar pose when upset.

She got out of bed and, with an efficiency honed from years of managing a household, proceeded to make her bed. Once finished, she turned to find him still at the window.

"I did try to tell you nothing happened yesterday morning, but you refused to listen. And I only drugged you that first night because I had to meet with Blackjack. I promise it will not happen again."

He slowly turned. "Oh, I quite agree."

The deadly quiet of his voice and the piercing glint of his gray eyes gave her a moment's unease. Still, against her better judgment, she said, "Just please do not treat me like a child now. In truth, I am no man's child. I have been taking care of myself for a long time. I do not need you or the noble Duke of Pemberton telling me what to do. I belong to myself, Devlin. And I alone will make decisions concerning my life and my future."

"Indeed." With a sardonic smile, he crooked a brow. "Then perhaps we should now address how skillfully you have steered your life into some rather dangerous waters, not the least of which is treason. Or, has it escaped your memory that you could be found guilty of conspiring with the enemy through acts of smuggling? You do recall we are at war?"

"Why are you being so cruel? You know I had no choice."

"The truth can be quite cruel, Christiana. Do you honestly believe that if captured there would be any leniency given you because you smuggled to protect your friends? Godolphin said the village came under suspicion by authorities not six months ago. Had your cleverly written coded letters been identified by that smitten lieutenant, no power on earth could have saved you from hanging."

Icy chills raced down her spine. Feeling as if she might swoon, she sat on the edge of the bed. He knew everything, all the dark secrets she'd tried to hide for so long—even from her friends. It mattered not that she wrote those coded letters to protect Blackjack from being captured. The authorities had indeed come to Bellewyck searching for him and other members of the Ravens, proving just how close the hangman's noose had been to her and those she loved.

Asking Devlin to remain silent about her identity was one thing, but for him to remain silent about possible treason would make him an accomplice. And now he had her diary, evidence that could be used against her and others.

"Do you intend to contact the authorities?" she asked in a near whisper.

He stalked to the bed, his eyes narrowed and his lips compressed into a hard, unrelenting line. Grabbing her by the shoulders, he pulled her to her feet and glared down at her. "You question whether or not I will see you hang?"

"Then tell me what you intend to do!"

"I intend to protect you," he said through clenched teeth. "I intend to see you freed from the blasted Ravens, and from any association with smuggling."

"And then what? What about Pemberton?"

He released her and combed his fingers through his hair, making several locks stand on end in a somewhat wild display. "For God's sake! I have repeatedly told you the Duke of Pemberton will not learn who you are from me."

"But you are so loyal to the duke. Why will you not tell him?"

"Does it matter? Is it not enough I care about you?"

"Enough to stay at Bellewyck Abbey?"

He laughed, yet it was caustic, more a sound of acute frustration than amusement. "Hear me well, Miss Petrovsky. Until you are willing to come forward and admit the truth about yourself, we have no future. I will *not* take you as my mistress, and I most certainly will *not* wed a woman who thinks it acceptable to live a lie."

"Is that an ultimatum?"

"Yes. Do you not see? You have surrounded yourself with deception and intrigue to such an extent it has become second-nature to you. Are you not brave enough to be the person you were born to be?"

"You think me a coward?"

"Far from it. I consider you the bravest woman I know. But your destiny is not to be a housekeeper. Why do you suppose Reliance struggled to protect you? Why do you think Mrs. Snow educated you so extensively? Servants and villagers risked their lives and sacrificed so much to see you received opportunities they felt you deserved. I daresay it was not so you could reward their efforts by becoming a servant or end your days swinging from a rope."

"I only wanted to keep them safe." Her voice trembled with emotion.

Devlin gentled his voice. "I know *why* you did it, sweetheart. What I want to know is why you *continue* to do it. Lord Bellewyck is dead. The threat to the servants no longer exists. Why then are you still smuggling? It cannot simply be a desire to do charitable deeds as the legendary white monk, not when you admitted to me in the grotto you hated smuggling. You must tell me the truth now, Christiana. Why are you still smuggling?"

"Because they won't let me go! I have tried. The night you arrived, I told Blackjack I wanted to quit the Ravens. He said it was not possible."

"What Blackjack says does not signify," he said with a derisive snort. "Rest assured, the first thing I intend to do is get you away from that bloody gang."

Something powerful about the way he spoke and the

steely determination in his striking blue-gray eyes compelled her to believe Blackjack would have no choice but to do exactly as Devlin demanded. At the same time, she couldn't help but wonder what other plans this man had for her.

"Suppose you do win my release from the Ravens, what next do you have planned for me?"

A slow grin came to his lips. "You have plans of your own, is that it?"

"I daresay my plans depend on what you do about certain things you have learned, namely what the White Monks did for me and how."

Devlin shrugged. "I have no intention of bringing the false set of books to light. What is done is done. Under the circumstances, the fact the servants stole from the brewery to care for you was rather commendable."

She realized her mouth was open, yet could do nothing but stare. He truly was her knight in shining armor.

"So, my dear Christiana," he said with a mischievous look, "if you are free of smuggling and no longer hiding as a servant, what do you want from life?"

"I-I only want the people I love to be safe and happy, to be cared for always."

He smiled, his gaze filled with understanding and compassion. "You need not worry on their behalf, my darling. Pemberton will be benevolent toward your friends, especially after learning all they have done to protect you from an unscrupulous guardian."

"You really think the Duke of Pemberton will be good to them?"

"No doubt whatsoever," he said with a rakish wink. His gaze quickly sobered and the desire in his eyes caused her heart to skip a beat. "Please tell me, Christiana. What do *you* want for yourself?"

Her throat constricted. "You," she whispered. "All I want is you, Devlin."

"There is much you do not know about me." His voice became husky as his eyes drifted and settled upon her lips.

"I only know I want you. I will always want you."

With a growl, he pulled her into his arms and captured her lips with uncontrollable passion. She moaned, melting into his embrace, twining her fingers through his hair. He no longer needed to coax and tutor her in the varying degrees of kissing or the intensely erotic copulation of their tongues.

Neither was she reticent about returning his kiss with equal ardor. The result turned explosive, making it difficult to stand, to think, or even breathe.

Then, with an almost wild roar of frustration, he pulled back, his voice gruff with passion. "Do not think for a moment I do not want you. But there are things I must do to ensure we have a future together. When all is settled, you will understand. Have no doubt, when that time comes, I will take you to my bed and never let you leave. Until then—make no mistake—you are mine."

CHAPTER TWENTY-FOUR

"Only the actions of the just smell sweet and
blossom in the dust."
~ James Shirley (1596-1666),
The Contention of Ajax and Ulysses

Devlin studied Christiana in the shadows of the warren. She wore her smugglers disguise, basically that damnable chimneysweep clothing with a ridiculous bag-wig, sweeping black greatcoat, and an oversized cocked hat. Seeing her tremble from the cold night wind, he drew up the collar of her coat and adjusted the hat.

"Explain again why it was necessary you accompany me tonight."

"Have you forgotten what almost happened the last time you went looking for Blackjack?"

He turned his attention back to The Eight Bells tavern. "What now?" he asked.

"We wait for the all-clear signal."

"The all-clear signal?"

"A green bottle in the eaves," Christiana said in a near whisper.

"Cloak and dagger nonsense," he grumbled under his breath. Still, he looked carefully for any sign of a bottle. "I see nothing. I best take a closer look."

"No," she said, placing a hand on his arm. "I can see; 'tis not safe."

Devlin glanced up and down the moonlit cobbled street. "No one is about. Nary a horse or carriage anywhere in sight. Might I add, if we stand out here much longer you shall be deathly ill come morning."

"When someone sets a trap, my darling, they usually like to be secretive about it."

Devlin crooked a brow. "My darling?"

She grinned impishly. "Are you not my darling?"

Gathering her diminutive figure closer to the warmth of

his body, he lowered his head to kiss her. She stopped his amorous intent with her gloved fingertips. "Just keep your eyes on The Eight Bells. 'Tis close to midnight."

"Ah, but of course, the witching hour. And what, pray tell, happens at midnight?"

Christiana stood on her toes and whispered, "Perhaps I shall take my true form and fly away."

"Your days of being a raven are over, my sweet."

She laughed ever so softly. "I'll have you know, given a choice, I should rather be a hawk—swift, silent, and deadly. No one would ever capture me and those that tried would wear my mark upon them forever."

"I must say, this blood-thirsty quality you have is rather unseemly." He looked back toward The Eight Bells, refusing to let her see how much he enjoyed their playful repartee. Feigning a stern expression, he muttered, "I am not amused."

"Yes, you are." Slipping her arms inside his greatcoat, she hugged his waist and nestled herself against his chest with a contented sigh. "Admit it, Devlin. This is exciting."

Despite the fact he was supposed to be meeting the villainous Blackjack and needed to keep his wits about him, he tilted her chin up and kissed her mouth, knocking her hat off in the process. He didn't release his gentle hold upon her chin, but studied her with somber regard.

Then, with a faint smile, he said, "Rest assured, my lovely, I intend to rid you of this fascination with danger and intrigue if it kills me."

"Do not say that," she whispered heatedly. "I could not bear it if anything were to happen to you."

"Nothing is going to happen to me." Rubbing her back, he held her more tightly against his chest. "Now remember, when we see Blackjack, you are to remain silent—as difficult as I know that will be for you. Mind your tongue and let me handle everything. I want no interference whatsoever."

She studied his face. "You are not the least bit afraid, are you?"

Devlin crooked a brow. "Little you know of me, if you think I fear this man or any of his companions. I fear neither death nor men. You, on the other hand, terrify me."

"Me? Why do I terrify you?"

Before he could answer, movement across the street caught their attention. Four men emerged from The Eight Bells—officers of the naval guard by their uniform. They spoke in hushed voices before walking off in the direction of the church.

"You see, it was not safe. What a nuisance they are."

Devlin followed the retreating men with his eyes. "Do not condemn them, sweetheart. They serve only to protect England and its people."

"How can you take their side? Just because they wear the king's uniform does not make them honorable—or better than anyone else for that matter."

"It is not a question of sides. Smuggling is illegal. No one is above the law, especially in times such as these. Justice is the very foundation of civilization. If everyone did as they see fit without heeding the laws set forth for a structured society, the world would be in utter chaos."

Christiana retrieved her hat from the ground and placed it back on her head. "Sometimes I wonder about you, Devlin Randolph."

He looked sharply at her. "What do you mean?"

"Only that to hear you speak, you should be a member of Parliament or something. In truth, I think it a waste for a man of your intelligence to be a steward. Granted, there is much I do not know about your past, but you are obviously educated and a gentleman of good family. You are well-spoken, a man of honor and principle. I cannot help but wonder how such a man comes to be employed by the noble Duke of Pemberton as a steward."

"Fate perhaps," he said with a shrug.

"Do you believe in fate?"

He looked at her then, her jewel-like eyes mesmerizing even in the yawning shadows of the warren. "I do now."

The moment of quiet intimacy was broken by the sound of horses. From their hiding place they watched a patrol of naval guards ride swiftly by as if in pursuit. Pushing Christiana further into the darkness, Devlin waited until the guardsmen were out of sight, the echo from pounding hooves fading into the night.

"What do you suppose that was all about?" he asked.

"Most likely, a rumor about a smuggling run tonight. The four men leaving The Eight Bells must have reported nothing suspicious at the tavern. And it explains why we saw no all-clear signal in the eaves."

"Do not gloat, my sweet," he said with a slight smile. "So, does this mean our meeting must be postponed?"

"It means ye passed the test," said an unfamiliar voice.

Devlin reached inside his greatcoat, attempting to withdraw the pistol he'd brought with him. Christiana stayed his hand.

What emerged from the darkness hardly resembled a man at all, but more a billowing cloud of blackness that Devlin soon realized was the man's sweeping greatcoat. A giant at least seven feet in height, the approximate width of an oak tree, stood behind Christiana.

Where the devil had he come from? For that matter, how long had he been standing in the shadows watching them?

"Come," the giant said, turning to walk deeper into the warren.

Devlin's jaw dropped open as he watched his petite Christiana meekly follow the bear-like man. She must have realized he wasn't directly behind her for she turned and smiled, her arm extended toward him.

"Come," she said.

Through the dark, winding warren they made their way to the beach and a row of weathered rope houses. Quite a common feature in fishing villages, the houses had been crafted from the hulls of discarded fishing boats. Sterns had been embedded deep into the sand, leaving the mid-section and bow standing upright. However, unlike other rope houses, the one they entered contained a secret entrance to an earthen tunnel.

For a man of such extraordinary height, the stranger moved through the tunnel with graceful ease. No outer light penetrated within and despite the timber-reinforced walls, Devlin had the uneasy sensation of being buried alive. Determined to not reveal his increasing discomfort, he followed in silence.

A door creaked open, releasing granules of sand, pebbles, and dust about their heads. The golden light of a lamp beckoned. The last to enter through the door, Devlin paused at the threshold. Hardly the den of a successful thief, their destination was a one-room cottage complete with a bed large enough to support the weight of the giant. A hearth for cooking, a cupboard, and a table with four chairs provided the only other furnishings. It resembled a place to keep one prisoner.

"Where is Blackjack?" he asked.

The giant added peat to the fire, then eyed Devlin with no

small amount of amusement. "Who the bloody hell do ye think I am?"

Devlin scrutinized the bearded stranger, noting the man's wild black and silver hair, heavily lined brow, and piercing cobalt blue eyes.

"*You* are Blackjack?"

"Aye," the giant grumbled with a menacing scowl.

Despite the fact the giant appeared robust, Blackjack was old enough to be Christiana's grandfather.

Raising a brow to Christiana, Devlin smirked. "You might have told me."

"I rather enjoyed your jealousy," she said with a twinkle in her eyes.

Blackjack glared at them. "What are ye two jabberin' 'bout?"

Christiana took off her greatcoat and hat, placing them upon the bed. "Mr. Randolph believed you quite smitten with me, Blackjack. I daresay he even suspected you had lecherous motives for keeping me in the Ravens."

"Did he now?" the giant said with a booming guffaw.

Not appreciating being the brunt of anyone's amusement, Devlin smiled sardonically. "Laugh all you want, but henceforth Christiana is no longer a member of the Ravens. There is no room or need in her life for smuggling—or you."

"Is that a fact?" Blackjack folded his trunk-like arms across his massive chest.

Devlin matched the older man's stance. "It is."

The smuggler studied Devlin in silence for a moment, then shrugged. Removing his cloak, he tossed it across the room to land with precision on the bed. Grabbing a bottle of fine French brandy and three glasses from a cupboard, he poured everyone a drink and pointed to the chairs.

"Sit," he commanded.

It became quite apparent the leader of the Ravens had no interest in opening the conversation. The man was much too preoccupied maintaining his bizarre game of intimidation. Leaning back in his chair, arms folded, he glared as if the heat from his eyes could burn a hole through a man's soul.

"Perhaps we should get started," Devlin said. "It is late and Christiana is tired."

Without looking away, Blackjack raised his glass and drained the contents in one swallow. Setting the glass down, he said, "Now then, what is this about her quittin' the

Ravens?"

"It's quite simple really," Devlin said. "Apart from the fact that if she gets caught Christiana could likely hang, she is my responsibility now."

"Ye take much upon yourself, steward," Blackjack said with a derisive snort. "Do ye not think the Duke of Pemberton might have cause to disagree?"

"The fact Christiana is the Duke of Pemberton's ward should make *you* uneasy. Trust me—you do not want Pemberton as an enemy."

Blackjack grinned and poured himself another brandy. "She's not been Pemberton's ward long enough for me to worry 'bout the man. Then there's the fact she'll be reachin' her majority soon enough."

Devlin leaned forward on his elbows and stared hard at the smuggler. "What she is now is all that matters in this conversation."

Blackjack snorted. "If ye think she can just stop smugglin' and walk away, ye're mistaken."

"I do not think she will stop smuggling," Devlin said with a deceptively calm voice. "I know it."

"Let me tell ye a bit about smugglin'." Leaning forward, the giant rested his forearms on the table and clasped his hands together. "A smuggler's life depends on secrecy. There's no leavin' a gang short of death. Now, I understand your concern for Christi, but she knows too much. Has seen too much. There's not a man in the Ravens who would let the lad they know as Christian walk away."

"My mistake," Devlin murmured, raising the glass of brandy to his lips. "I was under the impression you had control of your gang."

All good humor left Blackjack's face. "I advise ye not to challenge me, steward. I do what I can to protect Christi. She knew the rules when she joined. Too many lives have been lost because of loose tongues."

Devlin stood, determined to rein in his temper as he told this behemoth of a blackguard exactly what he thought of his dictatorial actions. "You do what you can to protect her? She *fell* from a cliff on your last run! For five years she has done your bidding, but no more. I might add 'tis only a matter of time before your gang discovers she is not a boy. How will you look to your men then? They will think you mad not to have noticed the truth or they will realize you have deliberately deceived them for years. If honor amongst thieves means anything, it is in your best interest as leader of the Ravens to let her leave now. Your men will never trust you again if they find out the truth."

Blackjack downed the contents of his second glass of brandy as if drinking water. He looked at Christiana with narrowed eyes. "Do ye trust this man, Christi?"

"With my life," she answered. "You know how much I have wanted to leave the Ravens, Blackjack. And he is right— 'tis only a matter of time before the others find out I am not a boy."

Blackjack jerked his head toward Devlin. "And what happens if he betrays ye? I'll not be there to protect ye then."

"She does not need your damn protection," Devlin bit out.

Blackjack growled as he slowly stood and stared down from his lofty height.

Devlin returned the stare. A moment more, then the smuggler looked away and crossed to the fireplace. Resting one of his beefy hands on the smooth, gray stones, he stared into the hearth. "Step outside, Christi. Mr. Randolph and I need to speak alone."

"I prefer to stay."

Blackjack spun around and in two strides yanked Christiana up out of the chair by the collar of her jacket. "I said get yer arse out of here."

His jaw clenching, Devlin imposed himself between Christiana and the giant. "Never, *ever* touch her again."

An amused look came over Blackjack until he noticed the pistol aimed at his belly. "Damn, I must be gettin' old. I should have noticed ye didn't remove yer greatcoat."

Devlin felt Christiana's hand touch his arm. Tears glistened in her eyes. For the first time, he saw how concerned she was for Blackjack's life.

He lowered the pistol. "Despite the fact that killing you would make things much simpler, Christiana considers you her friend. However, you best understand something, Blackjack. You have no authority over her whatsoever."

"I know of only one man who can claim authority over her now," Blackjack said with a distinctly cocky expression.

Devlin narrowed his eyes. He'd detected an unmistakable challenge in Blackjack's remarks since they started talking. It could no longer be ignored. Turning to Christiana, Devlin pulled her aside and had her sit on the bed. "Wait here, sweetheart," he said gently. "Try and get some rest. Blackjack and I will step outside to talk."

Her expression told him she didn't like the idea of them talking outside her presence, but she nodded.

Outside, the two men walked down a narrow path leading to a moonlit beach. The strong stench of fish and salt water permeated the air. Overturned fishing boats lined the shore, some tied off and some pulled far enough in where the returning tide couldn't dislodge them from the grip of the sand.

"How long have you known?" Devlin asked.

With a grin, Blackjack sat upon an overturned boat, his hands clasped together between his knees. "Not long after ye came to Bellewyck. I've friends in London. No one knew 'bout a man named Randolph hired by the Duke of Pemberton. They did tell me Pemberton's not been seen 'round town or at his family seat. Even more strange he went missin' when his steward came to Bellewyck Abbey. I'm a smuggler, not an idiot. I can put two and two together."

"And yet you've not told her."

Blackjack chuckled low. "I found myself more curious to wait and see what happened without interferin'."

Devlin sat on the sand, one arm draped over a raised knee. The sea lapped against the shore with gentle rhythm, and the wind combed through his hair like a lover's caress. Yet, the almost hypnotic peace and serenity could be deceptive. The wind could gust and howl, and the sea could rise up against a man and pull him to his death.

He steadied his gaze on the smuggler. "My knowing about your gang and its activities does not concern you?"

With a careless shrug, Blackjack said. "Like I said, I prefer to take a wait and see view on things—if ye get my meanin'."

Devlin nodded. "Cause any problems with her leaving the Ravens, and you and your gang will be—at the very least—in irons."

A dark look came to the smuggler's face. "Let me make somethin' clear, Pemberton. That girl is like my own flesh and blood. The only reason I let her join the Ravens five years ago was because I saw no better way to protect her from Bellewyck. And I sure as hell didn't want her joinin' up with the gang his lordship was dealin' with back then. If that meant recruitin' her as one of my men, so be it."

Devlin stood. "Even if your motives were a sincere desire

to keep her safe from Bellewyck, you endangered her life just as much—perhaps worse."

"Bah! She only went on special runs, and I kept her close by my side the entire time." Blackjack stood, hands bolstered upon his hips. "And if ye think I'll let her walk away with ye now just because ye're a duke, ye're wrong."

"You have no choice."

"P'rhaps not," Blackjack replied. "But ye will tell me now what yer intentions are since I'm fair certain from what I saw and heard in the warren that ye've taken her to yer bed."

Devlin raised a brow. Ordinarily, he wouldn't comment upon such an intrusive observation, but the smuggler had been watching them for God knows how long before he made his presence known.

"If you must know, I intend to marry her as soon as possible."

A broad grin spread across the giant's face, transforming his gruff features. "Ah, well, that's grand then." A moment later, however, his face had turned grim. "But when are ye plannin' to tell her who ye are? Ye've a bad time of it comin'. Ye must know what she thinks 'bout Pemberton."

"She does not know Pemberton," Devlin stressed. Frustration got the better of him; he walked down to the shoreline and shook his head. Blackjack was right; the longer he put off telling Christiana the truth about himself, the harder it would be.

He looked at the smuggler. "There are things I must do first. When the time is right, I will tell her."

Blackjack crooked a brow and scratched his full beard. "I suppose ye want me to keep silent about it then. And since I will be needin' silence from ye as well, seems we need a compromise."

"Very well,"—Devlin folded his arms across his chest—"the information I have about the Ravens will never be revealed, provided Christiana is released from the gang forthwith and you do not reveal my identity to her."

"And if I refuse?"

"Make no mistake Blackjack, the Duke of Pemberton is a very powerful man. I suggest you not tempt fate."

Pursing his lips together thoughtfully, Blackjack begrudgingly nodded. "Just remember, if ye dare hurt the treasure I am puttin' into yer keepin', I will see ye dead, *Yer Grace.*"

The moment they re-entered the cottage, Christiana came to her feet, circling about them like an eager puppy. "Well?"

"The man drives a hard bargain," Blackjack grumbled.

Christiana rushed into Devlin's arms, hugging him tightly. "Oh, Devlin, I cannot believe it's truly over."

"Not quite," Blackjack said as he poured himself yet another brandy. "How ye leave is at my biddin'."

"What the bloody hell does that mean?" Devlin snapped. "I never agreed to that."

Holding his glass up, Blackjack studied the brandy's clarity against the firelight. "It means there is only one way she can leave the Ravens with no questions asked." Looking at Devlin, he added, "Christian must die."

"Are you out of your mind?" Devlin bit out with deadly calm.

"Unless Christian dies, the Ravens will suspect he turned traitor and will hunt him down." Turning to Christiana, he added, "It must be believable, Christi—without question and witnessed by others."

"On a run perhaps?" Christiana suggested with an eagerness that made Devlin's blood run cold.

"Absolutely not!" Devlin bellowed.

"Rein in your temper, steward. I am not 'bout to let Christi get hurt now. We can stage the accident in such a way that I will be the first to reach her body. I will tell the others what happened and order them to abandon the run."

"And they will simply flee and leave you alone with her dead body?"

"Aye," Blackjack said. "The men suspect Christian is my son. My grief will be such they will not question the boy's death. And they will not want to get caught either."

Devlin started pacing. "I do not like it, but just for curiosity's sake, how do you propose Christian die?"

"I could fall from the cliff again," Christiana suggested cheerfully.

Devlin stopped short and bestowed his most disapproving scowl on her.

She offered a sheepish smile. "'Twas just a thought."

"It should be a hero's death," Blackjack mused aloud, a devilish glint in his eyes. "Christian should die protectin' the Ravens from capture."

"Oh, I would like Christian to die a hero," she said with quiet awe.

Devlin rubbed his brow, his head feeling as if it were about to explode. "This is madness—absolute madness."

"But Blackjack is right," Christiana said. "If I am to truly walk away from this life forever, it must be this way."

"It is too risky," Devlin argued.

"Not with both of us to protect her," Blackjack said. "And it'll not be a real smugglin' run."

Devlin lowered his hand and studied Blackjack. "Not a real smuggling run?"

"'Course not, but just the three of us will know that," Blackjack said.

With a heavy sigh, Devlin studied both Blackjack and Christiana. They were clearly determined upon this course of action, enough so they might proceed without his presence. What worried him most, however, was how logical a solution it seemed to their problem. *Still, with me involved every step of the way...*

"Very well, but I want it done quickly."

CHAPTER TWENTY-FIVE

"Whom men fear they hate,
And whom they hate, they wish dead."
~ Quintus Ennius (239-169 B.C.), *Thyestes*

"Do not ask me to do this, Devlin."

Despite Christiana's plea, Devlin continued to smile. He looked sinfully handsome in a superfine bottle-green jacket, ivory and gold embroidered waistcoat and buff-colored pantaloons. Boots polished to a glossy patina. Cravat fashioned into an impeccable knot. Granted, he appeared a respectable gentleman, but they'd gone marketing for the abbey, not shopping for expensive dresses.

"I am not about to go in there with you," she said.

"No?" Then, with a negligent shrug, he said, "Very well, if you will not accompany me, I shall be forced to guess about your preferences. Either way, I am of a mind to purchase a gown or two for you."

"Shops like this require appointments, Devlin."

Pursing his lips, he narrowed his eyes and peered into the shop's window. "I see no customers about. Besides which, ladies rarely venture out so early in the morning; they are home having a cup of chocolate and penning letters."

"How would you know?"

"I have two sisters and a mother. Believe me, I know."

Hearing muffled laughter, Christiana looked to her right. Nash leaned against the Duke of Pemberton's fine coach, clearly enjoying by their performance. Beneath her curious stare, the abbey's stable master sobered and turned his attention to the horses.

Stepping closer to Devlin, she spoke in a near whisper. "You are being ridiculous. A gown from this shop would cost a small fortune. And it is not proper."

A smile curved his lips. "Since I shall be your husband in the not too distant future, you best become accustomed to the fact I intend to spoil you excessively."

A twinge of excitement rippled through her belly at his words and the seductive promise in his eyes. The thought still seemed clouded in mist, like a dream she feared to embrace.

She looked down at the black cloak she'd worn to ward off the early morning chill in Folkestone, then raised her gaze once more to the dressmaker's shop. Judging from the two gowns on display in the window, the shop catered to a most wealthy clientele. For heaven's sake, the sign itself looked almost like a painting. Mrs. Harris, the name of the modiste, had been written with an impressive, sweeping elegance.

"Can we not look for another shop? I very much doubt Mrs. Harris would welcome me as a client."

"Come now, sweetheart," he coaxed in that sensuous, velvet voice that made it impossible for her to think clearly. "We agreed to enjoy Folkestone and see the sights. Consider this one of the sights. I might add, when I told Blackjack we were coming to market today, he felt it a grand idea to keep you from fretting about when *Christian* would meet his supposed doom. In truth, he told me about this modiste and that she arrives early to begin the day and greet new customers without appointments."

"How would he know about this modiste?"

Devlin laughed. "Granted I know not the intricacies of smuggling, but I suspect the lace, silks, and velvets Mrs. Harris uses in great abundance might explain the man's familiarity with her shop."

Unable to quell her amusement by his wit and insight, Christiana smiled.

Devlin extended his hand. "Come, take your first step into the future."

They entered the shop amidst a tinkling of bells. Christiana stood amazed in the most beautiful room she'd ever entered. The grandeur of the shop was more than she'd expected. A crystal chandelier and Chinese silk wall coverings made her feel as if she'd stepped into a garden. She smiled at the polished tables of inlaid, exotic woods, and a matching pair of peach-colored striped silk sofas. Even the thick, lush carpet beneath her feet made it seem as if she stood upon a cloud. If this was the type dress shop wealthy women frequented, what must their homes look like?

She felt a moment's panic, fearful the modiste would look down at just anyone walking in off the street, especially so early in the day. Yet, Mrs. Harris—an attractive woman of a comparable age to Devlin—could not have been more cordial or accommodating. However, it became rather obvious Mrs. Harris wanted Devlin's favor far more than that of her prospective client.

Watching Mrs. Harris flirt with Devlin progressed from awkward to exceedingly uncomfortable. As the woman's behavior continued, Devlin took evasive action. He spoke like some lovesick poet about the colors and fabrics he wanted used for his future bride—"The beautiful, beloved daughter of the late Count Alexander Petrovsky."

Christiana wanted to laugh aloud when Mrs. Harris deigned to study her, making particular note of her new client's simple pink muslin frock and tasteful, but nonetheless well-worn, black cloak.

From that point on, the exchange between Devlin and Mrs. Harris began to sound like a scene from a poorly written farce. And the longer the players remained on stage, the more embarrassed she felt for them.

Unable to observe the bizarre tableau a moment longer, she walked over to the shop's window, preferring to watch the comings and goings of people on the fashionable street. Although early, fine carriages with liveried servants traversed the lane. Among those that rolled to a stop, however, only courtly older gentlemen and dashing young rogues emerged.

Perhaps ladies really did drink chocolate and pen letters at this time of morning.

Glancing to her right, she noticed a magazine called La Belle Assemblee. Three ladies pictured on the cover engravings were arrayed from head to foot in what must have been the most expensive and exclusive fashion. Elegant plumes accentuated magnificent bonnets—fastened with jewels no less. The gowns were breathtaking, exquisitely feminine in design and composition, and complimented by fur-trimmed mantles. Even the velvet slippers had beautiful but impractical silk embroidery.

Balancing a Wedgwood saucer in her hand, Christiana sipped a cup of tea and stood before the window, listening absently to the ongoing discussion between Devlin and Mrs. Harris.

"I prefer this design," Devlin said.

"It is stunning," Mrs. Harris remarked. "But I fear not quite right for Miss Petrovsky. One must possess a certain understanding of the world to wear this particular gown. The lady must have confidence in not only her breeding, but her bearing. A woman wears the gown—the gown does not wear the woman."

"Indeed," Devlin murmured.

"I am never wrong about fashion," Mrs. Harris said with an undeniable air of superiority. "This design is intended for a woman who is more experienced about life and has a greater appreciation as to what such an alluring fashion might provoke in a man."

"I see. In other words, you believe this gown might prove too tempting for men should they see Miss Petrovsky wearing it."

"You misunderstood my meaning, sir." Mrs. Harris cleared her throat softly, then lowered her voice to a tone almost dripping with seduction. "I do not wish to insult the young lady, but your little Miss Petrovsky, however sweet and rustic her charms, is no doubt uninformed about desire, temptation, and its often unavoidable consequences."

"You are mistaken, madam," Devlin said. "Miss Petrovsky is neither sweet nor rustic, and I consider her sufficiently equipped and well-informed about both temptation and its consequences."

"Miss Petrovsky?" the modiste gasped with obvious disbelief.

"The Russians are quite a passionate people, you know," Devlin said. "As such, I am quite determined Miss Petrovsky acquire this gown as soon as possible. Have it done up in silk, gold, I think."

"As you wish," Mrs. Harris sighed. "I must say, you are a generous gentleman and one who is passionate about what he wants. To that end, I look forward to servicing those wants— whatever they might be."

With a pained expression, Devlin nodded. "Your dedication is noted, madam. Now then, what have you in the shop that Miss Petrovsky might take with her today?"

Christiana bit back another laugh. In truth, she might have been insecure and jealous had it not been for Devlin's scandalous and rather amusing retorts. Mrs. Harris could hardly have been more obvious about her desire to have Devlin in her bed. Despite her more refined surroundings, the woman behaved no better than brazen Millie Piehler whenever a handsome man entered The Mermaid Inn and caught her eye.

Returning her attention to the activity outside the shop, Christiana saw someone new had recently appeared across the street. He must have arrived on foot. She would have noticed another carriage driving down the street. His manner of dress seemed odd. If anything, he looked more like a poor fisherman than a servant or one who had coin to spend in any of these shops. Perhaps he waited for someone. That might explain why the man paced in front of the *Jas. A. Pearce, Purveyor of Fine Tobacco* shop.

The longer she watched the man's increasingly agitated movements, the more familiar he seemed. When a swiftly moving carriage passed, the man raised his head and looked her way. Good God! What was Snake Watson doing here?

A moment later, she knew. Two uniformed officers of the Royal Navy emerged from the tobacco shop and spoke with Snake. A sick feeling lodged in the pit of her belly. Although she wouldn't join the Ravens on any more actual runs, an important one had been scheduled for tonight. If Snake had turned traitor, everyone in the gang—including Blackjack—could be captured or killed before sunrise tomorrow.

Looking over her shoulder, Christiana saw Devlin arching his temperamental eyebrow at Mrs. Harris. Undeterred, the woman edged herself still closer to his side, twisting her body at an absurd angle to bring attention to her bosom.

"For God's sake," Christiana said under her breath.

Perhaps hearing her, Devlin glanced across the room with a questioning look. Their gazes held for a moment. "Come, join us, dearest. Mrs. Harris has some gowns we might acquire today, provided they meet your approval."

"I-I..." Returning her attention to the window, Christiana saw one of the soldiers gesturing for Snake to lead the way somewhere. Well, she wasn't about to stand here picking out gowns or listening to the ridiculous next act between the man she loved and Mrs. Harris. Devlin was more than able to fight his own battles with the dressmaker.

She couldn't delay a moment longer. Even now, if not for the unmistakable naval uniforms of Snake's companions, she might have difficulty following. Placing her cup and saucer on the table with a slight upset, she gathered her hooded cloak about her shoulders and ran out of the shop, the tinkling of bells sounding in her wake.

However unladylike it might appear, she dashed across the street and followed after the three men, ever mindful of keeping a safe distance. They walked quickly, heading in a direction away from the resplendent, respectable shops.

The marketplace.

Close to the harbor, the open market would be bustling with activity, a vast gathering of vendors and people, noise and distraction. The perfect place to plot treachery. When she turned the corner, she couldn't help but suck in a gulping breath. Vendors, one after another, loudly hawked their wares, everything from baskets of fish to freshly baked meat pies. Sounds and smells permeated the air, making it difficult to concentrate.

She strained to see her quarry above the crowd. Then, in a flash of color, she caught sight of the two officers turning toward a bookseller's stall, followed closely by Snake.

Slipping in between rows of makeshift shelves, she offered a grateful prayer the bookseller had such a large selection. The height of his shelves afforded her necessary shelter from being seen by Snake and his party.

A quick glance found the bookseller trying to convince a distinguished older gentleman to purchase several leather-bound volumes. Mindful of not drawing attention to herself, she removed the first book she saw on a shelf. Unable to quell a sardonic smirk, it read: *The Housekeepers Receipt Book; Repository of Domestic Knowledge; Containing a Complete System of Housekeeping*. With a heavenward roll of her eyes, she thumbed through the book's pages, feigning interest.

Stepping further down her row, her ears perked up when she heard the uncultured voice of Snake on the other side of the aisle.

"I tell ye 'tis t'night," Snake said. "Ye'll catch the lot of 'em, if'n ye do as I say."

"The whole lot of them, eh," one of the officers replied in a mocking tone.

"Aye," Snake said. "Come 'tween midnight and two and ye'll catch the Ravens and Blackjack in the act."

"Indeed," the second officer said. "What assurance do we have this is not a trap set for our men?"

"I've a notion," the first officer suggested. "Why not have Snake here come along with us?"

"Not bloody likely," Snake bit out. "Supposin' ye fail. They'll have my innards strung out on the beach for the gulls to feast upon."

"Why are you so intent on betraying the Ravens tonight?"

asked the first officer.

"I've me own reasons," Snake argued. "Besides, ye promised a reward for each one captured."

"So we did," the first officer murmured. "Still, if you want your reward as badly as it seems, you'll lead us to the landing site tonight."

"It ain't right," Snake whined. "I'll be spotted. I ain't goin' there t'night."

"Listen to the cur," the second officer scoffed. "He betrays his friends and when we want him to accompany us in their capture, he says it's not right."

"Right or wrong, Snake," the first officer said. "The only way to prove you're being truthful is for you to be with us every step of the way."

Snake swore under his breath, then mumbled his agreement to the terms.

"We'll be expecting you at half past ten," the first officer said.

Raising her gaze above the open pages of the book in her hands, Christiana watched the two naval officers stroll away into the crowd. She waited a moment to see if Snake followed—he didn't. Perhaps he went in the opposite direction? Closing the book, she turned to place it back on the shelf and saw an open space had been created from where the book had been removed. Even more upsetting, Snake's dark eyes stared back.

"Well, well," he said. "If'n it ain't young Christian."

Christiana turned to run, but Snake appeared and blocked her exit. Then his gaze took in the sight of her wearing a gown beneath her open ladies' cloak.

"I'll be damned," he said.

Kicking him savagely in the shin, she ran, trying to push her way through the congested crowd. Hindered by her skirts and the throngs of people, it took little time before Snake caught up, grabbing hold of her arm with a vise-like grip.

"I always knew there was somethin' odd 'bout ye," he snickered into her ear.

She struggled to get away, stopping when the unmistakable point of a pistol pressed into her side. "Keep walkin'," he ordered.

"I am not going anywhere with you, Snake. Go ahead and shoot me. You'll not get away with it. There are too many people about. Someone will catch you before you take two steps."

Just then, above the din of the crowd, someone yelled her name—Devlin and Nash. She willed Devlin to find her, hoping he might recognize Snake and surmise what had happened. But it was Nash who saw her first and called to Devlin.

As if in a waking nightmare, she watched Devlin turn his head to Nash, then follow the direction of the man's outstretched arm to where she stood. The ashen expression that came to Devlin's face told her he remembered Snake.

"Oooh's that," Snake whispered into her ear with his familiar cackle. "Caw, I remember 'im now. That's the bloke what came to The Mermaid Inn askin' 'bout Blackjack. Ye stopped Millie from killin' 'im. 'Twas the same night ye cut yer 'and."

Drawing closer by the moment, Devlin forcibly pushed his way through the crowd.

"If ye don't start movin', I'll kill 'im. Makes no difference to me."

"No," Christiana whispered, an anguished plea rising from her parched throat.

"Then start walkin'."

With a slight nod, she turned and moved in the direction Snake prompted, away from the open marketplace. Rather than go toward the harbor, where numerous fishing boats were moored, Snake pushed her in another direction.

Around a grouping of rocks, they came to an isolated cove. A lone skiff bobbed up and down in the shallow surf. She tried to think. All she knew was not to get in that boat, even if it meant being shot. She recalled all too well what the sea did to bodies it claimed, having witnessed far too many bloated, greenish-hued corpses washed ashore—some so ravaged by sharks they hardly resembled a person.

I'd rather die on land—but not without a fight.

"Why have you betrayed us, Snake?" she asked, hoping to distract the man.

The smuggler cackled. "Mayhap I got tired of bein' treated like a bloody fool. Ye always thought ye was better 'an me. All of ye thought ye was better 'an me. Well, I'll be rich after t'night. And I ain't gonna let the likes of ye spoil me chances."

"I never thought you a fool, Snake." She tried to keep her voice calm, listening to his footsteps—picturing in her mind's eye the distance she needed to take action. "You just always teased me. No one likes to be teased."

240

"Shut yer mouth! Mayhap I should let the Ravens see ye now. Women ain't allowed in the Ravens. That's the rule. Women have waggin' tongues, leastways that's what Blackjack always said."

Unfastening her cloak as she walked, Christiana said a silent prayer. Then, taking a deep breath for courage, she pretended to stumble. Swinging her voluminous woolen cloak about, she hoped to catch Snake off guard and make him drop his weapon.

It worked! She could hardly believe it. But as they both fell to the sand and shingle beach, a desperate struggle ensued. Again and again, her clothing hampered her movements. She screamed, but even to her ears the pounding surf drowned it out.

Out of the corner of her eye, she saw Snake's pistol—mere inches away. Managing to roll over onto her stomach, she started toward the weapon. Ignoring the sharp pieces of shingle cutting into her hands, she focused on kicking Snake. He was almost on top of her back, just as desperate to reach the weapon.

She screamed. She kicked. She crawled, ignoring the slicing pain in her skin or the blood oozing out of her palms. It glistened in the sunlight—so close she could almost touch it. But just as her fingertips grazed the silver barrel, Snake's longer reach proved true. Panting for breath, she looked up to see a flash of silver reflect sunlight followed by a sharp, burning pain and then darkness.

Whether it was instinct or luck, Devlin signaled for Nash to go toward the busy harbor while he checked the smaller cove. Then, racing around the bend of the coast, he saw a sight that made his blood turn cold. The smuggler known as Snake held Christiana's limp body in his arms, then all but threw her into a small boat, like so much rubbish.

Rage unlike anything he'd ever experienced compelled Devlin forward. He ran down the deserted beach, lunging at the smuggler. Small in stature, taken by surprise, Snake hadn't a prayer of defending himself. After two punches to the man's midsection and one clip to his jaw, the smuggler fell into an unconscious heap onto the wet, packed sand.

Turning to the sea, Devlin swore under his breath. The skiff had drifted out, pulled by the retreating tide. He peeled off his coat and boots. Running into the cold surf, he was waist deep and just about to dive beneath the swell of an incoming wave when he heard someone shout, "Watch yer back!"

Turning, he saw Snake, sea foam reviving him as it washed over his prone body. Still a bit dazed, the smuggler sputtered then began to fumble in his clothing for something.

Damn, he must have a pistol.

A quick backward glance to the skiff gave Devlin a moment's pause. He could still retrieve it, but not if he got shot in the back. Clenching his jaw, he returned his attention to Snake. The smuggler couldn't stand, but seemed determined to keep trying.

Against the pull of the strong undercurrent, Devlin swam back to shore. Each sweeping stroke cut through the water with clipped precision, despite the weight of soaked clothing compromising his efforts. Once gaining his footing, he stood and ran toward the shoreline. He stopped short.

Snake, a wicked smile on his face, had come to his feet— his weapon aimed where it could instantly kill a man. A shot rang out.

Instinctively, Devlin looked down at his chest despite knowing he'd not been injured. A quick look back to his attacker, however, showed Snake face down in the shallow water—shot from behind.

Looking about to determine who'd killed the smuggler, he saw Nash in the far distance, pointing to someone standing behind a closer grouping of rocks on the beach. Wiping droplets of water from his eyes, Devlin recognized the young man Christiana had been sitting with at The Mermaid Inn— the one she called Henry.

Weapon in hand, the young man ran toward him. "The skiff," he yelled.

Swearing under his breath, Devlin turned and saw the small boat containing Christiana's body drifting further out to sea. Racing into the water, diving through the ocean's retreating swells, he swam relentlessly toward the bobbing skiff. Wrenched from his soul and offered up with every determined stroke, he prayed.

Please God, let her be alive.

CHAPTER TWENTY-SIX

"There is a divinity that shapes our ends;
Rough-hew them how we will."
~ Shakespeare (1564-1616), *Hamlet*

"You are certain she is all right?"

The physician summoned by the proprietor of The Valiant Sailor Inn, nodded. "She will have a damnable headache, and likely some bouts of nausea. The villain hit her hard enough to bring about unconsciousness, but there is no indication of bleeding or confusion. She roused long enough to speak to me, and I observed no problems with her vision. There are some scratches and bruising on her hands and extremities from the struggle on the beach. I have left a pot of salve for them. She put up quite a fight, from what I can see. A brave young woman, I must say."

Devlin nodded, raw emotion constricting his voice. He escorted the physician to the door. "What about laudanum for the pain?"

"A small dose, no more," the physician said. "A natural sleep is best, not sedation. It is often prudent to wake the patient periodically during the night to ensure she does not drift into too deep a sleep. Remember, she should be able to focus, say a few words, and drink some liquids."

"Thank you, doctor."

"I daresay *you* could use some rest," the doctor said with a kind smile. "Take care you do not take ill from that icy water today. Some brandy would not be remiss."

Devlin grinned. "I quite agree, and thank you again."

With a nod, the doctor left the chamber. Devlin stood still a moment, his brow resting against the closed door. Though comforted by the doctor's prognosis, he couldn't stop thinking about the day's events and how close he'd come to losing Christiana—forever.

More exhausted than he cared to admit, he returned to a chair situated beside the bed and studied the steady rise and fall of her chest as she slept. Her face, pale as snow, looked serene, her slumber seemingly untroubled. A cut on her brow, just below her hairline, had resulted from Snake's blow. Although requiring a few stitches, the doctor's exemplary skill promised the scar would hardly be noticeable once healed.

Thank God it had been only a cut and not a bullet to her brain.

Devlin woke with a start, his heart racing, and looked quickly to the bed. She lay there—alive. It had only been a nightmare. Rubbing his jaw, he stood and wearily walked to the small hearth. After stirring up the fire, he returned to the bed and tried to wake Christiana. She didn't respond.

"Christiana, can you hear me? Wake up, sweetheart."

She made a fretful sound. He really couldn't blame her. It must seem every time she fell asleep, he woke her.

"Come now, Christiana, I need you to talk to me this time."

Her eyes fluttered open. "I am getting tired of this game, Devlin."

"Doctor's orders, my sweet."

She looked at him, then glanced about the room. "Why is it so dark and quiet?"

"It's late. I doubt anyone else is awake at this hour." With a loud yawn, he stretched his arms. "I beg your pardon. How do you feel?"

"I was dreaming," she whispered.

He quirked a brow. "Was I in this dream?"

"Perhaps," she said with a hint of a smile. Turning her attention to the window, she grew pensive. Suddenly, a stricken look came to her eyes. Sitting up, she cried, "SNAKE!"

"Shhh," he whispered, sitting on the bed beside her. "He is dead, Christiana. He will never hurt you again."

"But..." Fingertips touched the bandage on her head. "Oh God, is it too late?"

"Too late for what, sweetheart?"

"Blackjack," she said. Tears spiked her eyelashes. "Snake met with soldiers this morning, told them about tonight's run. Blackjack will be captured, Devlin. He will hang. They will all hang."

"Try to remain calm, Christiana."

"I cannot," she cried. "I must find them. I must warn

Blackjack."

"Listen to me, sweetheart," he said, taking careful hold of her bandaged hands. "You must not become excited. Now, if I promise to warn them, you must promise me to remain calm. Will you do that?"

"Yes, I-I promise."

"Then close your eyes," he whispered. "I will find Blackjack."

He waited until she'd drifted off to sleep again. As he situated the bed covers about her, Devlin felt a hand upon his shoulder. Startled, he turned to see who'd entered the room without his knowledge—only to find Blackjack and Henry.

"I was just about to look for you."

"No need," Blackjack said. "I knew Snake was betrayin' the Ravens; 'tis why I planned the run tonight. He'd met with those soldiers before. They always met outside that tobacco shop."

Devlin's fists clenched. His blood began to boil. "You planned this?"

Blackjack fluffed his wiry, full beard in a distracted manner. "Well...when ye told me ye were comin' to market day, I decided we might kill two birds with one stone. 'Tis why I suggested ye take Christi to Mrs. Harris' dress shop so early in the mornin'."

When Devlin just stared at the giant, Blackjack shrugged his massive shoulders. "I became acquainted with the widow when I needed to keep an eye on Snake. Ye might say Mrs. Harris and I do quite a bit of business together. She knew ye'd be comin' by the shop early; she did what was necessary to keep ye occupied."

"Mrs. Harris was involved in this scheme?"

The smuggler nodded. "Ye forget, I've known Christi a long time. If there is one thing she has no patience for, 'tis women who flirt with men. It bores her." He chuckled softly. "So, there wasn't much else for her to do but look out the bloody window. I knew seein' Snake talkin' with soldiers outside the tobacco shop would stir her curiosity. It did."

"She could have been killed today," Devlin bit out in a heated whisper. "What if I'd lost her in the crowd? What if Snake had shot her? What if I'd not been able to stop him before he got in that damn skiff with her?"

Blackjack shook his head. "I knew ye'd not let anything happen to her. Besides which, we were close by the whole time. My fishin' boat waited just around the cove. And Henry watched outside Mrs. Harris' shop to follow Christi. There was never a moment when she was out of our sight."

Devlin looked at the young smuggler. "He knew *Christian* was a woman?"

Blackjack put a hand on Henry's shoulder. "This one *is* my son. He has always known about Christi. He just never let on—not even to her."

"And I will be a witness to Snake meetin' them soldiers," Henry said. "I will be tellin' the Ravens that *Christian* died killin' Snake after learnin' the sod betrayed us."

Looking at Blackjack, Devlin frowned. "I suppose it never occurred to you to tell *me* this ingenious plan?"

The giant shrugged. "Sometimes 'tis better not to know. Mind ye, things didn't go exactly as planned, but I would've died before lettin' Christi get hurt—or the man she loves and intends to marry."

Somewhat mollified by the sincerity of Blackjack's words, Devlin nodded. "Thank you for that." Turning to Henry, he crooked a brow. "And thank you for saving my life on that damn beach today, although—I must say—you took your time about it."

With a sheepish expression, Henry scratched his head. "Bloody hell, Yer Grace. Ye surprised me when ye came back to finish Snake off. That was my job. I finally had a clear shot at the bugger and was waitin' for ye to swim far enough out to the skiff. Then yer man showed up yellin' for ye to watch yer back and ye swam back to shore. Damn if ye didn't keep gettin' in my way."

"I see," Devlin said with a wry grin. "Well, in any event, I am extremely grateful your aim proved true."

Henry grinned, but they were both distracted by Blackjack. The leader of the Ravens had neared the bed. Standing in profile, he looked at Christiana with a sad, thoughtful expression. Then, leaning down, he brushed a gentle kiss upon the crown of her head.

"Ye're free now, Christi," he said in a gentle voice.

When the giant turned about, tears glistened in his cobalt blue eyes. "Make damn sure she is happy, Pemberton, and keep her safe."

Bellewyck Abbey ~ Kent

Christiana walked through the winding labyrinth of the Shadow Walk, up from the underground lake where her secret chamber could be found. It was time, time to make peace with all aspects of her past. Having harbored the secrets for so long, it wasn't an easy thing to do. Yet, after what had happened in Folkestone, the knowledge that Devlin had risked his life to save her was more than she could bear.

Death had always been a menacing presence in her life, looming over her shoulder since childhood. On numerous occasions, in any number of situations, she could almost taste it—a foul and bitter mixture of ash and soot, the salty sea and the rocky shore. It followed her, at times it hunted her, but never had it felt so close she believed she would die, not until the morning on the beach in Folkestone.

A gift had been given, one she did not intend to waste.

The panel opened with hardly any sound, but the sudden movement created a noticeable draft. Flames in the hearth made a slight whooshing sound, then danced wildly about on the unseen current of air. Although expecting to hear a surprised Devlin shout some expletive, she didn't. And then she saw him.

Impeccably dressed, booted feet crossed at the ankle, chin resting in the palm of his hand, he sat before the fire—asleep. They were to have dinner together and he was napping? She stifled a giggle to see him like this—the man of her dreams with his lips pursed together like a little boy practicing the art of kissing.

A strange sensation swept over her—much like standing on the edge of the white cliffs on a summer day, looking down at the sparkling sea below. Suddenly, the wind swells into a wondrous balmy breeze, caressing and uplifting one ever so slightly until it seems possible to take flight and soar with it straight up into the clouds. It was a magical feeling, one of pure joy, and it happened every time she looked at Devlin Randolph.

I love him, her soul rejoiced.

"Are you quite through with your inspection?" Not moving his pose even a hair, Devlin opened his gray eyes—looked right at her.

"You beast!" She slapped his arm playfully. "I thought you truly asleep. You were not doing that awful snore."

"I am a man of many talents,"—he grinned mischievously—"and I never give the same performance twice."

She arched a brow at him. "Are we talking about the same thing?"

With a deep rumble of laughter, he stood. Pulling her into his arms, he kissed her mouth. "What are you doing in my room, wench?"

"We were to have dinner tonight, sir."

"Yes, but as a rule, I take my meals in the dining room."

"Not tonight." Pulling away from his arms, she walked over to the still open panel in his room. "Come with me."

He came to her side and looked at the gaping hole of darkness with an almost comical expression. "I know you are not happy about my leaving for London in the morning, but do you not think slapping me in irons is a bit much?"

With a soft laugh, she entered the opening to the secret passageway, crooking her finger for him to follow. "Come see my secret world, Devlin."

The invitation proved irresistible.

Much to his surprise, torches in ancient iron sconces lighted their way—although they were distanced a bit too far apart for his liking. Still, not wanting her to see how uncomfortable he felt in confined places, he followed. Every so often she paused, pointing out different markings carved into the walls indicating panels to certain rooms of the abbey.

"Rather ingenious," he murmured, paying particular attention to a crescent-shaped mark indicating her new bedchamber.

As they began a downward descent, she stopped. The flickering flame of a nearby torch cast a golden aura about her face. Standing before him in a new white muslin gown by Mrs. Harris, Christiana resembled an earthbound angel.

"Can you hear the water?" she asked.

Remembering what Godolphin had said about a lake running beneath the abbey, he bit back a grin. "As a matter of fact, I do."

With a smile, she squeezed his arm. "There is a lake beneath the abbey."

"A lake?" he replied with mock disbelief. "Was that not clever of the monks?"

Her laughter lilting through the Shadow Walk warmed his heart.

They continued walking, the stone path beneath their feet

growing slick. As the Shadow Walk's direction steadily continued, the winding descent made it seem as if they were entering the very bowels of hell. The sound of water dripping became louder, each droplet echoing into the darkness. When next they passed another torch light, he saw moisture glistening on the walls.

"Were you not afraid to come down here as a child?" he asked. "Without light from these torches, it must have been terrifying."

"By the time I discovered the Shadow Walk, I was no longer afraid of the dark."

He stopped short. "You were afraid of the dark?"

She looked at him and nodded. "It started just after my father died. I was five years old at the time. I would have nightmares and wake up screaming. Yet, even awake, the fear remained. I clung to Reliance's skirts, afraid to walk about the abbey alone."

With a delicate shrug of her shoulders, she continued walking. "Archie decided sweeping the chimneys would rid me of my fear. He summoned Mr. Hartwell and that was that."

"Did no one try to make him see reason?"

"Reliance tried. He told her if she contradicted his orders, she would be discharged. 'Tis odd, but I remember that day so clearly. Reliance stood behind me, her hands on my shoulders—and they were shaking. She told Tom she knew his lordship wanted me dead then. She had seen it in his eyes."

"She must have been a remarkable woman."

Christiana nodded. "She was wonderful and I loved her very much. She had the prettiest brown eyes. Such a tiny thing, too. Much shorter than me, but possessing such spirit and strength she seemed larger than life. When she put her mind to something, there was no stopping her. Jasper says I take after her in that respect, which is not always a good thing."

Coming to a split in the path, they paused. "If ever you come here without me, always take the left path. Remember, the right way is the wrong way."

"And what, pray tell, is down the right path?"

She studied him for a moment, seeming to come to a decision. "Oh, very well," she said with a sigh. "The grotto is down there."

"Grotto?" He quirked a brow. Folding his arms across his

chest, he pinned her with a hard stare. "Grotto as in the grotto you took me to the night I followed you to The Mermaid's Inn?"

She looked down and nodded. "Yes, I am sorry."

With a soft laugh, he pulled her into his arms. "I already knew about your little trick, sweetheart." He tilted her face up to look at him. "Godolphin told me about the lake *and* the grotto where you first met Blackjack."

"And they say women have loose tongues," she murmured.

"Speaking of tongues." He kissed her lips, anticipating the delicious moment when she would melt into his arms. It took no more than a heartbeat. On a breathless sigh, their mouths merged, their tongues entwining—slowly, tenderly then building with deep seductive spirals and increasingly heavy breathing until the kiss exploded into uncontrollable passion. He pulled back, forcing himself to simply hold her until he could gain control of his impudent, throbbing arousal. When he felt capable of moving again, he released her.

In the flickering light, he saw Christiana's passion-swollen lips and longed to taste them again. Raising his gaze from the temptation, he stared into violet-blue eyes shining like brilliant amethysts in the intimate lighting of the passageway.

"I love you, Devlin Randolph."

He swallowed hard. Had she just said she loved him, he might have responded in kind. Not that he'd ever said the words to any woman before. As a rule, they seemed to stick in his throat. Yet, he wanted to say them to her. Unfortunately, she'd attached his damn fictitious identity to her declaration. True, both names belonged to him—but hearing them together disgusted him now. Each time she innocently, often breathlessly, called him Devlin Randolph only served to remind him of his damnable masquerade and that bloody wager.

God help me if she ever learns about that.

"Devlin, is something wrong?"

He blinked. "No, nothing."

"Did you hear what I said?"

"Yes," he responded inanely. Uncomfortable with the awkward silence and the sudden sadness in her expression, he changed the subject. "Christiana, have you given any more thought to meeting Pemberton?"

"Yes," she replied softly. "You did say we could have no future until I was brave enough to step forward and embrace who I am. I do not want to pretend anymore, Devlin, and I do want a future with you. I just hope you are not wrong about the Duke of Pemberton and that he will not keep us apart."

"Oh, I am quite sure he will insist upon our marriage." Belatedly, he realized the sardonic tone he'd employed had been misconstrued by Christiana. Offering his best gentleman's bow, he smiled. "I beg your pardon, Miss Petrovsky, but I am exceedingly hungry. I daresay, if we delay any longer, I shall not be held accountable for my boorish behavior."

"Ahh," she said with a smile. "So, you are hungry?"

"There is one thing you must understand, my sweet." Taking hold of her hand, he steered her toward the path she'd just indicated—the left one. "As a rule, men think of two things only—sex and food. In that order, I might add. And since I have taken a vow of celibacy until after your relationship with Pemberton is properly addressed, that leaves my only comfort to be found in food."

Continuing downward, the path became even more slippery. Had he not been holding her arm, she would have fallen on two occasions. He glanced down at her new silk slippers with a wary eye. "It might have been better had you worn those old black half-boots."

"The woman wears the gown, the gown does not wear the woman," she said in mock imitation of Mrs. Harris. "Boys' half-boots with this ensemble? Good heavens!"

"Yes, well, I prefer the wrong shoes to you breaking your neck."

The sound of water lapping against stone became distinctive. When they turned a sharp corner, he saw why. They'd come to a vast cave and the mysterious lake beneath the ancient abbey's foundations, the entire area illuminated by glowing torch lights, He stopped, amazed at the wondrous formations emerging from the floor of the cave and those spearing downwards from the ceiling.

"My God, it resembles a forest of stone," he said.

Here and there he noted small, calm pools of water mirroring the formations with startling clarity. He saw the lake, but she prompted him to walk away from it, around another sharp bend, then another, until they came to a secret room. Although chilly, it glowed with candlelight.

"I thought candles were expensive and the abbey frugal," he said with a grin.

"This is a special occasion, sir," she replied, leading him by the hand to a table set for two, complete with linen, crystal and a silver epergne.

She proceeded to reveal, with graceful gesturing, the menu for their dinner. Given the temperature of the room, a cold repast had been prepared, including roast duck, ham, and lobster, as well as other dishes he spied including asparagus, seed cake, and a mouth-watering apricot tart. By God, she even had several bottles of wine. The careful planning she'd put into the lavish and very romantic display did not go unnoticed. He couldn't help but be impressed. The only thing missing were the musicians situated behind a screen in the corner.

Pulling her back against his chest, he whispered into her ear, "Your strategy for seduction is most impressive, my sweet. Bring a half-starved man to an intimate cave, serve up a delicious feast and ply him with wine, is that it?"

She turned about in his arms. "You think I have seduction in mind?" He crooked a brow in mute reply. "Oh, very well, 'tis true." She offered a mischievous grin.

At his resounding laughter, she playfully pushed him away. "For your information, I also had another reason for bringing you here. Look about you, Devlin. Look at the table— the silver, the dishes, the crystal. These are important clues."

He picked up a plate. Noticing the design, he frowned. "This is the Bellewyck crest."

She smiled.

"I brought it down here for safekeeping years ago. See? Of course, this is only a small bit of what I could save. My dear half-brother took most of the silver first. He believed I had broken the dishes in a fit of rage." With a soft laugh, she picked up another plate. "Are they not beautiful? You can see your face in them."

Before he could respond, she walked about the room, pointing to a few small, but fine pieces of furniture, beautiful tapestries, and other miscellaneous items. Not only did she convey their history and where they'd been placed in the abbey, but who had helped to bring them down to the Shadow Walk.

"You never cease to amaze me, my sweet."

"Of course, I intended to put them back after Archie died,

but that Mr. Higginbotham showed up so soon afterwards I had no time. He was such a nosy man—much worse than you."

His eyes cut to her.

Realizing the insult of her words, she smiled sheepishly. "Sorry, I didn't mean to insult you."

Pursing his lips, he tried to suppress a grin.

"In any event, I could hardly bring the pieces up while he conducted an inventory of the estate. He would have thought us all thieves!"

Devlin erupted in laughter. "Yes, I can well imagine how that might have looked to him. So, is it now your intent to use me as brute labor to carry these things back up to the abbey?"

"No," she said with a soft smile. "I wanted to show you my treasure room because now there are no more secrets between us. I feel so ashamed for the way I treated you when you first came to the abbey. When I was a child, dreams came easy. I would meet this wonderful knight and he would rescue me. But as years went by, I stopped dreaming. I stopped believing knights existed. But here you are. You leave tomorrow and—although I know you said you would return..."

He crossed quickly to her, cupping her face in his hands. "I *will* return, Christiana."

She smiled, but tears glistened in her eyes. By God, how could she still have doubts? "I am coming back."

"Well, when you do, these things will be in the abbey where they belong."

He hardly knew what to say as she walked away. She paused and looked into the corner, nibbling on her bottom lip as she was wont to do when upset or nervous about something.

"There are just two things I won't return; I want them."

Glancing about the room, he couldn't fathom what items she might desire.

She went to the corner, and revealed two portraits. He saw her resemblance to the woman instantly and slowly approached. "Your parents?"

"Yes. This is William Bertram, my father. I have some sketchy memories of him—bits and pieces really. This smaller portrait is my mother, Anna. 'Tis all I have of her." She stepped back a little and studied her mother's face. "I was named after her. Christi, because I was born on Christmas Day. The Anna part was for her."

"Christiana," he whispered.

She looked at him then, copious tears glistening on her porcelain cheeks. "Archie was going to burn it, but—" Overcome with emotion, she paused to take a shaky breath. Then, presenting a brave front with a smile that seemed wrenched from her soul, she wiped her face dry.

He went to her and pulled her into his arms. As she wept quietly, his gaze turned to the portrait of her mother kept safe for so many years in the Shadow Walk. Raw emotion burned his throat.

"But you saved her, didn't you sweetheart?"

CHAPTER TWENTY-SEVEN

"He knows not when to be silent,
who knows not when to speak."
~ Publilius Syrus (1st C. B.C.)

Pemberton House, Mayfair ~ London

Seated at the desk in his library, Devlin contemplated the contents of the small book in his hands. Like a disembodied spirit haunting the corridors of his mind, Christiana's diary had become both a godsend and a curse.

The words, at times painful to read, spoke more vividly about her shadowed world than any conversation they'd had. So much more than a frivolous journal, the diary showed in sharp contrast the love and guidance she'd received from the good servants of the abbey, as well as the depth of Lord Bellewyck's malevolence and cruelty toward his half-sister.

For their faithful service and devotion to Christiana, the servants and villagers would be rewarded. Yet, the disquiet in his soul would never be silenced until just punishment had been exacted upon those who sought to harm Christiana in any way. True, nothing could be done about Bellewyck, may he burn in hell. But one yet lived—one as much a part of the earl's sins as Bellewyck himself.

To that end, a virtual treasure trove of information from Christiana's diary ensured his trip to London would result in more than just her identity and inheritance being restored. Her detailed written testimony now enabled him to find unscrupulous men in London, blackguards of ill repute with whom Bellewyck had conducted business. Even more telling, she'd written about one man in particular—someone who'd worked hand-in-hand with Lord Bellewyck in his villainous acts. Apart from acting as an emissary to the earl, the man had taken particular delight in tormenting Christiana as a child. Glancing down at the open page, he saw the villain identified by name yet again.

Malcolm Vickers.

A clock chimed the early morning hour of three o'clock as the former servant of Lord Bellewyck entered the tasteful residence on a quiet, tree-lined street in Westminster. After removing a tiered greatcoat and beaver hat, he walked into the drawing room and lit a lamp. The first thing he saw was a well-dressed stranger sitting in a chair staring at him. The second thing he noticed—a pistol aimed at his chest.

"Good evening."

"Who the devil are you?"

"First things first, I'm afraid," Devlin replied. "Shall I call you Vickers or Smythe?"

When the valet paled and turned to leave, Nash entered the room, effectively blocking his exit.

Shaking his head, Devlin studied the reprobate with deadly calm. "Your hasty departure from Bath after the death of your former employer was both unexpected and suspicious, Mr. Vickers. Then again, I suppose you had your reasons."

"I know not what you are talking about," Vickers said. "What former employer?"

Devlin made a tsking sound with his tongue. "Allow me to refresh your memory. For the past fifteen years you were employed as valet to the Earl of Bellewyck."

"Never heard of him," Vickers sneered.

Devlin glanced at the longcase clock in the corner of the drawing room, a quiet rage building in his belly. "That is an intriguing clock you have there."

"Is it?" the former valet asked.

"I particularly like the family crest." Feigning interest in his pistol, he added, "Tell me, Vickers, do you know the definition of an entailed estate?"

Vickers frowned, but didn't reply.

Standing slowly, Devlin pocketed his weapon and approached the valet. "What about the penalty for theft and murder?"

"Who are you?"

Devlin stared hard into the dark eyes of the man who'd helped torment the woman he loved since childhood. "I am the Duke of Pemberton, heir to your former employer. And since that particular clock belongs to the Bellewyck estate, I should very much like to know how it came to be in your possession."

Beads of perspiration dotted the former valet's brow. "I-I assure you, Your Grace, I am not the man you seek."

Wanting nothing more than to throttle the man to a bloody pulp, Devlin folded his arms across his chest. "Is that a fact?" He walked a small circle about Vickers. "It is true, we have never met before."

A nervous smile played about Vickers' lips.

Stopping in front of the cur, he crooked a brow. "But there is someone here who has met you." As Devlin turned to the still open doorway, Virgil Higginbotham entered the room with a constable. "No doubt, you recall Mr. Higginbotham. Lord Bellewyck met with him the night he died."

Sweating profusely, Vickers swallowed hard.

"Now then, Mr. Vickers, how does a valet come to possess furnishings from the entailed estate of his former employer if not by theft? For that matter, how can a valet afford the lease of a town house in Westminster? And why would he give a fraudulent name on that lease?"

"Your Grace, I did not sign the lease on this house," Vickers blurted out. "'Twas leased by my employer."

"Ah, your employer," Devlin said with a nod. "Mr. Edmund Smythe?"

"Indeed, yes, sir," the valet acknowledged with a shaky smile.

"Where is Mr. Smythe at present?"

"He is, well, he is a sickly man," Vickers said. "Not long after I came to work for him, the poor man took ill. He...he has returned to his family home in Dorset, under the advice of his physician."

Devlin shook his head at the bald-faced lie. "And your explanation for having the Bellewyck clock?"

"It was given to me by Lord Bellewyck in lieu of wages."

"Then you admit you were employed by the late Earl of Bellewyck?"

Removing a handkerchief, Vickers wiped his brow. "Yes, yes, yes."

Devlin shook his head. "That is a pity. You see, Lord Bellewyck did not have authority to sell or barter with items belonging to an entailed estate. Had his lordship simply sold the clock outright and paid you from the proceeds, it would have been far better than having the clock in your possession. Then again, I also have evidence you not only advised Lord Bellewyck which items from the estate should be sold in

London, but handled the transactions personally."

"What evidence?" Vickers asked.

"There was a witness," Devlin said. "Someone had the temerity to document every item taken by you and Lord Bellewyck, as well as conversations proving you a most eager participant in theft."

"Who is this witness?" Vickers asked in a raw whisper.

"Did I not say?" Devlin shrugged his shoulders. "Ah, well, I suppose you have a right to know. The Bellewyck ward."

"There is no Bellewyck ward," Vickers said with a caustic snort.

"I beg to differ. Granted, you did your best to see her dead, but she is very much alive and well. Her name is Miss Christiana Petrovsky, daughter of the late Count Petrovsky of Russia, and the former ward of William Bertram, the Earl of Bellewyck."

"There is no such person."

"Permit me to refresh your memory yet again," Devlin said. "His lordship summoned her to Bath shortly before he died. Indeed, you personally escorted Miss Petrovsky to his bedchamber."

"Stop calling her that!"

"Tell me, Vickers, do you recall being sent out of the earl's room that night?" Devlin watched carefully as the valet grew suddenly pensive. There was a reason why his lordship did not want you present. You see, he gave Miss Petrovsky a strongbox."

"What strongbox?"

"A strongbox containing documents regarding her birth in Russia and the appointment of William Bertram as the child's guardian. It also contained the missing codicil to Archibald Bertram's Will, documenting not only Miss Petrovsky's identity, but the vast funds that were to be held in trust for her by your former employer."

"You are lying," Vickers said.

"I am the Duke of Pemberton. My reputation is impeccable. I suggest you not forget that."

Breathing heavily, Vickers rubbed his damp brow in a distracted manner. "It is not true," he rasped. "Those papers were destroyed years ago." Realizing what he'd said, the man walked over to a chair and sat down, cradling his head in his hands.

"I have enough evidence to put you in gaol this night for

theft, as well as the attempted murder of Miss Petrovsky," Devlin said.

Vickers looked up, his eyes wide with terror. "His lordship said no one would ever know. He said there was no proof—no record of her inheritance, her birth, nothing. He told me he destroyed all of it long ago and that everyone would think her nothing but a common servant."

"Why then did you think he summoned her to Bath?"

"To tell her what he had done," Vickers said. "To laugh in her face and tell her the fortune was gone—every bit of it—as well as the evidence about her birth. He wanted to crush her in the end and take away her future."

"Yet, he gave her the very evidence she needed to support not only her identity, but the fact he had robbed her of that inheritance. Then again, I suppose there was no way *he* could be punished for the crimes against her. After all, he would be dead. But there was someone else who could be punished, namely you."

"No," the valet whispered.

"No one else was involved," Devlin said. "The question remains—why would he betray you at the end of his life? What reason could he possibly have to turn against such a loyal and faithful servant? I have spent a great deal of time considering his possible motive. He could have simply implicated you as his accomplice, but there was more. He wanted me to look into the past, to give me enough pieces of the puzzle to see the greater picture. And then I recalled what his lordship said to Mr. Higginbotham before he died."

Vickers looked at the solicitor, confusion etched across his features.

"His lordship said 'death will not silence me,'" Higginbotham said.

"Bellewyck was not talking about the ward or her fate," said Devlin. "And since he was responsible for the theft at the abbey, he was not talking about that either. He was a selfish man, who cared only for himself. So, it stands to reason there was something he wanted discovered that affected him personally—and someone in particular he wanted punished."

"The poison," Vickers said in a raw whisper. "He must have found out. I only did it because he was taking too long to die and he kept talking about debtor's prison. He was going to make me go there with him. I could not go there."

"So, you poisoned a dying man."

"In his food each day," Vickers said with a nod. "No one was the wiser. Even his physician believed his decline the natural course of his disease."

"How convenient for you," Devlin murmured.

Just then the richly carved Bellewyck clock chimed.

"It wasn't murder...not really. You cannot murder a dying man. And I simply could not go to prison."

"Well, if it is any comfort, a different fate awaits you now."

CHAPTER TWENTY-EIGHT

*"Love reckons hours for months, and days for years; And
every little absence is an age."*
~ John Dryden (1631-1700), *Amphitryon*

Dark, ominous skies, a biting wind, and a steady
onslaught of rain seemed determined to follow the glistening
Pemberton coach on its return journey to Kent. Removing an
engraved silver flask from his greatcoat, Devlin took a
swallow of brandy. Temperate indulgence was necessary if
one wanted to ward off the ague, or so he told himself.

Feeling the coach slow and sway, he pulled back the
hunter-green velvet curtain and looked outside. They had
turned toward the village. In another hour, Nash would drive
the coach through the arched gatehouse to Bellewyck Abbey.

Anticipation at the thought of holding Christiana in his
arms made Devlin smile. He'd not intended to be gone from
Kent for so long—a fortnight at the most. However,
investigating the finances of Lord Bellewyck, seeking out his
unscrupulous associates in the rookeries and ultimately
finding that foul blackguard, Vickers, had taken well over a
month.

Closing his eyes, he pictured Christiana naked in his bed,
her enchanting deep blue-violet eyes half-lidded with passion
and her exquisite rose-tipped breasts arching toward him.
Arousal came swift and hard. Swearing under his breath, he
shifted in his seat, determined to bring his unruly body under
control.

Rather than spend the remaining hour watching tiny gold
tassels dance about on curtain hems, he opted for a short nap.
Stretching his legs onto the opposing seat, he folded his arms
across his chest and closed his eyes.

He awoke with a start.

Bloody hell, was someone pelting the coach with rocks?

Looking out the window, hail the size of peas bounced off
the road. His thoughts went immediately to Nash and the

horses. He heard the coachman shout for more speed. The dastardly hail didn't last long, but was replaced by a cross-wind so fierce it seemed death itself chased them down.

"Thank God," he murmured when the coach entered the stable yard.

As soon as they stopped, Devlin stepped down to help secure the coach and horses. After the four bays were dry, warm, and fed, he turned to the man he now considered not only an irreplaceable servant, but a valued friend. Slapping Nash on the shoulder, he commended the exhausted coachman's efforts and slipped him the flask of brandy.

Anxious to see Christiana, Devlin raced to the abbey in the downpour. He quickly searched the main rooms, disturbed by unlit hearths and shuttered windows.

He stood in the columned Great Hall, hands resting low on his hips. "Where the devil is everyone?"

Great claps of thunder, one after another, reminded him the tempest was at its peak. Candle in hand, he made his way to his bedchamber and removed his wet clothing. After donning dry clothes, he knelt before the fireplace and prepared to kindle a fire. Then, remembering the mechanism to access the secret passageway, he found the iron ring and released the door. Standing, he watched the wall panel open.

At once, he noticed some of the wall torches had been lit within the passageway. "She must be in the Shadow Walk with the others."

How long it took him to walk the winding path, he couldn't say although it seemed far longer than it had with Christiana's guidance. He didn't stop until coming to the split on the descending path. "The right way is the wrong way," he whispered, remembering Christiana's instructions.

He came to her secret room, noting that many of the items had already been returned to the abbey during his absence. Emerging once more into the yawning cave, he frowned. Frustration at not finding anyone became grave concern.

Opting to continue deeper through the cave, he proceeded with caution. Just when he was about to return to the abbey, he noticed a peculiarity in the floor beside him. He stared at a pool of water, clear as glass. A faint light flickered in the water's reflection, yet it wasn't the light from his torch. The light came from someplace else.

"There must be an opening on the other side."

Making his way about the perimeter of the pool, he found an earthen path. A torch flickered from an iron basket, and beside the basket was another door.

"There's nothin' to be done now but wait," Bertie said in a quiet voice.

Christiana nodded. She couldn't speak. Her heart ached far too much. Glancing across the room, she saw the somber faces of her friends. Tom sat at the table next to Gordon and Billy. Dearest Polly, always trying to be helpful, poured the men a cup of hot tea. They were here for her and each other, yet she felt strangely detached and very much alone.

Returning her attention to the fragile figure on the bed, she studied the shallow rise and fall of Jasper's chest. Taking hold of his now crippled hand, she thought about all the happy moments she'd spent in his company.

Does he even know I'm here?

Bringing his hand to her cheek, she closed her eyes.

"What's this," a thin voice said. "Weepin' over me."

Although his speech sounded slurred, Jasper had spoken. She smiled into his pale eyes. He looked to the far side of the room where the others talked in soft tones. "Gordon can take over the brewery. He knows the way of it. Billy can help him."

She nodded, determined to be strong.

"Is that damn steward back yet?"

"I received a letter yesterday. He promised to be back within the week."

With a slight frown, Jasper studied her. "There is somethin' I want ye to know." He paused, so long she thought he had not the strength to continue. Then, he spoke in a thread-like voice. "I was proud ye told him the truth. Ye'll have a fine future if ye put aside yer fears."

"I am so pleased you like him," she said and kissed his brow. "He doesn't think you do, you know."

An almost amused expression came to the brewer's face. "I like him well enough. More important, I trust him."

A rumbling sound distracted Christiana and she turned with a start to see Devlin entering the brewery through its secret panel.

"What the devil is going on around here?" His voice shot forth like a cannon blast. "There is a bloody tempest raging outside. Do you realize I have been looking everywhere for all of you? Fine welcome home, I must say. I race back from

London to tell you there is nothing to worry about and find the house completely deserted. Hell, I was even worried about you, Rooney."

Christiana's heart lightened to hear Devlin's disgruntled concern. With a sigh of relief, she looked back to Jasper only to see the old man's eyes slowly closing, a gentle smile lingering upon his lips.

Making his way through the far end of the brewery, Devlin frowned at the servants sitting around an oak table with stunned expressions. Then, he saw Christiana standing beside a bed, a bed in which Jasper lay.

At once, he understood the somber atmosphere in the room and the possible reasons for everyone being gathered in the brewery. As he neared Christiana, he saw tears glistening in her eyes.

"My God," he whispered. "What happened? Was he injured? Is he in pain?"

She swallowed hard and shook her head. "Not anymore."

CHAPTER TWENTY-NINE

*"'Tis fate that flings the dice, and as she flings,
Of kings makes peasants, and of peasants kings."*
~ John Dryden (1631-1700)

Devlin studied Christiana over the rim of his coffee cup. By God, hadn't he been patient enough? In the week since Jasper's death, she'd become quiet and reflective. Although he understood her love for the old man and the important role he'd played in her life, Jasper had attained the ripe old age of ninety-three—a remarkable accomplishment for any man. And if they were to be married posthaste, he had much to tell her—beginning right now.

"I spoke to my mother about you before I returned to Kent."

She looked surprised. "Your mother?"

"I do have one, you know," he grinned.

"Really?" A glimmer of amusement sparkled in her eyes. "And here I thought you had simply sprouted from my imagination."

"Ah, but you do have a delightful imagination, my sweet."

With a soft, telling blush, Christiana looked down at her plate.

"Are you not the least curious what I told my mother?"

"Well," she hedged, tapping the rim of her teacup with a fingertip. "I am considering the possibilities. It does tend to boggle the mind, I am afraid."

With a chuckle, he stood and extended his hand. "Come with me."

"Why?" she asked with a wary expression.

"Because, my darling, I have something to show you and, more importantly, something to tell you."

A short while later they stopped outside his bedchamber. Christiana delicately cleared her throat and eyed him suspiciously. "I do believe I have seen what you intend to show me, Devlin."

"Is that a fact?" he asked, opening the door.

She nodded with a coy grin and entered the bedchamber.

The first thing she saw was a hooded cloak of black velvet draped across a chair. Then she spied a cashmere shawl. From that point on she didn't know where to look. There was a pair of leather half-boots, five pairs of embroidered slippers, gloves, and even an exquisite ivory fan opened on the bedside table. Upon the bed lay three beautiful gowns and two night-dresses so fine and delicate they seemed impractical for sleep.

"How did you do this?" she asked.

"Polly gave me your particulars," he said with a wicked grin. "And, well, my mother helped with most of the selection. I am afraid my tastes are a bit too daring—more for my enjoyment than practicality."

"Your mother helped purchase these things for me? What must she think?"

Pulling her into his arms, he smiled. "She thinks I am determined to marry you."

"You told her you intend to marry me?"

"I did."

"But you have not spoken of the future since returning from London."

"I wanted to give you time to accept Jasper's death before I broached the subject. I sympathize with your sadness, sweetheart, but I have missed seeing you smile and hearing your laughter. And, having two sisters, I learned at quite an early age the surest way to see a woman smile is to gift her with a new gown or two."

"Oh, Devlin," she said. "You do make me smile. You will always make me smile—even without beautiful gifts. But such extravagance must have cost a small fortune. I shall be perfectly content being the wife of a steward, provided we live within our means."

He pulled away and walked over to a box on the bed that remained unopened. Rather than respond to her words, he spoke about the gowns and what his mother said were necessary underpinnings.

She crossed to where he stood, hugging him from behind and resting her cheek against his strong back. "I did not mean to sound ungrateful. This is a wondrous surprise—truly it is. I only meant 'tis not necessary to buy me gifts to make me happy. You make me happy, and I'll not have you in debt because of me."

He faced her. "And I'll not have you worrying about finances. Your happiness means more to me than anything, Christiana." His gaze focused on her lips, as if eyeing a treat that might spoil his dinner.

Pulling away, he proceeded to the door, rubbing his neck in a distracted manner. "Much as I hate to leave you right now, I have a meeting with some men in the village about repairs to the abbey."

With his hand on the latch, he looked at her with a seductive smile. "Once you have sorted through everything, select a gown to wear for dinner this evening. There is something important I must tell you."

They arrived en masse, a virtual entourage of gentlemen complete with extravagant carriages, liveried footmen, luggage, and meticulously groomed valets. Their arrival—announced not by servant or sealed missive—had been heralded by the sound of masculine voices shouting throughout the Great Hall with but one name upon their lips.

"PEMBERTON!"

Polly and Christiana looked up from admiring the few silver pieces recently returned from the Shadow Walk.

"What the devil is that?" Polly asked.

Christiana stood motionless. "Someone calling for Pemberton."

"The duke is here!" Polly shrieked.

Christiana shook her head, motioning for Polly to calm herself. "I will go see to our guests." As she headed to the door, she looked back at her terrified friend. "See if Mr. Randolph has returned to the estate. If he has not, tell Billy to fetch him from the village."

She tried to appear calm and composed as she walked down the long hall toward the group of men. It was difficult to not react to their boisterous, disparaging comments about the abbey. And if her suspicions proved correct, they were slightly inebriated.

"What, ho!" exclaimed one gentleman as he elbowed the tallest man in the ribs at her approach. "It appears someone yet lives in this ruin, and a vision no less." Straightening his coat, he combed a hand through hair resembling spun gold and pinned her with a thorough, most improper, head-to-toe inspection.

"Might I be of assistance, gentlemen?"

The tallest man frowned, his heavily lashed, emerald green eyes staring at her in a most unsettling manner. "Damn, woman, I hope you have not cost me five hundred pounds."

"I beg your pardon?"

"Pay him no never mind, my lovely," the handsome, golden-haired gentleman said with an air of sober civility. "Our business is with Pemberton. Kindly inform His Grace he has guests."

"I am afraid there must be some mistake. The Duke of Pemberton is not at Bellewyck Abbey. Neither have we received word of his impending arrival."

Three of the men began to laugh, prompting the gentleman with the golden hair to roll his striking blue eyes heavenward. "For God's sake, do be quiet. I am trying to converse with this lady." Returning his attention to her, he smiled. "Miss, uh...?"

Remembering her promise to Devlin, she took a deep breath for courage. "Petrovsky," she said. "My name is Miss Petrovsky."

With a bewildered expression, the man nodded. "Miss Petal-oar-ski," he repeated. "Permit me to introduce myself, Miss Pullski. My name is Mitchell, a close friend to the Duke of Pemberton."

In turn, Mr. Mitchell identified his companions. The youngest rogue with the decidedly infuriating manner of undressing her with his eyes was named Lord Wessex. The tall, green-eyed gentleman was introduced as Viscount Lyndon, and the muscular, robust gentleman with auburn hair was introduced as Mr. Walter Duncan."

"Hello," she replied.

"Hello," they responded in unison, smiling like idiots.

"Right then, Miss Petal-Petal-rumspree." Mitchell's inability to pronounce her name became most amusing, especially to his friends. He shot them another dark look. "Is there, perchance, a Mr. Randolph about?"

The faint amusement she felt died abruptly. "Mr. Randolph? Why, yes, there is a Mr. Randolph at Bellewyck Abbey. He is the steward."

"Damn," Mitchell mumbled, shaking his head.

"Hah!" Viscount Lyndon exclaimed. "Did you hear that? Mr. Randolph is the estate's steward. I believe that means I win, gentlemen."

"P'rhaps not," Lord Wessex said with a hiccup. "Since

Miss Petunia here knows nothing about Pemberton being at Bellewyck, I suggest we address the specifics."

"Very well," Lyndon said, folding his arms across his chest. "As I recall, Mitchell wagered the façade could not be maintained for even a fortnight. Clearly, this young woman knows nothing about Pemberton. Thus, Mitchell loses and I win."

Mitchell smiled sardonically. "Ah, but you wagered he could maintain the masquerade, but not discern the truth."

"What truth?" Duncan interjected.

"The truth about the servants stealing from the estate and murdering the ward," Lord Wessex contributed with another loud hiccup.

Duncan looked about the empty hall. "Suppose he's had the dastardly villains carted off to gaol then. That explains why no one's about."

"Excuse me," Christiana interrupted. "But what is this about the ward being murdered?"

Duncan looked at her with an expression of sadness and shook his head. "I think it best you not know the gruesome details, my dear lady."

"This is ridiculous," she muttered under her breath. "The ward was not murdered, gentlemen. Indeed, there has been no murder at Bellewyck Abbey."

"No murder?" Duncan asked. "The devil you say! Fine time to tell us, I vow."

Totally exasperated, Christiana looked to Viscount Lyndon. He weaved on his feet, his eyes narrowed as if trying to decipher a secret message only he could hear.

"Gentlemen, gentlemen," Wessex said. "I do believe I have gleaned the sum of it all. You recall I was the only one who had confidence in Pemberton. I wagered he would make a perfect spy, fool the lot of them, and expose their crimes. I do believe those were my exact words. Am I right, Duncan?"

Duncan scratched his head. "Bloody hell, I think that is right. What was my wager, Mitchell?"

"You made no damn wager," Mitchell bit out with clear frustration. "You never wager." Directing a comical glare at the young Lord Wessex, Mitchell added. "How can you possibly use him as a witness? Good God, man."

They all began to argue amongst themselves in a lighthearted banter. In truth, they reminded her of impulsive, reckless boys discussing a game of chance.

"What difference does it make?" Lyndon said. "The fact remains Pemberton left this estate and returned to town. We all agreed he was to remain here until Twelfth Night, at which time Pemberton said he would reveal the truth and have all the servants tossed out—or was it shipped off to Van Dieman's Land. Bloody hell, I cannot remember. But since he left Kent—well, he forfeits the wager and owes us each five hundred pounds."

"By jove, here's the fellow to ask," Duncan said.

Christiana looked to see a devilishly handsome and clearly out-of-breath Devlin standing in the open doorway. A moment later, however, the man she loved almost toppled to the floor when Polly, Billy, Gordon and even Tom Rooney slammed into his back from behind. Rather impressively, Devlin recovered his composure and walked toward her.

"Damn," Devlin whispered under his breath, adjusting his disheveled clothing. Had they already told her the truth? Looking at Christiana, he saw only bewilderment—not that he could blame her. "What seems to be the trouble?"

"Mr. Randolph," Christiana said. "These, um, gentlemen are looking for the Duke of Pemberton. I have tried to explain he is not here, but—"

"Come now, Pemberton," Lyndon interrupted with a deep laugh. "Makes no never mind what the lovely Miss Plum Pudding thinks. You were spotted in London and, as you know, that means the wager is forfeit."

Directing an exasperated glare at Lyndon, Devlin took hold of Christiana's arm and gently ushered her toward the library.

"What are they talking about?" she whispered. "Why did he call you Pemberton?"

"Christiana, come with me now and I shall explain everything in private."

He saw the precise moment when she surmised the truth. Her expression went from confusion—to doubt—to dismay. Still, as if reluctant to believe what her mind was telling her, she cut to the chase. "I hardly think the matter private any longer," she said, stepping away from him. "Viscount Lyndon seems to think you are the Duke of Pemberton. You have not corrected him. Why is that?"

Devlin glanced back at his friends, all of whom had become silent as the grave and sober as spinsters. Looking back at Christiana, he sighed. "I have not corrected him because I am the Duke of Pemberton."

"Caw!" Polly exclaimed into the ensuing silence.

Christiana hadn't taken her gaze from his. "No," she whispered.

"Yes, Christiana," he said, taking a step closer to her. "It is the truth."

Gently taking hold of her arm, he escorted her to the library. After closing the door, he led her to the small settee before the hearth. The dazed expression on her face almost broke his heart. He sat beside her, holding her hands in his. "Forgive me, sweetheart. I should have told you the truth before now, but knowing how you felt about the Duke of Pemberton, I decided to wait."

"Why?"

"You were beginning to trust me as the steward and I did not want to jeopardize that. Then we became lovers, complicating matters even more. I wanted to tell you that night in the grotto, but you were too determined to return to The Mermaid Inn. I was going to tell you again the next day, but that was when you told me you were the ward."

"I remember you wanted to tell me something in the grotto." She looked down at their clasped hands. "I thought 'twas something else."

"Do you also remember the things you said about Pemberton?" he asked. "Even after confessing yourself the ward, you made me promise not to tell him."

"And you replied the Duke of Pemberton would not learn the truth from you," she said in quiet reflection.

Devlin angled his head in an effort to better study her expression as she stared into the hearth. "My primary focus was to help you accept being Christiana Petrovsky and to remove all the dangers from your life. I also wanted to convince you that Pemberton was nothing like Lord Bellewyck."

She nibbled on her bottom lip, her chin quivering slightly. Tears filled her eyes, but she quickly blinked them away. "You should have found a way to tell me before now."

"Yes, I should have, but I didn't want to destroy the trust and affection you had for me as Devlin Randolph. In your mind and in your heart you had made love with a steward. Was I then to tell you the man who bedded you was the man you never wanted to meet?"

She looked at him then. "Was that why you said you never

would have made love to me had you known the truth?"

"Yes," he said. "And why I vowed not to make love to you again until everything was settled. How could I make love to you again when you did not know the truth about me? That would have been despicable. I had too much admiration and respect for you to do that."

Pulling her hands from his, she stood and went to the windows. She remained still for the longest time, then spoke in a quiet voice. "I understand why you kept silent, Devlin. I even understand why you thought pretending to be a steward might help you better learn what you came here to know."

She paused, looking down at her hands. "In truth, I suspected you were not who you appeared to be when first you came to the abbey. I thought you a spy for Pemberton—or that you might even be related to him in some way. I just never imagined you were Pemberton."

He walked over to her, wanting desperately to pull her into his arms. "It is rather ironic we both pretended to be someone else."

"Yes, very ironic," she whispered. She looked into his eyes. "Your name is not even Devlin, is it?"

"David," he said. "Although Devlin is the name by which my family has always called me. My grandmother pinned it on me when I was a baby. She was of Irish descent, you see. I did tell you Devlin is Irish for David, but I daresay she believed it better suited my mischievous nature." He shrugged. "I actually prefer Devlin."

"And those gentlemen are your friends?"

"They are indeed. They are really not a bad lot. We have been friends for years. I have known Lyndon the longest—since childhood."

"I see," she said. "Then perhaps you would care to explain this wager they kept mentioning. From what your friends told me, you came here believing us all thieves and murderers. Was it all a game to you, Devlin? Did you come to Bellewyck Abbey because of some wager amongst your friends?"

He went to his desk, opened a drawer and removed a leather packet containing some papers. After finding the one he sought, he held it up for her to see.

"When Higginbotham came to my home and informed me of Lord Bellewyck's death, I could not have cared less. I never even knew I was related to the man and had more than enough properties to keep my interests occupied. Then I learned Bellewyck had a ward, a child no one knew anything about and whom the servants at this estate claimed never existed. *That* was what prompted me to come here. You may as well know I have an Achilles Heel where children are concerned. I wanted to find the ward—or learn what had happened to it. In retrospect, I should have known you were the ward. But, my sweet, you had a clever answer for everything."

Christiana smiled sadly. "Apparently, we were both so busy trying to hide the truth about ourselves we could see nothing else." She took the document from his hand, giving Lord Bellewyck's Will a cursory glance.

"What about the wager?" she asked.

"It happened more out of boredom than intended cruelty," he sighed. "Lyndon suggested since I was coming to the estate, I could best learn what I wanted to know posing as a servant. Before I realized what had happened, wagers started being made about whether or not I would be able to succeed at the masquerade."

"More out of boredom than intended cruelty? Devlin, they said you believed us thieves and murderers. That you boasted about proving it and sending us all to Van Dieman's Land. Is that not cruel? Is it not cruel to wager with people's lives? Lord Bellewyck made wagers too, you know. He wagered on whether or not I would fall to my death. It remains a very vivid memory to me."

"How can you possibly compare me with Bellewyck?" he asked with deadly quiet.

Tears glistened in her eyes and she swallowed hard.

"For God's sake, Christiana, do you honestly think I would intentionally play with the lives of innocent people? Yes, the wager was wrong. Yes, I believed the worse about you all before I came here. I might add, when I arrived, my opinion seemed justified. You were resentful of my presence, secretive, guarded, and deceptive. You even drugged me. And though I understand the reason for such drastic measures, you *were* all involved in treachery. Still, I pursued the truth—despite how difficult you made it for me."

"Was seducing me a means to an end?"

He folded his arms across his chest. "By God, I will not respond to that insult."

"I see," she said.

"No, Christiana, you *do not* see. The fact you even ask

273

that question after everything I have done, everything I have tried to do to prove myself to you, is an insult."

Picking up the leather packet, he gave it to her. "Perhaps you should look these papers over now. I had intended them to be a wedding gift, but you may prefer to use them as the means for your freedom."

As he crossed the room, Christiana said, "Devlin, I *am* trying to understand."

He paused at the door. "Are you? I cannot help but think your mistrust of me now is because of a childhood fear that anyone with a title is just like Lord Bellewyck."

She blinked wide-eyed at his comment. Had his words struck a nerve?

"He is dead. The past is dead. I have tried to prove myself to you—again and again, Christiana. You must choose for yourself whether or not we have a future together. Whatever you decide, I will respect."

She looked down at the packet in her hands. "What will you do now?"

"My friends are waiting. I intend to see they have been made comfortable. I would very much like you to join us this evening for dinner. It will give you an opportunity to know them better. They are not perfect, nor always wise, but they are my friends."

CHAPTER THIRTY

*"What sunshine is to flowers, smiles are to humanity.
These are but trifles, to be sure; but, scattered along life's
pathway, the good they do is inconceivable."*
~ Joseph Addison (1672-1719)

Surrounded by her friends—including dear Nash who sheepishly admitted he'd been assisting the Duke of Pemberton with his deception—Christiana sat in numb silence in the warm kitchen of Bellewyck Abbey.

No one spoke—and with good reason. On the table were various papers from the packet Devlin had given her. One document stated a generous annuity had been established for each of the Bellewyck Abbey servants. Apart from that, the servants had been given a dramatic increase in wages reverting back fifteen years. Devlin had also designated a monetary gift to every person in the village for their dedication and loyal service to Miss Christiana Petrovsky.

With trembling hands, she set down the last paper she'd read aloud to her friends. The letter, a cordial correspondence from the Bank of England declared an account had been established in her name in which had been deposited the sum of fifty thousand pounds, representing the inheritance bequeathed to her by Count Alexander Petrovsky.

The papers also contained a newspaper clipping citing Malcolm Vickers, former manservant to the late Earl of Bellewyck, had been arrested in Westminster where he'd been living as Mr. Edmund Smythe. The charges included theft, conspiracy and attempted murder of a child, as well as the murder of Archibald Bertram, Lord Bellewyck. To all counts, Vickers had entered a plea of guilty.

"He could not make his lordship pay," Bertie said in an emotion-laden voice. "But God love the man for seeing that monster Vickers will dance for the devil soon enough."

"Vickers will hang for sure," Billy Darrow added.

"God bless the Duke of Pemberton," Gordon Darrow said.

"His Grace risked his life when Snake tried to kill Miss Petrovsky in Folkestone," Nash pointed out. "He would be dead now if Henry had not appeared out of the blue."

Nash's comment prompted everyone gathered to nod in agreement.

Polly smiled at Christiana. "And he loves ye, Christiana. It seems a trifle mad we ever feared such a man."

Just then the sound of loud, masculine laughter resonated from the hall. Christiana frowned. How can he be having such a grand time with his friends when she could think of nothing else but their argument? And she certainly didn't need reminding of all the wonderful things he'd done for her since they'd met.

"Sounds like they have gone into the Great Room," Polly said.

Bertie looked at Christiana. "Do ye suppose they will want some of Mr. Randolph's—I mean, His Grace's brandy?"

Christiana studied the anxious faces of her friends. They waited with bated breath for her decision.

"Get me the special ale," she said.

Polly and Bertie Lloyd looked at one another aghast.

"Not *that* special ale," she added with a shake of her head. "Fetch the White Monk blend Jasper invented. I want our guests to realize Bellewyck Abbey is not a ruin, but a respected brewery."

Tom Rooney nodded his approval and stood. "I will fetch it."

"Shall I serve it then?" Polly asked.

"We shall do it together," Christiana said.

A few moments later Christiana and Polly entered the Great Room to see Devlin seated before the fireplace with his friends, each of whom had dragged a piece of furniture closer to the hearth. As she approached, all five gentlemen stood.

"Hello," she said in a pleasant tone.

"Hello," they all replied, smiling in turn.

"I am not sure if His Grace has told you, but the servants at Bellewyck Abbey retire early. We are understaffed and, as you can well imagine, there is much work that must be done each day to maintain the estate."

Devlin bit back a grin when his friends looked about the spartan room, completely at a loss as how to respond to the cryptic remark.

"Before we bid you gentlemen good night," she continued,

"I thought you might like to sit before the fire and enjoy a mug of our special ale."

With a ready smile and a murmur of appreciation, his friends eagerly reached out to take a mug from the tray proffered by Polly. Devlin harrumphed to gain Christiana's attention. "Is that *your* special ale, dearest?"

Christiana smiled. "I daresay one cannot expect trust if one is not willing to give it, dearest."

"Oh, I quite agree." He picked up a mug and sipped its contents. Pausing after a moment, he looked to his friends who appeared baffled by his remark.

"Drink up, gentlemen," he said.

"Well, I shall bid you gentlemen goodnight then," Christiana said. "There is a candle on the far table for each of you. Another candle lights the hall and the stairs. I trust that should be sufficient light for each of you to find your chambers."

As Devlin raised his mug to his lips, he noticed Christiana staring at him in a most peculiar manner.

"It would be unfortunate should someone become lost and enter another person's room by mistake," she said. "Unless, of course, that was their intent. That is to say, some people might want someone to come to their room to talk."

Devlin gulped down his ale. Could she be any more explicit?

Never taking his gaze from hers, he slowly approached. When he stood a breath away, he leaned forward as if intending to kiss her mouth. He heard her breathing hitch; her rosebud lips parted on a quivering sigh. Then, much to her obvious surprise, he set his empty mug on the tray a now gaping Polly held, and turned away.

"Sweet dreams, ladies," he said.

Muffled laughter followed Christiana as she quit the room with Polly. Even worse, upon entering the now empty kitchen, Polly erupted in fits of laughter.

"What, pray tell, is so funny?"

Polly pressed her lips together, clearly struggling to rein in her amusement. "What were ye tryin' to do in there?"

"I was trying to tell him we need to talk." Christiana pointed toward the Great Room. "He is having a wonderful time, acting as if nothing unusual has happened today, and I am—"

"Ye're what?" asked Polly.

"Confused!" Christiana sat at the oak table, cradling her forehead in her hands. Her gaze lit upon the neatly tied leather packet with all the papers tucked safely inside.

"Are ye still upset about his pretendin' to be a steward?"

"No, I would have done the same thing."

"Is it the wager then?"

Another round of masculine laughter erupted from the Great Room, prompting Christiana to smile. "No, I cannot imagine Devlin being deliberately cruel toward anyone. And, after meeting his friends, I can see how the wager—however inappropriate—might have been born out of boredom. I never should have made such an issue of it. 'Twas cruel of me to compare Devlin and his friends to Lord Bellewyck. They are as different as night from day. I actually find them amusing and somewhat endearing."

Polly blinked like an owl. "Endearin'?"

"Full of mischief, like little boys."

"Well, one of those little boys—the one they call Wessex—had best keep his rovin' hands to himself. I almost forgot myself and kicked him when I helped Tom serve dinner."

Christiana nodded with a grin. "I saw the expression in your eyes."

The two friends sat together in the ensuing silence, the packet of papers between them on the table. "Do ye still love him?" Polly asked in a hushed tone.

"Very much," Christiana said.

"Then what is there to be confused about?"

"I do not deserve him, Polly. I did not think I deserved the man when I thought him a steward. How can I marry a duke and make him happy? I know nothing about his world."

"Ye already make him happy, and ye can learn about his world."

"But look at all the trouble I have been. When I think of what I said about the Duke of Pemberton—to his face, mind you—I could just die. I thought Pemberton cruel and selfish just like Archie, and all the time he was here trying to find me, trying to save me."

"He did save ye. He saved us all."

Christiana smiled at her friend through a misting of tears. "Yes, he did." She picked up the leather packet and looked at it.

"Well then?" asked Polly.

"I could do anything, be anything, if he said he loved me.

I would rather hear those words truly spoken in a heartfelt declaration than have fifty thousand pounds in the bank. I have waited all my life to hear those words, Polly. Without them, I shall always wonder if he married me because he is the duke and I but the virgin ward he mistakenly compromised."

"Perhaps 'tis easier for him to show ye," Polly said with a soft smile. "And he may yet say the words in time."

Sitting on her bed, wearing one of the scandalous new nightdresses he'd purchased in London, Christiana brushed out a length of long, black hair. No matter how hard she tried to think of something else, her thoughts kept returning to Devlin.

Surely he wasn't still in the Great Room with his friends.

Returning her brush to the bureau, she went to the window. Pulling back the blue and white toile curtains, she stared out into the night. "I will not go looking for him. If he wants to be with me, he will simply have to come to me."

"What if he's waiting for you to come to him?"

Turning with a start, she saw Devlin wearing a burgundy colored silk dressing gown—and apparently nothing else. He looked so seductive her heart skipped a beat, a wave of heat flooding over her body and making it difficult to catch her breath. Even more telling was the pronounced quiver she felt deep inside her body, as if he'd summoned her honeyed desire with a single glance.

When he turned away to close the panel, she breathed deep—determined to not let him see the effect of his presence. "You certainly have become comfortable with the Shadow Walk."

He faced her again, but didn't respond. Instead, he crossed the room, each step slow and seductive.

"I...um...did tell you it was called the Shadow Walk, did I not?"

He didn't answer, just studied her with silent intensity.

Becoming flustered, she said, "I know I mentioned it in my diary which—by the way—you still have not returned to me."

He stopped before her, a wicked smile curving his sensual mouth.

"Voila," he said, pulling the little red book from the pocket of his dressing gown like a clever magician. When she tried to take it from his grasp, he held it out of reach, teasing her. "Perhaps I should hold onto this." His low, velvet voice sent ripples down her spine.

"What do you mean?"

Devlin thumbed through the pages. "It does contain a great many passages about me. Indeed, I have within my grasp sufficient evidence to prove you love me with a grand passion—or did at one time."

"I still love you, Devlin."

"With a grand passion?" he asked, his brow crooked.

Trying to calm her racing heart, she whispered. "Yes."

A sinful smile curved his lips. "Then I believe this belongs to you, my sweet."

She took the book to her writing desk. "You have never told me, you know."

"Told you?"

Did he truly have no idea what she was talking about? Judging from the blank expression on his face, he must not. She nibbled on her lip, then caught herself and stopped. "You have never said you love me, Devlin."

"I see," he murmured with a nod. "Are the words so important, Christiana?"

"When one is faced with life-altering choices, yes, I suppose they are."

"I love your wit," he said with a slow grin.

She wasn't amused and, much to her surprise, he quickly became serious. "Christiana, to simply say I love you does not seem adequate. It certainly does not encompass the depth of what I feel for you."

He kept his gaze intent as he approached. "I listen for your voice when silence surrounds me. I look for your face when alone or in a crowd. I look at the deep blue sky and think only it reminds me of your eyes. I dream of you when I sleep, and you fill my every waking thought. Your laughter is food for my soul and a light in the darkness. Your smile warms me. Your courage humbles me."

Stopping before her, he pulled her into his arms, gently cradling her face in one hand. "I cannot remember my life before you. And I will not imagine my future without you."

Tears welled in her eyes, making it difficult to see clearly. She blinked, watching his mesmerizing eyes follow the trail of her tears down her cheek. With his thumb, he wiped them away.

"Do I love you?" He leaned closer until but a kiss away. "Let me prove how much for the rest of our lives."

Try as he might to show some restraint, Devlin trembled with an urgent need to make love to her. The moment he tasted her lips, he was lost. Their mouths melded, their tongues explored one another with voracious abandon. The cadence of their breathing became almost frantic as his hands swept over her body in long, lingering caresses. The almost sheer material of her nightdress slid easily beneath his fingers to mold her body in ways that made his rigid sex pulse with every erratic beat of his heart.

He broke the kiss, yet didn't release her from his arms. Her eyes sparkled like jewels. Her lips—plump, red, and wet from his recent plunder—made his mouth turn dry.

"There are no shadows or secrets between us now," he rasped. "And since I can stand no more of this torture, I shall have your answer now. I am the notorious Duke of Pemberton, former rake and impudent steward of Bellewyck Abbey. My darling Christiana, are you brave enough to marry me?"

"I will not share you with other women, Devlin."

He chuckled. "Yes, well, that rumor about a harem of mistresses is false, you know. In any event, you are the only woman I want—now and always. You possess my heart, my devotion, and my eternal undivided, insatiable attention."

"I want lots of babies."

"As do I."

"I will try to be obedient, but I shall always speak my mind."

"As will I," he said with a roguish grin.

"Can we spend time at Bellewyck each year?"

"I look forward to it," he whispered against her mouth.

Looping her arms about his neck, she smiled. "Then yes, I will marry you."

"Thank God." Seizing her mouth again, he used every bit of skill he possessed as a lover until she was moaning and trembling in his arms, completely oblivious to the removal of her nightdress until it had pooled about her feet.

With ragged breathing and on the brink of being too aroused to stand let alone walk, he lifted Christiana into his arms and carried her across the room, lowering her gloriously nude body upon the bed. Taking a step back, he said, "You recall the vow I made not to make love until your situation with Pemberton had been decided?'

"Yes," she sighed, her tongue darting out to lick her sensuous lips.

"It has been decided." He untied the sash about his dressing gown, watching Christiana's wide-eyed gaze as she studied his movements. The panels of his dressing gown opened. As the garment fell from his shoulders to the floor, the full heat of her gaze swept over his aroused body. When she stared brazenly with wanton wonder at the engorged length of his erection, it proved more than he could stand.

He slowly climbed onto the bed, arching over her body with his weight balanced on the outstretched palms of his hands. "Just to set your mind at ease, I had the foresight to obtain a Special License before my journey back to Kent. Rest assured, my love, we marry without delay. However, I fully intend to prove just how much I love you beginning here and now."

EPILOGUE

"Happiness is at once the best, the noblest,
and the pleasantest of things."
~ Aristotle (384-322 B.C.)

"I daresay this is the most unusual masked ball I have ever attended."

No sooner had the Dowager Duchess of Pemberton tactfully whispered her observation than an enormous gentleman galloped by dressed as a one-eyed pirate.

"Good heavens!" she exclaimed.

Amused by his mother's reaction to the boisterous merriment in the Great Hall of Bellewyck Abbey, Devlin laughed. Yet, despite her somewhat shocked sensibilities, he could see his elegant mother was truly enjoying herself. For that matter, so was everyone else.

Aglow with candlelight, the secrets and once foreboding shadows of the Great Hall had been completely vanquished. Instead of tomb-like silence, an orchestra played selections lively and at times hauntingly beautiful. The guests, resplendent in costume, were all amiable. With the exception of the smithy, Giles Yates—posing as the ungraceful pirate—it proved an intriguing challenge to identify each guest.

Suddenly, his gaze caught and held that of his wife. He certainly had no problem identifying her, despite the jeweled domino. Raising his glass of champagne, he saluted her. The longer he stared, the more telling her reaction. Even from across the room, she knew what he had on his mind. With a low chuckle, he finished off his glass of champagne and caught his mother watching him with a curious expression.

"Is something wrong?" he asked.

Her eyes sparkled with mischief. "For a man who once told his sisters he did not believe it necessary—or even prudent—to marry for love, you are quite the besotted husband."

"You think me besotted?"

"Devlin, you are so besotted with your darling bride that when the sun rises you likely perceive it as a tribute to Christiana."

"Is it not?" he asked.

With a soft laugh, Sophie Pemberton looked across the room to where Christiana conversed with guests. "I have always believed the best marriages are those based on mutual respect and love. I was blessed to find that in my marriage to your father. Your sisters have been equally fortunate to marry for love. And I am inordinately pleased that my only son has learned this truth—before he made the wrong choice in a bride."

She gazed at him with an expression he'd not seen since before his father died. "Love is precious, Devlin. Cherish it. Nurture it. But never take it for granted. I wish you and Christiana a long and happy life together."

He kissed her cheek. "Thank you, Mother."

With a gentle smile, she turned back to observe the dancing and struggled against another laugh. "Good heavens! Who is that brash rogue dressed like a wolf?"

Following the direction of her gaze, he saw the wolf behaving in an overtly dramatic, lascivious manner as he begged to partner an indignant, buxom shepherdess in the next dance. "That would be Wessex," he said. "And the shepherdess is my wife's maid, Polly."

Unable to hold back her amusement a moment longer, Sophie Pemberton laughed. When she saw people looking her way, she tried to hide her smile behind an open fan. Yet, the more she tried not to laugh, the more she found it impossible.

"Really, duchess, do control yourself," he said. Then, with his most elegant bow, he winked at her. "By your leave, madam."

He circled the perimeter of the room, greeting guests and otherwise conducting himself as a proper host. The fact his gaze kept returning to his wife couldn't be helped. She was stunning in a ball gown of gold silk, her hair swept up and adorned with ropes of pearls. It was all he could do to not pick her up and carry her out of the hall in front of their guests.

"Congratulations, Yer Grace."

Immediately recognizing the distinctive voice, Devlin studied his costumed guest. "Only you would be so bold as to come dressed like a highwayman, Blackjack."

With a shrug, the smuggler looked to the other side of the

room. Devlin followed his gaze. Christiana held hands with young Sarah Lloyd, the two of them laughing as a magician pulled an egg from behind Sarah's ear.

Glancing at the giant's awkward manner, it seemed obvious the smuggler had decided to stand behind the massive stone columns and watch Christiana from a distance. "Go speak with her, Blackjack. She will be delighted and surprised to see you."

"Did ye tell her ye invited me?"

"Tell my wife I went to The Mermaid Inn looking for you? After what almost happened the last time with that wench, Millie? I hardly think so. I've also not forgotten you gave Christiana that bloody blunderbuss years ago—or that she knows how to use it."

With a low chuckle, the Ravens' leader crossed the room, lingering in the shadows of the ancient columns. Then he walked up behind Christiana and whispered into her ear. With a cry of surprise, she released Sarah's hand and embraced the giant.

With a slight catch in his throat, Devlin procured another glass of champagne and crossed the room. He would give his wife another hour and no more. A husband could muster only so much control—and that control was fading fast.

Resplendent from the wondrous lovemaking she'd enjoyed earlier, in half-sleep Christiana snuggled next to her glorious husband's warm, God-like body and felt an empty space. Sitting up, she looked about the darkened bedchamber and found him seated at the desk, reading something by the almost spent light of a sputtering candle.

As quiet as possible, she tiptoed over. The handsome devil had her diary again. Determined not to laugh, she covered his eyes with her fingertips and whispered in his ear. "If you want to know what I am thinking, come back to bed."

With a soft laugh, he pulled her hands away from his eyes, kissing each palm. "For your information, my darling wife, I have written my own quote for the day."

Kissing the delicious corner of his plump upper lip, she whispered. "Is it a naughty limerick?"

"You wound me." With a hand to his chest, he feigned a frown, but spoiled the performance by smiling. "If you must know, I found myself unable to sleep for thinking upon what a beautiful, clever, caring, witty, and incredibly passionate wife

I have. There I was, wide awake in bed, listening to the soft, but contented snoring of my beloved." She slapped his arm playfully. "Then, lo and behold, I remembered a poem which captures my thoughts precisely. 'Tis what I would have composed were I so clever with words."

"May I read it?"

He pulled her down onto his lap and turned the diary toward her. She read the beautifully scripted words.

"To see her is to love her, and love her but forever.
For nature made her what she is, and never made
another. ~ Robert Burns
Happy birthday, my darling Christiana,
A lifetime is not long enough to love you,
an eternity would be too short.
You are my heart and my life. Always, Devlin"

"Oh, Devlin." She cried, kissing his lips. "If this is a dream, I hope never to wake." Then, overcome with emotion, she hugged his neck, breathing in the sandalwood, nutmeg and arousing manly scent uniquely her husband.

He held her close, gently stroking the length of her hair as she listened to the strong steady beat of his heart. "Christiana, do you remember what I said about dreams that day we first made love?" His voice was deep, rumbling against her ear from inside his chest.

She looked up at his face. "That one cannot find dreams in shadows?"

"Yes," he said then slid a hand beneath her hair to cup the nape of her neck. He pulled her close and kissed her—a slow, wet, deep, erotic kiss that all but curled her toes. She sighed and moaned, helpless against the magic of this man. He smiled against her mouth and nipped playfully on her bottom lip. Then, with a tantalizing, seductive smile that melted her insides, he whispered. "But I also said this dream has only just begun."

And it had.

Praise for Highland Press Books!

BLUE MOON MAGIC is an enchanting collection of short stories. Each author wrote with the same theme in mind but each story has its own uniqueness. You should have no problem finding a tale to suit your mood. *BLUE MOON MAGIC* offers historicals, contemporaries, time travel, paranormal, and futuristic narratives to tempt your heart.

Legend says that if you wish with all your heart upon the rare blue moon, your wishes were sure to come true. Each of the heroines discovers this magical fact. True love is out there if you just believe in it. In some of the stories, love happens in the most unusual ways. Angels may help, ancient spells may be broken, anything can happen. Even vampires will find their perfect mate with the power of the blue moon. Not every heroine believes they are wishing for love, some are just looking for answers to their problems or nagging questions. Fate seems to think the solution is finding the one who makes their heart sing.

BLUE MOON MAGIC is a perfect read for late at night or even during your commute to work. The short yet sweet stories are a wonderful way to spend a few minutes. If you do not have the time to finish a full-length novel, but hate stopping in the middle of a loving tale, I highly recommend grabbing this book.

Kim Swiderski
Writers Unlimited Reviewer
~~~

Legend has it that a blue moon is enchanted. What happens when fifteen talented authors utilize this theme to create enthralling stories of love?

BLUE MOON ENCHANTMENT is a wonderful, themed anthology filled with phenomenal stories by fifteen extraordinarily talented authors. Readers will find a wide variety of time periods and styles showcased in this superb anthology. *BLUE MOON ENCHANTMENT, the P.E.A.R.L. nominated anthology,* is sure to offer a little bit of something for everyone!

*Reviewed by Debbie
CK²S Kwips and Kritiques*

~ ~ ~

NO LAW AGAINST LOVE - If you have ever found yourself rolling your eyes at some of the more stupid laws, then you are going to adore this novel. Over twenty-five stories fill up this anthology, each one dealing with at least one stupid or outdated law. Let me give you an example: In Florida, USA, there is a law that states "If an elephant is left tied to a parking meter, the parking fee has to be paid just as it would for a vehicle." In Great Britain, "A license is required to keep a lunatic." Yes, you read those correctly. No matter how many times you go back and reread them, the words will remain the same. Those two laws are still legal. Most of the crazy laws in these wonderful stories are still legal. The tales vary in time and place. Some take place in the present, in the past, in the USA, in England, may contain magic... in other words, there is something for everyone! You simply cannot go wrong. Best yet, all profits from the sales of this novel go to breast cancer prevention.

A stellar anthology that had me laughing, sighing in pleasure, believing in magic, and left me begging for more! Will there be a second anthology someday? I sure hope so! This is one novel that will go directly to my 'Keeper' shelf, to be read over and over again. Very highly recommended!

Reviewed by Detra Fitch
Huntress Reviews

~~~

HIGHLAND WISHES - This reviewer found that this book was a wonderful story set in a time when tension was high between England and Scotland. Leanne Burroughs writes a well-crafted story, with multidimensional characters and exquisite backdrops of Scotland. The storyline is a fast-paced tale with much detail to specific areas of history. The reader can feel this author's love for Scotland and its many wonderful heroes.

The characters connect immediately and don't stop until the end. At the end of the book, the reader wonders what happens next. The interplay between characters was smoothly done and helped the story along. It was a very smoothly told story. This reviewer was easily captivated by the story and was enthralled by it until the end. The reader will laugh and cry as you read this wonderful story. The reader feels all the pain, torment and disillusionment felt by both main characters, but also the joy and love they felt. Ms. Burroughs has crafted a well-researched story that gives a glimpse into Scotland during a time when there was upheaval and war for independence. This reviewer is anxiously awaiting her next novel in this series and commends her for a wonderful job done.

Dawn Roberto
Love Romances
www.loveromances.com

~~~

REBEL HEART – Jannine Corti-Petska does an excellent job of all aspects of sharing this book with us. Ms. Petska used a myriad of emotions to tell this story and the reader (me) quickly becomes entranced in the ways Courtney's stubborn attitude works to her advantage in surviving this disastrous beginning to her new life. Ms. Petska's writings demand attention; she draws the reader to quickly become involved in this passionate story. This is a wonderful rendition of a different type which is a welcome addition to the historical romance genre.
I believe that you will enjoy this story;
I know I did!
~ Reviewed by Brenda Talley
The Romance Studio

~~~

IN SUNSHINE OR IN SHADOW - If you adore the stormy heroes of "Wuthering Heights" and "Jane Eyre" (and who doesn't?) you'll be entranced by Cynthia Owens' passionate story of Ireland after the Great Famine, and David Burke - a man from America with a hidden past and a secret name. Only one woman, the fiery, luscious Siobhan, can unlock the bonds that imprison him. Highly recommended for those who love classic romance and an action-packed story.

Best Selling Author, Maggie Davis,
AKA Katherine Deauxville

~~~

ALMOST TAKEN, by Isabel Mere, is a very passionate historical romance that takes the reader on an exciting adventure. The compelling characters of Deran Morissey, the Earl of Atherton, and Ava Fychon, a young woman from Wales, find themselves drawn together as they search for her missing siblings.

The romance between Deran and Ava is difficult from the start. This attraction soon becomes desire which turns to passion that no matter how hard they try will not be denied. Readers will watch in interest as they fall in love and overcome obstacles. They will thrill in the passion and hope that they find happiness together. This is a very sensual romance that wins the heart of the readers.

This is a creative and fast moving storyline that will enthrall readers. The character's personalities will fascinate readers and win their concern. Ava, who is highly spirited and stubborn, will win the respect of the readers for her courage and determination. Deran, who is rumored in the beginning to be an ice king, not caring about anyone, will prove how wrong people's perceptions can be. ALMOST TAKEN by Isabel Mere is an emotionally moving historical romance that I highly recommend to the readers.

Anita, The Romance Studio

~ ~ ~

With the eerie lyricism of M. Night Shyamalan, and a pinch of J.K Rowling, R.R. Smythe is the next 'big thing' waiting to happen. She offers a turn of the century horror-suspense that will easily capture the Young Adult audience with the tale that is both original and imaginative. While waiting for Harry Potter's swan song, discover a new voice, a new talent that shines.
~ Deborah Macgillivray, author of
***A Restless Knight** and*
The Invasion of Falgannon Isle

Also Available from Highland Press

Highland Wishes
No Law Against Love
Blue Moon Magic
Blue Moon Enchantment
Rebel Heart
Christmas Wishes
Holiday in the Heart
In Sunshine or In Shadow
Almost Taken
Into the Woods

Coming:

The Crystal Heart
Pretend I'm Yours
Recipe for Love
Faery Special Romances
No Law Against Love 2
Second Time Around
Dance en L'Aire
Enraptured
The Amethyst Crown
Eyes of Love
Almost Guilty
The Barefoot Queen

The Sense of Honor

Cover by SAS Designs
Cover photograph by Annette Batista
Printed in the United States of America

Ashley Kath-Bilsky

The Sense of Honor

Printed in the United States
117248LV00003B/62/A